THE HOVER

CEDRIC: BOOK 1

C. A. LEAR

To Tara —

Best wishes always!

[signature]

This is a work of fiction. Names, characters, places, and incidents either are the product of the author's imagination or are used fictitiously.

Copy Editing by Angie Chen

Cover Design and Interior Design by Kit Foster

First edition
10 9 8 7 6 5 4 3 2

For Martha.

.

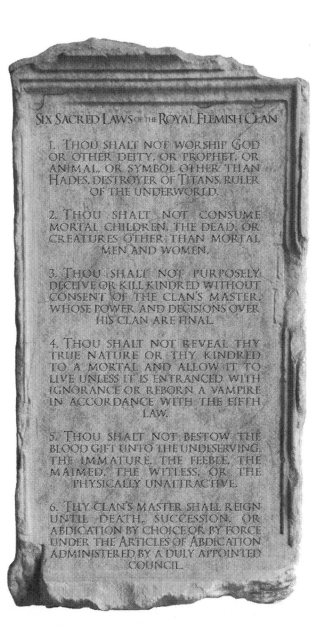

Six Sacred Laws of the Royal Flemish Clan

1. Thou shalt not worship God or other deity, or prophet, or animal, or symbol other than Hades, destroyer of Titans, ruler of the underworld.

2. Thou shalt not consume mortal children, the dead, or creatures other than mortal men and women.

3. Thou shalt not purposely deceive or kill kindred without consent of the clan's master, whose power and decisions over his clan are final.

4. Thou shalt not reveal thy true nature or thy kindred to a mortal and allow it to live unless it is entranced with ignorance or reborn a vampire in accordance with the fifth law.

5. Thou shalt not bestow the blood gift unto the undeserving, the immature, the feeble, the maimed, the witless, or the physically unattractive.

6. Thy clan's master shall reign until death, succession, or abdication by choice or by force under the Articles of Abdication administered by a duly appointed council.

1 - EAST FLEMISH BRABANT

JULY 1798

Cedric should have burned the bodies. His task might have been easier if he had, but he never again wanted to bear the sight and smell of charred human flesh.

He feared nothing before the unceremonious cremations. Now, he felt craven and confused—confidence eroded by doubt, pity, and loathing. Suddenly, a debate on the disposal of the victims crept back into his head. He quickly covered his ears as the voices pounced:

Shameful!

Clearly!

Cedric the coward!

Cedric the murderer!

"No!" blurted the boy, shaking his head.

Denial is the devil's defense!

Guilty as accused!

"I tried to save them, all of them," pleaded Cedric.

Half-heartedly!

Whole-heartedly inadequate!

"I...I..."

Worthless boy!

And now, they putrefy.

"No. They are—"

Buried or not, you know they'll rot!

One left.

Least you can do is burn it!

Ashes to ashes,

Dust to dust,

Burn it, burn it,

Burn it you must!

As the voices faded, he moved his hands to his chest and warily gazed up at the misty gray sky. The gold crucifix beneath his shirt felt sharp to the touch. "Where were you?" muttered Cedric.

He took up a flatbed wheelbarrow and pushed forward through the once productive farming hamlet of Linder, Cedric's home since birth. In the space of a few months, however, Linder had become diseased and desolate. Land that he and his father had farmed together reeked of pestilence. He saw no life, only death, and the voices of fear and guilt threatened his sanity. Yet, the despair which goaded him to end it all gained no favor as he labored on with obstinate purpose, pausing only briefly to hurl stones at scavenging rats, dispersing them back into the moldering wreckage of a barn long collapsed.

From a heap of sodden and twisted lumber, Cedric resumed salvaging the best planks, stacking them on the wheelbarrow, collecting rusted nails as he went. By noon, he was finished and pushing for home.

Outside the family's stone cottage nestled beside a pear orchard Cedric rummaged through the salvaged materials and started building a sizeable box with his father's tools. Each swing of the hammer, stroke of the saw blade, and thrust of the planer expended a measure of verve that in total would have sapped a man's energy by dusk, but not the boy's. Nothing was going to stop him. By midnight, the box was ready.

At first light, Cedric swathed his mother in a patchwork quilt, carried her outside, and gently placed her in the box. Removing a leather cord with the gold cross from round his neck, he clutched the pendant and was about to pray when a wave of panic coiled up his spine, bending his composure, throttling his nerves. He quickly moved away as bile spewed into his mouth followed by convulsive heaving. Nothing had prepared him for this, for what he was about to do. He felt irretrievably lost and trapped in a hellish nightmare from which he could not awaken. But he was awake, and so had been his mother until Death ended her misery. The moment his stomach settled, he curled into a ball and wept until his eyes burned.

Some four hundred fifty years prior, the Black Death came, reducing Europe's population by half in just a few years. The plague eventually receded, decreasing in frequency and scale. By Cedric's time, the disease was less common but no less deadly.

Cedric's father, Colson Martens, was a tenant farmer, owning little more than the tools of his trade, a plough horse, chickens, and goats. He sold and bartered cheese, eggs, fruit, and grains, affording his family a basic but comfortable life. Unfortunately, he was the first to fall ill. The initial symptoms were unremarkable: headache, fever, nausea, chills. A few days later, however, plum-sized blisters formed on his body followed by necrosis of the fingers and toes. Pain and weakness rapidly advanced. Mr. Martens died six days later, a day before Cedric's little sister succumbed to the same horrid disease.

Cedric secured the lid and slid the box into the earth beside his father and sister's graves. He then backfilled the plot and erected the third and final wooden cross. After placing fresh bouquets of red poppies on each grave-mound, he stepped back and scanned the landscape. There was no one to be seen. Everyone had either abandoned the village or died of the disease. Early on, he had helped his neighbors cremate their dead in shallow pits. Animals thought to have been infected were killed, and similarly burned and buried. Rats had infested the grain silos and fields throughout the farming community, and the landlord stopped coming round.

He lowered his chin and closed his swollen eyes. "I promise, Mother," the boy murmured. "I will go to Brussels and make a life there."

Cedric put on his father's cloak and tricorne hat, and placed a folding knife, blanket, loaf of bread, pickles, cured meats, and three silver guilders in a gunnysack. Together with a wooden canteen of water, he slung the weight over his shoulders and set out on a path that he and his father had traveled two years before.

It was the week of Cedric's fourteenth birthday. A kindly neighbor urged Colson to spend leisure time with his only son and lent him two young Friesian mares for the day. Cedric seldom rode horses. His father's plough horse was old, and he had asked Cedric not to ride her. It was as rare an opportunity to ride a horse as it was to spend leisure time with his father, and to do both was special indeed. Eager to go, Cedric mounted the mare and fell in beside his father.

Along the way, Mr. Martens shared experiences when he was Cedric's age—how he had met the boy's mother. "I was just seventeen when I first saw her," said Colson, gazing steadily forward as if focused on some distant visage of an angel. "She too was seventeen, amber hair, bright blue eyes—stunning! Every month, she came with her father to our village to sell baked goods. I always dropped everything to greet them. Good day, sir. Good day, miss, was all I ever said to them. I was smitten of the girl, you see, and pitifully shy. When I finally gathered the nerve to introduce myself to her, a month came and went and then another with no sign of her or her father." Mr. Martens shook his head. "My heart sunk when I heard of a plague in the baker's village. I thought she had come ill or worse. My parents thought differently. Why must you presume the worst? They asked. God willing, she is well.

"Was she alive and well? I needed to know," said Colson. "So I went to her village. A young man there asserted with great sorrow that a cursed disease had killed many, including the baker, his wife, and all his sons, but he added that the baker's only daughter had survived and was in the care of her godparents. Alive! I never felt more relieved. I went quickly to see her. Though grief-stricken, she appeared as beautiful as ever, and she remembered me. God in heaven had protected her! Not only was she pleased to see me, she asked that I visit her again. Thenceforth—"

"Thenceforth, everything, as you say" interjected Cedric, using one of his father's more romantic adages of youth, "was a wondrous blur."

After several more hours of traveling, they stopped on a shady knoll to rest. Far to the west Cedric saw an immense forest.

"That is the Sonian Forest," said his father. "It is part of a greater forest called Silva Carbonaria."

Cedric gasped. "It must be at least ten leagues across. What lies beyond it?"

"The walled city of Brussels."

"Have you been there?"

"Nay, but your mother has. Its streets are cobbled and clean, and its buildings are tall and beautiful. In Brussels there are many gainful opportunities for those who can seize them. Perhaps you will go there one day and do just that."

"Why not now?" blurted Cedric. "What I mean is, to see it if only from afar."

His father chuckled. "We must return these horses before nightfall."

"To the edge of the woods then, father? I wish to touch the trees."

Colson insisted that it was too late to journey any farther. So they turned back.

Brussels. Cedric knew little of the city or how to find it. It lay west of the Sonian Forest on the River Senne. That much he knew, but recollections of the route he had taken with his father had since faded. He would have to rely on others for directions. Providing the weather held fair and the path held true, he hoped to reach the forest inside five days.

2 - FATE OF FORTUNE

Cedric turned to gaze one last time at the ghost village of Linder. The cottage he had called home looked eerily smaller, like a lifeless body. Through the deluge of tears, it was hard to see the graves of his family and the larger mounds under which charred remains of animals and neighbors were buried. He turned and moved on, stepping into the next valley and then the next, trying to calm his emotions. He focused on the Sonian Forest and City of Brussels, hoping the meager rations he scrounged from larders would last. By nightfall, however, he had consumed nearly half the food and had yet to rid the voices of guilt and fear in his head that told him to go back, give up, and die.

Under a starry sky in a meadow beside a brook, he grieved himself to sleep.

The next day, sunrise on his back, he moved west. Grateful to his father for taking him riding, he recognized landmarks and knew that a farming village was ahead. By noon, he walked into the village and spent a coin on salted meats, apples, and bread. A farmer pointed him in the direction of the forest and said it was three days out. So far, so good, Cedric thought.

On day three, Cedric purchased similar fair in another farming community and continued on, assuming there would be other farms, villages, and travelers along the way. He ate plenty to maintain a brisk pace. By nightfall, however, he was again short on food and especially concerned that he had not come across any farms or village nor had he seen a soul.

On the fourth day, he started out early and expected to meet someone along the way who would point him in the right direction. Throughout the day, however, Cedric only saw empty fields and forks in the road with no signs to suggest right or left. Worse yet, an indefinable gray sky obstructed the sun and his ability to determine which way was west. Moving along paths of uncertainty, he began picking wild chervil and thistles chutes, stuffing them in his mouth and chomping them down like a goat in an attempt to stave off his hunger. Having the biggest appetite in perhaps all of Linder, Cedric was certain it was because he was the hardest worker there. His father had said this much. Cedric never imagined appetite to be his greatest weakness.

At dusk, he bedded down under his blanket and worried and hungered throughout the night.

The next morning, noisy crows in a nearby tree woke Cedric from his dreamless slumber. He finished his last crust of bread and slowly moved on. Unlike the busy and well defined roads he had taken with his father two years ago, nature had reclaimed the road beneath his feet—and as with the previous day, he saw no one and no signs of the forest.

He felt like the only person left on earth. Fear's voice rang louder in his head. He started pondering a demoralizing end, starving to death, west of nowhere, food for stalking crows and insects—his only companions. He was too far from anywhere to turn back. The road had blended into the landscape, but the sun was shining again. So he trudged on due west until exhaustion and the emerging moon convinced him to stop for the night.

The sixth day found Cedric in a bleary and weakened state of mind. His body felt too achy and heavy to move. He wanted to just lay there and sleep his life away. Sleep was easy. Sleep silenced his fear, but the noisy crows overhead roused him to his feet yet again. *Where is the Sonian Forest?*

His father had taught him to angle, hunt, and forage in the scanty wood near their home. Most forests, large and small, were bountiful. He knew that. He knew how to survive in them, where to forage, what to forage for, how to make weapons and tools and shelter from nature's offerings. He needed to find the forest soon, or truly abandon all hope of survival.

At noon, crouching beside a brook, chewing on watercress and refilling his canteen, he heard a faint rumbling. When he realized the sound was not only his stomach but galloping horses in the distance, he stood and saw two men fast approaching. He could hardly believe his eyes. It had been days since he had seen anyone.

Were they dangerous men? His stomach grumbled. Dangerous or not, those men may know the way to the forest. They may have food to give or sell. People are generally good and helpful, he reminded himself. Cedric waived his tricorne hat and stumbled forward to meet them. The horsemen slowed to a canter and then a trot. They circled their dark horses round the boy, peering down at him like griffin vultures.

"Good day, dear sirs," said Cedric, rotating, trying to keep eye contact.

Dressed in black, the men were bristling with polished swords and daggers. Cedric's father had warned him of strange men donning such weapons. Yet, the boy remained outwardly calm, telling himself again that people were generally good and helpful.

"Might I trouble you for directions?" Cedric's voice sounded feeble even to his own ears.

"See, brother?" said the elder of the two, his crusty smirk barely showing through his long, knotted beard. "Just as I thought, another lost boy. What is your name?"

"Cedric Martens, of Linder, sir."

"Linder?" said the younger of the two. "Never heard of it."

"Cedric Martens, eh?" said the elder. "My name is Fortune and this is my younger brother Misfortune."

The younger jeered at his brother, muttering, "I would have won it all back and then some."

"You sound like father, may he rest in prison," quipped the elder with a dismissing waive of his hand.

The circling horses were making Cedric dizzy. He tried to smile, but was uncertain his face was cooperating. "Mister Fortune, sir, I am en route to Brussels and hoped that—"

"Young Mister Martens," interrupted Mr. Fortune the elder. "I am certain you are a bright young man, and bright young men know that nothing of value is *gratis*."

"Sir?" said Cedric, furrowing his brow.

"Nothing worth having is free!" snapped the elder.

"Yes, sir," nodded Cedric.

"Good. Now then, what is your question? And be quick."

"How far is Sonian Forest from here and Brussels from there?" said Cedric. "Will you please recommend the best path to both destinations?"

To Cedric's relief, the men halted their horses. Mr. Fortune stroked his beard. "Have you any money?"

Cedric lifted his money purse and shook out the last coin into his hand.

Obviously unimpressed, Mr. Fortune's eyes wandered to Cedric's boots, breeches, and finally his unbuttoned waistcoat and shirt collar. "What is that round your neck?"

Cedric clutched the crucifix through his linen shirt.

"Come now, show it," said the elder man.

Reluctantly, Cedric lifted the pendant and immediately thought of his mother. A day before she died, she bequeathed the gold cross to him. It was generations old, a symbol of his faith, a priceless family heirloom.

The brothers' eyes widened. "Well, well, well...how fortune smiles upon you, Mister Martens," said the elder. "I shall answer one question in exchange for that pendant."

Cedric returned the pendant behind his shirt. "I...I cannot, Mister Fortune, sir," said Cedric softly.

Mister Fortune's eyes narrowed. "Two questions then?"

Cedric shook his head. "It belonged to my mother, and her father before her, and his father before him." He drew in a deep breath. "I beg pardon for interrupting your journey—"

Suddenly, the younger unsheathed a sword and slid its blade across his tongue. Startled, Cedric stepped back. Then to his surprise, the man tilted his head back, placed the tip of the blade upon his outstretched tongue, lifted the weapon to vertical, and swallowed it to the hilt. Without warning, Mister Fortune threw two daggers, both stabbing the ground nary an inch from Cedric's boots.

Mr. Fortune belted out laughter, causing the horses to stir and Cedric to take another step back. There was no escaping. They would simply run him down and either trample him with their horses or run him through with their weapons. Either way, Cedric prepared to fight. He was gangly but strong for his sixteen years, and he would not be defeated so easily. That is what he thought until his stomach cramped. Gripped by hunger, whatever strength he thought he had drained from his limbs.

The elder clicked his tongue and grinned while the younger brother pulled the dagger from his esophagus, wiped the blade dry with a kerchief, and sheathed it. Then peals of laughter between the men shattered the tension.

"Fear not, my boy," said the elder, struggling to keep a straight face. "Master of blades we are, en route to Luxembourg to entertain the masses."

"Reims after Luxembourg," added the younger.

"And Paris after Reims," said the elder. He tilted his head and tossed Cedric a curious look. "Have you any specialized skills? Juggling, perhaps?"

Giddy with relief and wonder, Cedric shook his head. "None of which I am aware, sir." Cedric retrieved the throwing blades and handed them to Mr. Fortune.

"Tis a pity," said Mr. Fortune. "We seek talent and financiers to grow our business." He pointed a knife at him and winked. "Should the gods bless thee with either talent or money greater than the weight of one guilder, do seek us out."

"Continue west on this road," said the younger. "The forest you seek is three hours by foot."

"But beware," said the elder. "The forest is dark—"

"And dangerous," added his brother.

Mr. Fortune carved a circle in the air. "Safer to go round it..."

"Or over it," said his brother, flapping his arms.

Cedric asked, "How many days round the Sonian as opposed to going through it?"

"Five days round it," said the elder.

"Two days through it," said the younger.

"Depending on the earth and sky," said the elder.

"And wolves," said the younger.

"And bears," chortled the elder.

"There are no bears, brother, for the witches ate them all," said the younger with a wink.

The elder leaned forward and whispered, "And the vampires ate the witches." He then chuckled as if it was all nonsensical fun and said, "If you must go through the woods, follow the streams and do not stop. Keep going until the trees are behind you and Brussels is ahead of you."

"Brother," blurted the younger. "The day is waning!"

"Then, we must go," replied the elder. The brothers aligned their horses and tipped their hats.

"Fare thee well, Master Cedric Martens of Linder," said the elder just as the brothers nudged their horses forward to a gallop.

"But, wait!" shouted Cedric.

"Follow the streams..." a voice shouted under the fading drumming of horses' hooves.

"Come back," whimpered Cedric. It was useless to shout. They could not hear him. He had neither gotten directions to Brussels nor any foods. Who were they really?

He drank water from his canteen and turned west with cautious optimism, wondering if anything the brothers had said about the forest was true.

3 - GODFORSAKEN

Sonian Forest appeared like an island in a sea of gradient fields. Aside from a painting, Cedric had never actually seen an ocean but imagined crows for gulls, fields for dunes, and buildings for boats. The farm ahead was huge compared to the farm he grew up on. It had not one or two but three grain silos, a large stable, ambling fields of wheat, and dozens of cows and sheep grazing in a meadow. It was a beautiful sight. Cedric's stomach encouraged him to go there and his mind wholeheartedly agreed. After all, he was not a beggar; he had money if only a guilder. The farmer might even invite him in for the evening meal and better still—offer a job on the farm!

Chickens clucked and strutted timidly as Cedric approached the house, looking right and left for anybody that might be outside. The house was a first-rate stone and timber building, much larger than the cottage back in Linder. He knocked on the door and waited for someone to respond. Stepping back, he moved his eyes across the farm but saw and heard no one. He stepped forward and knocked again, more aggressively this time. The door creaked open. *Strange to leave the door unlatched,* he thought.

"Hello?" said Cedric. "Is anyone at home?" He leaned in and looked, listened, and smelled. The kitchen was in full view. A door to a conjoining room was slightly ajar. Cedric's mouth began watering as delicious aromas emboldened him to enter the abode. A crust of bread on the counter and remnants of a meal for five on the table confounded Cedric. It was as if the family had suddenly vanished in the middle of their meal. He listened carefully and looked for signs of life but sensed no one else in the house. He rushed to the crust of bread, lifted it, paused to give thanks, and then shoved it into his mouth. It tasted glorious.

He placed his last silver coin on the counter to pay for whatever scraps he expected to find and turned to the table for leftover beans, pieces of mutton, and pickles. He lifted the stew pot and spooned out several mouthfuls. Just as he noticed that the fifth place setting was unused, a breeze entered through the front door followed by creaking hinges. The door to the conjoining room was moving.

He went to the door and peered inside. It was a bedchamber. The bed was neatly made, covered by a squash-green quilt with a pattern of red poppies. He moved sideways into the room a few steps, still savoring the flavor of stew. Then, from the corner of his eye, he saw them.

A high-pitched tone surged through Cedric's head and his limbs went numb. On the floor of the bedchamber, shoulder to shoulder, leaning against the wall sat a man, a woman, an older boy, and a younger girl. They reminded him of his family.

The man's head was resting unnaturally against the woman's, their necks mangled and possibly broken. Cedric's eyes jittered from side to side, desperately scanning for signs of life—breathing, twitching, anything—but the bodies remained deathly still. The red pattern on the bed was none other than blood. Blood was everywhere. He was standing in it—a drying and thickening pool. It was too much. His vision tunneled, turning gray at the edges. He would not allow himself to blackout. Inching away until his back unwittingly pushed the chamber door closed, he turned and ran nose-first into it. Panicking, nose throbbing and bleeding, he flung the door open and slipped into the dining table, knocking wooden cups and plates to the floor. He lurched out of the house, riling the chickens. He tripped and fell to his knees then quickly scrambled back to his feet.

Half mile later, muscles cramping, lungs wheezing, heart threatening to burst through his chest, Cedric threw off his cloak, placed his hands on a tree, and wept. Tears collected snotty blood from his nose, congealing and drooling in strings of goo from his chin. He could not blank out the horror he had just seen. He removed his gunnysack and fished out the folding knife.

Dangerous, said the fortune brothers.

Cedric was sick of danger, sick of death, sick of the judgmental voices in his head. He was starving, lost, and growing tired of what his life had become. *Godforsaken*, thought Cedric as he unfolded the knife and shakily held the blade out. The tool had belonged to his father. His mother and sister had knitted his blanket. The gold crucifix had belonged to his forefathers. Everything of his had belonged to family. He missed them. He wanted to join them, to be with them again. He looked down at his wrist and held the tip of the blade over a vein. One quick plunge would end his suffering. He took a firm grip of the knife, placed his wrist on the ground, and clenched his teeth. The voices of fear in his head ensured a painless death, passing out before the heart seized from blood loss. The tip of the blade pricked his skin as he trembled.

Suddenly, he recalled his mother's face. He recounted the sadness and concern in her eyes as they gazed upon him for the last time. She gave him the gold cross dangling from his neck and asked him to cherish his family and faith and start anew in Brussels. He promised he would. He promised.

Cedric reluctantly removed the blade from his wrist and clenched his eyes. He took in a few deep breaths to steady his heart and wiped off his face with an old kerchief. The sun had crossed its zenith—less than five hours of daylight remained. Coping with mind-searing trauma, he slowly gathered himself up and took a few timorous steps into the Sonian Forest.

Peering into the denseness, he saw little of the sky through the tree canopy. The Fortune brothers had told him not to stop. Two days deep, they said. Two days. Was that by foot or by horse? If only he had a horse. Surely there would be horses in the stable back at the farmhouse, but going back was out of the question. Aside from encountering the murderer, he was no horse thief and had no money left to give.

As long and difficult as the journey had become, as alone and afraid as he had ever been, the voices of fear and discouragement had not bested him. Determined to succeed, not only to find Brussels but to make a life there, he moved forward into the woods.

4 - MANCHESTER, ENGLAND

JULY 1798

At Hanging Ditch and Toad Lane stood Ravens Gate pub, and at its threshold stood a man who appeared sober until he finally moved. The building caught him as he toddled sideways against its redbrick wall, tilting his tricorne hat, scuffing his woolen coat. He muttered imprecations at nobody and pushed off, pausing and stumbling backwards, coincidentally, into Pierce van Fleming's care.

Pierce helped the inebriated fellow—a well-known butcher from the Shambles—to a hackney across the street and paid the coachman to take him home. Surely, thought Pierce, the man would have fallen prey to the dogs of delinquency had he not intervened. A reasonable concern, for all manner of scoundrels had slinked to Manchester after the collieries expanded and the cotton mills put Lancashire on the world's stage. He could almost smell the wicked, skulking and scheming in the shadows as he started back across the grimy street.

Before entering the pub, Pierce turned and saw a young woman, standing where the hackney had been. She was alone, a stranger yet strangely familiar, staring back at him with her iridescent-blue eyes. Her gown was of periwinkle-blue silk brocaded with silver-gilt foliate. Her hair was the color of ale foam, plaited and coiled under a jeweled tiara. Pierce knew of no formal affairs that evening. Was she a noblewoman, a wealthy foreigner, a ghost, or plain mad to be out alone in such a place?

He was about to go to her when a speeding carriage

suddenly crossed between them, and then another and another. After the noisy vehicles had passed, the young woman had all but vanished, as if she had been nothing more than an illusion. Pierce looked right and left for her but saw only graceless men, slogging about like ghouls. He heard nothing of her either, just the clattering of horses and carriages in the distance. Perhaps she *was* an illusion after all.

He shook his head, put whomever or whatever it was out of mind, and turned back to Ravens Gate pub. Minding the arched entrance, he removed his hat and stooped into the din. The front room was muggy with locals, arguing and joking behind plumes of pipe-smoke. They watched van Fleming make way to the counter where the publican stood ready for him.

"Good day, Mister Fleming," said the publican. He scooted a glass of bootlegged Speyside single malt to Pierce.

"Good day, Mister Clark." Pierce lifted the glass in thanks to the publican and scanned the room. The magistrate and chief constable were seated beside the front wall, playing a game of chess. The publican's niece was making the rounds, collecting empty glasses and engaging men in flirtatious gab. She glanced indiscreetly at Pierce.

"Aye, young Mister Fleming!" harked Farmer John O'Brian, drawing Pierce's attention to the backroom. "Come over, lad!"

Farmer John was in his middle years, portly and chinless, with a bulbous nose and a periwig snowing powder onto his shoulders. His moss-green eyes appeared asymmetrical, even more so when he drank, and especially on that evening—head half-cocked, bulging eye jutting forward as he spoke loudly of a boundary dispute for the umpteenth time.

Forcing a smile, Pierce brought his thoughts and whisky to the edge of a hearthrug on which John and his friends gathered in the glow of a coal fire. Pierce could not avoid the dispute as it involved his father, Hans, and now him. Yet, as Farmer John complained, Pierce's attention drifted inward.

Heir to his father's cotton empire, Pierce stood to become the wealthiest commoner in England, affording him exceptional courting opportunities with the aristocracy, according to his mother, who believed peerage followed by landed gentry to be the bedrock of English culture. Pierce held a different opinion. Nobles willing to marry practically anyone with financial means to afford their maintenance were as undignified as the commoner eager to marry them for trophy or title. He had no taste for that, none at all. He wanted instead to marry on terms of the heart, and took seriously his father's belief that *earning* one's title, respect, and prosperity was superior to inheriting them. Pierce saw the irony in his pending inheritance but resolved to honor his father's work ethic with like effort. Yet, some believed Pierce's New World values and industrial ambition had deceived even him into believing good fortune and freewill would be his.

Farmer John's booming voice buried all others in the room, and Pierce could no longer ignore it. "Mister Hans van Fleming comes along and tells me to stop building me fence! I'm building it on *his* land, he says! Hold on, I says. Me land map clearly shows the boundary goes from the old Scots pine to the west end of Brooks Bridge, which is exactly where I'm standing me fence!" Farmer John paused to address Pierce. "Young Mister Fleming, I was just explaining how your father swindled me two acres."

"Gentlemen..." Pierce entered the circle of friends and knelt in front of the inglenook. "My father swindled nothing, sir. Your land map is outdated and inaccurate."

"There is nothing wrong with that map! Got it from Lord Derby, I did, when I bought me ten acres from him. He needed money and I needed land. However, I count only eight acres now." No one knew how John came to afford acreage in Lancashire, or why Derby sold him any, but his success as a sheep farmer and producer of fine wool was irrefutable.

Pierce swallowed some scotch and waited for the burn in his craw to cool. "Actually, you still have ten acres, more or less. It is common knowledge the Scots pine on your map is gone. The tree you are landmarking is fifty paces off, and Brooks Bridge was relocated two-hundred paces upstream some fifty years ago. My father had the land properly surveyed, using a Ramsden theodolite which triangulates—"

"Rubbish!" blurted John. "You can't fool me with your ram's head triangular twaddle! My official map is generations old like the landmarks that must have grown legs and conveniently sauntered off two acres in your favor!"

It was like John to distort facts, but Pierce was unfazed. He imparted a thoughtful gaze to every man there, and then his face began to shine with a ticklish idea, a look that something remarkable was about to happen. His voice rang clearer as the fire glowed brighter. "I wager two acres, sir, that at thirty paces you cannot put a lead round in my head."

Overhearing the haphazard challenge and noticing John's dumbfounded expression, others outside the circle moved in for a listen as John's company scooted to the edge of their chairs.

John's eye blinked spastically. "Are you challenging me to a duel, Mister Fleming?"

"Not in the traditional sense, sir. Just take steady aim and pull the trigger. If your round finds my head, the boundary will be relocated to your fancy."

John rubbed his clammy face and locked eyes on Pierce. "So, I get back me land if I shoot you down at thirty paces?" Farmer John paused to think and then leaned back and laughed. "What folly is this? Hang for murder, I will!"

"For murder, perhaps, but not for self-defense. Your friends can attest to our dispute and agreement to settle by duel. Lend me a pistol and stage it we shall."

"You cannot cheat death forever, Mister Fleming, though some here might disagree." A few nods distracted John's bulging eye. "Suppose you lose. How will I recover me land?"

Expecting the question, Pierce answered in stride. "Magistrate James Smith is here. He prepared my testament last year. I shall have him amend it with instructions to revise the land map and to attach our boundary agreement to title were I to lose.

"What of your father, eh? He will be in no mood to look upon the man who's slain his son, let alone return the land to him."

"A reasonable concern...however, I assure you my father will honor our contract and seek no retribution, for that will be my final wish. You have my word. Now, sir, what is your wager?"

Farmer John rubbed his stubble where his chin might be

and glanced at his friends' keen faces. "Well, since you cotton people have no use for wool," grumbled John, "I offer me finest pig!"

Laughter erupted.

"A right fine pig, it is!" snapped John.

Though no love had been lost between the industries of wool and cotton, Pierce would have happily accepted a sheep to compliment the prize of silence. "I accept your fine pig...and Breanne," teased Pierce.

Farmer John sprung to his feet with agility so remarkable that his periwig—now atilt—nearly fell off. "Like I told you before, Fleming, stay clear of me daughter!"

John's friends jumped to restrain him and straighten his wig. It was no secret that Breanne, or Brea as her father called her, had eyes for Pierce. She was a blossoming woman of nineteen, with a petite nose, and chin so well defined, and eyes so symmetrical and brown, that all but John was skeptical of her paternal bloodline.

Pierce stood up and finished his drink. "All I want, sir, is an end to your land dispute. If I win, we shall speak no more of it and you shall deliver your fine pig to my father. Agree now and we settle tonight."

"Aye, if you agree to stay away from me daughter. What say you?"

Pierce nodded.

"We agree, then, to all three considerations," Farmer John said, bowing.

Pierce extended his hand.

John stared at the gesture with a curious face.

"It is a handshake, sir, to confirm our agreement," said Pierce.

"I know what it is!" blasted John. "Is my word not enough?"

"Go on, Mister O'Brian, shake his hand," egged the publican from behind the counter.

Scowling and scoffing, John reluctantly extended his hand. "What is next, kissing?" grumbled John as he took Pierce's hand, yanked it downward once, and turned away. "I will be waiting for you at me farm."

5 - DUEL AT THE ELM

A mob of spectators were already assembled at John's farm when Pierce and a very reluctant magistrate and chief constable arrived by coach. The entire way there, the magistrate and constable urged Pierce to break his agreement with John, arguing that the duel—scripted or not—was too risky. John was drunk and it was too dark to see, let alone aim a gun at someone's head. It was lunacy! Pierce considered their opinions but was motivated to stay the course. He desperately wanted John's ongoing boundary issue to end and believed extreme measures would achieve it. Besides, the so-called duel was really a calculated risk concerning target shooting. One's head is relatively small as targets go, and John would probably miss the tree entirely. The upshot was spectacle. People relished danger, daring, and dashing, as long as they could watch it from a safe distance. Who better than Pierce to provide it?

Pierce was not without jealous opposition. Some called him dodgy and brash, not to mention a womanizing swine, with too much daring and charm. Others felt he was unworthy of his wealth and wholly cursed. That his fortune was bound to someone's misfortune, and karma would make it right one day. Pierce *did* feel cursed, but not as much for behaving recklessly or having too much charm and wealth as for bearing a disturbing collection of scandalous secrets and deep-rooted demons. Indeed, van Fleming's self-image was of a grayer worth.

He saw the face of doubt in the mirror, of features obscured by a profound sense of detachment, as if life was not his to live, or that it belonged somewhere else and to someone else. His oddest little secret was an irksome invisible friend. It resembled a gargoyle, with leathery wings like a bat's. Its features were female but repellent like a perpetual stench that only he could smell. It always appeared when his exit from life was likely, and it would appear again within the hour.

John's wife and daughter, Breanne, came out to investigate the gathering of men.

"Is everything all right, Husband?" asked John's wife.

"Yes, yes," said John, approaching his wife and daughter.

"What is this about?" said his wife.

"A wager among friends is all. Nothing to see..." Noticing Brea's eyes pursuing Pierce, Farmer John stood between them and pointed to the house. "Nothing to see, I says! Go on, now. Go inside the house and don't come out 'til I say to."

After his wife and daughter returned to the house, Farmer John fetched his muzzleloader gun and Dragoon pistol and distributed oil lanterns to his friends. John successfully tested his gun on a log at thirty paces while Pierce pressed his back against the elm tree. With the crowd behind him, Farmer John brought forward a bottle of Irish whisky, handed it to Pierce, and awaited instructions.

Pierce drank a ceremonial mouthful and passed the bottle to a man who accepted the bottle with a jittery smile.

"From here, sir," said Pierce to John, "might I suggest that you walk thirty paces in that direction." He pointed to the half-moon.

"Aye," said John.

"I shall count to five. On five, will you please fire your weapon?"

"Aye."

"If I move before you pull the trigger or receive a round to my head, then you win."

"Understood," said Farmer John.

Pierce's eyes found Magistrate James Smith. "In the event Farmer John is successful, please administer my last testament, dear judge."

James nodded slowly, "Yes, but—"

"Thank you," interrupted Pierce, noticing ongoing concern on the magistrate's face.

"I have a question," said Farmer John. "Do I pulls the trigger on five or *after* five? In other words, is it one, two, *tree*, four, five, and then I pulls the trigger? Or is it one, two, *tree*, four, and pulls the trigger on five? And why does it have to be five? Why not *tree*?"

The drunken group spoke up.

"Aye, *tree* is accustomable," shouted one fellow.

"But five is more suspenseful!" said a bearded man.

"The convention is *tree!*" said another beside him.

"Shall we settle on four?" said yet another. Then laughter and joking broke out.

"Enough!" shouted Pierce. "It is not *tree*, you drunken buggers! It is three. Unless any of you would like to stand in my place, five shall be the count." Pierce waited for silence. "Right." He turned his attention back to John. "You, sir, shall say *fire* on five, right?"

John nodded.

"Are you ready, sir?"

"Aye." Farmer John lifted his musket and waited for the count.

"One, two, three, four, five...!"

"Fire!"

Pierce closed his eyes and shook his head. "Sir, you said fire after I said five. Please say fire the moment you pull the trigger on five. We must be certain you are pulling the trigger on five."

"Aye."

"Right, again. One, two, three, four,—"

"Fire!"

"Well done, Mister O'Brian, sir!" shouted someone in the crowd.

Chief Constable Gareth Turner imparted a worried look to Pierce. "I think you are making a grave mistake, Mister Fleming. This sort of activity ought to be outlawed, as the risks are—"

"The risks are great, I know," said Pierce. "Thank you again for trying to dissuade me. I appreciate your concern, but until such folly is prohibited, please officiate as a personal favor to me, Constable." Pierce placed his hand on Gareth's shoulder. "Besides, the accuracy of his aim is atrocious."

"That is what I fear," muttered Gareth.

As Gareth moved away, Pierce sensed a sudden drop in temperature, followed by a waft of rotting meat.

The apparition materialized to his left. Only Pierce could see her. The winged demon appeared as gruesome as a blood-soaked vulture, dreadful, grotesque, oozing of doom. If not for her leathery wings, bad skin, sunken eyes, and decaying teeth, Pierce thought she might have been an angel, not a scavenger, stalking him, waiting for him to die.

"I was beginning to wonder when you would show yourself," whispered Pierce with a whimsical smirk. "How does all at home in hell?" He turned his attention back to Farmer John.

John inserted a wad and round into the barrel and rammed it down. Then he added powder to the flash pan and cocked the hammer. "Ready here, Mister Fleming!" hollered Farmer John, as he leveled the gun to his shoulder.

"Ready here!" replied Pierce. He pointed the Dragoon at John and focused on John's gun muzzle. He drew in a deep breath and sounded the cadence, "One, two, three, four—!" The hammer sparked, followed by an explosion and flames from the muzzle.

Then silence.

Farmer John lowered his gun and peered through the smoke to where Pierce had stood.

"My God," said someone.

"Is he dead?" said another.

Viewing the spectacle from her bedroom window, Brea was beside herself with worry. How could she just stay in the house when Pierce was lying motionless? She had to go to him. Ignoring her mother's pleas to heed her father's wishes, she dashed out.

The crowd rushed to Fleming's collapsed body. James placed a lantern on the ground. Before he could get a closer look, Brea pushed through and knelt beside Pierce. She placed her trembling hands on his head and gently tilted his face upwards. "Mister Fleming?" said Brea, softly.

Brea, among other maidens of charmed sensibilities, considered Pierce's mannerism as neither high-brow nor high-class in the whitest sense of bland but colored in heroic peril to haunting affect. She was obviously enamored by this young man, this Apollo Belvedere personified. Pierce's face and form indeed resembled that of the actual statue of Apollo. Unlike the statute, however, Pierce typically wore durable coats, waistcoats, knee breeches, and riding boots to compliment his no-wig, no-makeup, equestrian brawn.

"Daughter!" barked Farmer John as he pushed through the huddle. "Leave him be! Go back to the house. Go on, lass!"

Brea felt something wet and slippery and lifted her hand to see—blood. Her face drained of color and she fell over.

After Farmer John removed Brea from the scene, Gareth moved the lantern closer to Pierce's face and explored the ground. James felt a lump on the side of Pierce's head and laceration to his ear and checked for a pulse. "He probably hit his head on this," said Gareth, patting a partially buried stone beside Pierce's head.

"He lives," sighed James.

"Here it is! Look here!" shouted a young man, probing a hole in the tree with his knife.

James shook Pierce and called his name a few times.

Pierce fluttered his eyes open and winced.

James and Gareth sat Pierce up against the elm. "Are you all right, Mister Fleming?" asked Chief Constable Gareth.

Pierce nodded and stood up.

Farmer John returned with an old, damp tea towel. "Mister Fleming, please tell your father that I shall deliver his pig on the morrow."

"Thank you, sir," said Pierce, gladly accepting the fabric and placing it over his wound. "And Breanne?"

"We agreed!" snapped Farmer John, waving his finger.

Pierce cringed at John's loud voice. "Is she all right?" whispered Pierce.

"You never mind her!" John glanced up at the man jabbing his knife into the hole in the elm.

Pierce placed his back against the tree where he had stood and watched the young man finally pry out the lead round located several inches high and to the right of his head. Pierce finally smiled. "Bloody poor aim, sir."

Farmer John squinted. "Do you honestly think I was aiming at your head, lad?"

At that moment, Pierce realized John had not wagered for land per se but rather for Brea. Pierce would have to stay away from her. Not a bad arrangement, as he only wanted to silence the land dispute, and he did.

The young man held the deformed projectile between his thumb and index finger as he examined it. He reached out to Pierce and placed it in his hand. "A memento, sir," said the man, nodding enthusiastically.

Pierce thanked him and placed it into his waistcoat pocket. He then glanced over to where the hideous apparition had appeared and recalled the attractive young woman in the blue gown from earlier that night. *Despicable creatures*, thought Pierce.

6 - THE BLIND SEER

C edric moved quickly among ancient conifer and beech trees through the Sonian Forest, suppressing his fear and sadness, stopping only to forage a bird's nest with eggs, and edible flowers and wild berries along a stream. At dusk, he found shelter in an earthen den in which bears may have hibernated in the days of bears—before the witches ate them all, according to the Fortune brothers. He gathered leaves to soften his bedding and placed a branch of dense foliage in front of the entrance.

Inside the den, Cedric ate some berries but was so exhausted that he nodded off as soon as his head touched the gunnysack.

It was a frigid morning when Cedric finally emerged from the earthen den. Determined to gather more food, perhaps a hare if he could devise a clever trap, he set out on a deer path. Soon, he stumbled upon a vine-covered hovel.

A trail of smoke arose from its twisted stone chimney. At first the building appeared warm and inviting, but he noticed no crops or livestock. He thought: *might this be a hunting cabin or the home of something dreadful—perhaps the monster that had slaughtered the farmers?* The Fortune Brothers had told him to keep moving. He had ignored their recommendation, sleeping in the bear-den, stopping to snoop. Perhaps he should go. Go now. He turned to leave, but it was too late. Someone or something was standing behind him.

It wore a pine-green cloak with a hood shading its eyes. Gripped in its bony hand with unkempt fingernails was a long, burled walking stick. A wicker basket hung from its right arm. Cedric wanted to reach for his folding knife but abstained out of fear. If only he had some makeshift weapons, a spear or bow and arrows.

"I... I beg pardon for my intrusion, sir," stammered Cedric. "I arrived here accidentally. Please allow me to leave, and I promise never to return."

A moment before panic set in, the figure set down the basket and pulled back its hood. Cedric was relieved to see an old woman instead of a monster, but he remained cautious.

She was slightly hunched, with ghostly features emphasized by her dark attire. A hint of blue was barely visible through her cloudy and seemingly unfocused eyes, and her thickly plaited hair was the color of dirty straw. She leaned her stick towards him.

"You arrived here accidentally because you are lost," snipped the woman.

Taken aback by her strange accent and candor, Cedric searched to defend his presence and possibly his existence. "I... I was hunting and... and exploring, madam."

"From where do you come?"

"Where, madam? East... Southeast of here."

She moved towards him.

He backed away.

"Please, madam, please stay your distance," insisted Cedric, hands lifting. But she continued until his back was pressed against a vine-covered pile of stones. By the time Cedric finally decided to take out his knife, vines were already coiling round his wrists, ankles, torso, and neck.

"What is this?" yelped Cedric. The more he struggled to free himself, the tighter the vines constricted.

"Be calm, boy, lest choking to death is your end." The woman sniffed and poked at him. "My name is Elida." She placed her hand on his heaving chest.

Cedric saw his reflection in her cloudy eyes.

"Your heart is heavy with sorrow and fear," said the old woman. "You have no home...no family. You have witnessed many horrors." She placed her soft hands on his grubby face, dragging her fingertips from his forehead to his jaw-line. "Neither man nor child," she commented softly as if speaking to someone else. Backing away, she pointed to a path that Cedric had not noticed—as if the ferns had parted to reveal a secret passage. "That way to food and shelter and life thereafter," said the woman. She pulled her hood up over her head and retrieved from her basket three small eggs and a cluster of wild berries.

The vines released him and he stumbled forward.

She placed the food into a small sack and tossed it to him. "You have little time. Leave the forest whilst you still can." The woman gathered up her basket and went towards the vine-covered hovel. The vines on the cottage moved like serpents as she approached it and chanted: *"A Roman on strings of malice shall rule, kingdoms of man and vampire shall fall, lest the strings of malice are severed by one, all shall be lost and ever forgotten."* When the door closed behind her, the vines stopped moving.

Cedric awoke from his delirium inside the bear den, weak, aching, and feverish. Everything appeared to be spinning. He was ill, very ill. He found the eggs and fruit gathered days earlier, or did he receive it from the old woman? Had he dreamt her? He forced himself to eat, hoping he would not throw everything up. He rubbed his aching head and peered outside. He could not recall where he had heard the warning, *leave the forest whilst you still can,* but had a sudden urge to obey.

He pushed the branch away from the entrance and crawled outside. The air felt especially cold and damp against his flushed skin, and he shuddered violently. Struggling to stay alert and on his feet, he stumbled along a barely visible path through a thicket of ferns. The path seemed to grow longer with each step, but the boy pressed on until he finally reached the edge of the forest.

A lush meadow spread out before him. No sooner had he staggered into the grass, everything went black.

7 - DEVIL'S PISS

Cedric felt the rigidity of a timber floor against his spine when he regained consciousness. He sensed a cavernous room, musty with traces of rust, vinegar, and wood. Sunlight shone through narrow windows, disrupting the monotony of large stone walls. He heard soft voices, which meant he was not alone. He felt better than he had in the forest, but his aching body resisted his desire to sit up. Cedric rubbed the blur from his eyes and noticed two short, scrawny legs beside him.

After a languid moment of silence, Cedric tilted his head a bit and saw a child standing there, perhaps five or six years of age. A few older boys were also in the room. One appeared to be soaking in a wooden barrel, grimacing and shivering. Another boy was napping, while two others talked quietly.

"Where am I?" whispered Cedric to the child. "When did I arrive?"

"You arrived a day ago," said an older boy, sitting at the crown of Cedric's head. The adolescent leaned forward and gazed down at Cedric, smiling warmly, strands of brown hair dangling beside his chestnut-brown eyes. "I overheard the guard. You were found unconscious in a meadow at the edge of the forest." He paused and continued to stare intensely at Cedric's face, as if trying to recognize it. "You were lucky the wolves had not found you first. Whatever were you doing out there?"

With the boy's help, Cedric sat up. He licked his parched lips and coughed. "Water, please," asked Cedric.

The older boy waved off the child to fetch water. "I am Jacob de Veen, of Galmaarden."

"Cedric Martens of Linder."

Jacob lowered his voice. "For how long were you in the forest, Cedric Martens?"

"One night, maybe two. I was ill."

"Obviously. Nobody in their right mind goes into the forest alone. Where were you going?"

"Brussels. Where are we?" asked Cedric again. ·

"Vos Castle, near Waterloo, I think."

Cedric was unfamiliar with lands west of Sonian Forest to make sense of Jacob's answer. Cedric rubbed the flannel shift between his fingers again and scanned the room for his things. "My gunnysack, clothes..." his eyes grew wider as he brought his hand to his chest and felt nothing there, "My cross..."

"They confiscated everything and burned our clothes," whispered Jacob. "Not only do they make us wear these gowns, they make us bathe in devil's piss." He glared at the soaking barrel against the wall. The boy that had been soaking in it was getting dressed.

Cedric shook his head and simpered with a huff. Not only had he been forever deprived of his family, not a single memento of their existence was spared. "Devil's what?" asked Cedric.

"In those wooden barrels is vinegar, garlic, and God knows what else. It smells like piss and burns like the devil!" Jacob giggled nervously as he eyed the guard standing in the center of the hall, whose horsewhip coiled around his shoulder and leather mask covering his face from nose to chin made him appear as menacing as an executioner. "The sentry will call upon you when it is your turn to dip."

"And if I refuse?"

Jacob ignored the question. The little boy returned with a wooden cup of water and handed it to Cedric.

"This is Master Twinkles, or Twinks as I call him," said Jacob in a brotherly tenor. "A dozen seasons old, he is, a young man of few words."

"Master Twinks, thank you for the water," said Cedric, smiling for the first time since he had left his village. Twinks reminded him of children in his village, of his little sister when she was his age.

Twinks recoiled shyly and moved to Jacob's side.

Jacob rubbed the child's head. "Even though they burned our clothes and make us bathe in devil's piss, they give us food and shelter in consideration of work."

"Work?"

"Servant's work. Two strange women come to select boys nearly every afternoon. Not a bad arrangement if you ask me."

"Fatten and serve us up, you mean," whispered another boy, eavesdropping from behind Jacob. "Rumor is nobody leaves the castle alive."

"How would you know?" replied Jacob, sneering at the boy. "You arrived just yesterday, too." Jacob turned back to Cedric. "He got the whip when he refused to bathe."

Suddenly, the odd boy went silent and lowered his head. Cedric noticed the guard pointing his whip handle at the boy. At once, he went to the barrels, stripped off his gown, and gingerly immersed himself in the smelly solution.

Cedric would do the same and eat a hot stew each day at noon. Not a bad situation in which to be, considering his predicament. He might have died in the meadow had he not been found and brought to the castle of rest and hearty-stew.

In the afternoon, two women entered the hall, one short and plump with a slight limp and a patched-over eye, the other tall, bony, and jittery like a squirrel. They huddled with the guard who, after a brief discussion, pointed out a boy.

It was all done rather quickly and quietly. The guard went to the boy in the barrel. The boy stood up. Then, the guard prodded him to follow the women outside. Each day, a new boy was brought in, and a boy was escorted out. Each day, Cedric and Jacob's friendship grew as did Twinks' fondness for Cedric. Although the tension of waiting and not knowing weighed heavily, not since before his family succumbed to the Black Death had Cedric felt positive about anything—least of all the future.

On the fifth day of captivity, Jacob and Twinks were selected to leave together.

Alone again, Cedric anxiously wanted to know where his new friends had been taken and if they were well. He prayed for them. He prayed for himself.

On the seventh day, Cedric was selected to leave.

8 - HAMLET THE PIG

Pierce's father, Hans, was restoring his high flyer phaeton in the carriage house when Pierce arrived at dawn. Hans was proud of his carriage collection and favored the high flyer for its elegance. At sixty years of age, Hans was slowing down. Wisps of gray hair barely covered his freckled scalp, and like Pierce, he refused to wear a periwig.

"Good morning, Father."

Hans turned stiffly to face Pierce, twitched, and smiled. "Your mother was inquiring your whereabouts."

"Right. Expect Farmer John to deliver a pig later today," Pierce said, anticipating his father's surprised expression. "I will explain it later, but please offer to shake his hand."

Hans saw dried blood on Pierce's ear. "You ought to clean that before your mother sees it."

Pierce nodded.

His father turned back to his wagon and lifted a polishing towel. "Care to join me this afternoon?"

"What are your plans?" asked Pierce.

Hans turned slightly so that Pierce could see the twinkle in his eye. "Rough shooting."

Pierce was surprised, for his father had not gone hunting in years.

"Bring the guns to the stable at noon," said Hans. "We shall ride to the pond."

"Clarks Pond?" asked Pierce.

Hans hummed affirmatively.

Pierce's fondest memories of his father were associated with hunting and angling. Preoccupied by the cotton business and pending retirement, however, Hans was usually too tired to recreate. Pierce left the carriage house for the well outside, rinsed off his face and ear, and hoped his mother would not notice his wound.

The cook, a young scullery maid, and Pierce's mother were busy in the kitchen when he entered. "Splendid morning, ladies," said Pierce.

The cook smiled. "Good day, sir."

"Good day, sir" echoed the scullery maid.

After a moment, his mother put down a bowl of partially shelled peas and stretched her back, sizing Pierce up in a way that made him feel culpable. Her usual interrogation started after a heavy sigh. "And where were you last night, Percy?"

"With friends..." said Pierce, standing sideways to hide his damaged ear.

"Fighting again?" said Mrs. Fleming, causing the scullery maid to smile.

"No, Mother."

Mrs. Fleming squinted at him. "Then why is there blood on your waistcoat, and dirt-stains all over?" Pierce's mother was observant to a fault. He truly felt that nothing could escape her notice.

"I fell, and that is the truth. I made a wager with Farmer John O'Brian and won fairly."

"What did you stand to lose, your head? And why wager at all?"

Pierce smiled at his mother's inquisitive nature. "It was a shooting contest," Pierce explained, "and my prize—"

"Answer the question," interrupted his mother. "What did you stand to lose?"

"I won a pig," said Pierce, evading her question again.

A faint snicker escaped the scullery maid as she stoked the fire in a stew-stove.

His mother huffed. "Is that all?"

"And John's silence. Honestly, Mother, his boundary squabbles grew tiresome."

"A pig, you said?" asked his mother.

"Yes. Hamlet the pig." Pierce kissed his frowning mother on the forehead and winked at the young maid to make her blush.

He then moved towards the stairs. "His name is Hamlet, on account he is to become bangers and ham."

"Naming an animal you intend to butcher is inappropriate. Nothing good comes of it, Percy!" shouted his mother as Pierce clambered up the stairs.

Pierce's parents learned early on that their son was peculiar. Whereas the physical pains of broken bones, bruises, and cuts typically instilled caution in maturing boys, Pierce had always remained stubbornly fearless. Surely, the adrenaline rush played a part, but the rush was not as much about feeling alive as it was about settling disputes and cheating Death. While it was not unusual for lonely and imaginative children to play with invisible friends of the genial sort, Pierce was a grown man, and his invisible friend, the angel of Death, hardly fit the mould. Why was Death enamored with Pierce? He oft wondered.

Pierce was nearly thirteen when he found himself on the roof of a barn. His father was bringing the merchant's wagon round below. It looked small from that height. Death stood beside him, uttering no words. Yet, Pierce imagined her voice, egging him on to jump. He was convinced that she was there to watch him die and collect his soul.

"Shut up!" snapped young Pierce at the apparition. "Jump, I will, when I am bloody well ready!" Finally, and not before he was ready, Pierce looked directly into her sunken eyes, stuck out his tongue, and leaped.

He landed on sacks of raw cotton as soft as pillows stacked high in the merchant's wagon. Death was hovering over him, as if waiting for him to die. But Pierce was alive and giggling.

"You ought to see the look on your hideous face!" shouted Pierce, wagging his finger at her. "Thought I was dead, did you? Ready to collect my soul, were you? Have you nothing better to do than follow me round like a rotting sack of filth?"

With medicine in its infancy and remedies that did more harm than healing, his parents maintained a low profile and attributed Pierce's unusual behavior to a remarkable profusion of energy, imagination, passion, and intellectual capacity. Indeed, Pierce was curiously brawny for his age. He was faster and smarter, too, learning to read at a high level by thirteen and solving problems with advanced logic and mathematics.

Death's frequent visits, however, confounded Pierce. She seemed obsessed by him, stalking him and repeatedly falling for his outrageous stunts. Whenever he inquired her business with him, she uttered nothing. But her face and posture were expressive enough to afford Pierce the notion that a grave secret was behind it all, and that one day he would uncover it.

At half past noon, Pierce and his father rode to Clark Pond. It was located at the farthest corner of the property, adjacent to land owned by the Clark family. The Clarks were Scottish. They owned Ravens Gate, Pierce's favorite haunt. Pierce and his father had spent many a day fishing in the pond and hunting grouse and pheasant. But on this day, Pierce's father was unusually reminiscent.

As they were following the spaniel through the grass, Hans stopped and turned to Pierce. "Son, do you remember how I found you?"

"Found me?" Pierce laughed. "How do you mean?"

"Actually, the spaniel found you...there," said Hans, pointing to a spot near the shoreline, "lying beside the pond. You were but a young lad, twelve or thirteen years of age. I thought you were sleeping, but..."

What? Was I lost?" asked Pierce, suddenly confused.

"Unconscious. I carried you home. Your mother was upset at first—"

"This is the first I have heard of it."

"It was not a serious event, really. You probably slipped and fell, striking your head on something. You turned out well." He tilted his head at the recollection and chuckled. "I had not thought of that day for years."

It was a question Pierce had asked himself. Yes or no was

too definitive an answer. He was physically and intellectually sound. His senses were keen, even more so than his contemporaries, though he never felt quite right, having no memories of a life before twelve years of age. Suffering a head injury explained his memory loss.

His father gazed into Pierce's blue eyes. "Why so concerned? That was many years ago." Hans suddenly noticed the dog, whimpering and quivering with excitement, nose on point. He leveled the gun and cocked the hammer. A soft whistle and nod signaled the dog to act. The spaniel lunged and a grouse took to wing.

Pierce let his father shoot first. He missed. Pierce then fired and brought down the game. The dog retrieved it and deposited it at Hans' feet. Pierce lifted the grouse, inspected it, and placed it in his father's rucksack. Pierce wanted to share his secret with his father—his amnesia—but kept quiet. He would not add yet another peculiar secret to the list of secrets his parents had collected from him.

9 - CASTLE RULES

Cedric's first full day as a castle servant started with Mum and Helga's morning visit, the same women who had escorted all the newcomer boys to the castle proper. They came to count heads and reaffirm the rules and servant's duties.

"Each of you is assigned a bed and a number," announced Mum in a voice that sounded lighter and younger than she appeared to be. "Your number is etched on your bed, and beneath your bed is a basket in which to store your belongings. You are required to sleep in your assigned bed. When asked to identify yourself, provide your bed number, not your name—unless of course your name is specifically requested. Now for the primary rules:

"Rule number one: thou shall not cast eyes upon any royal member of the clan without permission. Do not think of it lest you desire punishment—*severe* punishment.

"Rule two: No mirror shall be displayed or used in the castle. Do not ask why.

"Rule three: No servant shall enter royal chambers without authorization.

"Rule four: Except for the daily meal, served midday for a period of one hour in the dining hall, all servants shall be at work during daylight hours. Between the hours of sunset and sunrise, all servants must remain in their bedchamber. The royals tend to stay up late; thus, you may not.

"Rule five: Boys and girls shall not commingle. Yes, there are female servants here at the castle, and you shall not speak to them." Rule number five received griping exhales followed by austere glares from the head maid and her skinny assistant.

"No is no. There are no exceptions.

"Rule six: Disrupting the serenity of the castle and wandering aimlessly or curiously is prohibited. Your business here is to serve, nothing more.

"And rule number seven: Weapons are prohibited at all times. This includes anything pointed, such as a wooden fork or stake, or even an object that could be thrown to cause harm, such as a stone or large onion." This elicited giggles to the annoyance of the women.

"Punishment for violating the rules shall be severe and final with no reprieve. Finally, you are encouraged to bathe in the cleansing solution at least once a week. Helga and I do, and so should you."

"Explains why she smells like piss," Jacob whispered in Cedric's ear.

Mum noticed the boys and moved towards them. "Questions?"

Cedric cleared his throat. "Yes, Mum. There are thirty boys here. Are there thirty girls in the castle as well?"

Mum's eye twitched as she glared at Cedric's rosy face. "What is your name?" she asked sharply, limping towards him.

"Thirteen, Mum."

"Yes, I know," said Mum, her eye glancing at the number etched into the bed-leg. "Name?"

"Cedric Martens, Mum."

"Humph! You, boy, are not a guest here, and neither are the girls. You shall obey the rules and work for the generous consideration of food and shelter, and be grateful for it!" She glared at the others. "That goes for all you dirty-minded mongrels!" She quickly refocused her eye on Cedric. "My advice to you, number thirteen, is to avoid the girls, as they are *thirty* times deadlier than the plague. Is that clear?" She spun away only after he nodded in affirmation.

Cedric felt his question had been answered—thirty girls in the castle, thirty girls to be found. He observed Mum's frumpy anatomy, patched eye, and bad leg. *Perhaps a warmer Mum is trapped inside that cold shell,* he thought. *Perhaps intimidation makes most boys jump to do her bidding.* Cedric thought Mum imparted a wink, or was it just a blink?—hard to tell with one eye patched over.

The castle rules were established by the Royal Flemish Clan, an exclusive organization to which the elite pledged their allegiance. Other than being elite and the lords of the castle, nobody knew what The Royal Flemish Clan really was or did. It was believed that the organization was centuries old and that the head of the clan was a proper count who had hand selected all the clan's members. Many thought the clan was accountable to the Holy Roman Emperor, King Joseph II. Contrarily, some felt the organization worshipped the devil.

The first castle rule of the Royal Flemish Clan was not to look at the clan's elite—also called royals. Nobody considered breaking that rule for fear of punishment worse than death. The older boys told Cedric and Jacob of rape and dismemberment and not necessarily in that order—and feeding the body parts to pigs. Another penalty was disembowelment while chained inside a pen of hungry pigs. Death by iron maiden downsized for children, and the body quartered and fed to pigs was yet another punishment. Each story was progressively more horrible, and Cedric wondered about the ravenous pigs.

No one was certain of the truth, but after a few weeks, Cedric was certain of one thing: the population of orphans at the castle remained stable despite new arrivals nearly every day.

10 - THE CHASE

The chase always started in the shadow of a Dutch windmill. He fled by foot towards three enormous trees on a hill. His pursuers always caught him and beat him to the ground with wooden clubs. He never saw their faces or heard their voices. The final blow cracked his skull. The moment his heart seized, Pierce woke from the nightmare, unsettled and unrelieved. That was the start of Pierce's day, every day.

The nightmare provoked his curiosity. Who are the attackers? Am I the victim, or am I experiencing the victim's terror? What is the motive? When and where does the crime happen? The lack of answers left him frustrated. Busy work got his mind off such matters, and he wanted to be the entrepreneur his father was and every bit as successful, if not more.

To accomplish that, Pierce worked longer and harder than anyone else in the cotton industry. He grew sales and profits many times over and invested in the business as well as the communities of Lancashire. But no amount of work completely shielded his thoughts from *such* matters.

It was early afternoon when Pierce arrived at Ravens Gate, early enough to find Meghan Clark and her sister Grace still there. Disinterested in trends of her contemporaries, Meghan appeared plain, seldom in a wig or in French fashion, though such luxuries were available to her. She preferred simple day gowns of cotton to extravagant gowns of silk. Her ebony locks were voluminous and defiant, ignoring her attempts to contain them in buns, braids, and hats. Yet, no amount of plainness by nature or design could disguise her elegance, her pleasing physique, and the gleam of curiosity in her emerald-green eyes. Her sister—a year younger with hair more burgundy than ebony—stood beside Meghan, alerting her to Pierce.

"Good afternoon, Miss Clark, Miss Grace," said Pierce, bowing.

Grace turned to greet him. "Good afternoon, Mister Fleming."

"Your smile brightens the day, Miss Grace."

Grace giggled and flapped her winkers. "Yer too kind, Mister Fleming."

"And your dear sister?" asked Pierce, hoping Meghan would turn to greet him.

Grace wrinkled her nose. "A wee under the weather, she is. Wheedling her out of the house for a bit of fresh air was no easy task."

Meghan wanted nothing of Pierce, and her parents discouraged any association with him. Her Uncle Ewen explained that Meghan had always preferred books to boys, art to alcohol, and the past to the future. Though Pierce was enamored by her natural beauty and reticence, her disinterest and shyness attracted him even more so.

Meghan finally turned to acknowledge Pierce with a brief nod.

"Good day, Mister Fleming," said Grace, as she ushered her sister to where book-filled cabinets lined the walls in a quieter corner of the pub.

Hovering outside the entrance, two young women of puckish intentions were in an amorous mood, joking boisterously and coaxing Pierce to join them.

Meghan watched Pierce with revulsion as he went out to meet the indelicate women. "Father was right," whispered Meghan to her sister. "A scoundrel, that one is."

"Aye," giggled Grace, "a stallion of a scoundrel if you know my meanin'."

11 - A REGAL CAPTIVITY

A month had passed since Cedric entered a life of servitude at Vos Castle. His first chore was scrubbing the bedchamber and corridor floor with a small brush and pale of water. He scrubbed daily until new boys arrived and took over the task. Replenishing firewood was his next job. He split wood and restocked dozens of inglenooks, learning the lay of the castle and of prohibited places such as the girl-servant's bedchamber, the towers, and catacombs.

The girl-servant's bedchamber was located on the first floor. Cedric always moved slowly passed it, hoping for a glimpse, sound, or whiff of a girl his age, but all he ever saw was a locked door. He knew nothing the towers or catacombs, only what others had told him. The royals were believed to dwell in the towers, which made sense, but it was believed some also dwelled in the catacombs. The catacombs were a labyrinth of subterranean tunnels, burial chambers and dungeons—a horrid place in which to dwell, unless you were a roach or rat.

Making candles and torches was his next chore. He enjoyed the job and the candle shop in which he worked. It was a shack really, just outside and to the rear of the keep. It was peaceful there. An occasional guard checked in once or twice a day, but it was otherwise a sanctuary. Cedric was good at making candles, requiring no training. Samples of the various types of candles used at the castle—tallow, beeswax, spermaceti, and others with decorative twigs and leaves inside—were displayed and stocked in the candle shop. Cedric's job was to make certain candles and supplies were always available.

By September, replacing firelight was added to Cedric's chores. At first, he was to replace firelight outside the castle, but within a few days, his assignment included all areas inside the castle, including rooms off-limits to other servants.

If the catacombs included the dimmest rooms in the castle, the brightest rooms were located at the southwest corner of the keep. Known as the sunroom—due to its many windows—it was located on the top floor and contained plush Venetian settees, lounges, baroque commodes, tables, chairs and oriental rugs and runners on marble floors. The walls were ornately trimmed and paneled in fruitwood and adorned with fine oil paintings.

As Cedric quickly went about replacing candles in the parlor, he admired a portrait over the inglenook. He thought it captured the likeness of a count, his wife, and their infant son. It was magnificent, and Cedric wanted to believe that the eerie sensation of being watched was really the count and countess looking over him. The parlor expanded both ways into conjoining rooms, and more rooms beyond those, some of which were locked. Cedric was told to replace candles in all rooms provided they were easily accessible and unoccupied. He never expected to meet anybody in the sunroom.

It was a clear, late afternoon. The sunroom was Cedric's last stop before returning to the candle shop to clean up. Almost finished and anxious to leave, a young boy's voice broke the silence.

"Hello?" said the boy.

Cedric stopped what he was doing and dropped his gaze to the floor. "Please forgive my intrusion, sir," said Cedric.

"Identify yourself." The boy sounded much younger than Cedric, perhaps nine or ten years of age.

"Thirteen, sir."

The boy guffawed. "Is that your age or your name?"

"Neither, sir, my name is Cedric Martens of—" Just then, the weighty steps of a man entered the space. Cedric presumed the man saw him, but the man said nothing. The boy protested as he was being whisked away. After a moment of listening and worrying, Cedric quickly replaced the last candle and, before leaving, crept into the corridor to see where the man had taken the boy. To his surprise, the man, boy, and a woman were standing in the last room at the end of the corridor. He recognized them to be the people in the painting. The woman stood in front of the kneeling man and standing boy, her hands resting on their heads. They appeared to be meditating.

A week later, as Cedric was again replacing candles in the sunroom he heard nimble footsteps approaching, followed by a familiar voice.

"Hello?" asked the boy.

Cedric again looked down at his toes and waited, expecting the boy to recognize him. But to his surprise, the boy said as before, "Identify yourself."

"Thirteen, sir," said Cedric. Surely the boy would recognize the number and their brief encounter.

The boy guffawed. "Is thirteen your age or your name?"

"Neither. Sir, please forgive me, but do you not remember me? We had met last week."

The boy snorted, "Liar! Tell me who you are at once, or I shall report you to my father, Count Fredrick, and my mother, Countess Gerda." Before the boy could say another word, he was again whisked away by his father.

Cedric finished up and then crept into the corridor to see if the strange family was still there. As before, in the farthest room, the countess stood in front of her kneeling husband and standing son, her hands resting on their heads. Unlike before, however, without moving her shoulders or opening her eyes, the woman slowly turned her head unnaturally—nearly backwards—to face Cedric. Her grin quivered and widened to reveal canines of a predatory animal. Cedric instinctively turned and ran and did not stop until he arrived at the candle shop. Memories of the farmhouse massacre came back to him, cementing his fears. *What are those people?* Cedric thought, hoping he would not be punished for laying eyes on supposedly castle royals.

12 - THE RIDDLE OF THE COUNTESS

In the catacombs beneath Vos Castle, Countess Marie de Vos had been counting gold coins incessantly for three days. Save for one shiny gold piece wedged between her bosoms, she bagged the rest and flung them onto a pile of assorted bags and lockboxes stuffed with gold bullion, gemstones, and worldly commodities such as grains, beans, and buttons.

The chamber in which she counted had once contained devices of torture. Twelve sets of iron shackles fastened to the walls were all that remained of its cruel past. For decades, the chamber remained empty and locked, but after the countess wedded Count Marcel Marc de Vos, she started to store miscellaneous treasures there, and remodeled the room by building a storage loft, furnishing it, and raising the ceiling by punching through three floors above.

Searching for something new to tally, she lifted a Hessian sack and shook it curiously. "Lentils," whispered Marie, barely restraining her delight. She opened the bag and deposited the legumes onto a table the count received from Louis XIII. A boy servant arrived moments later. He waited patiently at the entrance, chin down, eyes closed, a sack of candles slung over his shoulder.

"Enter," said Marie, still admiring the heap of dried Masoor lentils. The boy moved quickly, replacing spent candles and leaving those still alit. He scraped drippings from candle holders, picking up scraps of beeswax and tallow. Torn between her desire to count lentils and observe the boy, Marie finally pried her eyes away from the table.

She saw a well proportioned adolescent with cropped

brown hair, but not too short as to sever the whimsy from his curls. He had expressive eyes—bright copper—and a pleasantly shaped nose and mouth. Were it not for his rosy complexion and ungainliness, he might have appeared mature from a distance. "Boy, what is thy number and name?" asked Marie.

He froze, mouth agape, eyes roaming the floor. "My number and name," whispered the boy dryly, inaudibly. He subtly cleared his throat and tried again. "Number thirteen, My Countess. My name is Cedric...Cedric Martens of Linder."

Drawn to his youth, Marie licked her narrow lips and counted his fingers and toes. "Thou art a newcomer to the castle."

Cedric stared at a splash of candle wax on the floor and nodded.

"How old art thou?"

"Sixteen years, My Countess."

"Tell me, Master Cedric, how many candles hast thou?"

"Fresh or spent, My Countess?" said Cedric in a calmer voice.

"Fresh, of course."

"Twenty-seven, My Countess," replied Cedric without hesitation.

"Explain."

"I have used twenty-three of fifty candles, My Countess."

Marie retrieved the gold coin from her cleavage and tossed it. It bounced noisily on the stone floor and landed on the splash of wax to which Cedric's eyes were affixed.

"Pick it up," said Marie. She watched him lift it from the floor and rub the gleaming profile of a man with the likeness of a Roman emperor. "What is it?"

"It appears to be a gold coin."

"It is an English Broad. Inscribed on the reverse is *pax qvaeritvr bello*. Dost thou know the meaning?"

"I know some English, but those words are unfamiliar, My Countess."

"It is Latin. It means 'peace is sought through war.' Lovely, is it not?"

"It is a heavy coin," said Cedric mildly.

Marie glanced at a pile of bags plump with coins. "I shall pose a riddle. Solve it and receive a worthy prize, including a one-time and confidential reprieve for viewing castle royals without permission." She studied his reaction, expecting nervousness, but the boy appeared impassive. "Countess Gerda informed me of thy offenses—both of them."

Cedric struggled to stay calm. If only he had not looked at the royals in the sunroom. "Please forgive me, My Countess."

"Solve the riddle and all shall be forgiven. Ready?"

"Yes, My Countess."

"Listen closely for I shall not repeat it." Marie gazed at the coin in Cedric's hand and enunciated the riddle with bell-tone clarity. "Were I to possess nine bags containing ninety Broads in each, how many Broads must I have at this moment?"

The math was simple for Cedric. "Eight-hundred and nine if the only one missing," he held the Broad closer to the candlelight, "is this one."

Marie's eyes narrowed. "And now that one, my clever boy, belongs to thee." She noticed Cedric stiffen with uncertainty. "It is thy prize. Keep it and speak to no one of thy reprieve."

"Yes, My Countess. Thank you. You are most kind and generous." Cedric placed the coin in his sack and continued to look away.

"Tell me, what became of thy parents?" She noticed his posture sag from the weight of her question.

"The Black Death," said Cedric softly.

"Ah, yes," said Marie as if she knew exactly how Cedric felt, "death by fleas so theorizes the oracle whose prophecies— according to the clan master—are infallible. Yet, how could a minuscule insect cause the death of millions? I recall the last great outbreak in Marseille as if it were yesterday. Its people were discolored and putrefying. They erected a wall round the city to contain the curse. Despite ample quantities of bloated bodies and pesky flies amid the rotting stench, I had a delicious time engaging the city's orphaned population." Noticing no change in Cedric's downturned expression, she smiled and brightened her tone. "Dost thou fancy my French taffeta gown, Master Cedric?"

Cedric stared at the entranceway. "Forgive me, My

Countess. Gazing upon a royal is prohibited, though I imagine your gown to be very beautiful."

"Beautiful?" huffed Marie. "Why not old and tattered? Imagine it soiled and smelly, as I have not moved from this chair in three days! Better yet, imagine no gown at all. Imagine my chilled flesh, every inch of it exposed for thy viewing pleasure." She paused to assess his reaction. "Art thou curious to see?"

Marie knew that the fairer sex was an irrepressible attraction for a boy of Cedric's age. She also knew that he had never before encountered the likes of her and was probably wondering why she was enticing him so. She watched him struggle not to view her even peripherally. He clenched his eyelids and remained still. Marie's eyes wandered back to the mound of red lentils.

"Leave," said Marie. As Cedric was exiting, she sank her long fingers into the pile of lentils, kneading it like a blissful cat, and thought of the boy as someone she might trust.

With gold Broad in hand and a pardon to ease his worry, Cedric anxiously awaited Jacob's return in the servant's bedchamber. It was dusk and Mum and Helga would arrive at any moment to count heads. As sunlight faded to moonlight and Cedric's worry mounted, Jacob finally dashed in through the open chamber door and sat down on his bed in a dusty thud. Cedric was relieved to see him and was about to show his gold coin when he noticed Jacob's fearful expression.

Jacob wiped away a tear and breathed heavily. Before Cedric could say a word, Mum and Helga stepped into the room. Helga's form appeared stretched and undulating, her fuzzy, pointed chin and hooked nose casting eerie shadows in the candlelight.

The room went silent as Mum and Helga started the headcount. Mum stopped in front of Jacob to assess his reddened face and puffy eyes. Helga held the lantern closer.

"You," said Mum, sternly. "Were you crying?"

"No, Mum," lied Jacob, managing to shape his mouth into a convincing smile.

"Are you sick?"

"No, Mum. Sorry, Mum. I always look this way."

Mum shifted her suspicious eye to Cedric and then back to Jacob. Finally, after some stressful heartbeats, Mum limped away with Helga burst-stepping behind her to the youngsters' beds. Jacob gestured silently for Cedric to watch them. Mum stopped at a vacant bed and nodded at her assistant to take note. Before the two women left the chamber, they stood by the entrance and glanced over at Cedric and Jacob. Then they closed and locked the door from the outside.

Whispering commenced shortly after their footsteps faded to silence. Cedric glanced at Jacob, then back at the vacant bed illuminated by moonlight through a narrow window. "Where is Master Twinks?" whispered Cedric.

Tears leaked from Jacob's eyes. "He must have looked at a royal, for I heard him being taken into the catacombs. I am certain it was he because..." Jacob covered his mouth to silence his weeping. "I heard his voice. He said my name. But then...screaming..."

Cedric sat quietly, trying to make sense of the unfortunate news. He put away the gold coin and glanced over once more at the empty little bed. Praying for Twinks's safe return, he pulled his blanket over his head and thought of his parents and sister whose charm was many times greater than her size. They meant everything to him and he missed them so.

The next day, a new little boy occupied Twinkles' bed.

13 - A GOOD WOMAN

The cotton mill in Ancoats was built alongside the Rochdale Canal, a waterway project that would soon make it possible to barge materials to and from Manchester. The mill was comprised of two massive masonry buildings, each one a hundred feet long, forty-two feet wide, eight floors high, with hundreds of windows and two new smokestacks. Hans and Pierce stood near the second smokestack, observing the installation of their second Boulton and Watt steam engine. The engine would turn thousands of mule spindles, replacing the waterwheel entirely.

Hans tapped Pierce on the shoulder and motioned for him to follow. Pierce turned to the millwright. "Mister Lowell," hollered Pierce. "Carry on, sir."

"Yes, sir," shouted Lowell, nodding and waiving enthusiastically.

Pierce caught up to his father at the rear entrance to the factory. It was Saturday afternoon, a quiet day due to no power to turn the machinery. They cut through the building to the front door and stepped onto the walkway. As they crossed the street towards the foundry, Pierce heard rain pattering on his tricorne hat. No sooner had they taken seats in a nearby tavern, thunder shook the building.

"Hope that engine is up and running by day's end," muttered Hans, emphasizing the truest challenge of the day was not the lightning storm.

A wench came to their table. Before she could greet them, another thunderous blast coerced her nervous gaze upwards.

"Do not worry, Miss Richardson," said Hans with a smile, "for lightning is attracted to worry."

The woman shook her head and drew in a deep breath. "Not such a good day, is it, Mister Fleming, sir?"

Hans nodded. "We will have two ales and soups, please, and—and those lovely biscuits with ham and cheese."

Miss Richardson's smile widened as she glanced at Pierce. "Very good, sir."

Hans watched Miss Richardson as she walked away and murmured, "Her father worked in the Rochdale Foundry next door. A marvelous tool maker, he was. Died of pneumonia, poor soul."

"I remember him," said Pierce. "He was a good man."

"Miss Richardson is a good woman. A good woman is what a man needs, Son."

Miss Richardson served the ale and went back for the food.

Pierce and Hans lifted their glasses. "*This* is what I need, Father." They drank down half their ale and belched. "I miss our time together over drink and food. The mill is—"

"The mill is our legacy," interjected Hans. "It defines us. It affords us the life we have. Do not forget that."

Miss Richardson brought out a large plate of ham, cheese, and biscuits and two bowls of vegetable soup.

Pierce lifted a biscuit and said, "Yes, by definition we are industrialists, successful and prosperous. I enjoy the work we do and the heart we put into it, but can we not also enjoy our prosperity? We used to go hunting, riding, and traveling abroad. I miss that."

Hans tasted the soup and then took a biscuit. He looked out the window at the angry weather and nodded. "Growing old is a dirty trick, Son, and the work is exhausting."

"That is why we need a holiday."

"That is why you will take charge of the Ancoats mill next month, and the Manchester and Liverpool warehouses next year." He smiled and tasted the biscuit. "Then I will relax and we can resume all those family activities you speak of—unless of course you become as I am now: overworked and tired."

Pierce chuckled. "Today, we are underworked and energetic. Why not go out on the town tonight?"

Hans raised an eyebrow.

Pierce lifted his glass. "We will drink, laugh, get into a little trouble, and come home late. Please, Father."

Hans bit off another piece of ham and biscuit and lifted his glass to Pierce's. "Very well, Son, but not a word of it to your mother."

Ravens Gate was not very busy when Pierce and his father arrived, soaking wet from the late summer's storm. They removed their hats and overcoats and hung them on a rack beside the front table. Soon as they sat down, Grace Clark came by.

"What a pleasant surprise to see you both, Mister Fleming, and sir," said Grace, her cheerful gaze bouncing between the van Fleming men.

"It has been a long time, Miss Clark," replied Hans. "How are your father and mother?"

"Well, and busy as always, thank you."

"And your sister?" asked Pierce.

Grace's smile faded slightly. "Meggy is a wee bit under the weather, as always. Drinks?"

"Ale," said Hans.

"Whisky," said Pierce.

When Grace left them, Hans said, "I remember when she was born. She has grown into a beautiful young lady, has she not?"

"She has."

Hans leaned in. "But you have eyes for her sister Meggy. I can hear it in your voice. She is a lovely girl as well. Remember when we used to barter cotton for ale with the Clarks?"

Pierce nodded.

"Gracie always came out to greet you, but not Meggy—no— at least not to where you saw her. She was a shy one, that Meggy."

Grace served their drinks. "Anything else I can bring you, Mister Fleming?"

"Another round, please, Miss Clark," said Hans. He lifted his glass and drank it empty. Pierce did the same.

The pub grew busier as the night grew shorter. Hans noticed a woman outside, standing beside their window. Every so often she would peer in and smile at them.

"What you need is a good woman, Son," said Hans for the third time that day. He glanced at the woman outside. "Not like that one."

"I know, Father," said Pierce, noticing Grace's unrelenting stares.

"Do you know why the Clarks stopped bartering with us, hmm?" asked Hans.

Pierce knew, but wanted to avoid the discussion. He had heard enough of the rumor.

"The rumor," said Hans, his voice slurring, head swaying.

Pierce held no interest for Grace, and the rumor was false. Yet, his father knew of it, which meant his mother probably did as well.

"I know the rumor is untrue, Son. I know you do not fancy Gracie. I also know what you do when you stay out all night. It concerns your mother, me as well. It is only natural that parents worry for their children." Hans closed his eyes, head tilting.

Pierce moved to stabilize his father. Hans placed his hand on Pierce's back and rubbed it. "Son, I am proud of you. You are going to steer our company into the future."

"Father, perhaps we should go."

"Nonsense!" Hans shook off Pierce's concern. "How often do I go out on the town with my son? Gracie! Gracie, dear! Another round, please!"

By closing time, Pierce and Hans were in no condition to ride home. Pierce took his father by hackney to the Broadmore Hotel. In the largest room on the third floor, Pierce helped his father to bed and took a sofa for himself. Throughout the night, Pierce looked after Hans, catching his vomit in a bedpan, feeding him water, and sleeping very little.

Late the next morning, Pierce and Hans arrived home, dehydrated with splitting headaches. Surprisingly, Pierce's mother said nothing unkind or berating. Instead, she asked the maids to draw down the bedchamber curtains and see to it they received plenty of water and strong coffee to drink.

The next day, Mrs. Fleming found Pierce and his father in the library. They had recovered from their hangovers and were enjoying a smoke. She closed the doors behind her and confronted them. The look on her face spelled trouble.

"Does our reputation mean nothing?" said Mrs. Fleming, with a biting austerity that captured Hans's full attention. "An immature son is one thing, but an immature father and husband is entirely another! Do either of you care about our reputation, our standing, the landed gentry from which I came, or the industrialist elite to which we belong? This sort of behavior is not only irresponsible but damaging!" Her words, tears, and frustration churned a stew of angst. "Is that what you want?"

All the while, Pierce kept an eye on his father.

Hans, nodding humbly and listening intently to his wife's fiery words, displayed a glint of satisfaction or perhaps amusement in his eye that Pierce had not seen in years.

"No, Wife, that is not what I want, nor was it my intention to shame us. It was only one night out with my son."

"It was an entire night of drunkenness!" In a moment of pause, she clenched her fists as if to summon the world's scorn, and then transformed her grimace and tension to a sudden calmness that impressed Pierce. "Dear Husband, you are no longer a boy. Please consult with me before engaging in hedonistic activities." Her eyes shifted to Pierce. "And you. What am I to do with you? Carousing at all hours, brawling and gambling like a hoodlum, talking to invisible friends. Grow up, Percy." Mrs. Fleming then turned and went to the door, opened it, and said, "Dinner is at five." Then she slammed the door behind her.

Hans lifted his glass. "Have I ever told you that a good woman is what you need, Son?" They touched glasses and drank.

14 - MARIE'S MUSE

"**O**pen the gates!" shouted a castle guard.

Two porters unlocked the heavy timber doors and let through a dusty black coach behind six gray horses with bioluminescent eyes, pulsating colors of citrine. With chins lowered, Sir Michael Livesey and his guards—who had been hurling javelins at straw targets—formed up to greet Headmistress Abigail van Ness.

After the coachman helped her out of the coach, Abigail headed for the castle, hardly acknowledging anyone and glancing briefly at the wooden spears and targets.

Sir Michael bowed and gazed at her periwinkle-blue silk gown. "Welcome back, Headmistress," said Michael.

"Thank you, Sir Michael," said Abigail, her eyes drifting from targets to castle. She continued on through the courtyard east of the keep. Approaching the side door, she saw a girl-servant exit the castle with a burlap bag slung over her shoulder. The girl tossed it onto a pile of bags on a cart, riling a buzz of flies. Abigail wondered if the pile of bags contained ordinary rubbish or something exceedingly dreadful. Noticing drops of murky liquid pooling below the cart, she turned to observe the sizeable building wherein new orphans were detained. Entering the keep, she moved swiftly through a narrow corridor to a large hall and arrived at the steps to the catacombs.

Weeding out husks and stems from a mound of rice, Countess Marie de Vos tweezed a grain between her bony fingers and lifted it for closer inspection. "Twelve-thousand and three," said the countess, her voice reverberating in the cavernous room. She placed the granule into a sack and listened to oncoming footsteps. Without looking, Marie waved the visitor in.

Abigail gracefully moved into the amber glow of candles and knelt at Marie's feet. She took Marie's hand in hers, pressed it against her smooth cheek, and kissed it.

"Welcome home, Abby," said Marie, still focused on the rice. "Sit with me. We have much to discuss." Marie beamed as Abigail took a chair at the table and observed the pile of rice. "A moment ago, I finished counting eighteen-hundred-forty-nine embroidered buttons from America. This is rice from Spain. Observe the standouts. Knights amongst peasants, are they not?"

Abigail wrinkled her brow and looked closer at the rice. "They all look alike to me, like grains of sand."

Marie clicked her tongue dismissively. "No two grains of rice, or sand for that matter, are identical. Each is different in size, shape, color, and wholeness. Some are curvaceous; some are straight; some are broken; some are clearly stunted or damaged. The differences are subtle but intriguing." She plucked out an exceptionally plump grain and held it between them. "For seldom do I discover one of incomparable luster, size, and shape... Twelve-thousand and four!" Marie flicked the grain into the sack and then snatched Abigail's hand. She inspected her smooth, slender fingers. "One, two, three, four, five... ten fingers, one in ten-thousand," mumbled Marie, as if distracted by something evocative, "one in ten-thousand..."

Finally, she focused her discerning eyes on the young woman's face. Abigail pulled back her pale blonde hair and leaned forward. When Marie's lips touched Abigail's ear, she murmured, "Confounded are gods upon high, for neither they nor the twinkling of stars in a milieu of darkness are as stunning as thee. Thou art a masterpiece of beauty and sensuality, my sweet Abby. Thou art immortal, mythical, and entirely mine."

Abigail looked away. "Yours I am, but I cannot see or feel that of which you speak, My Countess."

After a moment of silence, Marie belted out laughter. "Of course not, stupid girl, immortal beauty confounds even thee!"

"I do not believe we are immortal. We age and die as trees do, slowly if not cut down."

Marie shook her head. "Poor girl, endowed with nary a shred of romance."

As teenagers, Abigail and her little brother competed for attention. They constantly fought, resorting to all forms of trickery and mockery. Unfortunately, Abigail began to believe her brother's snide comments, that she was as ugly as a leach, and thus unworthy of the Priest's affections—a man she adored.

While her mother opposed Abigail's longing for the holy man, she desperately wanted to boost the girl's self-esteem. Because Abigail wished to be attractive, her mother crafted a vanity spell. The spell should have revealed Abigail's inner beauty more clearly instead of changing other's perception of her physical appearance. However, the latter came true. Indeed, acquaintances and strangers no longer saw a simple and charming girl. Instead, they saw their perception of physical perfection, an irresistible beauty. Only her family saw her for who she truly was. Her mother kept the corrupted spell a secret, and hoped it would eventually wear off—but it endured.

Oblivious to her mother's eternal hex, Abigail wondered how she came to garner the attention of men and women alike. She still saw the same girl in the mirror. It made no sense. The attention was unwanted. At church services, men stared and wives glared at her. Whenever she stared back at them, they looked away as if disinterested, only to latch their eyes onto her as soon as she turned away. No matter how unflattering she made herself to appear, the lustful and resentful gazes would not stop.

Suspecting a vanity spell, Abigail confronted her mother. "Do I look the same to you?" asked Abigail.

Her mother was busy in the kitchen, stoking the stove fire. After she closed the iron door, she wiped off her hands and took in a deep breath. "What do you mean, Abby?"

"When we go into town, people stare at me. At church, people stare at me. My friend Sara looks at me differently as well, especially her brothers and parents. Mother, may I ask directly—"

"Abby," interrupted her mother.

Abigail sensed sadness in her mother's smile.

"My daughter, no magic can improve on your natural beauty. Nay, you are blossoming into a gorgeous young woman, and one day you shall wed. Until then, please help me prepare the evening meal. Your father and brother are expected at any moment, and you know how hungry they will be."

As for Abigail's father, he was a man of few words and little understanding of female matters. With no family or friend to consult, Abigail sought the Priest's advice.

After the morning church service, Abigail found the priest inside the church, thanking his parishioners for attending mass. After the last person filed through, Abigail stepped up.

"Father, may I have a word in private?" asked Abigail.

"Do you wish to confess your sins, my child?" said the Priest.

"I seek advice, Father."

The priest nodded and led her to a room at the back of the church. He closed the door behind them and turned to her. "How may I help you, my child?" asked the Priest.

Young Abigail twirled her hair and gazed into his large, brown eyes. She had always admired his kindness through his eyes. "Thank you, Father." Abigail could not find the words she had planned to use and so uttered the first ones that came to mind. "Am I attractive?"

The priest stroked his goatee and gazed at her face as one might when looking for hidden intentions. "What do you mean, exactly?"

"I fear I am cursed, for people stare at me, as if attracted to me."

The priest began to move around her, scanning her up and down. Abigail enjoyed his attention. His judging eyes were unlike the others'.

"Who stares? When do they stare at you?"

"All and everywhere and always they stare at me. What have I done to deserve such unwanted attention? I try to ignore it, but I can *feel* their eyes on me." She shrugged and frowned. "Why? I am nothing—certainly nothing to look at, as my little brother would attest. Do you not agree, Father?"

"Agree?"

"Am I homely?"

"Are God's children homely?"

"My brother believes so."

The priest chuckled. "It is natural for siblings to taunt each other."

Abigail sat on his desk, slid back, and let her legs dangle. She pulled back her tresses from her face, draped them to one side, and observed him observing her. She liked his face, his well-groomed goatee and defined jawline. He was wonderfully attentive. She wanted to tell him everything. "It is the way people stare at me and what they stare at that concerns me, Father." Abigail cupped her hands under her breasts. "They stare at these."

The priest's eyes widened and he swallowed dryly. "Are... are these people acquaintances or strangers?

"Both, Father."

"Both?"

"Yes."

"Do they smile at you? People oft smile in passing."

"Men smile, but not at me, for their eyes roam all over my body. Women included. It is unnerving."

"I see. When did you first notice the staring?"

"A year ago."

"How old are you now, Abigail?"

A flush of excitement coursed through her at the sound of his voice uttering her name. He had never addressed her by name before, and she wondered if he was developing deeper feelings for her. "Nineteen years."

"Have you a suitor or someone special in mind?"

"I do, but mother forbids that I see him. She keeps me busy weaving. It is strenuous."

"I see. Well, my child, God has led you here because He means to save you." The Priest touched her forehead and drew the cross. "Blessed are we, for we are God's children, guided by our faith in the Father, Son, and the Holy Ghost. If there *is* a curse, it must be discovered and cast out.

"There is indeed something about you," said the priest. "I can sense it, an unnatural allure. Have you noticed any strange odors?"

"My brother emits strange odors," giggled Abigail.

The priest failed to see her humor. "Have you experienced intense nightmares or discovered strange new markings on your body?"

"My dreams are ordinary. I have a freckle on my arm."

He pointed to the center of the room and said, "Please stand over there and show me."

Eager to comply, Abigail went to the center of the room and lifted her sleeve. The priest then inspected a tiny spot on her wrist. He rubbed it with his finger, smelled it, and rubbed it again. The smell of thurible incense on his robe and his touch stimulated her.

"No," said the priest. "It is merely a freckle. Have you any unusual markings on your back?"

"I cannot see my back, Father."

"Will you please expose your back, then, so I may examine it?"

It was a request she had not expected. Lusting, fantasizing, and even flirting was hardly the same as exposing her backside. Why did he ask her to disrobe? Was he bewitched? "Undress... Here?" asked Abigail.

"Why, yes, of course. The mark of evil may be located anywhere on the body, especially in places not so easily seen. God willing, I shall find it."

Abigail thought carefully. They were alone in his office. She had him where she wanted him. Yet, something caused her to move to the door instead. "Please forgive me, Father. I cannot..."

"Cannot is the devil's word, my child. Negative thoughts are evil. They prevent us from achieving the greater good. Do not be afraid. I mean no harm."

"I do not fear you, Father. I fear *for* you." Abigail opened the door. "My mother is expecting me… to weave."

"Humans," hissed Marie. "Daft minions of a punitive and unforgiving man-God. Mortals unknowingly wallow in their own filth while believing they are righteous and deserving! Yet, when a goddess of legendary aptness—an Aphrodite and Venus together in one exquisite creature—rises above their squalor, instead of venerating her, they summon death upon her—upon you!"

Abigail wanted to forget the horrible ending to her former life, and hoped that Marie would digress no further.

"A witch," spat Marie. "They labeled thee a witch. Witches hath neither poise nor beauty. Witches hath no true power. After a witch gasps its last stinking breath, maggots come to consume the rest. Thou art a goddess!"

"You saved me from a horrible death, for which I am grateful—"

"I saved thee from them for me and others like me to revere, for we are unlike those ungrateful mortals. We embrace beauty. We preserve it. Embody it. We savor the taste and smell of it. And yet, my sweet goddess, thy stunning beauty is hardly thy greatest gift, now is it?" Marie stood up and floated to the center of the chamber, her resplendent gown flowing and shimmering like a stream of mercury. "Tell me about it. For what purpose does it serve?"

"You speak of *renatus*, My Countess."

Marie's eyes squinted as the corner of her lips lifted with anticipation. "Yes, the powers of necromancy. Explain it again, Abby. I never tire of the tale."

15 - THE RENATUS

Abigail moved to the center of the counting chamber. Many seasons had passed since she had contemplated necromancy. Her mother had died before she could pass the knowledge on completely. Even if Abigail had completed her training, performing the *renatus* successfully was not guaranteed. Only the most gifted sorcerers—a select few spread thinly across untold centuries—were ever able to do so.

"When Hades summoned the angel of death," began Abigail in a richer voice, "she brought forth the soul of an adolescent girl. Until then, souls wandered in the rift of absence and purposelessness, fading slowly like a stain in the fabric of oblivion. However, instead of keeping her soul in the underworld, Hades returned the soul and life to its corpse. He called this resurrection *renatus*. My mother called the resurrected being a revenant."

"Yes, go on," said Marie, completely engrossed in the explanation.

"The powers of necromancy were gifted to people of extraordinary magical prowess. In ancient times, such people practiced sorcery. They were revered. With the passing of time, however, they became the ire of religious leaders. People of magic were summarily demonized, hunted, tortured, and murdered in the name of their God."

"Yes, yes, yes," said Marie, impatiently. "Tell me, is a revenant a perfectly restored version of its former self?"

"Ideally, yes, but it would depend on many things: how the person died, the strength and skill of the necromancer, and the condition of the soul. A murder-victim's soul is the easiest of all to clutch because the soul seeks justice. There are risks, of course. A soul of bad character will ultimately produce a revenant of bad character. Even if the soul is ideal, pitiful witchcraft will undoubtedly produce pitiful results."

"It sounds like African *vodu* magic used in the French slave colonies. The witches there are wretched, as are the creatures they conjure—slaves really—mindless, clumsy, and ugly," said Marie.

"A proper revenant is not a slave. It retains all its former faculties and characteristics. All revenants have a common purpose, however."

"Which is?"

"To avenge their death."

"Then what?"

"I know not," Abigail admitted.

"Can a revenant be conjured to serve?"

"I know not," said Abigail, hesitantly.

"If I were to become a pile of bones, do you possess the skills to resurrect me?"

"I... I honestly know not."

"Abby, hast thou performed such magic? Say *I know not* once more and I shall eat thy tongue with a goblet of blood."

Abigail struggled to maintain a smile, for Marie's inquiries were delving deeper into the topic, and she knew Marie's threat to be genuine. "A human, no. A dog, yes," said Abigail, softly. "After conjuring my brother's sheepdog, it ran into the woods to hunt down its killer, an alpha wolf."

"Hath a dog a soul?"

"Hades is quite fond of dogs."

Marie rolled her eyes. "What about a human?"

"My mother conjured a human once."

Marie's eyes smiled. "Tell me more."

Abigail paced the room, hands clasped tightly. "My little brother was killed."

"Yes, murdered. I know."

Abigail closed her eyes as she told the story and remembered a childhood of magic, beauty, and wonder. She remembered the forest, the clearing, and a peculiar tree.

Because Abigail's parents could afford neither a public funeral nor a proper burial in the village for their slain son, they buried him in a peaceful clearing in the forest nearby an odd tree. Its copper leaves were sparse but brilliant. The bark was flaking and the branches were gnarled, hollowed, and dry like deadwood, but very much alive. The tree shimmered—sunny or not—releasing aromas of licorice root, sage, and leather.

Every week for a year, Abigail's mother hiked through the forest to her son's gravesite to place fresh flowers. Then, one evening, when the air was unusually warm and calm and the moon appeared blue and large, she returned to the gravesite one last time.

The wolves were nearby, howling, and Abigail felt a strange tingling in her fingers and toes as she trailed her mother. She hid behind ferns and observed her mother removing a *Mandragora* root from a basket. She placed it on the ground and gathered bark, leaves, and branches into a small pile over the root. She then placed her hands on either side of the kindling and gently blew on it until it ignited.

Standing beside the fire, she stared up at the moon for several heartbeats and began to recite an incantation, the words of which Abigail had never before heard.

The fire burned green and then red and grew in size and intensity. The flames began to form shapes in the likeness of people—strangers at first, then past relatives, followed by Abigail's father, mother, then her, and finally her brother.

The fiery likeness of her brother began to frolic round the deadwood tree, leaving tracks of copper flames in its footsteps, moving closer and closer to the tree as it circled the tree. When it was close enough to touch the tree, it placed both hands on it.

The tree burst into colorful flames.

The energy jolted Abigail to her feet.

Her Mother levitated on shards of lightning, surging from the earth. The deadwood tree scorched the night's sky with metallic colored flames. It was beautiful. Abigail wanted to enter the clearing and touch the fiery tree, but was levitating higher and higher. Though the fire grew in size and intensity, there was neither heat nor smoke nor burning smells.

Soon, Abigail felt the ground under her feet again. Forest creatures—reptiles, insects, birds, and beasts—peacefully gathered round the clearing. Abigail had no reason to fear them, nor did they of her, for all had come to witness the world's only necromancer.

Beside the burned out stump of what was the deadwood tree stood Abigail's brother, naked, expressionless, and beautifully restored. Her mother quickly wrapped her cloak round him and started back for home.

Abigail blinked and noticed that Marie and she were levitating high up in the dim of the counting chamber's ceiling space.

"Such an uplifting story!" said Marie with a piercing cackle.

Abigail was astonished to be floating. "How?"

"Levitation requires a great deal of energy as you pointed out in your story. An impractical means of travel, though strategically useful at times. So, what became of thy brother?" The women descended back to the floor.

Abigail stepped away and regained her composure. "On the night of his return, we celebrated with a feast, though he had neither appetite nor voice. I tried to speak to him, but he was deaf to me. Mother insisted that in time he would recover. His time, however, was fleeting. A few days later, he slew his murderers, the constable's twin sons. Like the revenant dog I had conjured, he left, never to return.

"The villagers saw thy brother, conjured by magic from the dead. Frightened by it, they hunted thee," said Marie.

"Yes. The entire village turned against us, including the Priest," said Abigail clearly disappointed. "Villagers came in the middle of the night, neighbors, friends, breaking into our home. They took us prisoner. The next evening, they brought us to the village center where Father and I were forced to watch them stone my mother to death." Abigail searched her emotions buried beneath layers of indifference, fading with time. She feared her hatred of Marie would fade as well. "Were it not for you, My Countess, I would have suffered my mother's fate."

Marie recalled Abigail's father's pleas for mercy. *My daughter is innocent,* he said. *Please show mercy and stop this madness. I beg of you! Take my life instead, my life for hers. Please let her go. Please!* She remembered those words and the scene in the center of the village—Abigail's dead mother, and Abigail...

Lying in a fetal position across her mother's body, Abigail braced for the first blow from none other than her childhood friend Sara.

Enthralled by Abigail's unearthly beauty, Marie snatched the stone from Sara. Sara was infuriated. When she tried to take back the stone, Marie plunged her hand into the young woman's gut and strung out her intestines.

The mob never had a chance. Marie disemboweled all of them. She covered Abigail with her shawl, and as all the villagers lay dying in the street, Marie approached Abigail's father. He trembled like a man confronting the devil. Before he was able to utter another word, she snapped his neck.

Marie took Abigail's hands in hers. "Enough talk of filthy humans and revenants. Anxious I am, now, to hear of thy trip abroad. What news hast thou?"

Finally, thought Abigail. "I found him, My Countess, the one." Marie appeared unmoved, but Abigail sensed her surprise.

"Does he bear the marks?" asked Marie.

"He does, on the palms of both hands."

"Where is he?"

"He resides in England, near Manchester."

"Is he blood related to thy master?"

She nodded affirmatively. "A wealthy Dutch noble wedded Count Marcel's distant cousin and bore him two sons. The youngest, Hans Marc van Fleming, married an English daughter of the landed gentry and traveled to Manchester to start a cotton textile mill. He has two daughters and a son who has come of age. His son is the chosen one."

"Related to Marcel..." grumbled Marie, with glaring skepticism.

"Yes, My Countess," said Abigail, unwavering.

Marie assessed Abigail's expression—or lack thereof. "This young man, is he of incomparable luster, shape, and size?"

"Yes, My Countess."

Marie's eyes began to glow. "Name?"

"Pierce van Fleming.

"Handsome?"

"Very."

"Bright?"

"Brilliant," replied Abigail.

"Popular?"

"Scandalously so."

Marie scanned Abigail's face. "Does he know of thee?"

"He saw me, My Countess, briefly from across the lane in Manchester. That is all. We exchanged no words. I left for London the morrow after, and for Oostende two days after that."

Marie nodded, turned away, and whispered her thoughts aloud. "Is my decrepit master right to believe the oracle? Am I wrong to doubt her? Suppose the oracle *is* right." She looked back at Abigail. "If the prophesy is true, who better than I to turn him? Who better than I to teach him and control him? There is much to ponder." Marie wrapped her long fingers around Abigail's neck and pulled her close. "I have missed thee, my sweet Abby." Marie whispered in her ear. "Thy silence begets thy life. Speak to no one of this. Dost thou understand?"

"Yes, My Countess."

"Good. Come to my bedchamber tonight. It has been far too long."

"Yes, My Countess."

16 - THE COLLECTION

The last morning of October found Pierce van Fleming waking from his nightmare. The crushing of skin, muscles, and bones seemed so real that his body ached of it. The wooden clubs, imprinted on his mind like chards of lightning, revealed nothing new of the killers. When he was able to move his arms again, he threw off the bedcovers and allowed his body to cool and nerves to unravel. It was a hellish start to his twenty-third birthday.

The house stood quiet when Pierce went downstairs, and his only pressing desire was to find his father. On his way out to the carriage house, he looked up and saw his mother, standing behind her bedchamber window on the second floor. She noticed him and waved. He was certain she was smiling— probably excited his sisters and their children were to arrive from London that afternoon.

Last night, Pierce spent time with his father in the kitchen preparing the birds they had harvested at Clark Pond. He could not remember the last time his father and he had cooked a meal together. Of course, his mother scolded them for making a mess of the kitchen, but the roasted grouse and smile it put on Hans's face was worth it. Even Pierce's mother's sense of humor returned after two glasses of sherry. *If only every evening was like that,* thought Pierce.

The idea of the entire family making a mess of the kitchen together warmed his heart. He wanted that. He *needed* that. Family time was something that had steadily diminished after his sisters married and moved to London, and work at the cotton mills became more demanding and stressful.

Pierce saw that the carriage house door was open. His

father was probably working on one of his prized buggies. He was anxious to ask his father to go on holiday to Southport. They ought to ride there and stay a few nights at the new Southport Hotel for some much needed father-and-son time.

As he stepped into the carriage house, Pierce found his father lying face-up on the floor beside his prized buggy. If not for the blood—fanned out like a red halo behind his head and a large carriage wheel lying across his chest—he appeared to be napping.

"Father!" Pierce quickly removed the heavy wheel and pressed his ear to Hans's chest. The man had no breath, no pulse. Pierce could not believe it. Then, he saw her—his invisible friend. She was hovering slightly above the floor, only her features completely rejuvenated. She was a beautiful angel aglow in bluish-white light, with smooth skin flushed with sorrow. Nestled in her outstretched hand was a dazzling orb, shimmering like a large star in a moonless sky.

"Wait!" cried Pierce, lifting his hand to the winged apparition. He felt panic and nausea and confusion all at once. "My father needs help. He needs your help." Pierce rose and stepped towards her. "In your hand... is that his soul? It is, is it not?" Tears began flowing freely. "Please return it. Please restore his life. I beg of you! It is not his time. It cannot be. His daughters and grandchildren are arriving this afternoon. He must be here for them." He placed his hands over his face and dragged them up through his dark, wavy hair. "This is not your fault. This must be a mistake. Mistakes happen."

Death looked upwards, as if distracted by something high above.

"No. Look at me!" growled Pierce. "You must return my father's soul at once, before it is too late! Now is the time. Can you not see that?"

Death remained unmoved by Pierce's plea.

"How may I convince you? What must I do? Tell me!" Pierce's eyes latched onto a folding knife on a workbench. He went to the knife, unfolded it, and pressed its rusted blade against his neck. "I shall give my soul to you, in exchange for my father's." He moved towards her. "Imagine it—my soul— finally yours! Have you not always wanted it? Have you not stalked me for it? Return his soul and I shall gratefully plunge this blade into my neck."

Death slowly extended her arm towards Pierce and flicked her index finger, causing the knife to fall. The blade landed vertically, its tip firmly lodged in the wood-plank floor beside his boot. Pierce crouched to retrieve it, but no amount of pulling or twisting budged it. Enraged, Pierce rushed her, but he ran through the manifestation as if it was a plume of vapor. He clearly saw her, still floating there, calmly waiting and undisturbed by his futile attempt to assault her.

Suddenly, a pinhole of intense light penetrated the roof and beamed down onto the orb. As it lifted and disappeared through the rafters, its rejuvenating effects dwindled, leaving Death recognizably ugly again—rotting, smelly, apathetic. She unfolded her gray tattered wings, lowering herself to the floor, gazing down at Pierce who was now on his knees, cradling his father.

"What are you staring at?" wept Pierce, trembling with rage. "Have you no decency?" Pierce managed a hateful smile. "Did you know that today is my birthday? Well, of course you do! And thank you for this most propitious occasion." He shook his head in disbelief. "Quite frankly, I expected something a bit simpler, really. Birthday wishes from dear father—but—but this?" He glanced down at Han's body and scowled. He glared back at those bloody tears oozing from Death's sunken eye-sockets and shouted, "Why are you still here? Get out, execrable scavenger of hell. I hate you! I hate you!"

With a single beat of her great wings, she lifted and vanished through the rafters like a phantom.

17 - DEARLY DEPARTED

Pierce's sisters arrived at the Fleming estate as scheduled. Chelsea was the eldest sibling, thirteen years older than Pierce. Her daughter, Emma, was fifteen, a brighter than average child and filled with enthusiasm for the cotton industry and adoration for her Uncle Pierce. Chelsea's sister was two years her junior. Her boys were three, five, and six years of age. The sisters had married financiers and moved to London. They returned independently to Manchester once or twice a year on holiday. Their husbands were friends and business partners, unable to come to Manchester as they were in France together on business.

Emma's task was to look after her three young cousins while the women consoled each other and arranged the funeral service. Their mother would not come downstairs, and Pierce mourned in private. With the main house and guest cottage occupied by women and children, he spent most of his time away from home, sleeping in his office at the cotton mill.

On the day of the funeral, Pierce returned home, hitched a team of horses to a buckboard wagon his father had so beautifully restored, and brought it round to the house for his mother and sisters to board. Emma and the other children took a carriage manned by Chief Constable Gareth Turner, who followed Pierce's wagon to a modest stone chapel on the north end of the estate.

After the minister led the coffin in to a place near the altar and the mourners were all seated, he recited passages from the King James Bible. Pierce barely heard the man's droning voice. He crossed his arms, stared at the eternity box, and tried to repress his feral emotions. He loathed tears—everything about them: the tacky wetness, the puffy eyes, compromised vision. He despised Death for taking Hans's soul in the first place and delivering it to God-knows-where. Pierce wiped the dampness from his face and pressed his kerchief against his reddened nose. *That horrid, spiteful demon,* thought Pierce, and he began to hammer his leg with his fist.

Suddenly, a delicate weight fell upon his arm. Nuzzled beside him was Emma, beaming with optimism.

Several days after the funeral, Emma searched everywhere for her uncle until she finally found him closed up in his office in Manchester. He appeared disheveled from a lack of sleep but never happier to see her. It was not difficult for her to convince Pierce to take the day to show her the town.

He took her to places her grandfather had enjoyed. He retold his father's stories of how he had met his wife and came to build a cotton empire in Lancashire.

The next day, Emma and Pierce rode horses across the farmlands. She was not the equestrian Pierce was. Whenever he jumped a fence, she waited for him to turn back and lead her round it or through a nearby gate, and Pierce never left her behind.

Emma toured the estate, met Hamlet the pig, whose springy tail wiggled in their presence, and discussed many ordinary topics, though such discussions always gravitated to the cotton industry. New machines, which made it possible to produce vast amounts of textiles in short order, fascinated her. Pierce brought her to the Ancoats mill to watch the spinning of raw cotton into thread. She learned how steam engines powered the looms that wove fabrics, and observed the fabric-dyeing process. Despite the smelly rivers, Emma enjoyed a flat-barge cruise along the Irwell and Mersey.

On the day Emma was to leave for London, she found Pierce at home, sitting at his desk in the library. She entered the room and patiently waited for his attention. After several ticks of the wall clock, he peeled his eyes from a document and smiled at her.

"Uncle Pierce, forgive my intrusion. We are to leave in the hour."

Pierce put the document down and stood up. "Yes, of course. Thank you for reminding me."

Emma lowered her eyes and stared at the desk. She recounted her grandfather sitting at the desk, reading documents in much the same way. "Also, I wanted to inform you of a story I had heard...about you."

Pierce moved to the side of the desk and crossed his arms.

"Something about a duel—with guns," whispered Emma.

Pierce shook his head. "I do not know what to make of that."

"The duel?"

"No. That people in London talk about me at all."

Emma giggled. "The Fleming Cotton Company is well known, and so are you." Emma pressed on about the duel. She wanted to inform her friend of the truth. "Were you ever involved in a duel, Uncle Pierce?"

"A proper duel, as defending one's honor?" Pierce said, moving to enact one. "With pacing," he made three strides away from her and turned. "With boxed and matched pistols?" He pointed an imaginary gun at her and fired an imaginary round. "Bang!" He collapsed to the floor and grabbed at his chest, coughing and wincing, and finally letting out his tongue. Pierce laughed and sat up. "Heavens no, my dear. I would be dead."

An hour later, as Pierce's sisters and children were boarding their London-bound coach, he took Emma aside and held out his fist. "I have something for you," said Pierce with a playful grin.

She extended her hand and received a small hunk of lead.

"One day, I shall tell you about the elm tree duel," said Pierce.

"So you *were* in a duel!"

"Come, Emma," said her mother, impatiently, from inside the coach. Chelsea smiled sadly at Pierce. "Can you manage, Brother?"

Pierce approached the coach with Emma and shrugged his shoulders. He then helped her aboard and took his sister's outstretched hand in his.

"I worry for you and for mother," said Chelsea. "Please send her to London if she worsens. I will care for her myself." Her dampened eyes scanned Pierce's sullen face. "Do take care of yourself, Brother. Though it is necessary that you tend to the business, especially during this unfortunate transition, it is essential that you take time to rest. Come visit us when you can. You are always welcome."

"Thank you, Sister," said Pierce. "Do not worry for me or for the business. I will send Mother to London when she is able to travel. A change of scenery will do her good. Farewell." He released her hand and stepped back.

"Goodbye, Uncle Pierce," said Emma.

Pierce nodded to the driver and the carriage pulled away from him.

18 - AT FIRST SIGHT

No one spoke as Cedric farmed alongside other boys outside the castle wall. Under the watchful eyes of guards—grim manifestations of men, dawning whips, daggers, and crossbows—the boys harvested carrots, beets, turnips, chard, and spinach. They formed a brigade, passing buckets of water from well to irrigation ditches. Farming was hard work but second nature to Cedric.

The boys filed through the castle gates and intimidating barbican, a narrow passage with high stone walls and gates at both ends. Cedric imagined boiling oil and flaming arrows raining down on raiders trapped inside the barbican. He looked up and saw four archers glaring at them as they filed through. Even in times of peace, the castle was a battle-readied fortress. Stopping at the well in the courtyard to wash up, Cedric suddenly caught a glimpse of a girl in a white servant's gown through a gap between rows of barrels about a hundred paces distant. She was carrying a sack of rubbish out to a cart. Judging by her physique, she was perhaps fifteen or sixteen years of age. He seldom saw any girls at all, and when he did, they were usually quite young.

Cedric crouched as if to adjust his sandals, but his eyes were squarely focused on the girl. When she turned, their eyes met. At the gap between the barrels, she stopped and crouched to adjust her sandals and peer back at Cedric. He thought she might have even smiled at him, though he could not see her face in detail from such a distance. To be noticed by a girl of his age was glorious. It was difficult not to jump and shout in celebration, but he managed to act as if he saw nothing unusual in the presence of the guards and other boys. Yet, he had not gone entirely unnoticed.

"What is it?" asked a young boy, approaching Cedric, staring at the barrels.

"Nothing," said Cedric, hoping the girl had gone inside before the boy or anyone else saw her. Yet, the boy kept looking and asking what Cedric had been staring at. Obviously, to Cedric's relief, the girl had not been seen. Relationships between boys and girls at the castle were prohibited. "Nothing," Cedric said again as he moved to the well.

A guard quickly closed in on the young boy who had moved away from the group to get a better look at the barrels. He gripped the boy's arm. "What is the problem here?" barked the guard.

The boy glanced over at Cedric, who was now washing up at the well. Cedric wished the boy would just shut up.

"That boy was staring at something over there," said the boy, pointing at Cedric and then the barrels.

"I see nothing," croaked the guard, squeezing the boy's arm. "What is your number?"

"Twenty-two. Let go of me!" The boy squirmed and then slugged the guard in the stomach, with the force of a pebble being tossed against a tree.

The guard lifted the boy off his feet.

"Put me down," shouted the boy, his legs kicking in air.

"Please put him down," said Cedric, approaching the guard, face dripping well water. "I thought I saw something over by the barrels, but as we can see, there is nothing there."

The guard released the boy. The boy fell to the ground. The guard pressed his boot on his neck to hold him down. "Your number?" said the guard to Cedric.

"Thirteen."

The guard glanced over at another guard nearby who then nodded and walked to Abigail, who was watching them from the threshold of the castle's main entrance. After Abigail nodded, the guard removed his boot from the boy's neck and backed away.

All eyes were on Cedric, now, who was helping the boy to his feet. "What is your name," asked Cedric of the boy.

The boy shrugged Cedric off. "Cornelius." He narrowed his

eyes and muttered, "You are up to something," as he pushed Cedric out of his way.

Noticing the stares, Cedric quietly queued up behind the other boys, keeping his head down, blending in, and marched into the castle for the night.

In the bedchamber Cornelius kept glowering at Cedric. Cedric asked him to stop it, but he kept on. Cedric would have told him about the girl if Jacob had not discouraged him.

"Other than an escape plan, he will not believe anything you say," said Jacob. "Cornelius is mad to escape, and he trusts no one."

"He should talk to Jefferson then," grumbled Cedric. "Jefferson has a new plan daily."

"Jefferson is full of hot air, and you...well, I see how the youngsters take to you."

Cedric shook his head. "I am no leader, and I have no plan. If Cornelius wants to escape, he should plan it himself and leave me out."

Escape plans were a constant source of entertainment and rumblings. Most boys enjoyed discussing them and wanted in on them. No escape to anyone's knowledge was ever proven to be successful. Notably, boys who were known to have developed proper escape plans suddenly disappeared, leaving behind those who were originally in on the plan. Why would they deviate from the plan, leave behind their co-conspirators? Boys like Cornelius, who got caught up in the hearsay of escape or die, feared they would be fed to pigs if they stayed another day. Irony was those who wanted to leave so badly usually disappeared without a trace, as if they really had escaped, like Cornelius had two days later. Everybody saw that his bed was empty. The next day, a new boy took number twenty-two.

Escape was farthest from Cedric's plans, especially now that the rubbish girl—as he so fondly called her—was on his mind. Occasionally, Cedric saw her from across the courtyard or from different floor levels in the great hall. He began to memorize the locations and when he had seen her to determine a schedule or pattern by which to follow, but no such pattern worked because his chores were seldom set to a fixed schedule. The only time he was at one place at the same time of day was after returning from farming to the water well an hour before dusk. It was during those times that he and she saw each other because that was when she usually took out the rubbish.

He was anxious to know her name, hear her voice, and perhaps experience her touch. He longed to know everything about her. If only he could spend a day with her. How wonderful that would be! Soon, she occupied a place in his heart alongside his late family.

19 - THE HIGH TOWER

Donning new leather armor and an old mortuary sword from England's civil wars, Sir Michael Livesey ascended the high tower at Vos Castle to the clan master's chamber. He moved steadily and effortlessly up the winding staircase, as if walking on air. When he reached the top, the master's guards bowed and requested that he remove his sword, scabbard, and dagger—a request that had always piqued him, though he would never show it. Having surrendered his weapons, they let him into a lavish room with colorful stained-glass windows that marked a once adventurous clan master.

After the guards closed the door and Michael was alone, he observed a collection of battle armor. An ancient Roman cuirass with a visor helmet of bronze and a sixteenth century knight's mail and plate armor suit had always interested him, but it was the clan master's newest addition that drew Sir Michael's attention.

The clan had adopted leather armor in the seventeen-fifties. Leather was easier to shape, dye, carve, and stamp than iron was. The clan master's vest incorporated bronze plating embedded between layers of leather to shield his heart from all sides. A raised collar protected the neck. Michael carefully compared his vest to the displayed version. They appeared identical with one fundamental difference: Sir Michael's vest lacked plating in the back, leaving him vulnerable to attacks from behind. Sir Michael appreciated the added protection the clan master's vest provided and decided to try it on.

Moments later, Count Marcel Marc de Vos entered the room. He was handsomely robust, taller than average, with long wavy hair and a gray beard cascading over a black tunic. His silver-blue eyes were wide-set, penetrating with sincerity that Sir Michael could always sense. To him, Marcel looked vital for someone so medieval—hardly the tired old clan master of rumor.

Marcel placed his hand on Sir Michael's shoulder. "Sit with me," said Marcel, moving on towards a pair of oriental armchairs in front of a cavernous inglenook alit and warm.

"Thank you for seeing me on short notice, Milord," said Sir Michael.

"It is always a pleasure to sit with you, old friend. What news do you bring?"

"Headmistress Abigail has returned from England, Milord."

"Ah, she has, has she? And from your homeland of all places," Marcel said, clasping his hands together and resting his chin on the tips of his fingers. "Did she find him...the *chosen*?"

"I cannot confirm as yet. But I am inquiring sources."

"Why not ask her directly?"

Sir Michael detected derision in Marcel's posture. "The countess told the headmistress to tell no one of the purpose of her voyage. I believe there is motive behind it."

"The countess has always harbored secrets," said Marcus simply. "Why must we act the fool?"

"If the headmistress offers her findings to you in confidence, then so be it. Until then, I recommend that we appear unaware so as not to alarm her. We have subtler ways of gathering information, Milord."

"Very well," said Marcus, finally.

"Milord, may I speak candidly?" said Michael softly, leaning in.

Marcel lifted his finger and nodded.

"Dare I say, the countess is conspiring against you. She continues to violate our laws, and believes you to be unfit. She and Domitian intend to remove you, and forcibly if—"

Marcel raised his hand and chuckled at Michael's suspicions. "How does one differentiate a woman's scorn from dungeon torture, hmm? To be certain, she loves power and despises weakness, and she would have me sleep with no one but her through the end of days. Monogamy, however, is not in my nature, and to accept my nature is not in hers. So, the bitterly jealous woman seeks solace elsewhere—in Domitian or a certain someone in England. Domitian wishes to succeed me and perhaps he will. Marie intends to control the next clan master and perhaps she will. But sedition?" scoffed Marcel. "Neither she nor Domitian would dare cross swords with me."

"But, Milord—"

Marcel raised his hand again. "In what year were you made, Sir Michael?"

Michael recalled the night Count Marcel had rescued him from English assassins in Amsterdam and then made him a vampire. "Sixteen-hundred and sixty, Milord."

What year is it now?"

"Seventeen-hundred and ninety-eight or nine... Please forgive me, for I scarcely know the days let alone the year."

Marcel grinned. "We have been together for nearly one hundred and forty years. In all that time, have I ever been wrong about such matters?"

"No, Milord, but I know a thing or two of allegiance and deceit. Ought we not to be vigilant at least?"

"Yes, especially against formidable opponents," said Marcel, turning his gaze to the fire. "Tell me again, Sir Michael, were you not a baronet in England?" Marcel stood up, his eyes still captivated by the flames.

Michael stood as well. "Yes, Milord."

"And why did you flee your country?"

Michael lowered his voice. "I would have been executed for high treason..."

Marcel turned to him and looked deeply into his eyes. "For regicide," clarified Marcel.

Sir Michael felt his master probing his mind for the truth.

"Yes, Milord, most likely hanged, quartered, and drawn had I stayed. However, my opposition of Charles the First was legitimate, for he had lost both civil wars and would have subordinated parliament to the throne and England to the Roman papacy had his powers been restored."

Marcel turned to find an iron rod beside the inglenook. "Yet, he was your king." Marcel took the rod and stoked the fire. "To whom are you loyal now, Sir Michael?"

Sir Michael Livesey dropped to his knee. "Milord, you are my maker and master, the only true ruler of this clan. I am your humble servant. I shall defend you with my life. My loyalty is yours, always."

"Please stand, Sir Michael." Marcel put the iron rod away and glanced up at a portrait of Countess Marie hanging over the inglenook. "As you know, the human count and son in the so-called sunroom are fed and protected by us so they may ensure our existence in this magnificent castle. But they are merely human, prone to fear and disloyalty, lest they are regularly controlled by Gerda."

For as long as Michael could remember, he had engaged in repetitive discussions with Marcel, much as people do when they age, and this discussion offered no new information. "Yes, Milord. Count Frederick's wife, Gerda, is a strong mind bender."

"The strongest I have ever known," Marcel said with pride. "After she bore his child, I made her a vampire. Now she is loyal to me and this clan. Yet, she still cares deeply for her human husband and son. Does that make her any less loyal to me?"

"You are her maker, her father, Milord. Thus her loyalty is yours. She will do anything you ask of her, even if it was to kill her human family."

Marcel chuckled. "How can you or I be so certain? Can I really trust her, or anyone for that matter?" He shifted uncomfortably. "I changed her—as I changed you—forcibly. She was bitter at first, but after I guaranteed the safety of her family, promising never to test her loyalty against them so long as she guaranteed to uphold her duty to me and the clan, she has never failed me. There you have it. Establishing mutual trust and understanding, ensures loyalty and the safety of our clan. For loyalty cannot endure without trust." Marcel's view moved to the displayed leather vest and then to Michael's matching vest. He smiled and said, "I trust you, Sir Michael. Your loyalty requires no persuasion, no tests or mind bending."

"True, Milord."

"Do you share in my trust, Michael?"

"I do, Milord."

Marcel gazed into Michael's eyes and placed his large hand on his shoulder, steering him towards the center of the room. "Now, tell me about London. Is it not a marvelous city?"

"It is, Milord," said Sir Michael, feeling the strength of Marcel's grip. His master was truly a powerful creature, thrice as old, thrice as strong.

"Is London not leading the world by way of industrious machines?"

"Many believe Manchester to be the industrial leader due to the invention of a machine that spins cotton into yarn and another that weaves yarn into fabric."

"These are fascinating times, Sir Michael."

"Indeed they are, Milord."

Marcel walked Sir Michael to the door. "Thank you, my vigilant friend. I grow tired and must rest. Inform me of what Headmistress Abigail has discovered in England."

"Yes, Milord. Shall I inform you of anything further concerning Marie and Domitian?"

"They concern me not. But perhaps you ought to sharpen your swordplay if you are so certain of rebellion."

"Very good, Milord," Sir Michael said, bowing. He retrieved his sword and dagger from the guards at the door, and spiraled his way down the massive tower, running his hands over the new leather armor with thoughts of England and betrayal at his core.

20 - THE SECRET PASSAGE

As Jacob and Cedric became trusting friends, confiding in each other and revealing their hopes and dreams for a future outside the castle, they befriended others, too—a boy named Nigel who was three years their elder. When Cedric asked Nigel how he had managed to survive for so long, the boy exclaimed that as long as you know where and when to hide, it was easy.

Castles fascinated Nigel. His father and grandfather were stonemasons who had built stately manors throughout Flanders and France. They had told him of hidden doors and secret passages built into mansions and castles. As the boys worked the land near the stronghold, Nigel discretely scratched maps of the catacombs into the soil, revealing secret doors and tunnels that he had supposedly discovered.

During their chores, Cedric and Jacob searched for evidence of Nigel's claims, pulling on candle sconces, pressing against walls, looking behind cabinets and statues. They found nothing of the kind, and Cedric was beginning to doubt Nigel. No other boy had exceeded three years in the castle, so no one knew for certain if Nigel truly had. But two-year elders did verify that he was there when they had arrived at the castle. Nigel kept drawing maps of secret doors and passageways in the dirt until one day a guard came to see what he was doing. Nigel quickly scratched away the diagram and the guard stood over him for the rest of the day.

One night, Jacob returned to the chamber only a dozen heartbeats before Mum and Helga arrived. After the women finished counting heads and locking the chamber door, Cedric heard Jacob's high-pitched whisper: "Cedric, Cedric, I found it. I found Nigel's secret door." Jacob leaned out so far from his bed that he had to support himself with a hand on the floor. "In the catacombs near the counting chamber is a candle sconce above a small door. We have walked passed it dozens of times."

Cedric shook his head. "I am tired, Jacob. Go to sleep."

"No, listen. It is true."

Cedric turned to face him.

"I opened the door and it was as Nigel described. Pull down on the sconce and the door presses inward just enough to slip through into a small tunnel."

Cedric's interest grew. "Did you go in it?"

"No. It was late. I had to figure out how to close the door so that I could return before the headcount."

"How does it close?"

"Lift the sconce to its original position. It is quite amazing. Are you in the catacombs tomorrow?"

Cedric could barely concentrate with the thought of a secret passage tunneling through his head. "I will be replacing candles."

"I will be scrubbing floors and collecting rubbish in the catacombs in the late afternoon. We can meet at the door and explore the tunnel together, yes?"

"Yes!" blurted Cedric. His outburst stirred other boys.

Jacob moved farther towards Cedric, with two hands on the floor now, and murmured softly. "It could mean the end of us if we are caught."

"What else is new? Have you seen people roaming the catacombs?"

"Seldom, if ever," said Jacob.

"Precisely. We just need to be quick about it. Let us meet at the door thirty minutes before dusk. We will have little time."

"Agreed."

"Oh, and Jacob?"

"Yes?"

"I saw the rubbish girl today," said Cedric.

Jacob smirked. "It is forbidden."

"And exploring secret passageways is not?"

"You will bring trouble to her and to you. Do you want that?"

Cedric rolled onto his back and closed his eyes as Jacob scooted onto his bench. "No," Cedric whispered, realizing that he had been fraternizing with the opposite sex, a violation punishable by God-knows-what.

21 - THE CHOSEN

The next morning, under a drab sky, Countess Marie de Vos entered the courtyard and gazed up at the high tower. She imagined Clan Master Marcel Marc de Vos up there, hibernating in his humongous bed surrounded by mirrors of all shapes and sizes. She wanted to count them and then kill him.

In his younger days, Marcel held bloodletting parties with the clan's women. Marie put a stop to it. She would share him with no other. Marcel had no immediate objections, for his main interest was Marie. They were very much in love and inseparable in the beginning. However, her frequent disregard of the sacred laws and placing the clan at risk embarrassed Marcel and wore thin his patience. Eventually, he blamed her for destroying their marriage and resumed his infamous orgies.

When Marie walked in on one of them, she was infuriated and humiliated by what she saw and flew down the tower into the counting chamber. Marcel came to the chamber only once during that time. Marie ignored his request to unlock the door and speak to him. He could have easily broken in but decided to let her cool off.

On the twenty-eighth day of her self-incarceration, she left both the counting chamber and Marcel, with no intention of reconciling their marriage. She made a bedchamber in the catacombs and spent her waking hours collecting and counting the castle's riches, letting her mind twist and her wounded heart fester.

Marie peeled her attention from the high tower to gaze at Headmistress Abigail, who was giving instructions to a group of boy servants near the gate. All the boys except Cedric Martens were staring at the ground. Cedric's eyes fixed squarely on Abigail's exquisite profile. It amused Marie to see the boy so boldly stunned by beauty. Marie waited for Abigail to finish and then waved her over. As Abigail approached Marie, Marie noticed Cedric turning and moving away from the group of boys, his attention now captured by the rubbish girl. *Interesting*, thought Marie.

The countess locked arms with Abigail and led her into the flower garden for privacy. As they moved deeper into the colorful foliage, Marie picked a rose and began plucking and counting each petal. "Hast Cedric Martens permission to cast eyes upon thee?" asked Marie.

"Yes, My Countess," said Abigail. "All servants have my permission."

"Interesting. It appears only one boy is daring enough to see you," said Marie.

"Yes."

"Is his name Cedric Martens?"

"Yes, it is. How do you know him?"

"That is not important. What is important is my decision to meet Mister van Fleming." Marie scanned for eavesdroppers and whispered in her ear. "Arrange my departure to Manchester with your lustful boy servant Cedric Martens. I rather like that boy."

"Yes, My Countess."

"Clean him and dress him in English fashion. Reveal my destination and business to no one, especially Domitian. I shall tell him myself if need be. Dost thou understand?"

"Yes, My Countess."

"And Abby, come to my bedchamber tonight. Bring a child, our youngest child." Marie noticed the gloom behind Abigail's smile. "Girl or boy, it does not matter."

Abigail lowered her chin. "I look forward to spending the evening with you again, My Countess."

"Liar," quipped Marie with a seething leer.

22 - LET GO

Nearly a month had passed since Hans's death. Pierce knocked on his mother's bedchamber door and waited, but there was no answer. "Mother, may I enter?" asked Pierce. Still no response, he opened the door.

His mother was in bed. Her breathing was shallow and dark rings around her eyes gave her a deathly form. She had been rapidly losing her appetite, weight, and energy. Pierce had summoned a doctor to examine her. He performed bloodletting and prescribed rest with a diet of eggs and beet juice. When his mother showed no signs of improvement, Pierce put her on a stagecoach with a nurse to accompany her to London. Chelsea and Emma would care for her.

Unfortunately, with both parents gone, the estate no longer felt like home, and Pierce no longer wanted to be there.

As weeks went by, he caroused more than ever, returning home occasionally. He was drunk most of the time and a miserable master of his estate. In the library one day, Pierce poured a glass of whisky from a decanter and sat down at his desk. The weather was foul and he decided to stay in for the night.

When he awoke the next day, his head was resting on the desk. The young scullery maid was kneeling beside him, carefully collecting shards of glass, placing them on a metal dish. His neck was sore, his head hurt, and he felt horribly drained.

"Good morning, sir," said the maid.

Pierce turned to her. The sound of glass dropping onto the plate sounded like gunfire. "Please..." said Pierce, cringing and rubbing his temples.

The maid stood up and slid a glass of water towards him. "Please, sir, have some water. I will start a bath for you. Your clothes are clean and ready in your bedchamber."

Pierce nodded and drank the water.

"I will come for you when the bath is ready, sir."

In his bedchamber, he undressed and put on a robe.

"Sir?" said the maid from the hallway. "Bath is ready."

Pierce followed her to the washroom where a large porcelain tub stood in front of a window overlooking the fields.

"Please take my robe, Miss Foster," said Pierce as he turned his back to her.

The maid reached around him and untied the sash. She then pulled the robe away from his body and folded it, trying not to view him as he went to the tub. Pierce saw her reflection in the window, and recalled his father's words about a good woman. Miss Foster was an attractive young woman of eighteen years. She had pale skin and straight blonde hair twisted into a bun tucked beneath her flimsy white cap. The blue apron covered most of her gown, but her ruffled chemise revealed more than Pierce's mother would have allowed.

"Thank you, Miss Foster. That will be all for now."

"Please ring the bell if you need me, sir. Fresh towels are here on the counter." The maid exited the washroom and closed the door.

Pierce slid in under the water. He stayed under until his lungs began aching for air. Drowning was a simple solution to his woes—all his troubles washed away, his body contained in this porcelain vessel. Just as he was about to inhale the water, he noticed a darkness looming over him, peering down at him. Pierce lifted his head and gasped for air.

"Bloody hell, you again!"

She was floating above him. Her rotting flesh appeared to be crawling with maggots under her gray skin.

He placed the back of his neck on the tub's ledge and shook his head.

"Stinking demon... Get out! You're not going to collect my soul today."

Pierce finished bathing, dried off, and went to his

bedchamber. He tossed the towel onto a chair and fell back onto his bed. On the side table, he noticed a full bottle of Scotch. He took it, pulled the cork, and drank an ounce.

By the time Miss Foster was knocking at his door, Pierce was fast asleep. She knocked again and waited, but he would not stir. She looked downstairs to see if the cook or the other maid was nearby. By the sound of things, they were in the kitchen. She placed her hand on the doorknob but hesitated. No, she would not enter.

When Pierce woke an hour later, he got out of bed, put his clothes on, and went downstairs. It was midday. The help was still there, and he wanted to be alone. He entered the library and closed the door. Thinking back to when his father and he had hunted and roasted grouses together, he was never happier. Pierce lifted a bottle of whisky and drank it like water. He then packed his pipe and lit it. Staring out one of the tall windows, bottle in one hand, pipe in the other, he smoked and drank until he was too intoxicated to stand.

The next day, he found himself on the floor beside someone placing broken bottle glass on a metal plate. Pierce took hold of the woman's wrist and pulled her on top of him. The plate and broken glass fell to the floor. She struggled to free herself of his grip.

"Please, sir," said the woman. "Please let go."

"Miss Foster, is this not what you want of me?"

Pierce tried to steal a kiss, but noticed that the woman was not Miss Foster at all. It was the cook, Miss Tibbits, forty years older and forty pounds heavier than Miss Foster.

"Oh! Please, forgive me, Miss Tibbits," stammered Pierce, letting her go. He sat up and rubbed his bloodshot eyes.

Miss Tibbits stood up and straightened her apron and cap. She did not flee from the embarrassment, though her eyes desperately looked for an escape. She opened her mouth but no words came out. She swallowed and tried again. "Sir, I...I can only imagine how terrible you must feel, losing your father and then sending your poor mother off to London. If there is anything I can do to ease your sorrow, other than the sort of activity Miss Foster..." Her hands lifted to her mouth to silence it. As the redness of her face began to drain, she forced a smile and said, "Let me help you onto the sofa, sir."

"No," said Pierce, lifting to his feet.

"Shall I fetch you some water then?"

"Thank you, that would be nice, and Miss Tibbits?"

"Yes, sir?"

"Please accept my apology. I am not myself, and Miss Foster is not to blame. I am obviously unstable, deplorable, a menace to everyone in this house. Because of that, I have decided to let the help go. I am sorry."

Miss Tibbits gasped. "But, sir—"

"It is a decision I shall regret, but it is for the best, Miss Tibbits. Please inform the maids and caretaker. I shall pay twelve months' wages to all."

The cook's chin dropped with disappointment. She lifted her gaze and nodded with a sort of dignity that she had done her best to care for the household. "Will that be all, sir?"

"Yes, thank you, Miss Tibbits."

After he was alone again, he took hold of a bottle of sherry from the table, opened it, guzzled a cup's worth, and glared at a portrait of himself when he was seventeen, standing beside his Belgian black stallion. He threw the bottle at the portrait. The shards tore the fabric, tilted the frame, and glass and sherry exploded all over the floor.

23 - DEAD END

At first light, the boy servants were ready and waiting for Mum to finish the headcount and remind them of their chores for the day. Cedric was to make candles with tallow and torches with pitch in the morning. In the afternoon, he was to replace spent candles and torches in the catacombs. Jacob's cleaning chores in the catacombs overlapped Cedric's; thus, they planned to meet at the small door near the counting chamber before dusk and investigate the secret tunnel behind it.

As daylight began to fade, Cedric walked from the counting chamber to the small door. Exactly as described, the door was located directly below a candle sconce. Water drained out under the door. He looked in both directions and listened intently for people. Aside from pendants of randomly dripping water on the ceiling, he heard little else.

He placed his hand on the sconce bracket and pulled downward. The strumming sound of cables lifting and pulling something behind the wall, followed by the grinding of stone on iron, and air drafting rapidly as the door opened, was something to behold. From his bag, he removed a small torch and lit it from the fire of another on the wall.

The doorway was hardly big enough to squeeze through, but he managed and soon found himself crouching in the stone tunnel. He peered into the breezeway and saw only darkness. He waited several minutes for Jacob. When the boy failed to show up, Cedric considered abandoning the investigation, partly because it was eerie and dark in there and mostly because time was running out, but curiosity spurned him on. So he moved quickly into the tunnel.

After several minutes of crawling, the space started constricting, forcing Cedric to shimmy on his stomach. A few feet from the outlet, he saw iron bars and rats exiting to a place with reeds swaying in the breeze outside. The smell, however, was of something rotting, like decaying flesh. It brought up memories of dead animals on the farm back home. The calf carcass he found at the edge of the farm smelled horrible, but not as horrible as the stench outside. It was truly sickening. He wanted to vomit. What was it?

By the looks of the sky outside, dusk was near. He had to get back to the bedchamber.

Cedric made his way to the entrance and tugged at the hidden entryway. Panic rose in his throat as he found the small door firmly shut. He could not pry it open. He prayed for Jacob to come free him and feared the headcount may have already begun. Worse yet, his torch had reduced to a glowing smolder. When he was about to surrender all hope, he heard tapping at the door.

"Cedric, are you in there?" whispered Jacob from the other side.

Cedric responded with frantic tapping at the door. "Yes. Yes. Open the door, Jacob. Please hurry!"

Finally, mechanical sounds of gears moving and the door shifting released Cedric from the shaft. Cedric gratefully tumbled out onto the wet floor.

"Pardon me, Cedric," whispered Jacob, as he and Cedric swiftly moved through the catacombs. "I found the door opened, but before I could join you, I thought I heard someone coming. I closed the door and hid in a chamber." He shook his head with embarrassment. "It was only a rat."

"I hate rats," muttered Cedric, as he tried to put the last days of Linder out of mind.

Cedric and Jacob rushed into the bedchamber a few minutes before Mum and Helga arrived.

After Mum and Helga had completed their tallying and locked the bedchamber door for the evening, Jacob turned to face Cedric.

"Did you reach the end?" whispered Jacob.

"Yes."

"Where does it lead?"

"Somewhere outside the castle," whispered Cedric.

"Can we escape through it?"

"An iron grate covers the outlet."

Enthralled by the discovery and recalling Nigel's simple method of survival, Cedric glanced towards Nigel's bed and saw that he was missing. Troubled by his absence, he glanced at Jacob to be certain he was still there and pulled the blanket up to his chin. Perhaps Nigel was trapped in one of his secret passages. Cedric hoped and prayed that Nigel would return, and then he fell asleep.

24 - THE HOVERING

Abigail waited at the entrance to Marie's bedchamber. Standing in front of her was a young girl.

"Enter," said Marie.

Abigail presented the girl.

Marie came to them, knelt down, and smiled sweetly at the child. She held a small cup of grape juice to the girl's lips and nodded for her to drink. The girl sipped from the cup then Marie led her to a settee smothered in beautiful pillows of all shapes, colors, and sizes. She lifted the girl onto the settee and turned to Abigail. Marie had always hoped that Abigail would hover with her, but she never did and Marie never forced her to.

The girl was entranced and calm when Marie sunk her fangs into her arm. A wave of euphoria swept Marie up into a hover. Suspended in air, as if lying on her back on an invisible table, arms and legs dangling slightly, Marie hovered several feet above the drained girl. The hover was not only the floating state of body but also the hallucinogenic and euphoric state of mind. The younger the child the more potent the blood, the more potent the blood, the more intense the hover was. A vampire's strength and speed was also greatly enhanced by child's blood. However, no vampire in their right mind fed on children or turned them into one of their own. It was strictly prohibited for good reason. To drink child's blood was suicidal.

The side effect was intense addiction, and rapid deterioration of not only appearance but also mental capacity. Insanity, rapid aging, skin soars, bloating and flatulence eventually plagued the addicted. To counteract this, more children and younger ones had to be consumed to maintain the desired effect. In the end, concealing ones addiction was impossible, and when discovered, the clan was always forced to destroy the addicted.

During the hover with Marie, Abigail was required to stay on guard, but she despised her role in being Marie's accomplice. She wanted to end it, end Marie, but the countess was Abigail's maker, mother, and protector. She rescued her from the witch-hunters. But sometimes she wished she had been left to die.

As Marie hovered, Abigail escaped into her imagination. She ran through a vast forest, as far and as fast as her legs would take her. Everything about the woods was vivid: smells, sounds, sting of conifer needles against her face and bare feet as she leapt over ravines and crags until finally reaching a clearing where the lone deadwood tree stood. It was at that moment, while standing beside the tree, that she admired its elaborate designs of glistening copper brocaded into its gnarled trunk and branches. The escape from the nightmarish reality, however, was ephemeral.

After the hover had gone its course and Marie had fallen asleep on her bed, Abigail wrapped the girl's body in a towel and carried it out. Standing in the corridor was Marie's trusted sentry, Isaac, ready to collect the body for disposal.

Back in her own bedchamber, high in the north tower, Abigail heated a cauldron of water over a fire. After an hour of bathing and trying to scrub away her associated guilt, she retrieved a mirror and wooden stake from a footlocker. She leaned the mirror against the locker and stared at the reflection of her naked body, a reflection that only she could see. In it, she saw her true self: her parents' daughter, a young witch with a wooden stake in her hands.

She felt its weight and dryness, the ridges of grain and the pointed tip. She always placed the point to where her heart ought to be, imagining where on the floor the opposite end of the stake would touch down if she fell on it, forcing the stake through her heart, reducing her despicable existence to bones.

As she had hundreds of times before, she placed the stake and the mirror back into the locker. After that, she put on a nightdress and slipped into bed with a glimmer of hope that had so far prevented her from impaling herself to death. Some called that glimmer of hope the prophecy. She called it Pierce van Fleming.

25 - REHABILITATION

When Pierce van Fleming stopped carousing and showing up at work, all of Lancashire noticed. It was common knowledge that he had sacked the help. The rumor was that he went stark-raving mad. That he might have even killed his father and then committed suicide. Bookmakers set odds, and Ewen Clark set Pierce's favorite bottle and glass on a high shelf, a cenotaph to a once great man.

Magistrate James Smith and Chief Constable Gareth Turner had known Pierce since he was a boy. They had respected his father and watched Pierce grow into the greatest industrialist of their time. Though Pierce's brawling and womanizing may have tarnished his reputation, he never claimed to be a model citizen, and James and Gareth never lost sight of the man they thought he was: generous, honest, and a loyal and reliable friend. Besides, they had investigated his father's death. Hans had slipped and fallen while mounting a wheel. The back of his head slammed against an area of floor paved in stone, fracturing his skull. The weight of the wheel pinned him down. It was a tragic accident.

Gareth and James had heard enough rumors. They went to the Fleming Estate and found horrible maintenance and starving animals. Weeds had taken over the flower gardens. The reflection pond had become a collection pond of debris. To a first-time visitor, the estate would have appeared abandoned. The horses were gaunt, the pig had collapsed, and Pierce would not come to the door when they knocked.

Gareth tried to open the door, but it was bolted. "What do you suggest, break in?" asked Gareth.

"Follow me," said James. He led Gareth to the back of the house and knocked at the kitchen door. No response. It was a modest door with a single panel, a simple brass knob and latch.

"Please stand aside, Mister Smith," said Gareth, squaring himself in front of the door, debating in his own mind how best to break in.

James gently placed his hand on Gareth's shoulder and pulled him aside. "Let us try this first." He turned the knob and opened the door.

The stench of rotting food alarmed them. Gareth found a small barrel with moldy food scraps and quickly took it outside.

"Mister Fleming!" shouted James as he continued on through the house. "Hello, sir? Magistrate James Smith and Chief Constable Gareth Turner are here to see you."

"Mister Percy van Fleming?" shouted Gareth as he joined the magistrate at the base of the stairs. "Hello, sir?"

As they were about to go upstairs, Gareth heard a noise, maybe a faint groan. He was not sure, but it came from the ground floor, possibly the library. They quickly moved through the gallery to the library and peered inside. Though the heavy curtains had been drawn, it was not so dim as to hide the silhouette of a man lying on the floor.

James and Gareth hurried in, the sounds of broken glass crunching beneath their steps.

"Mister Fleming," shouted James. He knelt beside him and tried to assess his condition. "Mister Turner, will you please open the curtains?"

Gareth did as he was asked and was shocked to see the room in shambles. Torn and busted portraits hung tilted, or not at all. A large mirror was shattered. Books were strewn everywhere. Sparkling fragments of bottles, decanters, and glasses coated the floor, and the room smelled of whisky and gin—and a befouled human.

James slowly rolled Pierce onto his back. Pierce moaned from the dozens of slivers of glass embedded in his body.

"Leave me," groaned Pierce.

"Gareth and I are here to help you," said James, matter-of-factly. "Some water, please, Mister Turner," whispered James to

Gareth.

"Leave me!" Pierce coughed. His eyes widened, staring at the corner of the ceiling. He lifted his bloody hand and pointed to the ceiling. "Leave me. Get out," groaned Pierce, as he faded from consciousness.

James glanced up at the ceiling and saw nothing.

Gareth handed a glass of water to James.

James splashed water on Pierce's face until he came to. "Mister Fleming, drink this," James said, pouring water into his mouth.

Pierce swallowed some and spit out the rest. His coughing drew Gareth closer. James handed the glass to Gareth to move him back, and he placed a pillow under Pierce's head. "Mister Fleming...Percy, listen to me, you are emaciated and lacerated. This is what we are going to do. First, we will remove the glass from your face and hands. Next, we will take you to your bedchamber to rest. Then, we will bring a doctor to mend you and help to care for you."

James and Gareth lifted him on the sofa and used a magnifying glass and tweezers to remove slivers of glass from his face and hands. They disrobed him, burned the filthy clothes, and cleaned his body with wet towels. When done, they dressed him in the cleanest nightshirt they could find and carried him to his bedchamber.

Two days later, Pierce was jolted from his cataleptic state. The light of day and sounds of people outside and inside the house confused him. His arms tingled. His hands were in bandages. His face stung. The reoccurring nightmare of being pummeled to death afflicted his entire body. He was too weak to sit up on his own. On the table beside his bed was a cup of coffee and bread and jelly on a tray. He wanted whisky but could not help salivating at the smell of the bread and jelly. His eyelids drooped. He was so tired. A knock at the door brought him back. He squinted to see and tried to speak.

"Ent..."

The door opened. A woman followed by two men entered the room.

"Good morning, sir," said Miss Foster.

Pierce was surprised to see his former scullery maid.

"Good morning, Mister Fleming," said James, "and welcome back."

"Good day, Mister Fleming, said Gareth, a smile forming on his face. "The doctor bandaged you up. You should be as good as new in a few days."

The maid helped him sit up and placed the tray on his lap. She spread jelly on a piece of bread and handed it to him. Pierce closed his eyes and took in the smell and taste of fresh baked bread and plum jelly.

"Despite your decision to remove the help," said James, "Miss Foster graciously agreed to come and nurse you to health. She is on loan, of course. Quite the cook as you should already know."

"Thank you," sighed Pierce, moving his eyes from James to the maid, uncertain if he was ready to go a whole day without brooding and stewing in drunken misery. For drink provided solace from the winged demon, the nightmares, his lack of identity, and the full weight of the business to bear. His kind and trusting father was the only man who seemed to truly know him—or at least accept him for who he was. Pierce felt as if he had lost his entire family and identity.

The maid curtsied and left the room.

"Your horses and animals are being cared for as well," said Gareth, cheerfully.

Pierce nodded. "I am indebted to you."

"Indeed you are," chuckled James. "Now I must leave you in good hands. The missus awaits." He placed his hand on Gareth's shoulder as he turned to leave.

"I do have one request, Mister Fleming," said Gareth. "I would like to take one of your black Belgians out for a ride one day—with you of course."

"Please do, Mister Turner. With or without me, you are welcome."

"Splendid! I shall return tomorrow then. Good day, sir." Gareth left the room.

No sooner had the men left did Miss Foster return with a boiled egg and water.

Pierce felt awkward to be tended to by the maid he had sacked, yet, there she was and there he was in need of her services.

"Miss Foster, I do not know quite how to say this so I shall simply say it. I am ashamed."

"Sir...?"

He let the dust in his mind settle.

"I am ashamed for my actions towards you. I was lost in my sorrow. As for your current employment, I am gratefully pleased. There is no finer man than Magistrate James Smith, as you know. He and my father were dear friends." Pierce felt strangely emotional and had to stave off tears.

She smiled and curtsied. "It is my pleasure to see you well, sir. Your appetite appears to have returned."

Pierce masked his sadness with a smile. "Indeed it has, thanks to you."

"Mister Smith has restocked your larder with instructions to fatten you. Tonight's meal shall consist of doe venison, roasted grouse, celery ragout a la Francoise, mashed pea, pastries, and cake with walnuts and raisins." She backed to the door and shied her eyes to the floor. "Will that be all, sir?"

"Yes, thank you, Miss Foster." Pierce observed the daintiness of the scullery maid as he had many times before. She was a pretty young woman, a good woman. Pierce's mother had drawn a line between the servants and the served. She would not condone a union between them.

Two years prior, Mrs. Fleming had introduced Pierce to eligible daughters of the industrial elite. She even approached families of title who sought male suitors of wealth, but nothing came of her efforts. Pierce reminded her that he would not marry for title or class alone—that love, beauty, passion, and mystery were far more important. Each time he expressed that opinion, he did so with Meghan Clark in mind.

26 - THE CHALLENGE

From Edinburgh to Manchester, Meghan Clark's family operated a total of six pubs, including Ravens Gate. Meghan had just turned twenty-one and her parents were undertaking a challenging task of identifying suitors for her—challenging in that Meghan found all suitors to be unsuitable. Stubborn as she was, with an insatiable interest in art and books, her parents placed little pressure on Meghan to wed. They felt Grace would be the first, for unlike Meghan she preferred ale and lads to books and art.

Meghan's father and Uncle Ewen had inherited a large collection of books, most of which were shelved at Ravens Gate—her only reason for going there. Women of good standing seldom visited pubs and much less drank in them. Wenches were more common, such as Meghan's younger sister Grace, who worked for her uncle at Ravens Gate. The Clarks allowed their children to work at the pubs from sixteen years of age on, but required them to return home before nightfall.

That never stopped Grace from slipping out of the house while the family slept. She attended late-night parties with the hedonistic children of the burgeoning middle and upper classes. Unfortunately, a disgraceful rumor circulated amongst her riotous acquaintances, alleging Pierce van Fleming had deflowered Grace at one of those parties—the reason her parents detested him. They forbade their daughters from speaking to Pierce. While Meghan tended to obey her parents' wishes, Grace tended otherwise. Her attraction to Pierce grew despite her parents' loathing of him.

Pierce had not gone into town in weeks and was becoming restless in the empty house. Miss Foster had returned to James Smith's household, and despite the nightmares, Pierce slept well and woke more rested than ever before. Coincidently, the winged demon had not visited him in weeks.

The first order of business was to bathe and groom and find something clean to wear. With only one set of fresh undergarments to spare, he put on his best dress, placed his washing in a sack, and mounted his horse. Traversing a labyrinth of ginnels to a community of Stanley cottages on the outskirts of town, he dropped off his washing at a laundress and rode into Manchester. Then by foot, he followed the pavement to Shambles. Approaching a well known butcher's shop, he could not believe his eyes. Two doors ahead, Grace Clark was entering a boutique. Then, he heard a familiar voice and stopped at the doorway to see Meghan Clark inside the butcher shop. Sometimes life has its way of granting wishes, he thought as he stood in the doorway.

Meghan thanked the butcher and turned to leave.

A mix of anxiety, exhilaration, and confusion came over Pierce. Never before had he felt so unprepared.

"Mister Fleming, what an unexpected surprise," said Meghan, slowing to a stop, unable to exit with Pierce blocking the exit.

"Mister Fleming?" said the butcher, pointing his knife at him. "What a wonderful surprise to see you, sir! Been looking for you, I have. Do you remember the time when I was so *kaylied* you paid a driver to take me home?"

"Which time are you referring to specifically, Mister Whitman?"

The butcher slapped the counter and coughed up a throaty laugh. "The missus says it was you who rescued me from me faults that night."

"You would do the same for me, Mister Whitman."

Seriousness befell Mr. Whitman's face. "Indeed, sir, I would. Will you please accept me finest black pudding in appreciation for your kindness?"

"I accept, Mister Whitman," said Pierce, removing his hat and bowing awkwardly in the narrow space of the entrance way. His eyes locked onto Meghan as he straightened his posture. "Good day to you, Miss Clark." Locking eyes with her was as rare as a Thames whale, and he relished the brief moment.

"Good day," said Meghan, cautiously moving forward, squeezing past the man-obstacle.

Pierce's mind searched for something clever to say, something to engage her. "Miss Clark," said Pierce. "May I please have a word?"

She stopped and turned to him.

Pierce smiled gratefully and continued. "For some time, now, I have wanted to..." A voice in his head beseeched him to slow down, "to ...to challenge you." *That was dreadful*, said the voice in his head. "What I meant to say is to present an opportunity."

Meghan scrunched her face, trying to make sense of him. "What sort of opportunity, Mister Fleming?"

"You and I have something in common—a fondness for horses. I believe you enjoy fox hunting as well as riding competitively."

She nodded hesitantly.

"Thus, I would like to challenge you to a horserace from Johns Gate to Brooks Bridge."

Meghan shook her head as if he had suggested a trip to the moon.

"Quite frankly, Mister Fleming, I cannot see the point. Any activity involving *us* would be awkward, if not inappropriate."

"Miss Clark, if I may—"

"No thank you, Mister Fleming. I must decline yer offer. Now, if you will excuse me, I have an appointment to keep."

"Yes, of course." Pierce bowed. "Please forgive me."

"That will not be necessary. Good day, sir."

"Thank you, Miss Clark. Good day, Miss Clark!" He watched her cross the thoroughfare and began to assess the damages—what he said, how he said it, what he should have said, or not have said, and so on. A tap on his shoulder startled him from his retrospection. Expecting the butcher, he turned to find Meghan's sister standing there, her auburn tresses gathered up, her green eyes catching a glimpse of Meghan turning a corner out of sight. "Fancy meeting you here, Mister Fleming," said Grace in a playful tone. "What on earth did you say to my sister to frighten her off like that?"

"Good afternoon, Miss Clark," Pierce said, bowing politely. "She is keeping an appointment."

"Or making a hasty getaway," quipped Grace.

Pierce struggled to compose his disappointment in Grace's snippety comment.

Her eyes blanketed him from face to boots, as if to admire him or to make him feel uncomfortable. She moved a little closer. Her air felt not of anger but of desire. He had felt it before from her.

"You challenged Meggy to a horserace," said Grace, her bright eyes focused on his lips. "I fancy a horserace. Did you know that she and I used to race horses? Guess who won most of those races? Me, of course." She giggled mockingly. "Unlike my sister, I would have accepted yer challenge. Winner takes all, if you know my meanin'." Grace leaned in with a flirtatious grin.

Pierce stepped back and checked his pocket watch. "I apologize for taking up so much of your time, Miss Clark." He bowed and put on his tricorne. "I, too, have an appointment to keep."

Grace's eyes drifted downwards as she curtseyed slightly. "Aye, Mister Fleming. Good day, then."

He tipped his hat. "Good day, Miss Clark." As Pierce ambled along the walkway, he heard Mr. Whitman hollering from the butcher shop, "Mister Fleming, sir, you forgot your pudding!"

27 - SIBLING RIVALRY

Absorbed in stories of the New World, Meghan had not noticed her sister creeping up behind her in the parlor. Grace stopped behind Meghan's chair and imagined a spider suspended from the ceiling. She lowered her index finger to the top of Meghan's head and twitched it just enough to frighten her out of the seat. Much to Grace's amusement, Meghan lowered her head and attempted to shake off the phantom spider. Duped again by her sister, Meghan threatened to throw her journal at Grace. "That was no nice," grumbled Meghan as she plopped back down on her chair.

"Sorry, Meggy," Grace said. She tried to run her fingers through her sister's luxurious locks, but Meghan swatted her away.

Grace giggled and said, "Remember when we was young, and you got new clothes and I got yer old ones. Now *that* was no nice."

"That was none of my doin'," reminded Meghan.

"I know, but it was no nice all the same. You always got the best things, Meggy. Even yer hair is thicker, and yer eyes are greener. I want 'em. I want the best things, too," said Grace.

"What if my hair was yellow and my eyes were black as pitch?"

"Better still."

"You always long for what you don't have, Gracie, and longing to be something you just aren't."

"Speakin' of longing, I saw you, yesterday, with," she lowered her voice, "Pierce van Fleming."

"Is that so?" said Meghan, her eyes drifting towards the

window. "And I saw you spying on me from the shop next door."

"I was no spying. I was looking out for you," muttered Grace.

"So what's yer business, Gracie?" Meghan wanted her to get to the point and leave.

Grace leaned in. "I want to know yer true feelings for our winsome Mister Fleming."

Meghan sat back in her chair and thought about her sister's big ears. Meghan crossed her arms and shook her head. "You have mother's hearing and father's meddlesome nature, a dangerous pairing," said Meghan.

"So?" said Grace.

"So, it will bring you trouble, Gracie."

"Do you fancy him?"

Meghan kept her growing curiosity of boys at bay with literature, as the idea of marriage and children terrified her. Besides, Pierce was an egotistical industrialist of whom her parents greatly disapproved—hardly the most available bachelor in their eyes. "What sort of man challenges a lady acquaintance to a horserace? I thought a minted lad like him was...more conventional," said Meghan.

"Pierce van Fleming is many things, but conventional is no one of them. So, you *do* fancy him then."

"No," said Meghan.

"Will you marry him if he asks you ta?" asked Grace.

Meghan wrinkled her nose and shook her head. "Yer mad, Gracie O'Brian!"

"Aye, maybe so."

"Undecent and senseless..."

"All that, too, now?" said Grace.

"Aye!" said Meghan. "I barely know him, and he seldom crosses my mind—you know that." Meghan's eyes narrowed. "What is this *really* about, Gracie?" Something in Grace's eyes and flushed cheeks began speaking volumes to Meghan. "You! It is you!"

"Me?" said Grace, taken aback by her sister's accusative tone.

"I knew you fancied him, Gracie, but so strongly? I had no idea. Well, you needn't compare our feelings for him. I have none. But I recommend that you consult Father afore you make permanent arrangements with that minted Mister Fleming."

"Rubbish!" shouted Grace. "Why are you seein' him against Dad's wishes?"

"I told you, Am no seein' him!"

"Liar!" spat Gracie.

"You can have him!"

"Maybe aye can and maybe nay and maybe he can't see past you!" said Grace.

"What does that mean?"

"Am no yer pathetic shadow!"

"What are you talking about?" demanded Meghan.

"Am no blind! I see him lookin' at you! And I see you lookin' at him! Even if I fancied the man, you stand between us!"

Meghan's mouth dropped. "How can you possibly be jealous when there's nothing to be jealous of? We both know, Father will no allow us to see Mister—"

"Dad needn't know..." Grace's eyes jittered and then settled on Meghan's face. "That's it. Slyer than a fox, you are. Keeping it secret until the time ripens. Then bonnie-wee Meggy gets everythin' again, including Mister Pierce van stinking-Fleming! And what does poor Gracie get? Nothin', nothin', nothin' again!"

Meghan felt her blood fuming with anger. It was not about Pierce but her sister's character. "Ironic how someone by the name of Grace can exude so much pride, lust, envy, and gluttony. Maybe it serves you right! Maybe you deserve nothin' nice. After all, it was yer disgustin' rumor that pushed him away!" Meghan lifted her hands to her mouth as if to catch those words—too late.

Grace sprung to her feet, hurt and ire bursting red on her face. There was little Meghan could say or do to lessen the sting.

"Oh, Gracie, I apologize," murmured Meghan, realizing spite was a common trait and they ought to control it.

Grace stormed out of the parlor with unnerving thoughts of Pierce and Meghan together and a growing determination to end them.

28 - THE ROMANS

Marie found Domitian laughing noisily in the company of two men behind the castle. Domitian twitched when he saw Marie approaching and hurried to meet her. "There you are, my love!" sang Domitian. "I have been looking for you. Will you not join us in a game of archery?"

Marie gazed out at the target and noticed a human male—half-naked, blindfolded, and gagged. He was bound to an old gate propped up against a tree, and three arrows within inches of his body. By her expression, Domitian knew she was displeased.

"A human target in broad daylight, Domitian? Really?" said Marie. She approached one of the men. "Art thou Italian?"

Domitian whispered in her ear: "Representatives of the Roman Clan, they have come at my request to discuss our plans,"

"Please excuse us," said Marie to the Italians. She pulled Domitian aside by the collar. "Thou hast violated thy castle rules in the open."

"Rules? Since when have they mattered to us?"

"They matter when others might be watching. Violations in the open bring unwanted attention."

He nodded. "Yes, yes, you are right, but these men have journeyed long and far. I was doing my best to entertain them."

Marie turned her eyes to the human target.

"He trespassed somehow... and... and was wandering," stammered Domitian. "I assure you, my sweet, this shall not happen again."

"Trespassing? He appears to be a castle worker. Remove his

memory and return him to work, or eat him in the shadows—anything but this."

Domitian clamped his lips together.

Marie shook her head. "Tell me about our guests."

Domitian moved closer and whispered, "Because the Romans feel Lucius instead of Marcel ought to have been elected ruler of the League, these men are eager to oust Marcel."

"Yes, but can we trust them? What is to stop Lucius from taking advantage of our weakened state of affairs? Why would they not absorb us and all of Flanders?"

"Impossible. Those men killed Lucius nary a week ago."

Marie gasped.

"No one but us knows. They have entrusted us with that secret. Like Marcel, Lucius was too old. Their new clan master is not interested in ruling the League. He wants to take back Italy, to remove the eastern threat, and then move his influence eastward against them. They will help us if we help them."

Marie peered at the Roman vampires with a residue of doubt.

"Very well, but take them to where no loyalists lurk. This place is crawling with them," Marie finally said, shifting uncomfortably.

She followed Domitian back to the awaiting Romans.

"Orfeo Donati and Sergio Boccarossa of the Clan Roma, may I introduce Countess Marie de Vos of the Royal Flemish Clan?" said Domitian.

Both men kissed Marie's hand. "We are spellbound by your beauty and hope to form a lasting and prosperous friendship," said Orfeo.

"Thank you," said Marie. "Domitian speaks highly of thy clan and recent changes and strategies. I favor them."

"Eh, shall we quickly finish our game and seek a less conspicuous venue in which to speak?" said Domitian. He pointed at the man tied to the tree as Marie took an arrow out of his quiver and lifted a bow. "The game is to shoot three arrows as close to the mortal as possible, without damaging it, of course. The closest arrow wins, and the winner draws first blood."

Before Domitian could utter another word, Marie released an arrow into the man's forehead, killing him instantly.

"Dear me, please forgive my poor aim," said Marie.

The hungry Romans ran to drain the man while still warm. Marie tossed the bow and quiver at Domitian's feet, and marched off.

29 - PRIDE AND TEMPTATION

On Friday afternoon, Pierce decided to leave work earlier than usual. He knew Meghan usually visited her uncle's pub at half past noon. A part of him wanted to remove Meghan from his thoughts, but Pierce was unlike most men, and Meghan was unlike any woman he had ever known. Besides, his ego would not allow him to ignore her—or her to ignore him.

Ravens Gate was quiet when he arrived. He went to the counter with hat in hand and observed the empty room.

"You're starting early, Mister Fleming," commented Ewen Clark, as he poured Pierce his usual glass of Speyside whisky.

Pierce lifted the glass and swirled the amber liquid.

After a moment, Meghan's uncle placed his hands on the counter and leaned forward for a serious word. "Mister Fleming...I know the rumor concernin' Gracie is false, but it hangs over my brother's head like an axe blade. He wants you to stay clear of his daughters and this pub. I told him that you were here when they were no, but being here this time of day puts you in the path of his daughters."

"I have the highest regard and admiration for you and your family, Mister Clark. I can assure you and your brother that I am no threat to your nieces."

Ewen retrieved a wet glass to dry. "Supposing me brother and you were on good terms. Unless you're Plato or Socrates, Meghan will pay you no mind. And Gracie, poor lass, she's of a different mind entirely. I recommend that you stay clear of that one."

Pierce nodded as he watched Meghan and Grace approaching from across the street. He turned to Ewen and smiled.

Ewen shook his head. "Ta my brother's dismay, I defend you, Mister Fleming, because I know Ravens Gate is yer away home. But you will no be welcomed here if you bring grief tae my brother and his family."

"I appreciate your concern and advice, Mister Clark. I would expect nothing less." Pierce looked seriously into Mr. Clark's patina-green eyes with an intensity that made Ewen stop drying the glass. "I mean your nieces no harm and shall protect them with my life. You have my word."

"I believe you, Mister Fleming."

Pierce finished his whisky, placed the glass upside down on the counter, and approached the Clark sisters, who were moving to Meghan's favorite corner of the room—the book case.

"Good afternoon, Miss Clark, Miss Grace." Pierce bowed.

"Good day, Mister Fleming," replied Grace.

"Why are you here so early, Mister Fleming?" asked Meghan.

"I came to see you, Miss Clark. May I have a moment of your time, please?"

Grace's smirk became a frown. Meghan signaled her sister to give them privacy. Grace made Pierce step aside as she stomped towards the counter.

Pierce held his hat to his chest and smiled. "Please forgive my intrusion. I came to finish our discussion, concerning the horserace."

"Really, Mister Fleming...?"

"I believe you will see the importance after I discuss the prize."

Meghan looked across the room at her sister, who was glaring at them, whispering animatedly to her uncle. "Do you intend to bribe me by dangling a prize in front of my nose, Mister Fleming?" she asked.

"A bribe is not a prize in the truest sense of sport. You stand to gain little if you lose the competition."

She closed her eyes for a few seconds, but he was still there when she opened them. "What is this prize?"

Pierce smiled and leaned forward as if to confide something

crucially important. "The prize is a very old publication of *Metamorphoseon*." Pierce noticed her posture straightening and her eyes widening. "You see, I have a sizeable library and thought you might like to win a rare book from my collection."

"Ovidii," murmured Meghan.

"A Roman poet I believe."

Meghan nodded. "*Metamorphoseon* was his masterpiece."

"You stand to own it if you are successful."

Meghan glanced at her sister again and frowned. "Not that I can or ought to, but...when?"

"On the morrow."

She shook her head. "Not only is the request unreasonable, but so is the timing. I can promise nothing." She looked back at her sister and uncle once more and displayed a torn expression.

"Thank you for your time, Miss Clark. I hope to see you at Johns Gate on the morrow." Pierce bowed and exited before she could say another word.

30 - THE RUBBISH GIRL

Cedric Martens found the rubbish girl in the kitchen with the cook and two other girl servants, quietly preparing a stew in a large cauldron. Normally, Cedric would not have been allowed to share space with girls, but Abigail had sent Cedric with a list of provisions and a basket in which to collect them. Though the rubbish girl and he had been exchanging glances for some weeks, they had no opportunity to meet and talk until a few days earlier.

Cedric had just finished replenishing candles in the catacombs, and she had just finished collecting linens to wash. She was elegantly petite with light-brown eyes and fleshy lips. Cedric took hold of the basket of linens and carried it outside for her. He set down the basket at the washing basin beside a well and saw her face in the sunlight. She blushed and turned away. Cedric quickly looked to see if anybody was looking. When he saw no one, he whispered, "My name is Cedric, Cedric Martens of Linder."

"I am Lily Janssen of Oplinder."

"Oplinder?" blurted Cedric, too loudly.

She quickly placed her hand over his mouth and they lowered to a crouch. When she was convinced that no one had seen or heard them, she removed her hand.

"I have been to Oplinder many times," whispered Cedric excitedly.

"I know who you are. I recognized you the first day our eyes met. Do you know William de Wilde?"

"De Wilde...William...yes, tall, twenty years of age? If memory serves well, I think his father was a blacksmith."

"Yes. He is my cousin on my mother's side."

Cedric was beside himself with glee and saw clearly that Lily was, too. Vos Castle was the last place he expected to meet someone who had known him before the plague.

The plague...

A cloud of questions suddenly threatened to dampen his spirits. What happened to her family? Why is she here? How long has she been here? Cedric had heeded his mother's advice, not to go to the nearby villages such as Oplinder, to go without delay to Brussels where jobs were plentiful for honest boys with strong backs and useful skills.

"William told me about you and your family," said Lily, her smile fading. "Your father, mother, and younger sister...What happened to them?"

Though others had inquired about Cedric's family—Countess Marie, Jacob and other boys—he always struggled to reply, as if the words formed into a stone and dropped into his chest. "Black Death," he finally murmured.

"I understand," said Lily, clearly saddened. "My parents and twin brothers also died of the plague. William's family took me in, but soon after, they became ill and died. There was nothing left, no reason to stay. William and I headed west to our uncle's farm. When we arrived..." Seriousness and fear came over Lily's face.

Cedric reached out to calm her. She was trembling with fear.

"We arrived at my uncle's farm after dusk," Lily continued. "Something came out of the house." She squeezed his hand and her face appeared angrier than fearful now. "It...it attacked William and carried him away."

It sounded incredible. "What was it, or who was it?" asked Cedric.

Lily shook her head. "It was dark and it happened so fast, but I believe it was not of this world. I...I ran into the house and called out to my uncle, aunt, and cousins, but no one replied. I took a lantern and started searching. I found them in a bedchamber, lined up against the wall." Her hands covered her face. "The blood..." She leaned into Cedric.

As he held her close, a flood of horrific memories of the farmhouse massacre threatened to rile Cedric's emotions as well. He stiffened at the probability that he had arrived at her uncle's farm the day after Lily had. What happened to William? Had the monster return for her? How did she end up at the castle? Realizing that they had spent too much time in hiding together, Cedric scanned for spies.

"I wish to stay and console you, but I fear for your safety," Cedric whispered in her ear. "May I see you again?"

Lily smiled and nodded affirmatively. Certain no one was watching, they stood up and parted ways.

On three occasions over the next two months, Cedric and Lily met in secret. Cedric learned that the monster returned for Lily soon after she discovered the bodies in the farmhouse. It attacked her from behind, knocking her unconscious. Lily regained consciousness in a room at the castle, locked up with other girls. She never saw William again. Cedric also learned that she was almost a year younger than he. She enjoyed cooking and knitting and swimming at night in summer. Like Cedric, she missed her family. She missed her home, and wanted to escape the castle. Cedric promised to take her away with him someday. She liked that and let Cedric hold her hand whenever they whispered confessions.

Lily saw Cedric enter the kitchen and quickly went to him, backing him out into the corridor. The cook came and placed her hands on her hips. Cedric handed a slip of parchment and the basket to the cook.

After the cook read the parchment, she dropped it in the basket, turned to Lily, and shoved the basket into her stomach hard enough to push her back a step. Then the cook swiveled around and said to Cedric, "Stay out of my kitchen."

Lily read the parchment, which included handwritten instructions requiring Cedric to give the list of foodstuff—five day's supply of salted meat, dried fruit, and nuts—to Lily at the kitchen. Interference by the cook or any royal was prohibited by orders of Headmistress Abigail. She smiled and peeked outside at Cedric, who waved her over.

Their hearts raced. Their attraction was obvious. Now they were together once more, a wondrous occasion by any stretch.

"Cedric, what is this all about?" whispered Lily, clearly excited and worried all at once.

Cedric saw that the other girls were busy preparing food and the cook appeared to be ignoring them. Satisfied that nobody was watching, he slid his hand behind her and pulled her closer. Then he whispered in her ear, "I think I will leave the castle."

Lily gasped so loudly they both looked to see if anybody in the kitchen had noticed.

Lily pulled away. "Wait here."

Cedric stood where he could spy on the girls. They shot glances at him. He moved out of their sight and leaned against the wall where, out of the corner of his eye, he saw Jacob replacing candles farther down the hall.

A few candle-changes later, Lily popped her head out of the kitchen and smiled at Cedric. He no longer detected sadness behind her eyes, and it was the first time he noticed her blonde hair curling out beneath her cap. Brushing his hand against hers in a way that made her flush, he took the basket of food.

"Thank you, Lily," whispered Cedric.

Lily's eyebrows sloped with concern. "You promised to take me with you."

"I cannot take you this time. I will return for you and we will leave this place together."

His words made her smile again. "Where are you going?"

"I know not."

"When will you return?"

"As soon as I can..."

Lily quickly looked right, left, and behind. She then kissed Cedric on the lips, a brief and glancing kiss—his first kiss. It left him speechless. Lily's eyes moistened. "I promise to wait for you, Cedric Martens." She squeezed his hand and then returned to her post in the kitchen.

Never make false promises, his parents had always told

him. Cedric had yet to fulfill his promise to his mother—to go to Brussels and start anew. How might he fulfill his promise to Lily when his life belonged to others?

As he curved his way up the west tower stairs, Cedric's heart grew heavier. He no longer wanted to leave—not without Lily. Castle-life may have been dreary and dismal, but it was a little brighter now, thanks to Lily. She replenished what little hope he had left for a better future. Starting a new life with her in Brussels occupied his thoughts until he arrived outside headmistress's bedchamber door.

When the door opened, Cedric stared down at Abigail's hemline.

"Master Cedric, please come in," said Abigail.

Cedric entered the chamber and set the basket of food down on a table. He no longer looked at Abigail directly, despite having permission to do so. Whereas Lily was a pretty girl of fifteen, Abigail was a stunning woman of nineteen. It was hard to pry his eyes away once they latched on to her beauty. Besides, he did not want to disrespect Lily by lustfully staring at the headmistress. *Never again,* thought Cedric.

He gazed out a window. The view of the countryside was riveting from that height. In the distance he saw rooftops.

"A day's journey beyond that village is the seaport village of Oostende," said Abigail. "You will go to Oostende, and from there you will voyage across the sea to London. London is the largest city in England. Now, please remove your clothes," said Abigail.

Her request caused Cedric a moment's pause. "All my clothes, headmistress?"

"Yes. I promise not to look too closely."

Half-heartedly, Cedric obeyed, taking off and handing his clothes to her. Abigail tossed his smelly garb into the fire and retrieved a rag from a kettle of hot water. She wrung it out and then proceeded to scrub his back. No one had scrubbed him clean since he was an infant, and he remembered none of that. The sensation felt a bit too nice.

She left the rag on his shoulder, moved to the window, and said, "Finish up and dry off with the towel on the bed."

After Cedric finished scrubbing himself clean, Abigail told

him to toss the rag into the inglenook. He watched the damp material sizzle and smolder as she fingered through garments on the bed.

She handed him a new long shirt and he put it on. After pulling up new stockings, he tucked his long shirt under his crotch and put on a new pair of breeches. Abigail then helped him put on a white steinkirk kerchief, and had him slip into new leather shoes and an elaborately embroidered blue waistcoat. Finally, he put on a dark blue woolen coat with sterling silver buttons and black tricorne. Cedric looked down at his clothes. He had never worn such clothes before. They looked and felt expensive.

Abigail opened her footlocker, pushed aside the wooden stake she had held to her chest so many times before, and retrieved the mirror. Leaning it against the locker, she moved to the side and said, "Cedric, see how handsome you look!"

Cedric gazed into the mirror at what might have been someone else, for he hardly recognized himself.

"Do you like it?" asked Abigail.

Distracted by his own reflection, his response was nothing more than a nod.

Abigail walked behind Cedric with a black cloak and draped it over his shoulders. "You will need this to keep you warm."

Cedric turned to the window. "May I ask a question, headmistress?"

"You may."

"Who will I accompany on this journey?"

"Countess Marie de Vos. She asked for you by name."

Cedric stiffened and swallowed dryly.

"Do not fret, Cedric. Avoid eye contact and serve her faithfully. You will be her liaison, her messenger, her eyes and ears. Do you understand?"

"Yes, headmistress."

"You will arrive in London and continue on to Manchester by coach. The countess intends to meet someone very important in Manchester. You will help locate him. I had pockets tailored into your breeches and waistcoat. In a pocket you will find a map. On the map, you will find his dwelling place and various other places he visits regularly. His name is

Pierce van Fleming. Please repeat that name."

"Pierce van Fleming," mumbled Cedric to himself.

"Once more and louder, please."

"Pierce van Fleming," said Cedric.

"Yes."

As Abigail explained how he ought to conduct himself on the voyage, Cedric sneakily looked for Abigail in the mirror.

"It is your choice not to view me directly; however, you do not have permission to view my reflection." She took away the mirror and placed it back into the chest. "You must not speak of this mirror or any other you may have seen. Do you understand?"

"I do. Thank you, headmistress."

"The carriage will arrive at sunset. You are to help the driver with the Countess's luggage. It will be impossible not to look at her, but avoid direct eye contact." Abigail said, continuing to observe the boy's features, his playful brown hair, smooth skin, straight nose, and the sounds of his heart pumping blood throughout his well-defined build. She wondered if he was yet a man or still a boy. Had he been a man and not the Countess's escort, she would have drained him. "We must go now," whispered Abigail. "The Countess's luggage is in the foyer and the carriage will soon arrive."

31 - THE RACE

When Meghan finally arrived at Johns Gate to accept Pierce's challenge to a horserace, he had already been waiting there for over an hour and was grateful for a relatively warm but cloudy December's day. She rode astride, as men do, wearing fox hunting attire: buff breeches, black boots, white shirt, red coat, and black hat. It was her intention to win the race, if not for sport then for a rare book that had occupied her thoughts through the night. She could not help but notice Pierce's fetching stature beside his black Friesian steed. The scene reminded her of a portrait hanging in the parlor of her grandparent's home in Scotland. She thought back to the first time she had seen Pierce. He and his father had come to her family's farm with textiles to trade for ale. She was only ten and shy but curious about the van Fleming boy, admiring him from behind trees and fences. But that was long ago. He was not the one for her, she reminded herself.

"Good day, Miss Clark."

"Good day, Mister Fleming." She dismounted with ease and fed her horse a carrot.

"Words cannot describe how enchanted I am to see you again, Miss Clark."

She acknowledged his compliment, nodding slightly. "Thank you for waitin'."

"No trouble, no trouble at all."

Meghan smiled, gently scratched her horse's cheek, and stared at Pierce's satchel slung over his shoulder. "Have you the prize?"

"I have."

"May I see it?"

Pierce opened the satchel and lifted the book just enough to reveal the title before easing it back into the leather container.

She was disappointed, as if cheated that he retracted the book. "And if I lose? What do you stand to gain?"

"Why, the pleasure of your company, Miss Clark."

"Then I suppose you've already won." Her eyes narrowed with determination. "Brooks Bridge is a mile distant. Is there a particular route, or rules to this race?"

"Any route, and only one rule: ride to win."

Meghan admired his horse—Belgium black, sturdy and powerful, but hardly a horse to race. She noticed Pierce's eyes, surveying her horse.

"That is a handsome animal, possibly Darley?" asked Pierce.

"All I know is he likes to run." She turned and mounted the animal. "Since there are no rules, Mister Fleming, I shall be waitin' for you at the finish." Suddenly, her horse lurched forward into a gallop.

Pierce was surprised by her boldness. He mounted his horse and kicked it into motion.

Meghan knew the lay of the land and was prepared to jump the brook ahead and the hedgerow after that. With a twenty-length head start, she shifted forward and jumped the brook and then the hedgerow with ease. Behind her, Pierce was in stride but making little headway.

The next obstacle was a stand of trees on the lower right side of a hill. A path over the hill went to the left away from Brooks Bridge but was devoid of obstacles. The trees, however, appeared to be spaced close enough to slow down a horse. She decided to veer left onto the path. When she glanced over her right shoulder, she saw Pierce entering the stand of trees at full gallop.

Meghan felt her horse decelerate on the incline. On the downside of the hill, however, she accelerated and veered back on course at the very moment Pierce burst out of the trees. When their paths converged, Meghan realized that he had caught up to her.

A wooden fence, stream, and meadow were all that remained between them and the finish at the bridge. Neck and neck, they pushed their horses to run faster. They jumped the fence successfully, but the stream posed a problem for Pierce as Meghan chose the narrowest section, leaving a wider part for Pierce to jump. His horse made it across but lost traction on a muddy bank.

Mud-splattered and trotting towards the finish, Pierce found Meghan, standing beside her horse on the old stone bridge, gazing up at rainclouds. "The trees over there will provide shelter," said Pierce, pointing to a nearby stand of sycamores.

They lashed their horses to the trees, and Meghan followed Pierce to a wicker basket on a quilt in the center of a clearing. He had obviously planned the picnic.

"I really must go," said Meghan, standing at the edge of the clearing as if it were a cliff.

Pierce sat down, reached into the basket, and retrieved a bottle of sherry and a loaf of bread. "Your home is over the hill no more than ten minutes' ride. That is why I chose to finish at Brooks Bridge." He waved his hands over the bounty. "This was meant to be your consolation prize had you placed second. Considering your commanding head start, the consolation prize goes to me."

"No rules, ride to win, remember?" Meghan said while stepping onto the quilt.

Pierce held the book up to her. "And won, you did. Please, accept your prize, along with a friendly toast to victory. This sherry is Spanish and this bread is homemade."

The leather-bound edition lured Meghan closer to take it. "Bake the bread yourself, did you?" said Meghan, her eyes squarely focused on the book now in her hands.

"Yes, this morning."

She glanced over at him and raised an eyebrow. "You can't be serious." She lowered herself onto the blanket and smirked. "I never thought of you as a baker."

"A baker, an angler, a traveler..."

"And industrialist..." added Meghan.

"Yes, of course," replied Pierce. He handed her the book, poured sherry into a pair of glasses, and gave her one. "To a much deserved victory." He lifted his glass. "Congratulations,

Miss Clark."

They drank, and then she carefully examined the book binding.

"May I ask you something, Miss Clark? Why are you so interested in literature?"

Her eyes grew wider as they found his again. "Not only literature, Mister Fleming—history, philosophy, and art, especially art. What I wouldn't give for the opportunity to visit all the world's art museums and libraries. I rather fancy the feel of a book in my hands, and I enjoy writing almost as well." She finished her sherry, removed her gloves, and ran her fingers across the binding. "The only good is knowledge and the only evil is ignorance."

"Socrates," said Pierce, remembering what Ewen had told him about her love of philosophy.

Meghan was impressed he recognized the quote. "You are a man of many surprises, Mister Fleming."

"Dare I ask to be called by my given name...in private at least?"

Meghan ignored the question and began turning pages.

Pierce refilled her glass and placed the bread between them.

She gazed through the trees, the effects of the sherry reminding her of love and sensuality yet to be discovered. "To me, the world beyond the horizon is unimaginable," Meghan said, tasting her second glass of sherry. "Yet, I want to imagine it—no, experience it. I want to know the world, Mister Fleming." Meghan drank some more and smiled some more, not a restrained smile but a smile that accentuated her dimples. She was clearly feeling the effects of the sherry, the victory, and the trophy. She tore off a piece of bread and placed it in her mouth.

"How is it?" asked Pierce.

Her eyes squinted with pleasure. "Absolutely delicious! Thanks to you, I am honored and overwhelmed to be here. And, Mister Fleming, whose name of Flemish origins begs the question, why did yer family settle in Manchester of all places? Oh, and do you enjoy readin'?"

Meghan's Scottish drawl charmed Pierce. "My parents originally came to raise sheep and spin wool. We have a modest collection of old books decorating the library walls. I have been known to read on occasion."

"An unlikely pairing...books and you."

"Well, I may not be as avid a reader as you are, but I do enjoy a good story told in good company."

"Are you a good storyteller then?"

"That depends on whether you are a good listener."

Meghan laughed. "I am. When I was a wee lass, I listened to my father weave tales for hours." She finished her second glass of sherry and handed back the empty glass. She looked down at the book and then up into Pierce's steel-blue eyes just as the first drops of rain pelted the leaves. That was the cue to leave. She quickly placed the book under her jacket while Pierce gathered up the blanket and stuffed everything into a basket.

Before mounting up, she placed the book in his hand. "Will you please keep it dry and safe 'til I can fetch it?"

Pierce gladly agreed. He expected her to leave at once, but she lingered, gazing up at him in a way that warmed his heart. He gently placed his hand on her shoulder. She closed her eyes and tilted her head back revealing plump and parting lips. He wanted to accept her invitation—and normally would—but he backed away and bowed like a prince. Her eyes thanked him, and then she turned to her horse.

As he saw her off, he wondered if they had finally become more than acquaintances.

32 - A PLAN TO END HIM

A chilling breeze followed Domitian through the catacombs to Marie's bedchamber. The chill was a strange phenomenon with no adequate explanation. Some believed it to be spirits of the dead stirring from the deepest tunnels while others attributed it to a drafty old castle. Domitian glared at Isaac, Marie's faithful sentry, standing perfectly still in the doorway.

"Sentry," said Marie, her eyes rolling with annoyance at Domitian's jealousy of the sentry. "Please close the door and wait outside."

After the door closed with a loud clang, Domitian forced a smile. "Where are you going and what is his name, my love?"

"What on earth do you mean?" said Marie.

"You know exactly what I mean—the one! The one over whom you obsess. The one whom you are going to meet. Oh yes...yes, yes, yes, you are! A servant boy is loading your luggage onto a carriage this very moment. Admit it...you are leaving to seek him out."

"Art thou cross?"

Tugging wrinkles from his tunic, Domitian pursed his lips.

"Yes, Domitian, my dear, thou art correct," said Marie calmly, as she opened her powder box.

"So, my love, please tell me, what is his name?"

"Why does his name matter to you?" said Marie while powdering her face.

"*Why?*" Domitian approached her. "It matters to me that you would leave without a word! It matters to me that you would consider—even for one moment—that this man could be the one. It matters to me that you might not return at all, and—and I shall hunt him down if he is the cause!"

Marie chuckled. "Hunt him down without knowing his name or his whereabouts?"

Domitian began to wince and huff.

"Thy discomfort is quite entertaining, my dear," Marie said, smirking.

Domitian crossed his arms, tapping his boot and pouting with impudence.

"Calm thyself, Domitian. I intend to expend the so-called one, the mortal."

"Expend as in kill?"

"What else?"

"Nothing would be more reassuring, if he was not a special sort of man."

"He is just a man."

"You would not journey to meet him if he were *just* a man. You would send an assassin instead." He brought his hand to his jaw and tapped on his cheek. "Why did you not order Abigail to end him when she was there?"

Marie giggled and lifted a small glass vial. "She is a beautiful spy, not an assassin. Besides, I need to get away from this place." She glanced at him and smiled. "Do not fret, my dear. I shall have him killed lest he kills himself." Marie shook the vial and removed the cork.

Domitian observed her face. "That...that look is why I am concerned."

Marie placed her index finger over the vial's opening and turned it upside down.

"You have never killed a vampire."

Marie righted the tiny bottle and removed her finger. On it was an oily red substance. She rubbed it between her finger and thumb. "It is true, I have never retired a vampire of mine own hands, but there are other ways."

"I wish to go with you. I shall finish him off for you."

"No."

"Please, My Love. Take me with you."

"Thou shall stay and tend to our business while I am away."

"But, of course," said Domitian in an upbraiding tenor.

Marie rubbed the red substance onto her lips.

Domitian's eyes widened with a new thought. "There is nothing to stop you from obtaining evidence to falsify the oracle's prophecy, is there? Such evidence would strengthen our case against Marcel."

"What evidence?"

"A sort of proclamation, renouncing the man's right and privileges to the Royal Flemish Clan. Think of it as assurance, in case the man somehow survives your visit."

Marie's reddened lips widened and puckered. "Why would the council accept such a document?"

"It cannot hurt to try."

She opened her jewelry box. "Very well. Have it ready by dusk."

"So soon?"

Marie rummaged through her jewels, ignoring the question.

Domitian nodded. "Dusk it is. But I have one more request."

"What is it?" Marie asked, turning to face him with a ruby and diamond necklace draped over her hand.

"Do not let anyone connected to that man survive—what is his name?"

Marie handed him the necklace. "Pierce van Fleming."

Domitian scowled as he clasped the necklace on her. "Yes. Him."

"Art thou satisfied now?"

"I have never been more dissatisfied in either of my lives. I hate this man," he said, placing his hands on her shoulders and kissing the side of her neck. "Please consider my request. Before van Fleming dies, feast on his family and friends. Expend them all. Please do this for us, my love."

Marie placed her hand on his face. "Discard thy worries, Domitian, for thou art the future master. That much we know."

33 - THE RUMOR

A week into the New Year, Meghan rode sidesaddle to the Fleming Estate, dressed in a riding habit, both legs firmly secured round the pommels. As before, she left home quietly without telling her family where she was going. She planned to ride to Ravens Gate after retrieving her book. Her uncle Ewen would vouch for her whereabouts, and none would suspect her of visiting Pierce van Fleming. None, except her sister Grace, for she had stalked Meghan to Fleming's house and was spying on her from behind a stand of trees.

Pierce greeted Meghan in the courtyard. After stabling her horse, he showed her into the house. It was her first time there.

"How does your mother in London?" asked Meghan, ignoring the book resting on a curio cabinet in the foyer.

"She is doing as well as can be expected. Thank you for asking."

"It must be lonely here without yer family. At least you have the help."

Pierce's eyes dropped.

Meghan listened to the silence and saw evidence of an untidy home. "Where is the help?"

Pierce's face appeared crestfallen. "I sent them away."

Meghan was surprised the rumors were true but dared not to inquire. Sensing his embarrassment and wanting to avoid an awkward topic as much as he probably did, she clasped her hands and smiled.

He moved towards the gallery and said, "Care to see the library?"

"Aye, very much so," said Meghan, relieved to move on.

The library was a sizeable room with four large windows, wood-paneled walls and ceiling, and columns of bookshelves so high that a wheeled ladder was necessary to reach the top shelves. A large desk stood at the center of the room. Leather armchairs, sofa, and a rack of clay pipes doused the room in scents of leather, tobacco, and wood—masculinizing the space so much that Meghan began to redecorate it in her mind. After turning 360 degrees to take in the space, she gravitated towards a collection of Greek classics. Spotting one in particular, she looked back at Pierce for permission to remove it.

Pierce swept his arm out. "Please..."

She carefully removed the book and opened the cover. "It appears to be a very old edition of Homer's *Iliad*. Have you read it?"

"No. Have you?"

She nodded. "Some."

"You are welcome to take it."

She shook her head. "It belongs here, in yer library." She shelved the book and turned to him. "Surely you come here to read from time to time."

"I come here to drink and smoke from time to time."

Meghan giggled at his frankness.

"Well, at least the room is being used for something," chuckled Pierce.

"Would you mind if I came here to read, Mister van Fleming?"

"Mind? I hereby appoint you official librarian of the Fleming Estate. Please come as you will and do as you please, for this room and its contents are henceforth in your charge—with exception of the spirits of course. Fancy a drink, Miss Clark?"

"Meghan or Meggy is fine. No alcohol, please. I am still recovering from two glasses of Spanish sherry and a horserace!" Meghan's vibrant smile faded to seriousness. "May I ask you something of a personal nature, Mister van Fleming, concernin' my sister?"

"Only if you call me by my given name."

"Will you, Pierce?"

"Yes, of course, Meghan."

"The rumor—you know the one? Pardon my frankness but, it claims that you had deflowered my sister." She was pleased to see Pierce's troubled expression to the accusation. "Do you know how the rumor started?"

Pierce paced the room in thought. "I believe it started as a rude joke at a late-night gathering your sister was attending. I know of some of the people at those parties. Many are pampered rascals of wealthy parents—reputably lacking credibility, speaking with tongues in cheeks. There is no truth to the rumor, Meghan. I never attended those parties, and I never touched your sister."

Meghan simply wanted to know Pierce's thoughts on the matter and was satisfied with his explanation. "I believe you," she said. "My sister is to blame. Because of her and that scandalous rumor, my parents are against you. They refuse to acknowledge or even consider the rumor as nothing more than a vulgar joke. Sometimes, I do not understand them."

Pierce gazed out a window, the very same window Grace was spying through from behind a hedgerow. "I believe your parents are doing what they are supposed to do—guard their children from harm. Truth is I am no saint, and rumors abound in my world. I frequently see my name in newspapers, and seldom in a good light. I admittedly live life a bit recklessly at times and will not deny it. Considering that, I think your parents' opinion of me is quite understandable."

Meghan shook her head in disagreement. "My parents are inflexible. They forbade me from seeing you. Now, I fear what they might do if we are discovered together." Meghan's face wilted with sadness. A rush of emotions began to overwhelm her. "Am I wrong to disobey my parents, to distrust my own sister?" She felt heaviness in her heart and closed her eyes, squeezing tears onto her cheeks. She wanted to melt into Pierce's arms like a frightened child. "Why must this be so complicated? Why must guilt accompany joy? Nothing makes sense." She felt his hand on her shoulder, inviting her to lean forward, and she did. She felt his warmth and allowed her face to rest against his chest.

"Love can be complicated," whispered Pierce.

It took three ticks of the clock to process what he had said.

She pushed him away. "Love? Is... Is that what you think this is? We hardly know each other." Meghan remembered her sister's words: *Pierce is a scoundrel, addicted to whisky and harlots.* If true, then what does that make me, wondered Meghan. Why am I here with such a man?

Yet, Pierce had always treated her with kindness and courtesy. He made her feel vital, emboldened, even becoming. He was not as his sister had described him to be.

She bit her lower lip and gazed up at him with mixed feelings. His face was young but mature and with whiskers for lack of a razor. "In matters of the heart," said Meghan, "I believe you to be experienced. You ignore the rules."

"Arbitrary rules," added Pierce.

"Arbitrary by your definition," rebuffed Meghan. "Tell me, ought I to heed my family's warnings? Ought I to sacrifice my happiness for those who do not see what I see, or feel what I feel?" The room felt smaller, quieter, and *love* no longer seemed unattainable. Her eyes followed his jaw-line to his lips as she lifted to his chest, hesitating to touch him again, noticing that he would not stop her. She had never before observed a man or felt for a man in such a way. Any other time and she would have retreated, but suddenly everything felt natural—primal.

She placed her hand behind his neck. A shot of excitement lifted her to her toes. The sensation of his mouth on hers was intoxicating. His large hand cradled her head, and her heart raced to be with his.

They moved to the sofa on which she reclined and pulled him to her. Meghan wanted to unbridle herself, to be unhindered by guilt and fear. Her sister was wrong. Her parents were wrong. She tried to ignore their voices in her head, warning her to stay clear of Pierce van Fleming, but it was no use. Their words flowed like venom, judging him, condemning him. She turned her face away from his and murmured, "I cannot."

Pierce instantly stopped and moved away.

Meghan stood up and straightened her garments.

"Meghan, if I offended you in any way—" began Pierce.

"No, I am the offender, and I must apologize for my actions.

I... I am clearly out of character and ill-prepared to cope with...with... This!"

"Meghan—" Pierce reached out to her.

She moved passed him towards the doorway. "I am a foolish girl, an inexperienced guilt-ridden cacophony of confusion." She quickly moved out of the library and to the foyer where she waited for Pierce to let her out.

Close behind her, Pierce saw that she had not taken the book. He retrieved it and gave it to her. She thanked him and followed him to the stable outside.

Waiting outside the stable, Meghan struggled to control her emotions. Guilt, sadness, fear, joy, and longing distracted her from what she really wanted—happiness with the only man who had ever excited her, challenged her, respected her, held her close and kissed her on the lips.

After Meghan was saddled and settled, her eyes finally found Pierce's. She saw in them a light of concern, of longing, and loneliness that touched her heart. She backed away and said, "As disingenuous as this may sound, I *do* enjoy our visits, Pierce."

As before, Pierce watched her leave, but this time he saw a glint of happiness peaking through the uncertainty in her eyes.

34 - DINING OUT

The coach ride from Vos Castle to the seaport at Oostende took several freezing cold hours on roads rutted and slickened by ice and snow. Cedric rode beside the driver. It was his first coach ride. The sounds of wheels turning, the vehicle creaking, and six black horses trotting and snorting steamy puffs, exhilarated Cedric. It was different from the horse ride with his father—the day he set eyes on the ominous Sonian Forest. The strength of a horse was remarkable, but the combined strength of a team of horses pulling a loaded carriage steadily for hours was stupendous.

When they finally arrived at the harbor in Oostende, Cedric helped the driver unload the luggage onto a loading dolly. The shipmaster soon arrived to greet Marie. He was a sizeable man in both height and girth, with dark blonde hair, weathered skin, and crow's-feet wrinkles from squinting so much. He bowed deeply and kissed Marie's hand.

"It is an honor to have you aboard again, Countess," said the shipmaster.

"Thank you, Eric. Why must we disembark from Oostende? Bruges is more charming."

"So it is, Countess, but the River Zwin is shallow with silt and no longer navigable."

"Such a pity. I hear the population there is dwindling as well."

"It is. Shall I escort you aboard the ship, Countess?"

"Please. Take the boy and my things and I shall return tonight. I wish to dine alone in town." Marie shifted here eyes to the boy. "This is Master Cedric. He will show me to my quarters upon my return."

"As you wish, Countess," said Eric, bowing once more.

Cedric bowed as well, not knowing what to say.

That evening, Marie de Vos walked along the harbor, listening intently for a place to dine. She followed her ears towards the merriment of people. Located on all four corners of a busy street were four taverns, beautifully alit in torches, candles, and oil lamps. The street intersection was teeming with sailors speaking languages that even Marie could not understand. Through the windows of one of the taverns she saw young women dressed in colorful gowns. Some wore torn stockings or no stockings at all. They freely visited any man who might afford their company.

She entered the busiest of the four taverns and started counting: thirty men and twenty-four women, chatting, laughing, and dancing to music of a violinist accompanied by a crew of scraggly sailors singing odd songs about their ship's rigging.

"Dare I say, I'd be the luckiest mariner if you were to join me tonight," said a young man to Marie.

Her first thought was to tear out his throat, but something about that place made her feel as bawdy as a harlot. She smiled. "Join thee?"

"What I meant to say is I would be honored if you accepted my company. May I offer you a drink?"

She liked his American accent and forwardness. "When I was twenty, I enjoyed champagne."

"That must have been yesterday. Please wait here while I fetch us a glass of bubbles." The sailor made his way through the crowd towards the bar as Marie observed a buxom young woman, sitting on the lap of what might have been a ship's commander by the look of his uniform.

Suddenly, Marie felt a hand on her shoulder. She turned to find a different sailor, grinning and belching foul intentions. The added pang of rotting teeth and gums repulsed her. Before he could say a word, she glared into his mind and revealed her true image to him. Instantly the man's pupils dilated and he backed away in a panic. Marie laughed and began counting wicker lamps and candles.

"There you are!" said the American sailor, handing her a

glass of champagne.

Marie took a sip. It tasted sour, but she smiled and said: "It is delicious. Thank you."

"Where are you from?" asked the sailor.

"A small village south of Brussels," replied Marie in his language. "And you?"

"Virginia. My ship arrived yesterday with a cargo of tobacco and cotton. We set sail for Portugal tomorrow." He stepped back to take a good look at Marie. "Dare I say you are the prettiest thing my eyes have seen in years? Where did you say you were from?"

Marie smiled at his informality. "I have always wanted to meet an American. I much admire your country's newfound freedom. Were you involved in the war with England?"

"My father, two brothers, and I served in the Continental Army under Commander Washington. Unfortunately, I am my parents' only surviving son—discharged five years ago."

"Fascinating, I would like to learn more. Shall we continue our discussion someplace secluded?"

The eager sailor led her outside to a quieter part of town where they sat on a carved wooden bench in the evening shadow of a stone building. As the American described life in Virginia, Marie tried to remember what it was like to be a young woman with desires for romance and hopes of marriage. He was an attractive man and perhaps the type she would have fancied for a night or two. But after Marcel dehumanized her all those years ago, such dreams and ideals became extraneous.

"How old are you?" asked Marie.

"Why I'm twenty-five as of last month." The young man stared into Marie's eyes. "I say, Miss Marie, your eyes are beautiful and aglow like hot coals."

"They like what I see," said Marie, scenting the man's blood, tobacco, and whiskey. Her eyes pulsated as she enticed him to move closer. She let him kiss her cheeks and then her lips. The American was quick to act out his passions. His hands moved to her waist and Marie felt strangely aroused, so much that her incisors and fingernails elongated uncontrollably.

On watch for people, she saw an older couple moving towards them along the walkway. "Relax, my handsome young sailor," whispered Marie. Then, she bit into his jugular vein. He moaned and held her tightly as his blood surged into her mouth. The couple walked by quietly, trying not to stare at what appeared to be an inappropriate display of affection by inebriated foreigners.

Cedric was waiting at the top of the gangplank when Marie arrived. He immediately straightened his posture as best he could while looking down at his boots. "Good evening, My Countess. Shall I show you to your quarters?"

Marie followed Cedric to a door on the bow side of the top deck. He opened it and let her in. Just as he turned, he felt Marie's hand on his shoulder and saw her fingers for the first time. They were youthful with beautifully manicured nails.

"Cedric, thy clothes fit thee well."

"Thank you, My Countess."

"Good night."

"Good night, My Countess."

35 - CONFIDENCE AND CONSENT

Two weeks had passed since Meghan Clark's visit to the Fleming estate. Pierce looked for her in town and at Ravens Gate but found nothing more than a greater longing to be with her.

Ewen explained that she had gone to Scotland to visit her grandparents and had not returned. Pierce fought his urges to seek her out. He was torn between doing too much and not enough. What was the correct timing and dosage for doing anything at all? It was a delicate and agonizing dilemma because their relationship—what it had become or had yet to be—was on the hush. Going to her family's home was out of the question.

A week later, near the end of the workday, Pierce heard three taps at his office door. The general manager opened it.

"Yes?" said Pierce.

"Excuse me, sir, but a Miss Meghan Clark here to see you. She said that you are expecting her."

Pierce was expecting no one. "Uh, yes, of course." Said Pierce quickly rising from his desk, pushing the chair back into a credenza. He straightened his waistcoat, closed a drawer, and hastily organized loose papers into a pile. "Thank you, Mister Felton. Please show her in."

Felton stepped aside to allow Meghan through. Then he bade Pierce a good evening and closed the door.

Pierce smiled brightly. "Miss Clark...Meghan, what a

wonderful—"

"—Surprise? Aye, for me as well," she said, moving into the center of the room. She removed her gloves and placed one over the other, folding them in half, unfolding them, then folding them again.

"I cannot adequately express my relief and joy to see you, Meghan. Your uncle said that your return from Scotland had been delayed. I feared illness may have befallen you."

"I am quite well—if madness is the new well." She spoke curtly and focused on a large pane of glass overlooking the mill's operations. She moved to it and gazed out at a cacophony of overhead flywheels, pulleys, and belts connected to rows of spinning mules. A boy in a white apron diligently inspected the machinery, engaging and disengaging gears like a man with many years of experience. She turned to Pierce and smiled nervously. "It is an impressive mill."

"Thank you." He noticed her green and gold bodice, tightly fitted over a white taffeta gown, less voluminous than the trend but transcendently stylish. She had obviously arrived by buggy.

She dropped her eyes to a piece of thread on the floor. "I apologize for coming unannounced. I was returning home with supplies and thought to..."

"Thank you for coming," Pierce said, pulling a chair out for her.

"I prefer to stand, thank you."

He then got out two glasses and a bottle of whisky from a cabinet.

"None for me thank you."

Pierce nodded and poured himself a glass and leaned against the desk.

Meghan moved back to the center of the room. Her eyes moved from side to side as if searching for words she had composed but lost along the way. She gripped the gloves tightly and scanned the floor for the thread. "I wish to speak freely, Mister Fleming, to finish the conversation we had started in the library, but my thoughts are not as organized as I had hoped them to be. So I will say what comes to mind if you can bear it." She glanced up briefly at his face.

"Yes, of course." Pierce noticed her use of his surname. It sounded dry and distant.

She nodded as if giving herself permission to divulge a deep-rooted secret and looked upon him with a tremulous smile. "Matters of importance to me have suddenly become irrelevant. My...my thoughts have become unclear. I have lost my appetite for not only food but also literature and riding, among other activities I used to enjoy. I have come to tell you that—that nothing has been the same since our last visit." Again, her eyes moved from his face to the scrap of fiber on the floor. "Honestly, I thought the horserace was a pointless and crass invitation from a calculating man. After all, you are a shrewd industrialist. I know now that it was wrong of me to judge you or to consider my family's judgment of you. My only excuse is that I was as I am now, confused and naive.

"Furthermore, I have concluded that what I hear and what I know of you is inconsistent and contradicting. A scoundrel you are not, a puzzle perhaps, but not a scoundrel. I wish to see all the pieces of your puzzle fitted into place so that I may take in the entire picture of you." Her eyes moved back to his. "I have come to ask this question: Who is Pierce van Fleming, really?"

Pierce exhaled like a deflating balloon.

"You needn't share all the pieces here and now," said Meghan in a softer tone, "but I wish to see deeper into the mysteries of you."

Pierce's mind began to race. He was a man with murderous dreams, no childhood memories, and an invisible friend called Death. He felt like a man without a face. How could he explain it without revealing all those blasted secrets? How might she react to such truths? Then again, no one had ever cared enough about him to know more.

"Who am I?" said Pierce. "I have been asking that question for as long as I can recall, which is not very long, for I have no childhood memories before twelve years of age." He paused to gauge her reaction. She appeared mildly surprised. "The only thing I can remember is a crow perched in a decrepit tree at the center of a strange forest."

There, he said it. He had never revealed that secret before. His family knew nothing of it. It felt cathartic to share a morsel.

"Shall I continue?" he asked.

Meghan moved to the chair and sat down. "Aye, please."

He placed his glass of whisky in front of her and poured another glass.

She placed her wrinkled gloves on her lap and took the glass.

"I suffer a reoccurring nightmare of being chased and beaten to death," admitted Pierce.

"Are you sure the victim is you?"

"I presume it because I see it happening through the eyes of the victim. No matter how fast I run, they catch me, and beat me with wooden clubs until the moment of death—when I wake up."

"Dreadful," she trembled. "Do you know who the murderers are?"

"No. I cannot see their faces, but their hands appear to be very young." Pierce watched her wet her lips with whisky. "I wake up every day from that nightmare, terrified to be alive. Perhaps that is why I stay awake for as long as I do—to delay the inevitable re-enactment. Yet, the hours of awareness are not without its haunts." Pierce swallowed a large amount of whisky and put the glass down. "An invisible apparition as hideous as a decaying gargoyle appears wherever and whenever I am in harm's way. Only I can see it."

Meghan's face remained concerned and interested. "Why do you think it appears to you and only you?"

"Perhaps it is waiting to collect my soul."

"How terrifying."

"Yes, almost as terrifying as my banker," Pierce joked, feeling somewhat liberated from his secrets. He was willing to reveal more, but not everything. He would not explain his scar-riddled body. There was no reason to unless she saw them, and there was no reason to see them, though he hoped for one.

Belts and gears in the mill stopped turning. Silence fell like a blanket of fog. Dusk was fast approaching.

Meghan stood as Pierce went to light a kerosene lamp.

"Pierce," murmured Meghan, so softly that it might have been mistaken for a sigh. When Pierce turned to her, Meghan lifted her hand and placed it in his.

Pierce moved closer to her and touched her cheek. The kiss came quickly, passionately, lingering with a delicate intensity that casted away all doubts concerning her feelings towards him.

"I have a place in town," said Pierce. "We can meet there whenever you like."

Pierce was owner of the Broadmore Hotel in Manchester. He kept a private suite on the second floor, a sizeable space with a washroom and loo with running water, and a coal stove on which to cook. They met every Tuesday at noon. They played cards, read aloud to each other, discussed philosophy, and kissed passionately whenever she was in the mood. Over several weeks, their love grew stronger. All the while, Pierce remained a gentleman, never suggesting or even implying that they form a sexual union.

Though she hid her feelings well, Meghan's virgin curiosities and growing desire to act on them was becoming unbearable. She had fallen deeply in love with him. Consequently, she wanted commitment and permanence. She was certain of his love for her, but not of his commitment to her, and she dared not to ask. Meghan thought it would be inappropriate, but was sneaking in and out of a man's hotel suite appropriate? The lines between proper and unseemly became blurred. Her sister had told her of women's influence over men. That few men could resist the advances of a pretty, young woman. As uncomfortable as the idea was to Meghan, why not try to influence Pierce with her beauty? Would he like that? She wondered, and then decided to try it—to make the next rendezvous unlike any other.

36 - LONDON TOWN

With gothic edifices awash in chilling rain and thousands of tall ships and boats jamming the River Thames, London at night appeared endless and menacing to Cedric. Approaching a million inhabitants, it was a monster of a city, rife with depravity, filth, noise, and intemperance. Cedric knew little of those things. His only concern was for the countess, her comfort, her safety.

The sailors allowed Cedric to help set the gangplank on the larboard side. Then he went ashore to secure accommodations for Marie. Uncertain of where to begin, he wandered from wharf to town, memorizing landmarks along the way. A few side streets later, he came upon a main thoroughfare flowing with people. He looked up and down the busy street and heard a friendly voice.

"Aye, young governor! Over here! A merchant standing beside a shack of wares blew smoke through his bushy moustache. "My, my, my, what a handsome lad you are. May I be of service?" He placed his pipe on a stand and removed an umbrella from a bunch of others. "On days like today, what you need is a brolly to keep you dry!" He opened the umbrella and twirled it against his shoulder. "I've a handsome selection for only ten P."

It had been a while since Cedric spoke English, primarily because few people in Flanders used it. However, his grandfather was English, and his father Colson spoke it well and frequently to Cedric and his sister. So, he let the words tumble out of his mouth, hoping the merchant would understand them. "May I try it...the brolly?" mumbled Cedric, now dripping wet.

"Sorry? Would you like to try it?" asked the merchant.

"Yes, please," said Cedric, somewhat relieved the man was able to guess the gist of his words.

"Indeed, you may! You may, indeed!" The man held the brolly out to Cedric.

Cedric took the umbrella and instantly thought of Marie. "Is this... the biggest one you have?"

"Aye, it is, and made in France that one is—guaranteed to keep you dry for only twelve P."

"Twelve P? I thought you said ten P each."

"Ten P for the smaller ones, governor. This one is French-made, and bigger than the others. That said and because I intend to earn your trust, it can be yours for just one and sixpence, a fine price for a fine French-made brolly if I do say so myself."

Cedric thought for a moment. "Is a shilling not equal to twelve pence?"

"So it is. It is indeed. What say you then, young master, wet and shivering or dry and warm?"

Cedric retrieved three shillings from his money purse. "I shall pay a shilling for the brolly, and another shilling for your assistance."

The merchant looked ecstatic and confused all at once. "Assistance, young governor?"

"I must book the finest room in the finest hotel in London, and secure a coach ride from port to the hotel for my countess."

Eager to earn his shilling, the merchant hollered at a hackney parked across the street. The driver waved and brought the carriage round.

"Mister Michaels!" said the merchant to the driver. "Please take this fine young lad to the Sheffield Hotel and return for his countess here at the Quay!"

The driver nodded cheerfully, stepped down, and opened the carriage door. Cedric paid the merchant and took the brolly into the hackney.

The Sheffield Hotel in Westminster was just two blocks from Buckingham House. Cedric booked their finest room for Marie and the least expensive one for himself.

Back at the ship, he found two sailors standing beside Marie's luggage under an overhang on the pier. Cedric asked the hackney driver to stow the luggage as he fetched Marie. Cedric was wary to focus his eyes on his boots as he approached Marie's stateroom. Before he could knock at the door, it opened. The hem of her gown was all he saw as he sheltered her under the brolly.

"Cedric, is everything arranged?"

"Yes, My Countess."

Across the deck and gangplank and to the hackney, Cedric continued to shelter her from the weather. The driver greeted her kindly as she boarded the sparse carriage.

"All aboard, please," said the driver to Cedric.

"Sir, may I ride outside with you?" asked Cedric.

The driver tilted his head and paused a second or two. "Sorry, lad. Passengers must be inside at all times. Besides, it is a foul day for an outside ride-along."

"Cedric," said Marie, "get in."

Reluctantly, Cedric closed both his brolly and eyes and boarded the carriage. Avoiding even the possibility of seeing her reflection, he sat opposite of Marie and pressed his nose against the window. The whole time, he felt her staring at him.

Instead of dwelling on intimidating circumstances, he took in the largest city he had ever seen. The endless tapestry of cluttered streets and people rushing like disturbed ants diverted his attention from the royal lady sitting across from him.

A few minutes later, the hackney stopped in front of their hotel just as the rain paused to greet the evening. After Cedric escorted Marie to her stateroom, he chartered a stagecoach to Manchester. The journey from London to Manchester typically took three or four days, depending on the weather—too long of a carriage ride with the countess, he worried. She told him to check in with her once at dawn and again at dusk, rapping three times evenly with a slight pause before the fourth rap. He was told to enjoy the city alone, as she would do the same.

Before daybreak the next morning, Cedric knocked at her door as instructed.

"Good morning, Cedric." Her words rang clear in his head,

though the door remained closed. "Remove thy coin purse and hand it to me."

When the door opened, Cedric averted his eyes and handed over his coin bag, wondering if she would leave him with no money at all.

"Take it," said Marie, holding out another bag stuffed with coins.

Each morning, Cedric exchanged his nearly-full coin purse for a replenished one. Each day, he was at liberty to spend as much as he had. Cedric quickly discovered pub culture, coffee shops, and the local cuisine of mostly boiled fare and dairy foods. Each time he reached into his coin purse he thought of humble beginnings, a loving family, and their tragic end. So much had changed. He was no longer hungry or cold. He appreciated the two women who made it possible for him to travel abroad. All the same, he missed Lily terribly and wondered if she still missed him as much.

On the fifth day, Cedric helped load the luggage onto the stagecoach and took a seat beside the driver. Outside the city, Cedric wondered if Marie de Vos was enjoying the scenery of rural England from inside the seven-passenger, leather-upholstered carriage as much as he was enjoying it from the driver's bench. After thirty arduous miles of countryside, however, Cedric was aching to rest. When the horses finally stopped at a coach inn near dusk, Cedric helped unload the luggage, booked two rooms—the largest for Marie and the smallest for him—and settled in for the night. And so they traveled in stages for three days until finally arriving at the Irwell Hotel in Manchester.

The building was located on the corner of Deans Gate and Market Street Lane. It was raining when they arrived, and Cedric struggled not to look at Marie or touch her as he ushered her to the hotel under the brolly. As before, he booked two rooms and visited the countess at dusk. Yet, on that night, he received no answer at the door. He rapped again, repeating the cadence, but nothing. When he turned to leave, he was startled to find a young woman standing behind him. At first, he thought it was a stranger and politely excused himself. As soon as he noticed her gown and satin shoes, a rush of embarrassment and worry backed him against the door.

"Good evening, Cedric," said Marie.

He turned away. "Please forgive me, My Countess. I had come to ask if there was anything more—"

"Relax, stupid boy. My fascination of thy discipline has worn thin. This is not the castle. We are no longer governed by its rules. Look at me directly."

Cedric closed his eyes. Looking away had become as comfortable and appropriate as staring into a used chamber pot was not.

Marie directed her will at Cedric. "Look at me, Master Cedric," ordered Marie.

He felt her finger touch the bottom of his chin, tilting his head up. Still, Cedric's eyes remained closed.

Marie giggled as an adolescent girl might when charmed by a handsome boy. "Thou hast nine freckles, four to the left and five to the right of thy nose. Now, gaze upon me. I promise not to bite."

He lifted his eyelids slowly.

"What dost thou see, a withered old woman, a monster of mythical proportions?"

"You... You... I—"

"Stammering can mean many things, Cedric—stunned, stimulated, intimidated, enchanted, or just plain stupid."

Cedric felt all of that—curious, too. "You... You are young and beautiful, My Countess," murmured Cedric.

"Not stupid after all," said Marie with a giggle.

"But I had thought—"

Marie lifted her index finger to his lips, leaned in, and kissed him on the cheek.

Cedric wondered if she sensed his nervousness. He felt his heart racing and his jugular vein throbbing and rising to the surface of his neck. It was a dizzying sensation.

She suddenly pushed Cedric aside and opened her room door. "Good night," said Marie, hastily closing the door and locking it.

Cedric stood in silence in the hallway, heart pounding, fully aroused and mystified by what had just happened.

He made his way down to the ground floor and entered his

room. Peering at his reflection in a dressing mirror, he began to reason aloud. "What just happened? She looked to be twenty-three or four." He touched his cheek and neck where she had kissed him. "Bizarre," said Cedric, as he rubbed off a sticky impression of the countess's lips.

In the morning, Cedric went upstairs and knocked at Marie's door as instructed.

"Good morning, My Countess. May I be of service?" After a few seconds, Cedric heard her voice, as if her lips were tickling his ear, even though the door was closed.

"Go seek a man named Pierce van Fleming," said Marie. "Find him and watch him with discretion. Observe his home, his friends and family, where he goes, what he does. Keep me informed. Go now."

"Yes, My Countess." Excited to start the second phase of his mission, he removed from his pocket Abigail's map of the places Pierce van Fleming was likely to be.

37 - TENACIOUS DIFFERENCES

"**P**ierce van Fleming's courtin' yer daughter," hissed Grace at her parents. "I saw 'em together, riding, drinking sherry, and embracing at length."

Her mother lifted her hands to her chest and gasped while her father remained calm.

"I followed her to Mister Fleming's house. She went there to retrieve a book, but then I saw 'em through the window...kissing," accused Grace.

Mrs. Clark lifted her hand to silence her daughter. "What can our Meggy possibly want with that horrible man?"

"Is it no obvious?" grumbled Mr. Clark.

"I can stop 'em," said Grace confidently.

"How?" asked her father.

"By showin' her the drunken devil that he is!"

"Settle down, Gracie," said Mr. Clark, shaking his head. "I will talk to her."

"Aye," nodded Mrs. Clark. "Meggy will listen to you, my dear."

"She will no listen!" insisted Grace. "That devil has cast a wicked spell on her, and nothin' you say can remove it."

Her father rubbed the back of his neck while he sorted things in his mind and fished out a clay pipe from his coat pocket. "What do you propose', Gracie?" he asked while gently tamping the pipe-bowl on the palm of his hand.

Grace moved from side to side and rubbed her hands together. "Mister Fleming has an appetite for harlots. 'Tis only a matter of timin'. I can arrange it so Meggy catches him in the act."

Her father shook his head. "You will do nothing of the kind,

Gracie. No, I will talk to her. She will listen to me."

Meghan was reading *Metamorphoseon* in the parlor when her father entered. He closed the door and took a seat across from her, clay pipe jutting from his mouth, wisps of smoke trailing upwards.

She marked her place and calmly placed the book on her lap. "Good morning, Father."

"What are you readin', lass?"

Meghan glanced down at her book. "A collection of poetry of supernatural myths."

Mr. Clark tilted his head back and blew a column of smoke through his nostrils like an old dragon. "How did you come to possess such a book?"

She remained silent, a glint of concern in her eyes.

He laughed quietly and shook his head, forcing himself not to probe too deep, too soon. "Aye, hundreds of books, we have. Perhaps we ought to open a public library, eh?" He sucked on his pipe and puffed smoke rings, watching Meghan's restrained delight to see them. "Tell me, have you plans for today, lass?"

"None yet, why?"

Her father stood his pipe on the side table and stared at her book. "Thought we might go ridin', perhaps to meet yer new friend."

Meghan's eyes widened. "New friend?"

Her father lifted his pipe and resuscitated the smolder to an orange glow, then wedged the mouthpiece into the corner of his grin. "Meggy, you are such a lovely child and smarter than anybody I know, a daughter to make a father proud. I only want the best for you."

She shifted uncomfortably and gripped her book. "What is this all about?" said Meghan. "What did Gracie tell you?"

Mister Clark paused for a moment as if to reconsider his intent, but then his eyes found hers and he stayed the course. "Can you look me in the eye and tell me you aren't seein' that man, that Mister van Fleming?"

Meghan looked away. "The rumor is as false as yer impression of him."

"That remains to be seen. Have you spent time in his company?"

"Ever so brief and seldom and in the presence of Gracie," which was not entirely true.

He removed his pipe and shook his head. "Rumor or no, he is bad, Meggy. Certainly no good for any daughter of mine."

"How can you possibly know that, Father? How well do you know him? Have you exchanged ideas with him? And why do you not trust my judgment?"

"Because you lack experience!" boomed Mister Clark, leaning forward. "I needn't know him to understand his type! I know what he does after hours, where he goes and stays until sunup. True or no, the rumors paint a scandalous picture of him! Yer navigatin' uncharted waters in the fog, child. I am here to guide you back into the light."

Meghan took in a deep breath. "I have listened to you all my life, Father, and have always obeyed you, usually without question. I cherish yer love and wisdom now as ever before. That said I shall no longer subscribe to arbitrary requests concernin' my happiness and future."

He stomped his boot violently, shaking the floor and Meghan's nerves. "It is yer future and happiness I mean to protect!"

Meghan shook her head. "It is yer precious reputation you mean to protect."

He crossed his arms and cracked his neck. "Aye, that, too—"

"Then it is no about me," quipped Meghan.

Her father's face turned the color of exasperation between heliotrope and ruddy. He pointed his pipe at her. "Now you listen to me, child!"

Meghan sprung to her feet, clasping her book to her chest. "Am no child!"

"Yer actions show otherwise!" He loosened his collar and stood up. "Yer mother and I forbade you from seeing him, yet, you defied us. Why, Meggy? Reputation is important, but not only our family's, yours as well. Can you not see it?" He stepped towards her. "We love you and trust you. We know you will make it right." He lowered his voice but not the intensity. "Henceforth, you shall not so much as speak to Mister van Fleming. Do not acknowledge his existence. Do not acquaint yourself with any of his acquaintances. Make the wrong choice again, lass, and I shall hunt him down myself and put a stop to it, as God is my witness! Do you understand?"

Meghan contained her emotions. "Am sorry, Father, but no. I do not understand. Who I speak to is my business. And love is always the right choice." She moved to the door. "Will that be all, Father?"

Mr. Clark dismissed her by turning away.

Grace was right. Meghan would not listen. Mr. Clark found Grace in the foyer, sitting on the stairs. A nod from him was all she needed to set her scheme into motion. He removed the pipe from his lips, leaned against the balustrade, and exhaled smoke. Then, as if forced to make a regretful decision, he nodded, without fully understanding Grace's scheme or how it would impact all their lives.

38 - A DEPLORABLE TRICK

A month after Meghan's father had strongly forbid her from seeing Pierce, Meghan arrived at the Broadmore Hotel. Carefully planned, her rendezvous with Pierce was to be an incomparable experience. She had bathed the night before and moisturized her skin with rose balm. Her undergarments and gown were the easiest in her wardrobe to unfasten, and her hair—lavender scented and loosely drawn up—would fall and drape over her shoulders when released by two pins. Nervous and excited, she imagined how her carnal exploration would play out, how it might feel to be with Pierce, a man, finally, unbridled.

Meghan entered the dining room through the back of the hotel. Pierce was not there. Once before, she had to go upstairs to fetch him. He was usually tired in the afternoon, and prone to nap if given the chance. As she gathered up her gown and was climbing the steps to the second floor, she imagined him on his bed in slumber, breathing sweetly, as vulnerable as a child. Approaching the door to Pierce's room, voices inside puzzled her.

Noticing the door was ajar, she pushed it open to find Pierce lying beneath a woman on his bed. The woman's hemline was hiked up to her hips, her pale arse partially exposed, thrusting forwards and outwards. Meghan gasped. She had not recognized her sister in the ebony wig.

"Get off," said Pierce repeatedly.

Meghan gave no thought to where she was running to. She just wanted out. Stumbling in the lobby, she burst out onto the street and proceeded to her buggy a block away.

By the time Pierce was able to determine the direction she

had gone, she was already driving away. He called out her name and ran after her, but she kept going.

Grace was in the lobby when Pierce returned. She spat on his shoe.

"Why?" asked Pierce.

"Yer a scoundrel, and yer money doesn't change that. Sooner or later you will betray her. So, it is over. You will stay away from her. Do you understand me?"

Pierce's first inclination was to silence Grace into oblivion for what she had done, or at least to beat the spite out of her. Death was there, circling high above the lobby like a baleful spectre. "If I am a scoundrel, then what are you?" snarled Pierce. "It was *you* who betrayed your sister, not I." He glared up at Death. Her rotting grin was as repulsive as Grace's presence. Everything about that moment sickened him. He felt his heart tearing and shriveling in a void of confusion, exasperation, and lonesomeness.

Grace left Pierce alone to slump to the stairs, taking a seat on the third tread. He thought through the events leading up to Meghan's arrival, trying to reconstruct them, desperate to determine how they were possible. He hoped Meghan would allow him a chance to explain.

Meghan was not only devastated by what she saw and believed to be the ultimate betrayal, but also ashamed not to have heeded her parents' warnings. When she arrived home, she ran to her mother who sat in the parlor knitting a scarf. Meghan fell to her mother's feet and rested her tear-drenched face on her knee.

"Child, what is it?" her mother asked, acting surprised. Truth was the parents were waiting for Meghan to return home in hysterics. Another truth was they were duped by Grace. Grace told them she would hire a beautiful harlot to arrange a secret rendezvous with Pierce. The woman was to inform Grace of where and when the rendezvous would happen. Catching Pierce with another woman would be as easy as leading Meghan to a library. Grace would simply take her to the scene of the betrayal. That was the scheme. Grace never told them that she would play the harlot.

Her parents consoled Meghan, and suggested that she go to her grandparent's estate in Scotland. She loved it there. The house contained many of her childhood memories, as well as a magnificent library. It took little convincing her to go.

Pierce's arrival at their door the very next day, made it all too clear to Meghan that she had to leave. Mr. Clark mixed words with Pierce. He was not overly rude, but firm, asking him to leave and to stay away from his daughter. Pierce had sense enough not to explain how Grace had tricked them. That would cause more damage upon damage.

A month passed. Pierce sat in his office at the Ancoats cotton mill, trying to focus on business. He felt every bit as heartbroken and numb as he had on that deceitful day at the hotel. He thought of Meghan constantly—of where she was, what she was doing, how she felt about him, of what might have been. Perhaps Grace and her parents were right. Perhaps he truly was unfaithful and unworthy. After all, his proclivity for carousing and womanizing was among his greatest flaws, and he knew it.

Meghan would not respond to any of his letters. The Clark family prevented him from contacting her. Eventually, his evening pursuits became epidemic. Several different women and a brawl a week kept him busy at night, as he lost hope of ever reviving their love and finding love again. He figured that it was only a matter of time before he died in a brawl or was killed by the hands of a jealous lover. How elated Death would be if that were to happen, he thought.

Meghan's departure to Scotland remained a secret. Her parents feared Pierce would pursue her there if he knew. They burned his letters and sent messengers to tell him to stay away. He received no service at Ravens Gate, and Ewen would no longer speak to him.

At her grandparent's home, Meghan woke at midnight with a fever and burning sensation in her lower abdomen. Unable to sleep through the discomfort, she lit a candle and started rereading one of her favorite books: *The Life and Opinions of Tristram Shandy, Gentleman.* Reading relaxed her, shifting her focus away from what felt like severe cramping. She read until the light of morning brightened the room.

Unwell as she felt, she kept it from her grandparents. Worrying them over a stomach ache was unnecessary, she told herself. It was nothing serious. It would pass. And by noon, the pain lessened. Feeling better than she had a few hours before, she decided to confess her ailment to her grandparents. They wanted to fetch a physician, but Meghan convinced them not to. That she was well enough to go riding that afternoon.

By evening, however, the pain returned with a greater intensity accompanied with abdominal spasms, nausea, chills, and vomiting. Meghan suffered through the night and masked her suffering while in the company of her grandparents. This went on until the third day, when the pain was so intense she could no longer stand upright.

A physician arrived in the afternoon to find Meghan moaning into a pillow. After listening to her heart, timing her pulse rate, and inspecting the insides of her mouth and ears, he started depressing her abdomen with his fingers. When he applied pressure to her lower right quadrant, she yelped so loudly that her grandparents came to the door.

"Is everything all right in there?" asked the grandfather, pushing the door open just enough to peek in. The grandmother was standing on her toes behind him.

"If everything was all right, I would not be here, Mister Clark," quipped the doctor. "Have you wine, sherry, or whisky, sir?"

"I have whisky."

"Will you please bring me two glasses, one half-filled with

whisky, the other empty, and a teaspoon?"

"Right away," said the grandfather, turning and prodding his wife to help him fetch the items.

The doctor placed his hand on Meghan's forehead, and then lifted her eyelids for a look at her pupils and commented: "You have a mild fever and a rapid pulse rate. I noticed ulcerations on the tip of your tongue. Explain your symptoms and when you first noticed them."

"Four days ago," said Meghan, cringing from the pain. "I woke with a fever and stomach pain. The pain has grown worse. I have chills and nausea.

"Do your symptoms include diarrhea, constipation, loss of appetite, and vomiting?"

"Yes."

"For how long have you had a fever?"

"Four days."

"Blood in your stool?"

"No."

"The symptoms are likely caused by an infection in the lower right quadrant of your abdomen. The cause of the infection is difficult to isolate. It might be food poisoning, ulcerations, gallstones, but I believe it is an intestinal obstruction." He fished out a few small jars from his bag and arranged them on a side table. After the grandparents delivered the requested items, the doctor poured half the whisky in the empty glass, and carefully measured in a muddy liquid, a clear liquid, reddish powder, and what appeared to be sugar. He stirred the concoction with a spoon then licked the residue from it. "It is ready."

"What is it?" asked Mrs. Clark.

"Laudanum." The doctor lifted a spoonful of the analgesic to Meghan's lips. She swallowed it. "Give her two teaspoons every four hours."

"Yes, of course," said Mr. Clark, masking his worry with a faint smile.

The doctor lifted the other glass of whisky and drank it down. Then, he leaned in close to Meghan and said with a softened tone: "The medicine will ease your pain so you can rest."

Truth was the doctor had seen those symptoms before and knew about appendicitis. He had read about the disease, but up to that time, only one appendectomy had been performed in England. Unwilling to risk an invasive procedure he was ill-equipped to do, he told Meghan's grandparents to keep her comfortable and to call him back if her symptoms worsened.

39 - THE DARK GIFT

Cedric Martens had been spying on Pierce van Fleming for weeks. He learned Pierce's daily routines: working, eating, carousing, and lusting. The man caroused every night but somehow managed to work at the mill reliantly Tuesday through Thursday. Friday through Sunday was another matter.

On Friday night, the boy led Marie to King's Ransom, a seedy pub on the west side of Manchester, just as Pierce was exiting the pub. Marie was delighted to see that Pierce was as Abigail had described him to be—tall and fetching.

"Well done, Cedric," said Marie. "Now, go back to the hotel and wait for me there."

Cedric's shoulders drooped, and he nodded obediently. He reminded himself of his servant status. His opinions were weightless. Yet, he wanted more to do. He wanted to be more involved. He was a pretty good negotiator. He had bartered and traded goods. He negotiated the umbrella and arranged all transportation and lodging in England. His command of the English language was rapidly improving. If only she saw his potential, he told himself.

Without Cedric, Marie followed Pierce to an inn a few blocks away where he met up with two young women, sloppy on cheap gin, standing beside a gas lantern. Marie followed them into the inn, slipping past the front desk and gliding up two flights of stairs. The room door was left unlatched. Marie pushed it open enough to view them kissing, undressing, and laughing boisterously.

To Pierce, it was just a typical Friday night, but the night was hardly typical, for behind the door stood Countess Marie de Vos. The bed was out of view, but she was able to see their reflections in an oval mirror on the wall. Pierce's hedonistic qualities, his womanizing prowess and physical presence tantalized her. Endowed and muscular with bullish stamina, Pierce van Fleming was far more than she had expected. When the *ménage à trois* finally slowed to a panting heap of sweating flesh, the countess pushed the door open.

Pierce sat up and said exactly what she expected him to say.

"Come in, dear madam. Please join us!"

She stepped into the candlelit room, closed and locked the door, and announced herself in Brabantic Dutch. "I am Countess Marie de Vos of Flanders. I have come for my cousin Percy."

After a curious moment of silence, one of the women sat up and chortled.

"We speak English here your majesty, and you're a bit tardy. As you can see, we've already *come* for your cousin Percy!" mocked the woman with a Dutch accent, drawing laughter from the other woman.

"And you're a bit overdressed I might add!" said the other, jiggling her breasts.

Marie was a blur when she moved, wrapping her elongated fingers around both women's necks, pinning their bodies against Pierce's. As the women succumbed, Marie peered into van Fleming's eyes. Hers were hazel, mesmerizing and beautiful as they glowed and pulsated to the racing beat of his heart. Six beats later, Marie squeezed one woman's head off with her right hand. Blood gushed from the severed neck as the torso wheezed and convulsed. Marie then sunk her fangs into the other woman's throat, ripping out arteries, muscle, and cartilage. The woman bled out lavishly.

Marie laughed hysterically, pieces of flesh wedged between her teeth.

"My dear Abigail was right! Of incomparable luster, shape, and size thou art. Might my feeble and unfaithful master be right after all?" She placed her hand on Pierce's head and pulled him into her blood-drenched chest. "Be calm my sweet prince. Fear not." She kicked and pushed the woman's corpses to the floor and started counting his eyelashes. "One, two, three, four...this may take a while," giggled Marie.

Pierce tried to fight her off, but was like a fly caught in a web.

"God," he muttered.

She paused to look about the macabre scene. "Where, Percy? I see no one else. Hast thy God forsaken thee?" She pressed her lips to his forehead, leaving a bloody imprint.

As Pierce's eyes searched wildly for a weapon, he saw the reflection of Marie's dress in the wall mirror, but the woman cast no reflection.

"Behold thy future!" said Marie. "Damn it to Hades if poor Domitian was not right. How could I possibly kill thee?" She combed his hair with her fingers. "Such a beautiful head... Thou art an Eros amongst mortals. I must have thee, oh yes, in every way! Be still now, my prince. Be ready to rise above the loathsome filth of your god's inhumanity." She held his face to hers and surveyed his fearful expression. "Henceforth thou art my son, my muse, my love. In darkness on earth, forever immaculate, betrothed, and powerful we shall be."

She easily overpowered Pierce, running her bloody hands over his naked body, supplanting her mouth on his neck, swallowing his blood. Astonished at the unusual sweetness of his blood, her eyes rolled back and she levitated over him. Too drunk with ecstasy to ponder why a man would taste like a child, she hovered.

Marie woke before dawn. Pierce was still lying where she had all but drained him to death. Yet his heart was still beating and the puncture wounds on his neck had scabbed. She sniffed him like a curious beast.

"Art thou man or boy?" said Marie. She brushed his hair aside and ran her finger along the ridge of his nose down to his lips and across his throat where she squeezed a drop of blood onto her finger and placed it into her mouth. She could no longer taste the sweetness of youth, but rather the earthly salt of the dark gift. She caressed his muscular frame and straddled him. He was sturdy and beautifully marred. She counted his scars, all twelve of them.

No, she would not kill him. Not yet. He had potential.

By the witching hour of the second eve, Pierce van Fleming

became the progeny vampire of Countess Marie de Vos.

40 - DEPARTING LIGHT

"Thy thirst for human blood is irrepressible," said Marie to Pierce as she entered his bedchamber in the Fleming house. It had been three weeks since his turning. She sneered at his suffering as he lay in bed, writhing and flinching. "Starvation is unpleasant, is it not? Nausea, fever, paranoia. The agony slowly intensifies, churning thy guts, crinkling thy skin, stinging thine eyes. Beware, my wanting prince, for the *frenzy* draws nearer."

"The *frenzy* is of no concern," muttered Pierce, hair clinging to his clammy forehead.

She stared at him with condescension and took air into her nostrils. "Canst thou smell it? Humanity's ever-present stench? The furor of crows flying overhead irritates thee, does it not?"

"Nay, they are no bother," said Pierce, though he knew she was right. Quarrelling crows grated his nerves. The bedpan, albeit empty, polluted the air. His skin was creeping with discomfort. Such malaise threatened to snuff out the smolder of human consciousness that by chance had survived his transformation.

"Death," growled Pierce. "That bloody demon has cursed me."

"Nonsense," snapped Marie. "In three weeks' time, thou hast fed on rodents and one diseased old man. No wonder thy mood has grown foul."

"Death must have had a hand in this."

"Death, death, death. Always dwelling on pointless mortal concerns." said Marie, moving to an armoire. "Why torture thyself? End thy suffering. Dine with me. Dine like the dark prince thou art."

Pierce rolled out of bed onto his knees. "Tell me, please, why are you here?"

"Really, stupid man, I had already told thee—"

"Enough!" spat Pierce, covering his ears. "Thee, thou, thy. Your outdated tongue is what irritates me."

Marie's eyes suddenly shifted to the doorway. "Yes, what is it?"

Cedric remained just out of view in the hallway. "Forgive my intrusion, My Countess. May I be of further service this evening?"

"No," said Marie. "Retire to the guest cottage. Stay there until summoned."

"Thank you, My Countess."

Marie turned to Pierce. "I happen to fancy early English."

"Who is the boy?" asked Pierce.

"A servant, nothing more, though he possesses admiral qualities. Thou...or rather *you* shall learn to manipulate the weak-of-mind to do your bidding during daylight hours." She opened the armoire. "You are the chosen one, so says the oracle. The clan master believes in her premonitions. I am, however, skeptical." She started counting garments.

"Why does the clan master believe in the oracle?" asked Pierce.

Marie fingered through Pierce's wardrobe: "Six long shifts, six britches, six waistcoats, and six kerchiefs, all every bit as outdated as my English." She clicked her tongue with disdain. "Really, my passé prince, where is *your* panache?" She closed the armoire. "The oracle is a witch from the Norse world, one in a long line of oracles who have come to dwell in the forest. The master believes them to be guardians of the clan."

Pierce sat down on the bed and fell back. "What is your master's name?"

Her smile parted to reveal a perfect row of teeth. "Count Marcel Marc de Vos. Presumably five centuries old, he has ruled the clan for over four of those centuries. According to the oracle, someone like you will succeed him." She gazed at his hands. "You bear the marks. You are from an island nation. You fit the description."

Pierce puffed air of annoyance between his lips. "Rubbish,

all of it." He sat up and rubbed his stinging eyes. "The prophecy is false, for I shall never leave England."

"Come dine with me tonight, Percy. You need not suffer the frenzy, lest you intend to mutilate the boy."

Pierce glowered at her. "Frenzy or no, you mutilate all your victims. You tore those girls to pieces at the hotel."

"They should not have insulted me."

"They will be your undoing. You will hang for what you did."

Marie laughed. "Who will know? I took the inn's registry and disposed the bodies. With no evidence or witnesses, your constables will have nothing more than an unsolvable mystery to ponder. Really, Percy, you have much to learn."

Despite Pierce's resistance to her and his new reality, he found himself tagging along beside her at dusk, his mind traipsing back and forth between reluctance and desire. One moment they were in a carriage, then they were walking in central Manchester the next. The monster in him wanted to attack the crowds, but a persuasive undercurrent prevented him from going berserk. Was Marie controlling him?

They walked upon a thin blanket of snow towards a young woman standing in front of a brick building. Her lips formed a smile and incomprehensible words on steamy puffs of breath. Pierce's ears felt as if they were filled with water. He recognized her face but could not place her. The woman led them into the building and upstairs to her flat. Marie placed a small bag of coins on a table and started removing the woman's shawl.

Pierce awoke the next morning to find his mouth latched to the young woman's thigh. Marie was picking out chunks of flesh from her bloodstained teeth with a splinter of bone. He released the leg and sat up. Bloody bed sheets clung to his naked body.

"Grace," murmured Pierce, as he gazed upon her body.

"What?" Marie asked, wiping her mouth with a bed sheet.

"That was her name. Did she say anything about me?"

"Just some dribble concerning her sister..."

Pierce had not thought of Meghan since his turning. Memories and his feelings for her surfaced like random bubbles in a murky pond: her book fetish, the horserace, the day Grace bludgeoned their young and fragile love to pieces. He wanted to know of Meghan's whereabouts. Was she well and happy, perhaps married with child? He recalled his promise to Ewen Clark, that he would not harm the Clark sisters. So much for that. Not only was he a liar, he was a bloodthirsty killer. The only way he could protect Meghan was not to speak of her, never to seek her out, and to bury her memory under layers of regret.

Marie slipped off the bed and placed her hand on Pierce's shoulder. "How do you feel now, my sweet prince?"

Pierce focused on the gaping hole in Grace's neck. He should have been horrified, but found the scene to be no grizzlier than a carved goose at dinner. Why?

Why did he feel so apathetic, so numb? Had his senses and physical strength been greatly enhanced at the expense of his morality? He struggled to find a conscience, to regret taking part in the woman's demise. Meghan's sister Grace was a spiteful woman, he reminded himself, but undeserving of this. Why do I not feel guilt and devastation? I committed murder. Murder! I know the difference between right and wrong and...and I shall vow never to kill again, without moral justification, of course, for instance self-defense. I would sooner feed on rats than on innocent humans.

He attributed the fog of indifference to the shock of being turned. He gazed steadily into Marie's eyes. "I feel strong," whispered Pierce. "Incredibly strong."

41 - MORE IS MORE

The typical day of working long hours and carousing had changed for Pierce. He slept six hours, worked six hours, and spent the remainder of the day at his estate. He wanted to be alone. He no longer suffered nightmares. Death no longer visited him. He hunted game on his property, staving off the frenzy with animal blood. It extended his will to forgo murder for over two months, but his cravings for human blood would not relent.

As Pierce tended to his horses in the stable, he smelled Cedric standing at the doorway. By then, Pierce had learned to decipher various scents, accentuating one by suppressing others. Pierce found it amusing that the boy was taking to him, showing the gumption to serve him even though he was still in the countess's employ. Perhaps he was just plain bored, cooped up in the guesthouse with nothing better to do.

"Mister Fleming, sir, may I be of service?" asked Cedric.

Pierce paused and turned to the boy. "Tired of doing nothing, are you?"

Cedric smiled after Pierce smirked at him and quickly took up a shovel. Pierce backed away, watching the boy shovel horse dung into a wheelbarrow. He was strong and obliging—much in the way Pierce had been at his age. Pierce smelled the boy's blood, sensed his rising body temperature. Pierce distrusted himself. Marie taught him to act on his instincts, to attack and feed discretely. He was thirsty and alone with the boy. The urge to act grew stronger. He took a step towards Cedric. Might he control his thirst for blood? To test his will, Pierce filtered out all scents—save Cedric's. Instantly, Pierce's eyes began pulsating and his incisors elongating. Pierce's vision narrowed and sharpened, and he crept towards the boy.

The horses stirred.

"Cunning," said Marie, jarring Pierce's moment to a standstill. Her voice came from just outside the entranceway. She wore a cloak powdered white with snow. "Persuading the boy to do your dirty work, are you?"

Pierce turned away from Cedric. He felt ashamed.

"Come with me," said Marie. "Let the boy finish up." Pierce followed Marie into the snow-covered courtyard. "Had I not arrived a moment sooner, Cedric would be dead or dying," said Marie. "Perhaps I should have allowed it. As always, you lack nourishment." Marie stopped and turned to Pierce. "Humans eat animals. We eat humans. Our kind requires quality sustenance, for without it, we will grow weaker and more vulnerable. You wish to live among humans. The way to do that is to feed on them discreetly. Come, I will show you."

"I will stay here," said Pierce.

"You will do as I say," hissed Marie.

From inside the stable, too far away to hear their conversation, Cedric gazed out at them.

"Boy," shouted Marie. "Mister Fleming and I are going away on business for a few days. Take care of the estate and turn away all visitors."

"Yes, My Countess."

"And ready the cabriolet," said Marie as she turned towards the house. "We shall leave in the hour."

At Marie's request, Pierce parked the buggy in a secluded location. From there, they walked into the village.

"Relax, my stubborn prince," said Marie to Pierce. As they entered a crowded tavern, Marie's eyes moved across the room until they caught the gaze of two young men. Eye contact and a smile was all it took for them to join Marie and follow her outside. The foursome walked to a brothel where two young women joined them as quickly as the men had. Pierce saw that the men and women were entranced. They said nothing but smiled and eagerly followed them to the buggy.

It was that moment Pierce realized Marie's power. She controlled not only four humans, but him as well. It was not that she forced her will upon him. He could have easily blocked her out and walked away. It was his loathing of the blood-craving that welcomed any form of relief. She relieved him of it. It must have been the same for the men and women. They were naturally attracted to her beauty, and probably bored and intrigued, and thus accepting of her persuasion.

In the lush hills of Alderley Edge, Pierce gathered blankets that Marie had brought and spread them out beneath a stand of trees. Except for the company and drastic manner of intentions, the spread reminded Pierce of the surprise picnic he had made for Meghan following the horserace. The young men made a fire close enough to warm them. Marie then gestured for everyone to join her on the blanket.

Marie's eyes gazed up at Pierce, who refused to partake. "Come, Percy. Join the company of beautiful people." She tapped a young man on the shoulder and whispered something in his ear. As the man began to undress a woman, Marie went to Pierce, standing beside the buggy, arms crossed.

"Entertained by this sort of thing, are you?" asked Pierce curtly.

"Are you not?" rebutted Marie. "There was a time when this was all you did. Have you forgotten?"

"No. I recall those times, happy endings, with everyone still alive and well."

Marie placed her finger on Pierce's lips. "Do not forget that it is I who governs your urges. They will rule your actions when I release you. No rats, no rabbits, no sickly old people on which to feed—not tonight. Tonight's happy ending shall be as it should be, with us still alive and well." She slowly released her mind from his, allowing his hunger to overwhelm. Then, she led Pierce into an undulating orgy of pleasure.

In the morning, Pierce awoke to a grizzly scene. He sat up and scanned for Marie amongst blood splatters and mismatched body parts.

"Slept well?" asked Marie, sitting in the buggy, counting river pebbles collected in a tricorne hat. She appeared clean and dressed. "Wash in the river, my sweet prince. We may socialize amongst your precious humans without killing them now."

Pierce had never felt guiltier and yet more invigorated. He felt as if he could fly, and his senses were never keener. The snow shimmered in the early morning light, and he could hear and smell things as far away as the city. After cleaning up and returning to the buggy, Marie tossed a shovel at his feet.

"Hurry, it is getting late," said Marie.

When they arrived home, Pierce found a note on the door. It was from Chief Constable Gareth Turner.

> *Dear Mr. Fleming,*
>
> *Cedric was injured in a robbery. He is recovering in my care. Please collect him upon your return.*
>
> *Regards,*
>
> *C. C. Gareth Turner*

42 - RETRIEVING THE BOY

At his modest home in Stockport, Chief Constable Gareth Turner greeted Pierce at the door. "Mister Fleming, good day, sir. Thank you for coming."

"Good day, Constable. I came as soon as I received your note. How is the boy?"

"Come, come inside," said Gareth, fanning his hand, backing into the house. "Where on earth have you been? James and I worried you might have died in that old ironstone mansion of yours. Good God, man, you look dreadful!"

"Knackered is all. I have been out of town on business," said Pierce, following Gareth through the house into the parlor where Cedric and Magistrate James Smith were sitting.

"Good God, man, you look dreadful!" said James, repeating Gareth's comment with a wink when he saw Pierce. He stood up to shake hands. James squinted at Pierce. "Really, though, are you well?"

"Exhausted is all," said Pierce.

"Out of town on business," said Gareth of Pierce.

Pierce glanced at the bloodstained bandage round Cedric's head. "How is he?"

Cedric shifted his glazed-over eyes to Pierce.

"Better," said Gareth. "He could scarcely speak two nights ago. Apparently, he was attacked and robbed near the old dairy."

"The doctor stitched him up," said James

"Cedric," said Pierce. "How do you feel? Are you ready to leave?"

"Why leave so soon?" said Gareth. "We really do need to talk, in private. Let us go into the kitchen for some tea."

Pierce nodded. "Master Cedric," said Pierce. "Please wait here. I will come for you shortly."

In the kitchen, the men sat quietly as Gareth's wife, Margaret, poured everybody a cup of tea. After she left them and several sips in, Gareth broke the silence. "There is something amiss in the boroughs."

"Indeed," said Pierce. "What do we know about Cedric's assailant?"

"Well, nothing as yet," said Gareth.

"I should like to fund the investigation," said Pierce.

"Thank you," said Gareth.

"On a different matter," said James, glancing over at Gareth, expecting him to share an important topic they had obviously discussed.

"Right," said Gareth. "People are disappearing. The first report was filed several months ago. Two young women, a hotel clerk, and a married couple went missing."

"People have gone missing nearly every week since then," said James. "Foul play is at work. Blood and flesh have been discovered where the victims were last seen."

Pierce gazed out the window at a pair of crows in a tree. "Any theories or leads?" asked Pierce.

"None so far," said James.

"I have noticed a trend," said Gareth. "At first, the missing persons were of all ages, but since the first report, missing persons have been getting younger."

"Younger? How many in total are reported missing?" asked Pierce, wondering if they had accounted for all murders committed by Marie and him.

"Fourteen," said James.

"Seven men, seven women," added Gareth. "I have constables questioning those who saw them last. We are searching the rivers, lakes, and farmlands for evidence but have found nothing yet. With no leads, we may as well be fishing for sharks in the Irwell."

"Do we have enough men to enforce order?" asked Pierce.

"I continue to commission men, and the consortium of industry leaders continues to fund us," said Gareth.

Pierce put his cup down and smiled. "Constable and Judge, I

really must go. Thank you for looking after Cedric. Please allow me to fund your investigations. Shall we meet again next week to discuss your progress?"

"That would be fine," said Gareth.

"Fine," said James.

Pierce gathered Cedric, and James and Gareth bade them a good day.

43 - RETRIEVING THE COIN

In the kitchen at the Fleming mansion, Pierce stood at the stove frying eggs while Cedric sat quietly at a table.

"Boy," shouted Marie as she entered the kitchen, "Who did this to you?"

Cedric remained unresponsive.

"Cedric, answer me now. Who attacked you?"

"He is not well," said Pierce. "He suffered a head injury and is lucky to be alive."

"Weak, and now stupid?" Marie leaned against the wall and crossed her arms.

Pierce served the eggs, poured a cup of milk for the boy, and sat down at the table beside him. After a moment, Cedric lifted a fork and shoveled eggs into his mouth.

"We ought to replace your bandage after this," said Pierce.

Cedric finished all his eggs and turned to Pierce.

"Four men took my coin," whispered Cedric.

"Coin or coin purse?" asked Pierce.

"Both," said Cedric.

"What coin?" asked Pierce.

"It was an English Broad," said Marie. "The boy won it by solving a riddle."

Pierce remained focused on Cedric. "Cedric, can you describe your assailants, age, height, voice, clothing, anything?"

Cedric sat very still, then closed his eyes and spoke, "I had gone into the city for supplies. In the Shambles, I met four men—eighteen years of age, medium-build. They spoke Dutch. They seemed friendly."

"Dutch," said Pierce.

"Dutch sailors," clarified Cedric.

"Dutch merchant ships are moored in Liverpool," mumbled Pierce to himself. He leaned over and committed the boy's scent to memory.

"Really," muttered Marie, "do you plan to sniff them out like a dog?"

Pierce ignored her. "Cedric, do not leave the estate." Pierce got up and rushed out of the kitchen.

Marie followed him outside to the stables. The horses became unsettled when she entered the building. Pierce motioned her to back away. He then saddled up his Belgium black stallion and led it outside. Why the horse was calm around Pierce confounded Marie.

"Why do you care?" said Marie from a distance. "The boy and the money ought to mean nothing to you. It is capricious folly to carry on like this."

Completely ignoring her, Pierce mounted the horse and rode off.

Based on Cedric's information, Pierce went directly to the Port of Liverpool. It took little time or effort to track Cedric's scent to a Dutch merchant ship. Pierce hopped aboard and followed the scent below deck where he found three sailors gathered round a table.

"I wager a shilling!" said a blond man with a hairy face.

"It is all you have!" said another.

"Nay, I have one more including this hat. I wager all of it for your gold coin."

Pierce came out of the shadows. "That is a beautiful and rare gold coin."

The young sailors were startled to see Pierce. They reached for their daggers.

"Who are you? Why are you here?"

"A friend," said Pierce, as he stared at Cedric's hat perched on a sailor's head. "A friend of the true owner of that hat, the gold coin, and the money purse on the table."

"The coin belongs to me," claimed the sailor as he lifted his dagger. The others followed his lead.

Pierce moved quickly, snatching the coin, using his mind and body to deflect their attacks, causing them to thrust their daggers into each other. The last Dutchman standing slightly wounded dropped his dagger on the table.

"Hat, please," said Pierce, holding out his hand. The man placed it on the table. "Come here," ordered Pierce, peering deeply into the sailor's twitchy eyes. Pierce concentrated, forcing his will on the man. The Dutchman finally nodded and went to Pierce.

"Turn around, please," said Pierce. The man obeyed. "Tilt your head to the side and pull back your collar." When Pierce saw that his neck was grimy and smelly, he wiped it clean with whisky and whispered in his ear, "No mercy for the wicked." Then he drained him dead.

The next day, Cedric woke up to find his hat, gold Broad, and money purse on the side table.

44 - UNEXPECTED GUESTS

"We could have simply given the boy another bag of coins," huffed Marie, pacing the kitchen and glowering at Pierce as he palmed a cup of tea. "And why do you insist on making tea? Everything you do is nonsensical. A complete waste of time!"

Pierce held the cup to his lips and inhaled the aroma. "You are right, Countess. We could have simply given Cedric more money and a new hat."

"It is unnatural..."

Just then, the sounds of a hackney arriving outside drew their attention away. Pierce went to the foyer and opened the door. He stepped onto the porch, dreading the thought of visitors, for no one was safe in the presence of Marie. He watched the coachman step down and open the carriage door. Then, out stepped Pierce's niece, Emma.

Pierce's worry swelled as he went to her. "Dear niece...!"

"Uncle," cried Emma.

Pierce took Emma's hands and gazed at her youth. "This is quite an unexpected surprise."

"Have you not received my letter?"

"I...I do not believe so, no."

"Then I apologize for arriving unannounced, Uncle." said Emma, appearing distraught.

"What is the matter?"

"With a heavy heart, I bring sad news," Emma said, tears forming. "Your dear mother..."

Pierce folded his arms around her. After a moment of sorrow, for which Pierce searched deeply within, Emma stepped back. "The doctors did all they could. We comforted her until her last breath. I am terribly sorry, Uncle." Emma glanced at the window to see Marie, grinning eerily at her.

Pierce saw Cedric standing in front of the guest cottage. "Had I known you were coming—"

"I intend to stay in the city, but wanted to make my arrival known."

He waved at the coachman. "Take her to the Broadmore Hotel. Do you know it?"

"Aye, sir."

"Good. Ask for Missus Porter. She will settle your fee." He turned back to Emma. "You do remember Missus Porter?"

Emma smiled and nodded.

"Ask for the Fleming suite." Pierce gave her money. "Shall I meet you tomorrow afternoon?"

"Thank you, Uncle."

Pierce saw her off and returned to the house. As he entered the library, he noticed a portrait of his mother hanging on the wall beside another of his father.

"Who was that delicious morsel?" said Marie, falling in behind him, licking her lips.

"Just a messenger bearing news of my mother's death."

Marie went to the collection of crystal whisky decanters. Lifting a bottle, she removed the stopper and scented its contents before pouring a glass. After tasting it, she brought the glass to Pierce. "I have no preference for whisky."

Pierce breathed in the smoky fumes and downed the booze.

"Your niece is very lovely," said Marie. "I would very much like to meet her. What is her name?"

"There is no reason to meet her. She is of no concern to us."

"Relatives are always concerning."

On the surface, Pierce appeared unruffled, but deep down he feared for Emma's life. The incestuous thirst Marie spoke of usually resulted in the total annihilation of a vampire's former human family.

"I will spend time with her on the morrow," said Pierce, back stiffening with fear for his niece's safety, "and then she will leave. We shall not see her again. I can assure you of that." Pierce left Marie in the library to count books. He tempered his anger, telling himself Marie would not pursue Emma. There was no reason to. Why go all the way to London for one girl? Still, unable to defend his niece against the countess sickened him. Marie was either too powerful—physically, mentally, supernaturally—or he was too weak. He felt her manipulation, as if she had planted a sliver of herself in the center of his mind. It was a constant struggle to fight it.

The next day, Pierce met Emma at the hotel as planned. He helped her into the buggy and drove to a village away from the crowds, chance meetings, and especially Marie. They sat in a quiet tavern and ordered a meal. This was Pierce's first attempt at eating cooked food since his turning. The ale smelled of sweaty old saddle and tasted sour. Next, he tried roasted lamb. It smelled musky and burnt. He forced himself to swallow it, washing it down with stinky sour ale.

"I loved grandmother dearly," said Emma.

Pierce thought of excuses not to finish his meal. "Emma, may we change the subject?"

Emma nodded. "Yes, of course. How insensitive of me."

"No, no, it is just that...I had not seen my mother for a year, and a lot has since happened. I am deeply grateful to you and your mother for her care." The deeper truth was guilt—exhumed from the wreckage of his mind—for sending her away and then avoiding her in hospice.

Emma smiled sadly.

"Emma, what are your plans for the future?"

"Well, as I have been interested in helping you with the business, I had plans to move to Lancashire."

Had Pierce never met Marie, he might have been ecstatic to bring Emma into the business, but it was all Pierce could do to blanket over the scent of her adolescent blood, stinky ale, and musky lamb. His primary concern was Marie. She would harm Emma if given the chance. Pierce smiled and lifted his glass of ale to Emma's cup of tea.

"Emma, I look forward to your move. The business needs you. I need you." They drank. "Timing is very important. I ask that you wait until we both agree the time is right to make the move. Until then, I encourage you to pursue your education. Have you considered college?"

"College is for men. No woman to my knowledge has gone to college. I thought you might educate me in ways of the business."

Pierce chuckled. "True, few women have gone to college, but that should not discourage you. Why not be the first woman to attend Oxford?" He pushed aside the beer and food and leaned forward. "Listen, I will teach you everything I know about the business, but will you at least consider college?"

"Yes, of course."

"Good. I will speak to your parents about it."

"Thank you, Uncle."

"I want you to return to London in the morning. I will have Missus Porter arrange it."

"When will I see you again?"

"Soon. Please do not share our agreement with anyone until I have discussed it with your parents."

After the meal, Pierce escorted Emma to the hotel and bade her a good night. On the way to the buggy, he failed to identify Marie's perfume among the myriad of odors.

Marie watched Pierce maneuvered his buggy into traffic. She had been watching them nearly the entire day. Taking mental note of Pierce's fondness of his niece, Marie gazed through the hotel window at Emma climbing the lobby stairs.

45 - GLUTTONY AND GUILT

As time wore on, James and Gareth reminded Pierce of the expanding list of missing persons. The fact that Pierce was responsible for those missing persons profoundly bothered him, but why? Vampires were supposed to be unfeeling and unremorseful. Yet, Pierce cared. His cursed desire for human blood tormented him like a reviled addiction he was powerless to stop. He felt guilt and self-loathing, deserving of death and eternal damnation for what he had done. He begged God and Satan to smite him down and damn his soul to oblivion, presuming he still had a soul. When his prayers went unanswered, he questioned the existence of heaven and hell, seeing no value or validity to religion. What happened to the winged demon of souls? Why had she abandoned him? Was it his immortal state that repelled her? Was dying a mortal's privilege? He worried he might never die.

Marie's immediate remedy for Pierce's ailment was to feed on as many humans as possible—and the younger the better. Unwilling to concede, yet supernaturally compelled to partake in the ways of the vampire, Pierce grew physically stronger, but profoundly dejected. As he and Marie stalked central Manchester, Pierce read people's expressions, wondering if they could see the killer in him. Immersed in a steady flow of people, Pierce suddenly stopped. Marie stopped with him and followed his stare to Farmer John's wife and daughter, Brea. They were on a collision course. Without a word, he took Marie by the wrist and led her to the other side of the street.

"Unhand me!" seethed Marie, pulling away and slapping his face. "Do not forget your place."

Pierce noticed others trying not to stare at Marie's sudden outburst. "I beg pardon, Countess, for I know those people. I know them all too well and thought to—"

"The first rule of survival is to act as they do amongst them. Is that not what you have always wanted, to be amongst them?" She observed Brea walking beside her mother. "Might I say, your friends look absolutely delicious especially the girl. How old is she, Cedric's age?"

"She is older," said Pierce, "an adult." He moved into Marie's view. "Dear Countess, please understand, they are well known in this community, and they are my friends. We cannot—"

"Yes, we can, or at least *I* can," said Marie, stretching her neck to get another glimpse of the women.

"Please, I beg of you, not them."

Marie turned to Pierce and smirked. She placed her hand on Pierce's desperate face and said, "Some friend you are—to exclude them from our dinner party. Show some appetite, my prince."

To Pierce's relief, Marie continued in a direction away from Brea and her mother, leading him instead to an abbey where an elderly nun greeted them in a courtyard.

"Good day, Missus Devos!" said the portly nun. "I presume you have come for Robert?"

"Yes," said Marie. "Sister Kelly, this is my husband."

"Pleased to meet you, Mister Devos. Thank you for coming."

"The pleasure is mine, Sister Kelly," said Pierce, playing along to appease Marie.

"Will you please excuse me? I will fetch young Robert."

"Please do," said Marie.

The nun rushed into the hallway and met up with another nun, whispering and disappearing into a distant chamber.

"Why are we here?" asked Pierce"

"We are about to become parents."

"I thought I had seen everything," muttered Pierce. "But this..."

"We have come for only one insignificant orphan. Or would you prefer that we kill them all? Perhaps we should."

"No."

"I am doing this for you, Mister Devos. Avoiding—how did

you call it—careless gluttony?"

After a moment of crossed-arm silence between them, the nun returned with the young boy. Standing behind him, she placed her hands on his shoulders.

"Master Robert is ready, Mister Devos, Missus Devos," said Sister Kelly.

The nun knelt to Robert and said softly, "Master Robert, these kind people are Mister and Missus Devos. They are your new parents. Are you not the luckiest boy? Show your appreciation and go to them. Go on now."

Clearly frightened, the boy backed himself into the nun. She chuckled nervously.

"He is a shy one, but they always are." She gave him an encouraging nudge. "Go on."

Marie smiled and looked into his eyes. The entrancement was always the easiest through the eyes. Suddenly, the boy walked to her and put his arms around Marie's waist.

"All is well," said Marie, patting him on the head.

"It is truly God's will," said the nun with a sigh of relief. She put her hands together. "This is a perfect union. God bless you both." The nun handed a small bundle of the boy's articles to Pierce and smiled sweetly, grasping a crucifix dangling from her neck. "Those are some of Robert's favorite things. Peace and happiness be with you, Mister and Missus Devos."

46 - THE WICKED SICKNESS

Marie and Pierce entered the confined lobby of the Lancashire Greens, a small inn on the outskirts of town. The host barely greeted them. Marie gave him the eye and he quickly handed a room key to her. The room was small, containing one bed, an old divan and chair, and a rickety armoire. Pierce sat down in the chair and stared at the boy. He could pass for Cedric's younger brother.

She walked Robert to the couch, sat beside him, and placed her hand on his knee. After a few ticks of a pocket watch, she rolled her eyes up and the boy's eyes did the same. Whichever way she moved her eyes, the boy's eyes followed in synchronicity. "Is it not amusing...mind bending?" said Marie to Pierce.

"No," said Pierce.

"You should see what Gerda can do. She is the clan's mind bender. I saw her bend six vampires and six humans all at once. She made the vampires believe they were human and the humans believe they were vampire—oh the hilarity that ensued!" Marie saw that Pierce was not amused. She shook her head with disdain and said, "There are six sacred laws of the Royal Flemish Clan, supposedly chiseled in stone by none other than Hades' master stonemason. That tablet was conveniently lost, of course, never to be found. Nevertheless, the first rule is not to worship God or Zeus or any other deity or symbol other than Hades, Lord of the Underworld."

"Why worship anything?" asked Pierce.

"Indeed. Why? Seldom do I follow rules, and faith is an exploitable flaw."

"When you were human, which faith exploited you?"

"I was born into the catholic faith," a giggle escaped her smirk. "I married Marcel in a church to appease my parents and the priest. After receiving the dark gift, I wanted to kill the priest for what he had done, but Marcel stopped me."

"What had the priest done?"

"It was long ago and no longer important. What remains of my faith is a bag of gold crosses I have collected over the years—eighteen to be exact."

"So, then, do you believe in nothing now?"

Marie responded with silence.

Pierce nodded as if he had understood a wordless explanation. "Please, go on...the sacred laws?"

"The third law is never to deceive or kill another vampire. I value some aspects of this rule. I have never killed kindred."

"I gather you have passed over the deception aspect just as you have conveniently passed over the second law: not to feed on infants or adolescent humans." Pierce suddenly noticed the boy quaking with fear. "Does he hear us?"

"It would appear so, no thanks to you." She placed her hand on the boy's knee again and said, "Fear not, little boy. Close your eyes and ears to us. What we say and what we do are of no concern to you."

An instant calm came over Robert.

"Not as skilled as Gerda, but skilled enough," said the countess. "Where was I? Oh yes. In our former lives, we learned of morality, ethics, logic, and civil duties on which all but one of our clan laws is based. The child's blood law is based on false assumptions."

Pierce scoffed. "It is my understanding the law prohibits child's blood because it is toxic—"

"If that were true, then explain why I am here and well."

Pierce had no explanation. His experience was nil, his knowledge inadequate. Yet, hunting humans of any age presented a moral dilemma in his muddled mind.

"A child is to an adult as a calf is to a cow," expounded Marie. "Do humans not eat veal?"

"Children are not calves. They are not slaughtered and eaten. They are the future of each generation of humanity and are thus cherished and protected under the eyes of God. "

Marie laughed. "I fear your humanity misleads you just as religion misleads humanity. I follow no rules, and all humans are food. As for religion, all are created by humans to control humans. You wanted to know if I believed in anything or nothing. I believe our kindred are weak to be influenced by man-made concepts. The Cainians are the perfect example. They believe Cain to be the first antediluvian vampire because he received the dark gift from God. Really? If that were true, then we ought to worship God as our creator. After all, God is the greatest nemesis of all. His inability to forgive is matched only by his profusion to punish. Speaking of fallen angels, there is the Palladists, Luciferians, and owed to ancient mythology the Hadesians. God and the gods, Satan and Hades, all created in man's egotistical image." Marie closed her eyes and stretched her mouth open, exposing her fangs like a wild primate. She seemed tired and aged with wrinkles on her face. "Enough talk." She put her arm around the boy. "You must be very tired, my sweet. Mummy is going to put you to sleep now."

The boy breathed deeply, steadily. Marie's eyes glowed and pulsated as she inspected his arm and coaxed a vein to swell up beneath his skin. She fed calmly, with a sort of deference that disturbed Pierce. After a generous taste, her lips curled with pleasure. Her skin blushed with restored youth. She gestured for Pierce to join her.

"No," said Pierce.

Marie giggled liberally.

Pierce watched her levitate and hover.

"Come hover with me, Percy."

Pierce felt Marie forcing herself into his head. He closed his eyes and turned away, but he was hungry and too weak to fend her off. As he struggled to retain control, his body was already kneeling before the boy. When he refused to sink his fangs, Marie took hold of his hair, placed her lips on his, and transferred blood into his mouth. She clamped his jaw closed, forcing him to swallow.

All ill thoughts melted away as Pierce literally became lighter than air. He hovered, face up, arms out, legs bent at the knees, aware but not awake. It was like being in a dream of infinite joy. At first he experienced the sensation of floating until he could no longer feel his body. He could see it, from any perspective, like a spirit in the room, watching others hover.

When the light of morning illuminated the aftermath, Pierce wept. Marie wrapped the body in linens.

"We must leave before the maid arrives," said Marie. "The hover causes us to lose all sense of time."

"You were wrong about the dangers of child's blood, Countess. It will destroy us all."

"Enough dribble. You never touched the boy." She tilted her head at Pierce. "What *did* you imagine in the hover, hmm? Did we kiss? Did you act out your filthy desires on me? Anything you can imagine is yours to enjoy whilst in the hover. Were your previous exploits so different?"

"Yes, they were. No child was ever involved, and no one died. You are a monster. I shall never understand you, and the worst of it, I shall never understand the monster I have become. You ought not to expect me to join your clan of perversions."

Marie coughed up a mocking chuckle. She removed a paper document from her handbag and placed it on the table with a bottle of ink and a quill. "This is a waiver of your rights and claims to the Royal Flemish Clan," she said in a business tone. "Your signature shall memorialize the end of your affiliation to the clan and to me. You shall be on your own, a rogue, forever shunned by our kind. This document is also a promise that you shall never step foot in Flanders. Break this promise and you shall be bound in chains, locked in an iron box, and indefinitely buried alive."

Pierce approached the table and began reading the waiver. "Brilliant," he said, dipping the quill and signing the document. Marie waved the paper to dry, then gathered her handbag and left Pierce behind to clean up.

The next day, Pierce watched children working in the factory at Ancoats. His father had hired the orphans, believing work was better than begging. Pierce had thought nothing of it since he, too, had worked in the factories from childhood, but his situation was unlike theirs. Theirs was one of survival whereas his was one of privilege. He instructed his general manager to pay each child a full day's wage for a half day's work from two o'clock to five o'clock, and they were not allowed to work on weekends. The general manager asked Pierce to consider the impact to production and profit.

"Concerning production, schedule more adults for the morning shift, but not so many as to displace the orphans in the afternoon," replied Pierce. "Concerning profit, leave that to me."

"Yes, sir."

"Clear out ample space in the old warehouse. Bring in beds and linens and paint for the walls. Make the place presentable and comfortable for its orphaned tenants. Hire two teachers and a cook, and purchase school books. They are to study in the morning and then come to work after their midday meal. I'm putting you in charge of this project."

"Yes, sir. If you don't mind me asking, sir, are we going into the orphanage business?"

Pierce considered the question. The abbey took in orphans whenever they could—seemed it was never enough. "It is not a business."

47 - THE CURE

Cedric sat in the guest cottage at the Fleming estate waiting for Pierce and Marie's return. Memories of his father, mother, and little sister flashed across his mind. He recalled how happy they were until the plague came. He promised his mother he would seek a new life in Brussels. He nearly died trying. As horrible as the castle was, he owed his life to being there, and he would not have met Jacob or Lily.

Lily. He longed to see her again. She touched his heart in ways no one ever had. The feel of her skin on his, her lips on his, her sweet voice and promise to wait for his return, lingered like a beautiful sonnet. Suddenly, he felt compelled to go to the front door. Would it not be grand to find Lily standing at the threshold outside? He imagined it as he entered the foyer. He heard neither knocking nor sounds of any kind to lure him there, yet there he stood, hand on the door knob, ready to embrace his Lily.

He opened the door and was startled to see her... "Good evening, My Countess," said Cedric, bowing.

As if she had not been waiting at all for the door to open, Marie entered the cottage at full gate, went straight into the kitchen, and sat down at a small table.

"May I offer you tea, My Countess?"

"No. Sit."

Cedric still felt uncomfortable in her presence, and found her youth to be peculiar for someone so old. Marie found Cedric equally peculiar—difficult to read or to persuade.

Marie retrieved a document from her handbag and unrolled it across the table. She then handed Cedric a quill after dipping it in ink.

"Sign it," she demanded.

"May I inquire what it says, My Countess?"

"Pierce and I have agreed to part ways. Unfortunately, no level of effort convinced him to return with us to our lovely castle. He insisted that we formalize our separation with this document. He has signed it, as you can see, and as witness you shall, too."

"But I did not witness—"

"It does not matter! Sign it."

Cedric reluctantly signed his name at the bottom of the document. Then Marie took back the quill and returned everything to her handbag.

Cedric could feel her eyes on him. It was unnerving.

"I require your assistance, Cedric."

She had never before asked for his help, and seldom used his name. She simply barked orders. The change in tone was unexpected.

"Yes, of course, My Countess."

"I want you to perform a task. It is not only important to me but also to Mister Fleming. However, he must not know of it. It must be our secret. Do you understand?"

Cedric nodded. "The task is a secret, My Countess."

"If you complete the task, I shall bestow upon thee the clan's highest honor: a hero's welcome at the castle. Additionally, I shall recommend your membership to the Royal Flemish Clan. Would you like that?"

Cedric knew nothing of the clan's true nature only that they were an elite group of people— albeit eccentric—and wealthy beyond his imagination. He could not believe it. "I...yes, My Countess. Thank you."

"Excellent! Cedric, do you swear your allegiance to me? Will you do as I ask without question?"

"Yes, My Countess."

"Even if the task is awfully unpleasant?"

Cedric reasoned that she might want him to clean a chamber pot or muck out Hamlet's pigpen again. "Not every task is pleasant, My Countess."

"True." All the while, Marie gazed into Cedric's eyes and

ever so subtly began to mind-bend his mood and judgment. "Pierce suffers from a debilitating ailment." Marie took out a wooden stake from her handbag. "This will cure him of it. I need for you to plunge this into his chest directly over his heart whilst he sleeps." Marie placed the wooden stake on the table in front of Cedric.

Cedric's jaw dropped. Surely, she was joking.

"For the cure to work, it must penetrate his heart."

Cedric stared at the sharpened stake.

"But if the stake penetrates his heart, he will die," he said.

"No, Cedric. It is a remedy," continued Marie with a steady tone of reason. "Pierce suffers from bleeding heart syndrome. It causes loss of appetite, depression, tremors, fever, and paranoia. Perhaps you have seen the symptoms."

"I cannot recall seeing him eat anything, and he does seem unhappy and nervous most of the time," replied Cedric, thoughtfully.

"Yes, well, this stake is made from a type of wood that will cure him. After a minute or so, you are to remove it and help him to his feet."

Cedric lifted the wooden stake. He felt its weight and touched the pointed end. It was not a thick piece of wood, about the width of a broomstick handle, tapered and smooth. He placed it on the table and frowned. "But what if I miss his heart? It is very risky."

"It is, but you will succeed. I have confidence in you, Cedric."

Cedric lamented. "May I think about it, My Countess?"

Marie stood up abruptly, knocking the chair over. The boy's mind was like an iron door, locked and impenetrable to her.

"You may not! Just because I allow you to escort me, look at me, and sit with me does not make you my equal. I made you my personal servant because I thought I could trust you. Was I wrong? Ought I to have chosen someone else?"

Cedric lowered his head. He felt ashamed to have upset her.

"Please forgive me, My Countess."

Marie walked behind Cedric and placed her hands on his shoulders. "Cedric, do you remember a servant by the name of Jacob?" asked Marie in a calmer tone.

Cedric frequently thought of Jacob, what he might be doing

at the castle, if he had discovered other secret passages, or made new friends.

"Jacob was your friend, was he not?"

"Yes, My Countess. He was my dearest friend."

"And like you, he came to replace candles in the counting chamber. Did he speak of that?"

"He told me nothing."

"I see. Well, Jacob told me plenty about you, as well as someone very dear to your heart. Do you know of whom he spoke?"

Cedric's parents and sister came to mind, and then—

"Lily," said Marie. She sensed Cedric's pulse accelerating as she gently stroked his neck with her long index fingers. "Such a lovely girl of fifteen, she is. Lush blonde hair, fair, smooth complexion, and eyes as blue as hyacinths. What a divine couple you should make."

As Cedric recalled Lily's farewell kiss, he brought his fingers to his lips.

"Your first kiss lingers, yes?"

"Jacob told you?" asked Cedric softly.

"Jacob was quite a talkative boy. He was also curious, perhaps too curious, and duly punished for it. I fear you shall never see him again."

Cedric could not believe his ears. He turned to her. "Please, My Countess, please tell me what happened to Jacob."

"As concerned as you are of him, should you not be more so of Lily?"

Cedric's tone wavered as his heart sunk. "Is she...?"

"Alive and well?" said Marie. "She is—at least for now."

Cedric swallowed dryly as a glint of hope lifted his spirits.

"However, it is a pity that you and she had fraternized, violating a basic castle rule. Why, Cedric? Why did you put dear Lily at risk? She trusted you."

Cedric began to sweat. If only Jacob had not talked about them. "We greeted politely in passing," Cedric said, rubbing his sweaty hands together.

Marie lifted her hands from his shoulders. "Do you suppose kissing and casual greetings are the same? Or do you suppose I am stupid enough to believe it?" snapped Marie. "Tell me, what happens to those who disobey the rules?"

Tears fell from his eyes.

"Tell me!" boomed Marie.

"Severe punishment," Cedric said, turning away. "I am at fault. I deserve to be punished, not her. Please, My Countess, show her mercy and punish me instead. Please, I beg of you."

Marie laughed. "Be careful what you beg for, Cedric." She stood beside him. "I have the power to forgive and the power to grant a crown a month for as long as you shall both live, but only if you do as I say."

Cedric lifted the stake slowly.

"Tonight," Marie said. She walked to a cabinet, pulled open a drawer, and began counting utensils. She retrieved a two-pronged meat fork and tapped the prongs against her teeth, listening to the tone of the fork. "Well?"

"I will do it tonight," said Cedric, "for Lily's sake."

Marie took the fork with her and left Cedric to administer the cure.

48 - BEARER OF TERRIBLE NEWS

An hour before dawn, Cedric quietly entered the main house and ascended the stairs. He was fatigued for lack of sleep and troubled by what might happen to Lily if he failed. The senseless seemed strangely sensible, and all Cedric wanted was to cure Pierce of his ailments and free Lily of Vos Castle.

With stake in hand, he paused in front of Pierce's bedchamber door and recalled Marie's instructions. Pierce must be asleep, Cedric reasoned. The stake must puncture his heart. Then he must remove it after a minute and help Pierce to his feet. Cedric entered the room and crept towards Pierce's bed. Pierce was lying on his back, very still, as if dead. The boy lifted the stake over Pierce's chest and thought of Lily. He closed his eyes and struggled to steady himself. It must penetrate the heart, he told himself. He would not go through with it and lowered the weapon.

The sound and smell of Cedric jolted Pierce into action. He immediately took hold of Cedric's arm.

Pierce confiscated the stake. "What sort of madness is this?" whispered Pierce angrily.

"I was asked to cure your ailment. That is the truth, Mister Fleming, sir."

Pierce shoved Cedric across the room and got out of bed. He ran to Cedric and lifted him by his shirt collar with one arm, stake still in his other hand.

"Did Marie put you up to this?" Seeing that Cedric was speechless with fear, Pierce released him. "Wait here." Moving quickly down the hall, Pierce opened the door to Marie's bedchamber and saw that she had gone and had taken all her belongings.

Pierce and Cedric sat in the kitchen, staring at the wooden stake resting between them. Pierce placed his hand over his chest and wondered if Cedric would have gone through with it.

"The countess told me the stake would cure you," said the boy.

"Elucidate me."

"She said that you suffered from bleeding heart syndrome. It was the cause of your depression and loss of appetite. The stake would cure you—"

"A stake through my heart would certainly end my suffering," griped Pierce.

"Sir, I felt the method was wrong..."

"Did you, now?"

"I admit confusion, but I would not go through with it even though the countess threatened me."

"What threat?"

"She would harm Lily if I refused."

"Lily?"

"I met her at the castle. She is still there, waiting for me, and I must return to free her."

"I can only imagine the danger she is in."

"We fraternized. It is not allowed."

"Separating boys from girls is not so unusual—"

"You do not understand the danger she is in. I must return for her!" Cedric felt helpless and betrayed by a woman he had revered. She was obviously not who she seemed to be, and perhaps the clan was not what it seemed to be. "I have nothing, no family, no money. Lily is the only thing that matters to me. I must free her from that—that horrible place!"

Pierce stood up. "So, the chivalrous squire intends to storm the castle and rescue his princess from the wicked old queen, eh?" Pierce chuckled quietly. "How far do you plan to go with no money?"

The boy had nothing to say.

"Come, fresh air will clear our heads," said Pierce.

They went outside and stood in front of the ironstone house, watching the dawn of a new April. Pierce thought of Cedric's tragic losses, his dangerous journeys, his love for a girl, and his quest to save her.

"You will not survive," said Pierce, observing Hamlet the pig wallowing in his pen, "especially if there are others like the countess at the castle."

Cedric let his frustration out on a rock, kicking it towards the pigpen.

"Feelings of love such as yours must be motivating in times such as these," said Pierce. A tremor shook Pierce as he felt the effects of starvation. He thought about his ability to stave off the hunger for longer periods. The tremors and fever still accompanied his growing need for sustenance, but holding out for more than a week without feeding on anything had become tolerable. Pierce crossed his arms and squinted from the brightness of day. In the distance, he heard a horse and noticed a plume of dust about a mile away.

"We have a visitor."

Cedric saw no one. He listened intently, but heard nothing. "Are you sure?"

Pierce took in the chilly air. "Chief Constable Gareth Turner."

A minute later, Chief Constable arrived, his horse stomping and snorting with energy. Gareth tipped his hat.

"Mister Fleming, there's terrible news concerning Farmer John and his family. You had better come."

49 - UNUSUAL SUSPECTS

When Pierce, Cedric, and Gareth arrived at Farmer John's house, the old elm tree where John had shot at Pierce and Brea had fainted at the sight of his blood was bursting with new leaves and the melodious music of fidgety thrushes. Grazing sheep dotted the misty meadows as the sun dried up the dew. Yet, on this day—this picture-perfect day in the countryside—a crime scene investigation was underway at Farmer John's house.

Deputy Constable Byron Lloyd greeted Pierce, and then took Gareth aside.

Beside the pigpen where Hamlet had been born stood two young men. They were staring at Pierce and Cedric. Pierce noticed them, too, and wondered if they were related to Farmer John.

"Chief Turner," whispered the Deputy Constable, "we have incriminating evidence that you and—well—Mr. Fleming must see."

Gareth glanced over at Pierce.

Pierce waved at the boy. "Master Cedric, wait here, please."

The drapes in the house were open, shedding light on family memorabilia, trinkets, and portraits awash in odors of hours-old death that only Pierce was able to smell. A hallway bisected the house and two bedchambers. In the bedchamber to the right lay the bodies of John and his wife.

"A weapon of some sort penetrated the skull through their eyes," said Byron. "There is no evidence of struggle. It's as if they were killed in their sleep."

Gareth moved closer and saw a hole where Farmer John's eye used to be. "Weapon?" asked Gareth.

"Searching for it," said Byron.

Pierce had seen Marie stab her finger through her victim's orbits and was certain that she was the murderer. He reasoned that she wanted to get the parents out of the way first so that she could entrance Brea uninterrupted. The horrific scene in Brea's room left him with little doubt of that.

Marie's moniker was all over Brea's naked body, lying across the bed on her back, pale and withered. There were puncture wounds up and down her arms and legs, piece of neck torn out with minimal evidence of blood loss. Pierce imagined Marie entrancing Brea, feeding from her arms and legs, cleanly at first and then puncturing the carotid artery. For the finale, Marie bit off a chunk of neck muscle and spit it out. As Pierce scanned the floor for evidence, he heard a young constable enter the room, followed by splashing sounds and the sharp odor of bile. The man apologized for vomiting and exited abruptly.

Deputy Constable Byron opened the window and saw that the two young men outside had moved into view. He turned away and approached the body, pointing to the abdomen. Pierce and Gareth moved in for a closer look. Written in blood below the navel was Pierce's name.

Pierce was confounded. He had hoped Marie would leave Manchester without incident. He felt foolish for trusting her at all, but the vampire in him had been measurably compelled— whether by entrancement or his nature he could not be certain.

"Mister Fleming, why do you suppose Brea wrote your name in blood?" asked Byron with an incriminating tone.

"We cannot be certain she wrote it," replied Gareth. "Had she...then why upside down?"

"Good point," said Byron. "Perhaps Mister Fleming can answer such questions."

Gareth took in a deep breath and nodded. "It is a matter of procedure," said Gareth to Pierce. "You and the boy will need to be questioned."

Cedric watched Deputy Constable Byron escort Pierce out of the house.

"Hey!" said one of the young men that had been watching them from a distance. "Is he the one, the-one-and-only Mister

Pierce van Fleming?" asked a man in an accent distinctive to Belfast.

"He is," said Deputy Constable Lloyd—to Gareth's displeasure.

The man chuckled derisively as he glared at Pierce. "Well, well, well. If it isn't, the infamous, Mister Van Fleming. I am Paul O'Brian and this is me brother, Patrick. Our late Uncle John spoke of you and your father, unfavorably I might add. Something about swindling his land and having shameless eyes for our sweet cousin Brea," said Paul in a spiteful tone as he began to swagger closer.

Patrick pushed his brother aside and lurched towards Pierce.

Gareth quickly moved between Pierce and the brothers. "Paul and Patrick," said Gareth, "please accept my condolences. Everyone here thought highly of your uncle and his family, and we are committed to bringing to justice those responsible for this crime."

"Those responsible, Chief Constable? Shouted Patrick "Why, the killer is standing beside you," he growled, leveling his finger at Pierce. "Just look at him. Guilty as the devil, he is! How else can you explain it? He's the one! The murderin' devil!"

Byron joined Gareth to restrain Patrick. Paul stood behind his fuming brother, a grin on his face.

"Pierce van Fleming, your day is comin'!" growled Paul.

"You are a murderer," shouted Patrick, struggling to get by the deputy constable. "As God is my witness, you will hang for this!"

With other constables holding the O'Brian brothers back, Gareth, Pierce, and Cedric got on their horses and went into town.

In many ways, Chief Constable Gareth had been like an elder brother to Pierce. Several times, he had locked Pierce up when he was too drunk to fend off conniving men and women. He never imagined that one day he might lock him up for murder.

Confused and concerned, Cedric stood beside the inglenook, awaiting Gareth's return in the Constable's front office. He gazed out the window at men on horses. Some of them were constables he had seen at Farmer John's house, including the

O'Brian brothers among them. When Patrick O'Brian saw Cedric through the window, Cedric turned away much as he had in Marie's presence.

When Gareth finally returned with Deputy Constable Byron, he motioned for Cedric to sit with them. Byron took a seat as Gareth lifted a yellowing meerschaum pipe and began to load it with tobacco from a tin can.

"Cedric Martens, where were you yesterday morning, afternoon, and evening?" asked Gareth as he tamped the tobacco with his thumb.

Byron took a pad of paper and a rod of graphite wrapped in string and started sketching.

Cedric sat down and was relieved to see that Patrick and his brother had moved from view. "I was in the guest cottage at Mister Fleming's estate in the morning," said Cedric. "I was there all day."

Gareth took a long piece of kindling, placed the end of it in the inglenook, and used it to light his pipe. Flames shot up after each enthusiastic inhalation, until the tobacco glowed orange. Gareth knocked the flame off from the kindling and returned it to a brass cup among other slivers of wood.

"Can you prove it?" Gareth asked.

"Well, I was alone for most the day, but the countess visited me."

"Countess? Pierce had not mentioned anything about a countess," said Byron.

"Countess Marie de Vos of Flanders. She is a true countess, married to Count Marcel Marcus de Vos."

"What is her relationship to you and Mister Fleming?" asked Gareth, as he took a seat.

"I was a servant at her castle in Flanders. I escorted her from Oostende to London and from there to here. Mister Fleming graciously let her stay at the main house while I occupied the guest cottage."

"What was her business with Mister Fleming?" asked Gareth.

"I know not, sir."

"How had Mister Fleming come to know her, and where is she now?" asked Byron, as his eyes moved back and forth between the sketchpad and Cedric.

"They met near a pub called King's Ransom."

Gareth coughed on the smoke.

"The countess left yesterday. I believe she is returning to Flanders," added Cedric.

"From which port?" asked Byron.

"Uncertain...London or perhaps Liverpool. She left without a word."

"Why do you suppose she left so abruptly and without you?"

"On several occasions I expressed desire to stay and work for Mister Fleming. He is much too busy to maintain the property himself, and he has no staff. I have farming and carpentry skills. As for why the countess left so abruptly, I know not."

"Speaking of farms, were you acquainted with Farmer John O'Brian and his family?" asked Deputy Constable Byron.

"I never met them but knew of them through Mister Fleming. He spoke highly of them."

"Where was Mister Fleming yesterday?" asked Byron.

"He was at the estate through the morning, went into town in the afternoon, and returned home shortly after dusk."

Byron continued to sketch. "Why did he go into town?"

"I apologize for not knowing why. Seldom had Mister Fleming and the Countess discuss their business with me."

"Cedric, have you noticed anything unusual about Mister Fleming's behavior? Exhaustion, shortened temper, paranoia—anything?"

"No, sir."

"How has Mister Fleming treated you?" asked Gareth. He blew an impressive smoke ring followed by a smaller one through it.

"He has always treated me with kindness."

"I see," said Gareth. He glanced over at Byron. "Have you any more questions, Constable?"

Byron shook his head, as he continued sketching.

Gareth put his pipe down. "Cedric, do not leave town. We may need to speak with you again, yes?"

"Yes, sir."

"You may go."

"You cannot possibly believe Mister Fleming is guilty of murder, can you?" asked Cedric. "I know he fancied Mister O'Brian's daughter."

Gareth rubbed his temples and exhaled streams of smoke through his nostrils. "Go home, Cedric."

Down the hall, behind iron bars, Pierce was recalling Cedric's interrogation and the crime scene. Pierce felt shame and sadness for what had happened to Brea and rage and hatred for what he had become.

After Cedric left the office, Byron held his sketch up for Gareth to see.

"The likeness is uncanny," said Gareth.

50 - ASHES TO ASHES

Cedric arrived at the estate eager to work. He tended to the horses, cows, chickens, and Hamlet the pig. He skimmed out debris from the reflection pond and polished the carriages. He worried for Lily. He worried for Pierce equally and could not stop thinking of the farmhouse massacre he had discovered near the Sonian Forest. The O'Brians appeared to have been killed in the same horrible manner. Was *she* the monster? Trying to distract himself from worry, he worked until midnight.

Every morning, Cedric kept vigil for Pierce's return. He spent the entire day finding something to do, making noticeable improvements to the estate. He painted the fence and shored up the sagging gates and stable doors. Then he oiled the hinges and latches—anything to keep himself busy and useful.

Because the O'Brian brothers were lingering outside the constable's office, Gareth feared for Pierce's safety and kept him locked up. On the third day, Pierce heard the jingling of keys and watched warily as Gareth unlocked the cell door.

"You are free to go as long as you stay in Lancashire," said Gareth. "Mister O'Brian's family, including Paul and Patrick O'Brian, were seen celebrating Brea's birthday in Manchester past midnight. We believe the murders happened while you were at home sometime between one and six o'clock that morning." Gareth placed his hand on Pierce's shoulder and looked into his sunken eyes. "Tell me your alibi is true."

Pierce stepped out of the cell and said, "It is, constable. I am not the killer." Ironically, he *was* a killer and struggled not to drain Gareth of his life that very moment. Luckily for Gareth, Pierce had become proficient at controlling his hunger and urges, focusing on unappealing aspects of the human body, such as repulsive odors.

"I believe you," said Gareth, "but the O'Brian brothers do not. Beware of them."

"Thank you, Constable."

Pierce mounted his horse and left the city. In his weakened state, he labored to stay upright in his saddle and went slowly into the countryside. About a mile from the Fleming estate, Pierce lurched from a sharp pain in his back. Then his horse reared up, throwing him to the ground and fleeing in a scare. Pierce got to his feet and felt an arrow lodged in his back. An oncoming horse careened into him, slamming him to the ground. Another arrow penetrated his shoulder. He managed to stand again but was too weak to run.

The O'Brian brothers encircled Pierce, reloading crossbows and taking shots at will. Arrows penetrated his leg, arms, and midsection. Patrick took careful aim and shot an arrow through his neck.

Pierce fell to his knees. Another arrow entered his side. He recoiled in agony and fell over. The brothers tied a rope around his ankles and hoisted him into a lone tree, and shot one last arrow into Pierce's stomach. Their laughter faded into the chiming of fire alarms in the distance.

Swinging at the end of a rope, Pierce saw the orange glow of fires on the horizon, reducing his factories and warehouses to ashes. His first thought was of his father. Hans had put his life into the cotton business. He taught Pierce everything about it. The business was the only tangible thing tying Pierce to his home, his family, and his humanity. Now, the fires marked the end, and Countess Marie de Vos was responsible. He may have been a troubled man of dubious qualities before she came, but now he was completely defeated, stripped of everything he held dear; all for the best, perhaps, never to quench his thirst for blood again. He closed his eyes and wished for Death to come, while fading thoughts captured images of his sisters, nephews, and Emma safe in their homes, oblivious to the tribulations and horrors of his ending, even though Marie was still out there somewhere, lurking in the yet-to-be-discovered ruins of their legacy.

51 - SAVED AND SACRIFICED

Cedric was returning to the guest cottage when the galloping of a horse drew his attention. It was Pierce's horse. Cedric ran to the distressed animal, noticing an arrow protruding from its haunch. He led the ailing stallion to the stables and saddled up a fresh horse.

It did not take long for Cedric to come upon the silhouette of a man dangling against an orange backdrop of a city ablaze. Cedric quickly maneuvered the horse beneath Pierce and untied the rope, letting him down slowly, draping his body over the saddle. Cedric then secured Pierce to the saddle with rope and walked the horse back to the Fleming Estate.

Cedric helped Pierce into the house and sat him beside the inglenook. Pierce's eyes were sunken, his face gaunt and colorless. Cedric stepped away and gasped at the sight of a half-dozen arrows protruding from Pierce's body.

"Master Cedric," trembled Pierce. He retrieved a folding knife from his pocket and handed it to the boy.

Cedric unfolded it and saw that the blade was old and worn.

Pierce pointed at the arrow protruding from his neck. "Remove the fletching." After Cedric cut away the feathers, Pierce pointed at the arrow's tip. "Pull it out."

Cedric took hold of the arrowhead and steadily extracted the wooden shaft. An hour later, Cedric had successfully removed all the arrows. Cedric brought strips of cloth dipped in alcohol with which to wrap Pierce's wounds.

"Mister Fleming, sir, I think you need to see a doctor."

Even in his weakened state, Pierce felt his eyes pulsating and tried to control himself by smothering Cedric's scent with the alcohol-drenched cloth held to his nose, but he kept trembling and sweating as the frenzy threatened to overwhelm him. He needed nourishment, and by then, no amount of distractions could drown out the sound of Cedric's heartbeat or the smell of his blood.

"Leave me. Go now. Go to the guest cottage," Pierce pleaded urgently.

Cedric backed away. "But—"

"Get out. Now!" snapped Pierce.

Confused, Cedric exited the house.

Pierce turned to the fire and trembled with pain. He had gone nearly three weeks without feeding. Starvation, pain, and the process of healing were draining what little strength and control he had left. After a moment of discordant thoughts, he staggered to a cabinet and pulled open a drawer. He retrieved his father's old military saber and staggered outside.

The blood scent was strong. From smell alone, he knew exactly where Cedric was. The candlelight in Cedric's room glowed softly behind the boy's silhouette as he prepared to sleep. Even in Pierce's weakened state, Cedric was helpless to defend himself against a frenzied vampire. Pierce continued past the cottage towards the pen where Hamlet slept. Unaware of Pierce standing over it, the pig snored steadily. Thoughts of the elm tree duel, his mother scolding him for naming an animal he intended to slaughter, and the odd mix of animal and human blood cluttered his mind.

The saber came down through the top of Hamlet's head. The pig let out a grunt and convulsed slightly. Pierce withdrew the saber and plunged it into the pig's throat, severing its carotid artery—and then, he fed, pacifying the frenzy.

52 - THE ESCAPE

At first light, Pierce bridled two horses to the buggy and stowed blankets, wooden buckets, salt, water, canned foods, and money. It was time to leave and not a minute too soon.

"Gather your things, Master Cedric," said Pierce. "We must leave, now."

"Yes, of course. You look much better, Mister Fleming."

"Thank you, Master Cedric. Now, get moving."

Cedric followed Pierce to the front door. "When are we expected to return?"

Pierce opened the door and muttered, "Never."

In the buggy, as Pierce shook the reigns, he sensed men approaching and cut across the fields, taking farm trails to the east.

Unaware of Pierce and Cedric's hasty getaway, Gareth and one of his constables arrived at the abandoned estate. They had come to report news of the fires, which had started at Pierce's cotton mill, now sweeping across the city. Presuming Pierce and Cedric had gone into town to support the fire brigades, they left.

Pierce took a lesser-traveled route to the southeast. It would add hours, perhaps days, to their journey to London, but it was unlikely anyone would recognize them along the way. As it was for the O'Brian boys, the fires were a diversion, affording Pierce a lengthy head start. The constables would be too occupied with the emergency to notice his absence for at least a day.

After dusk, Pierce steered off the road, maneuvering through stands of trees until finally stopping in a clearing. It was dusk and Cedric was astonished at how well Pierce was able to navigate the woods, especially in his physical state of recovery.

"Are you all right, Mister Fleming?" asked Cedric again for the third time.

"Yes. You need not ask me again. I will live on." Pierce tossed Cedric two blankets.

Cedric smiled. "I feared for your life. It is no small miracle you are as well as you appear to be."

"I am lucky, indeed, thanks to you. I may not have survived without your help."

"Who attacked you?"

"I thought you knew," said Pierce.

"The O'Brian brothers?"

"Yes."

Cedric found a soft area behind the wagon to spread his blankets out. "Are they the reason we left so hastily?"

"Not exactly, no. I am fairly certain they are sailing for Ireland as the city burns." Pierce noticed apprehension in Cedric's face. "I did not murder Farmer John and his family. They were in the city until midnight, and I was home by then."

"I am sorry for your loss, Mister Fleming. I had lost my entire family to the Black Death. I wandered for days after I had buried my mother, trying to find my way to Brussels. I promised her that I would go there and start a new life. Fortunately or unfortunately, I was found and brought to Vos Castle."

Pierce leaned against a tree upwind from Cedric and gazed up at the constellations.

"The castle is dark and cold—filled with strange people like the countess and homeless orphans like me to serve her."

Pierce thought of the child Marie had adopted and killed. He thought of her addiction to child's blood and the taste of it, the addicting effects. He closed his eyes and sighed. "Orphans?" asked Pierce.

"Yes. They come to the castle from all over in search of food and shelter. Guards detain them in a large building beside the castle. They make them bathe in devil's piss. After several days of that, they move into the castle to serve the royals."

"Devil's piss?"

"Vinegar and garlic, I think. We were forced to bathe in it at least once a day."

The reason for devil's piss was obvious to Pierce. It was not only to cleanse but also to repel vampires. Certain things such as vinegar, onion, and garlic repulsed vampires. Pierce figured that the dipping solution acted as a vampire repellent to help the newcomers survive long enough to become proficient at their chores. "Devil's piss probably kept you alive, Cedric."

"I was told it cured the Black Death and other diseases. If only I knew of it before my family succumbed..." Cedric closed his eyes and dropped his chin.

Pierce knew little of the plague and nothing of cures, but clearly felt the boy's sadness. "Tell me, Master Cedric, how are the orphans treated at Vos Castle?"

"We received one big meal a day, and worked from dawn to dusk. There are many rules. Punishment for breaking any one is severe and final. Orphans disappear without a trace while new ones arrive each day."

"What sort of punishment and what becomes of the punished?" asked Pierce.

"I know nothing of how they are punished, where they are taken—if they are locked away or sent away. Many believe the castle to be a prison. I held a different belief, until recently. After all, I met Lily and Jacob there and was well fed and sheltered. I was never punished even though I broke the rules. I revered the royals. I believed them to be generous and honorable, especially Headmistress Abigail."

"You are kind and brave, Master Cedric, trusting of people to a fault. However, the countess is not who she appears to be."

"I realized that when she threatened to harm Lily if I failed to harm you. I have also seen things... things that defy reason."

"Such as—"

"I laid eyes upon a royal family, not once but twice. Both times they appeared to be meditating, in a room at the end of a long hallway. The man and the boy were kneeling and the mother stood facing them with her hands on their heads. Her back was to me on both occasions. I left without being noticed the first time, but she knew I was there the second time because she turned her head impossibly backwards to see me. Her eyes were closed but her mouth was...was grinning or...or snarling..."

"How do you mean?"

"Her teeth were freakishly long and sharp like an animal's. Frightens me to think of her, it does. I also happened upon a farmhouse wherein a family was horribly massacred. I cannot recall in detail their injuries as my only desire at the time was to flee, but, the blood..." Cedric suddenly quaked and focused his eyes on Pierce's. "Lily was abducted by some sort of monster at that very same farmhouse. She was taken to the castle. Might the monster be one of them, a royal?"

Pierce wanted to say yes even though he had no proof. He knew very little about the clan, the members, how many they were, whether all or some were like Marie—conniving and evil. Revealing to the boy the existence of vampires might not be prudent as yet. "There are many unexplained things in the world, and monsters of all sorts," said Pierce, focusing on the blood-thirsty beast inside him.

"Lily is my reason for returning. Will you help me rescue her, Mister Fleming?"

"I will gladly pay your way back to Flanders, Master Cedric."

"Thank you, and will you join my quest?"

Pierce intended to hunt down the countess, not rescue people even though a part of him wanted to. Pierce's reason for living was still a mystery to him. He spent most of his adult life working, lusting, fighting, and lamenting over what it all meant. His was an odd life to be certain—a life that he was just beginning to reckon. He longed to see the angel of death again, to beg for her forgiveness, to offer his soul if he still had one to give. All the same, he had no desire to end his life just yet. There was simply too much to do, too much to discover—or so he wanted to believe. What was his purpose? Why was he so different from Countess Marie? Why was his hunger for revenge as strong as his thirst for blood? Could he live a peaceful life? Could he fall in love again?

He refused to revisit his feelings for Meghan Clark. He refused to believe that love could be so pure and lasting. He had spent countless nights with countless women, and the enjoyment was mutual to say the least. Yet, he loved only Meghan Clark, the raven-haired beauty from Scotland. She captured his attention so completely. She was unlike any other, ignoring him at first, then opening up to him like a fresh bouquet of roses. She was a beauty that shattered his notion of what beauty ought to be. Love happened and ended all in the lifespan of a rosebud.

"Mister Fleming, please come with me to Flanders. You can return to Manchester afterwards. Lily and I might return with you if you allow it. We have skills. I am a good carpenter and farmer, as you know, and Lily can cook and clean."

"As I said before, there is nothing in Manchester to return to, Cedric."

"But your business—"

"Ashes—"

"You can rebuild it."

Pierce smiled at Cedric's confidence in him. He reminded him of his dear niece Emma. "No. I have always wanted to see the world. Today is as good as any to start."

"Flanders should be your first destination."

Pierce chuckled at Cedric's doggedness. "I must first visit my sisters, especially my dear niece. In fact, I would like to introduce you to her."

"What is her name?"

"Emma. Now, get some rest, Master Cedric. We shall travel fast and far in the morning."

As Cedric drifted to sleep, Pierce's hunger for human blood depleted whatever relief and nourishment he had yielded from Hamlet. Pierce moved deeper into the woods, up wind from Cedric, with uncertainties and challenges weighing heavily on his mind. He needed to be in London to withdraw large sums of money and to book passage out of England. There would be no more than a day before the constables would discover his retreat and give chase. He could not return to Manchester. His life there—if ever it was *his* life—had clearly ended, and all because of *her*. His maker, his nightmare. Ironically, she became his reason to live, at least long enough to exact merciless retribution for what she had done to him and to his friends.

53 - PRESUMED GUILTY

Chief Constable Gareth returned to the fire, which had spread beyond the cotton mills and overwhelmed the brigades and water pumps. In the midst of the chaos, Deputy Constable Byron handed a message to Gareth. "What is this?" Gareth asked, glancing at the slip of paper.
"A serious problem, sir."
"How could anything be more serious than this?" Gareth unfolded the paper and held it up to the firelight.

Dear Honorable Chief Constable,

At great risk to my family and myself, I accuse my uncle, Pierce van Fleming, and his fledgling accomplice, Master Cedric Martens, of foul play concerning missing persons in the Burroughs. Together, they indiscreetly killed men, women, and children and buried their bodies in the surrounding woods and fields. A list of victims and a map of the burial sites is hidden in the kitchen along with a two-pronged meat fork used to drain their blood.

Before my uncle causes further harm, please apprehend him.

Respectfully,

Emma (M) Borden

"God in heaven," muttered Gareth. He clenched his eyes, as the singular task of apprehending Pierce suddenly became his priority. After Gareth did indeed find a list of names and burial sites, as well as a bloodied two-pronged meat fork in Fleming's kitchen, he called his men to investigate the burial sites. He had hoped the whole thing was an elaborate hoax and to find no substantial evidence. But he was wrong.

Bodies were exhumed, and Gareth received a court order from Magistrate James Smith to arrest Pierce van Fleming and his accomplice, Cedric Martens, of fifty-five counts of murder. Because the fire was believed to have started at Fleming's cotton mills, Pierce was also the prime arson suspect.

Gareth sent a letter to Emma to verify that she had written the note and was willing to testify against her uncle. It was difficult for Gareth to accept Pierce as a heartless murderer and arsonist. Fleming had his reckless peculiarities but never came across as dangerous. Perhaps there was another side to Pierce, a darker side. He could no longer contain the story. Gareth ordered the images of Pierce van Fleming and Cedric Marten to be published on the front page of *The Manchester Mercury* and resolved to apprehend them at all costs.

54 - THE HIGHWAYMEN

Cedric had slept soundly in the clearing, and the weather had been dry and mild. He got back on his feet, yawning and stretching for the third time as he looked for Pierce. The buggy was there, but not Pierce or the horses. Aside from singing birds, he heard little else in the still of morning. His anxiety mounted as thoughts of Pierce in trouble or being abandoned and alone again coaxed him into the woods within eye-shot of the buggy. After several unsuccessful laps round the buggy, Cedric began calling for Pierce. "Mister Fleming," shouted Cedric. A pair of crows took wing. "Mister Fleming, where are you?"

Pierce emerged from the woods. "Here."

Relieved and upset, Cedric shook his head. "Where were you, Mister Fleming? I became worried."

"I beg pardon, Master Cedric. The horses required food and drink, and you required sleep. A grassy meadow and a brook are only a few minutes' walk. I shall take you there for food and water."

After the horses were bridled and secured again, Pierce and the boy set out to gather food and water. They went through a clearing of tall grass and into a valley where a brook meandered through it, and beside the brook was a slain deer. Cedric clearly saw that the animal was field-dressed. He looked around for a hunter but saw only Pierce.

"I ambushed the stag," said Pierce.

"How?"

I waited quietly beside the brook. The deer was unaware of me as it drank. I took it down by its legs," Pierce revealed his knife, "and then cut its jugular." He pointed at the animal's neck.

Cedric saw the puncture wound. Back in Linder, before the Black Death, Cedric might have scoffed at such a story, but he had seen many strange, terrifying, and wonderful things during his travels, and attributed them to peculiarities common to peoples and places uncommon to Linder. "As incredible as that sounds, the deer is slain," said Cedric, forcing himself to believe his eyes. Pierce had never given Cedric reason to distrust him. The boy marveled at Pierce's generosity, courage, and miraculous healing powers. If Pierce said he ambushed the deer and had not killed the O'Brian's, there was no reason to doubt him. "Is it legal in England to poach wild game?" asked Cedric.

Pierce knelt beside the deer and unfolded his knife. "Is it ethical to let men starve for such a law?" Pierce asked as he began skinning the animal. "The question of guilt is irrelevant to our goal, is it not?" said Pierce, as if he had read Cedric's mind. "If we are to stop the countess, we must leave England. And as strange as things may seem, stranger things surely await us." Pierce continued to separate the skin from the flesh with his blade. "What is our first priority?"

Cedric helped Pierce tug back the hide. "Go to Flanders?"

Pierce paused. "No. It is to leave England."

"But, Lily—"

Pierce pointed his blade at Cedric. "We cannot discount other destinations if a ship to Flanders is not ready to depart when we are. The risk of waiting is too great, do you not agree?"

Cedric wanted to disagree, for the only risk he saw was Lily's safety and safety of the other orphans. But Lily was his priority. "How are we to stop the countess if Flanders is not our destination?" asked Cedric.

"We can go to Flanders from wherever we end up, for if we do not survive, your Lily will have no champion. Do you understand?"

Cedric nodded. "Yes, Mister Fleming. I understand. Our first priority is to leave England." Cedric stored his hopes for Lily in his heart and then helped Pierce butcher the game.

They traveled two days more, bypassing toll collectors, sleeping in forests, and cooking salted venison over a fire. Cedric told Pierce about his home village and his family—and about Lily. He wanted to learn more about Pierce, about his childhood, but Pierce claimed not to have childhood memories.

Pierce shared stories of his father, sisters, and his carousing adventures in Manchester but never revealed his true nature, or that he was responsible for many of the Manchester murders.

Back on the road, an hour before dusk, Pierce saw the silhouette of four men ahead, including a woman, a horse-drawn buggy, and three saddled horses. He brought the wagon to a stop and listened.

"What is it?" asked Cedric, who was sitting behind Pierce with instructions to keep a lookout for pursuers.

Pierce continued to stare at the men and noticed their weapons. "Highwaymen, I think."

"Highwaymen?"

"Robbers..."

Cedric could not see them clearly at such a distance. "Is someone being robbed?"

The robbers pointed their pistols at an elderly couple and ordered the man to empty his pockets. The man pulled out a pocket watch, a comb, and a coin purse. His wife offered up a small handbag.

"Are we going to help them?" asked Cedric.

The boy's sense of care and responsibility of his fellow humans confounded Pierce. He searched his conscience for a glimmer of his former ideals, but recalled Marie instead. Was he becoming jaded by his guilt? Was he finally losing what little humanity he had left? "They are not our concern," said Pierce.

"A crime is being committed. If we are able but unwilling to stop it, are we not condoning it? If we condone it, are we not accomplices?" said Cedric sensibly.

Pierce's plan was to flee England as quickly and quietly as possible. Rescuing others was not part of that plan. Yet the boy had stirred something ingrained in all men with souls worth saving. Pierce turned to Cedric.

"We do not condone crime. It is simply none of our business. It is too risky to get involved." The look of disappointment on Cedric's face tugged at Pierce's conscience. "Oh, for God's sake," grumbled Pierce. "Come on then. Sit beside me."

After Cedric positioned himself on the front bench, Pierce gave him the reins. Cedric shook the leather straps to get the horses moving again.

"Faster, much faster..." said Pierce, standing up. "Stay to the left of them and maintain speed a furlong ahead after I jump. If I fail, continue on to London and book passage out of England. Money is in my satchel. Do you understand?"

Cedric nodded.

As they rapidly and noisily approached the befuddled people, Pierce moved into position and jumped. His boot heel found a robber's head, and he knocked the other two down with his outstretched arms. Seeing that he had not killed them, Pierce turned to the husband. "Have they taken anything of value?"

With much confusion, the man nodded.

Pierce saw the man's periwig with some coins, a handbag, and a pocket watch on the ground. He retrieved the watch and handed it to the man. "Quickly, collect your property and go! Whilst I deal with them." Pierce turned his focus back on the highway robbers.

"Thank you, sir," murmured the wife, as she grabbed her handbag.

The man and his wife got into their buggy and quickly drove away.

Two of the robbers finally got to their feet. They pointed their pistols at Pierce while rubbing the backs of their necks.

"Your weapons are empty," said Pierce, sounding as annoyed as he appeared to be. As the third man on the ground was regaining consciousness, the other two decided to attack Pierce. Pierce simply knocked them to the ground. He confiscated their pistols, bent the brass barrels like chicken wire, and threw them at their horses, scaring them off.

"I would advise you to acquire more dignified occupations

and comfortable walking shoes. You are going to need them."
Pierce wanted to feed on them, kill them all, but knew Cedric
was watching.

Cedric was effusive when Pierce returned to the wagon.
"Mister Fleming, sir, you were magnificent, a wondrous blur! I
had never seen anything like it. How on earth—"

"Cedric, I was lucky not to have been injured or killed," said
Pierce sternly. "We have little time. Please, take the back seat
and keep watch. We must reach London by nightfall."

Several hours later, a toxic blend of industrial waste, rotting
carcasses, and raw sewage scorched Pierce's nostrils. "Smells
like London," mumbled Pierce, as he recalled his father's
aphorism: *If there ever was a place where too much is a wee
bit, London is undeniably it.*

Shops were closing when they rolled into the city. Pierce
kept going all the way to Billingsgate. Cedric guided him to the
street where he had purchased the umbrella for Countess
Marie, and then to where Marie's ship had been moored. Many
of the shipmasters and crews were going out on the town or
retiring deep in the bellies of their merchant vessels. Even the
street-sellers had closed for the night. The only thing left to do
was to stable the horses and find lodging.

Pierce drove to the outskirts of the city where he felt safe
from London's police. He left the dusty buggy and horses with
the only stable master still available. Cedric managed to book
rooms at a modest inn nearby. That night, Cedric slept in a bed.
Pierce, on the other hand, could not rest. Weak and hungry, he
was in need of nourishment. As Cedric slept and Pierce stalked
the streets, a copy of *The Manchester Mercury* arrived by post
boy service at Westminster. Londoners would soon learn of the
Manchester Killers.

55 - MANCHESTER'S MOST WANTED

Chief Constable Gareth Turner, Deputy Constable Byron Lloyd, and three of their men arrived at Magistrate John Smith's office in central Manchester. On John's desk was the message supposedly written by Emma Borden, yet unconfirmed as she failed to respond to Gareth's post sent by courier three days earlier. In John's hand was a court order for the arrest of Pierce van Fleming and his accomplice Cedric Martens. Nobody knew for certain where Pierce or Cedric had gone. All but Gareth considered Liverpool.

"The reason why Liverpool makes sense is proximity," exclaimed Byron, patting his plump belly. "A short distance by horse, it also has a sizeable port. Only problem is, had they gone there, they would be well on their way to God-knows-where."

"Perhaps that's where they belong," said one of the men.

"Good riddance to 'em!" said another.

"Precisely why Liverpool is out of the question," countered Gareth. "Searching for a nameless ship bound for God-knows-where is a fruitless endeavor. I believe Pierce and the boy fled to London. I know Pierce quite well and—"

"Know him?" cracked Byron, followed by a mocking chuckle that jiggled his weight. "The man is a murderer, Gareth, and an arsonist."

"Alleged," clarified Magistrate James. "A jury of his peers will determine innocence or guilt."

"Look," said Gareth in his defense, "I have known Pierce since he was a child and find it hard to believe that he would kill a fly. He has always cared more for others than himself, especially his family and friends. He has saved lives, for God's sake!"

A young constable stepped forward. "But he is a heavy drinker and a brawler capable of violence. Was he not involved in countless brawls, including a duel with Farmer John?"

"It was no duel," said James emphatically. "It was meant to settle a land dispute, and it worked. Pierce not only won the wager but also John's respect. I know this because I was there."

"And John's daughter, Brea, fancied Pierce," added Gareth.

"Apparently his past deeds have influenced your perception of his more recent ones," countered Byron. "We are all aware of his investments and influence. His financial support of our policing effort is admirable, but the evidence against him is mounting. Can you not see it?"

"I can," said Gareth, with a troublesome tone.

"Excuse me, Chief Constable," said a young man interested in getting back to the original point, "but why London, sir?"

"There are several reasons," said Gareth. "The distance is quite far, yet advantageous. It will buy him time, as the front-page news has not yet arrived there. It is the largest city in which he can hide—with the largest port from which he can easily embark to anywhere in the world. More importantly, his family and money are there. I believe he will visit his sisters and banker. If we leave now, changing horses along the way, we might arrive in London before he has time to embark."

"London," groaned Byron. "It will be next to impossible to find them in a city so immense."

"Agreed," said Gareth as he lifted the front page of the Manchester newspaper. "But this headline and your sketches are currently en route to London. By the morrow, their faces will be posted all over the city." Gareth folded the paper and placed it in his satchel. "Prepare to leave for London in the hour."

56 - THE MAYFAIR MASSACRE

Pierce and Cedric lifted their collars, placed tricornes on their heads, and stepped out into the frigid London morning. The streets were quiet and smelled of soot and horses, and Pierce was grumpy with hunger.

"Never a hackney around when you need one," muttered Pierce. After several blocks, they spotted a carriage parked at an intersection, its driver snoozing under a horse blanket.

Running and jumping onto the carriage, Cedric stirred the driver.

"Excuse me, sir, would you please take us to the Pool?" asked Cedric.

The driver yawned and stretched, dropping an empty bottle of gin onto the footboard. Stumbling down from his box, scarcely sober or awake, he held his hand out, into which Pierce placed five pence.

"Legal Quays, eh?" muttered the driver. "A hazardous place, it is. Foreigners, thieves, drunkards..." He belched loudly and opened the door. "Pardon me, north or south, governor?"

"North Pool, please," said Pierce, as he fanned away the malodorous vestiges of cheap gin on the man's breath.

At the Pool of London, Pierce considered merchant ships bound for the continent, any continent. Charted destinations were not as important as the departure time, despite Cedric's desire to return to Flanders. Though many ships were to leave that day, Pierce would not embark without first meeting his banker and visiting his sisters.

To each ship's shipmaster who would agree, Pierce secured passage for a shilling and a promise to settle in full upon departure. By morning's end, they had booked a dozen ships, some of which were destined for Africa, North and South America, Australia, and Europe, including Oostende.

As they walked between wooden cargo crates, Cedric speculated that the countess had tallied the dense forest of ship masts gently swaying on the Thames and relished the thought of her losing count. Cedric had not questioned Pierce's booking spree, figuring he had good reason. The ship to Oostende was a two-mast brig anchored at the farthest end of the North Pool near the center span of London Bridge. Cedric wanted to board that ship, which was scheduled to leave with the tide the next morning. With his stomach groaning for nourishment, the boy checked his coin purse and stretched his neck in search of a restaurant or coffeehouse.

"Mister Fleming, are you hungry or thirsty?"

Pierce felt the weightlessness of his coin purse. "No. Why?"

"That coffeehouse over there appears to have food."

Pierce glanced at his pocket watch and then at the quay. "Very well, but we must be quick."

Located at the confluence of Lower Thames Street and London Bridge, The Strand Coffeehouse was like thousands of other coffeehouses scattered across London. Its collection of literature and news from around the world was nearly as impressive as its commanding view of the bridge. Cedric saw no women but rather a dozen men seated randomly on eclectic chairs and sofas, reading a newspaper or a book with a cup of coffee in one hand and cigar or pipe in the other. A few men were engrossed in conversation about local and world affairs.

"Are you not thirsty for something, Mister Fleming?"

Pierce shook his head. "Nor hungry."

Cedric watched as Pierce's eyes found the bookshelves. The boy smiled and ambled to the counter.

Drying a porcelain cup, a bartender with a full beard and a Middle Eastern fez smiled at Cedric. "Good morning, young master."

"Good morning," said Cedric, observing the tassel dangling from the man's hat.

"Would you like a cup of coffee and something to nibble? We have walnut cake and delicious pea soup today."

Cedric furled his brow. "Pardon me for asking. What is

coffee, exactly?"

The barman scooped coffee beans from a bag and said, "We roast the coffee beans, then grind them. We poor boiling water over the grinds to make coffee." He scooped out some grounds from a container and tilted it for Cedric to see. "This is a Turkish roast. We also have Arabian, Persian, and a new Italian roast."

Losing interest, Cedric gazed over at Pierce who was reading *The Gazetteer* beside a window.

"Might I recommend the Italian? Its flavor is mild but with lingering bravado," said the barman.

"Yes, please," said Cedric.

The man neatly arranged on a wooden tray a cup of coffee, clotted cream, two lumps of sugar, a square of walnut cake, and a bowl of soup.

Cedric took his tray to where Pierce was sitting, easing himself onto a sofa and placing the tray on the knee-level table.

Pierce was turning a page every second.

"Mister Fleming, are you reading or looking at pictures?"

"I am gleaning."

"Gleaning what? News of us?" whispered Cedric, as he blew the steam from his coffee.

Pierce glanced at Cedric. "Yes, and we hope to be sailing before any news of us arrives."

Cedric sipped his coffee and recoiled slightly.

"How is your Italian coffee, Master Cedric?" asked Pierce.

"Mild, with lingering bravado," said Cedric with a bitter face. He stirred in some cream, added a lump of sugar, and wondered how Pierce knew it was Italian.

After a few minutes, Pierce put the newspaper down and checked his watch.

"Good news is no news," said Pierce. He peered out the window. The streets and sidewalks were finally showing signs of life as merchants swept the walkways in front of their shops.

"Please finish up, Master Cedric. We really must go."

After the coffeehouse, they traveled by hackney to Pierce's sister, Chelsea's, townhouse in Mayfair, about two blocks from Hyde Park. Pierce intended to discuss his testament and distribution of business assets with her. When they arrived from a distance, however, Pierce's hopes crumbled.

Eight of London's police inspectors were combing the residence. Pierce and Cedric moved away and continued round the corner where Pierce leaned against a tree in obvious distress.

"Mister Fleming?" said Cedric with concern.

Pierce buried his face in his hands as the faint odor of death and of Marie's perfume fouled the air. It was useless to stay and grieve. The countess intended to ruin him, to destroy him, and perhaps she would succeed, but he would not go down without a fight.

"Come on," said Pierce as he moved towards their awaiting hackney.

Pierce was not surprised to find the police at his other sister's home as well. "The banker," whispered Pierce wryly.

When they arrived at the banker's offices, Pierce immediately noticed the familiar odor of death. "Can you smell it?" said Pierce.

"Smell what, Mister Fleming?" asked Cedric.

Pierce kicked the door open and entered the building.

They quickly moved to the back office to find the mutilated remains of the banker and his clerk. The money vault was left wide open and empty. Pierce surmised that Marie had compelled the bankers to unlock the vault and then slaughtered them.

That night, Cedric tossed in his hotel bed with horrific images of the day, while Pierce roamed London Town tormented by rage and sadness inside a dense fog of confusion.

57 - MISS MOONRAKER

Pierce returned to Chelsea's house and entered through a bedchamber window on the second floor. Emma's room was as she had left it, dolls from her youngest years propped up like bookends on a shelf, her favorite books between them. On the dresser, beside porcelain figurines of a prince and princess atop a music box rested the lead round he had given her. Pierce felt its weight, its deformity, like the guilt festering inside him.

He exited the house with the realization that Marie had murdered his entire family, destroyed their businesses, and stolen all their money. His need for vengeance and blood merged.

On a rooftop beside a row of chimneys bellowing coal smoke, Pierce crouched and waited in the rain. Even four flights up, the rankness of the city twitched his nose, but a keen smell proved unnecessary where pleas for mercy rose up from a narrow alleyway.

At ground level, a man wielding a knife held a young woman against her will. The alley was dim and isolated. "No, please, please let me go," begged the woman. She pleaded over and over until a shadowy figure descending behind the would-be rapist surprised her. Just as the man turned to see what she was staring at, he suddenly lifted into the soggy sky at an incredible rate of speed.

Back on the roof, Pierce drilled his message into the criminal's mind: *No mercy for the wicked,* then consumed his life. Pierce dangled the dead man's coin purse over the edge and dropped it in front of the shocked woman.

Well nourished and moving on in a foul mood, Pierce came

across a noisy bawdyhouse off The Strand where harlots outnumbered patrons three to one. Inside stood a throng of prostitutes and men of apparent wealth, inebriated and tempted to deflower a young woman. She was made to stand on a table in nothing more than her undergarments.

It was common for homeless girls from the country to seek work in London. Old bawds like Kitty Sinclair prowled for them at stagecoach stops, targeting the prettiest ones, offering food, shelter, and work. Such offers were seldom refused.

"Is she not the loveliest flower you have ever seen?" shouted Kitty Sinclair to the unruly crowd, her harsh voice slicing through the noise.

"What is her name?" hollered a customer.

"We call her Miss Moonraker," announced Kitty, "for she comes to us from a pond in Wiltshire."

The men laughed for the odd story of smugglers hiding French brandy in Wiltshire ponds had gotten round. Whenever officials found smugglers attempting to rake in the submerged brandy barrels, the smugglers claimed to have been raking in cheese or rather the moon's reflection on the water's surface.

Two prostitutes standing beside the woman began to loosen her corset to the delight of the customers, who were behaving like wild dogs on the hunt. Two of them pooled their money and offered six crowns, another offered twice that amount. Pierce watched from outside with strained curiosity. He told himself that it was none of his concern, but the goings-on unnerved him, and he was still in a very foul mood.

"Twelve crowns?" scathed Kitty Sinclair. "Either you are blind or impoverished! Surely, this virgin is worth a king's ransom. Show them why, ladies." The bawdy women briefly lowered the woman's corset to reveal her undeveloped chest. Five men offered twenty crowns, but the first group tossed thirty at Kitty Sinclair. "Thirty crowns to the five gentlemen going once, going twice, going—"

"Fifty guineas!" shouted a drunken nobleman standing beside his friend.

Kitty Sinclair's eyes widened. "We honor men who recognize the value of quality. Fifty gold guineas to the fine lads from Whitehall, going once, going twice, thrice..." she paused to scan the room and noticed customers slinking away. "Sold! All right, ladies, to the red room with them!"

On the roof of the building, Pierce saw through windows a room with walls covered in red and gold wallpaper and numerous mirrors, pillows, and linens of red on a poster bed. The window was slightly open, and because it was a business, he was able to enter without permission. He closed the window behind him, and slipped behind the curtains.

The door to the red room opened and the young woman entered followed by the Whitehall men and two prostitutes. Before the prostitutes were able to say a word, the men pushed them out and closed the door.

They moved to the young woman, backing her towards the bed. "Now, Miss Moonraker," said one of the men as he removed his hat and cloak, "no harm shall come of you. My colleague and I simply request that you undress slowly, is all." His friend had already removed his breeches and was unbuttoning his shirt when a third voice cut through the moment.

"Ignore them. Do not undress."

The two men turned to the voice.

"What is the meaning of this?" demanded the man with no breeches. "Who are you?"

"Is this some sort of joke?" asked the other. "Leave at once."

Pierce stepped into the candlelight and gazed steadily at her. She reminded him of his niece.

"Are you deaf?" shouted the breeches-less man, now advancing on Pierce. "If you do not leave, I shall—"

Pierce quickly gathered both men by their necks and hurled them through the window. Glass and moutons fractured as they tumbled onto the roof outside. He then moved a cabinet in front of the door and handed the man's breeches and cloak to the woman. "Here, quickly, put them on," instructed Pierce.

Stunned and confused, she was slow to respond.

"Please do it now," urged Pierce.

The bawdy women were starting up the stairs to investigate the alarming sounds.

Pierce cleared away the broken window glass and motioned for the girl to come closer. He helped her out onto the roof and then joined her. The Whitehall men were stunned and bleeding on the roof but alive. Pierce supported the girl as they carefully made their way to the back of the building. "Close your eyes," said Pierce, as he held her tightly. He jumped into the alley, let her on her feet, and quickly lead her to an inn a few blocks away.

After checking into a room, the girl let the cloak drop to the floor and started to take off the oversized breeches.

"What are you doing?" asked Pierce.

"I have no money," said the girl.

"You do now." Pierce removed a heavy moneybag from his belt and tossed it onto the bed. "You have nearly fifty guineas." Pierce opened the window for another rooftop exit.

"Wait," said the girl. "What is your name?"

After a moment's thought, he looked back at her and said, "Pierce, just Pierce."

"How do you do, Mister Pierce? My name is Angelica, just Angelica."

Pierce offered a glancing smile and stepped out onto the roof to listen to horses in the street below. Chief Constable Gareth and his men had just arrived.

58 - FORTY-SOMETHING SOLDIERS

Circumnavigating puddles, Domitian meandered through the catacombs like a wretched cat. His anticipated visit with Marie distracted his senses from the random dripping of groundwater seeping through cracks in the ceiling, and the pungent odors of mould and rat feces. As he approached her bedchamber, Marie's sentry bowed and stepped aside. Domitian paused and smiled at him.

"Isaac van Bourgondien," said Domitian as if his mouth was stuffed with beans. "I do like your name."

Isaac stood expressionless. "Thank you, Sir."

"You seem happy, Isaac."

"Your happiness brings me greater happiness, Sir."

Domitian's eyes narrowed. "Were I unhappy, would my unhappiness bring you greater unhappiness?"

"Yes, Sir."

Domitian whispered in Isaac's ear, "The next time I feel sad, expect company." Domitian chuckled quietly and started to move on, but stopped and backed up to Isaac. "Sentry, for how long have you served the countess?"

"Nearly fifty years, Sir."

Domitian smiled and nodded as he finally moved away. He found Marie in her silk-lined sarcophagus, sleeping soundly with a pleasant, almost childlike calm. Admiring her beauty, he noticed a blemish on her temple. He then observed her neck and found one there, too, slightly larger and glistening of moisture. He reached out to touch her face. She grabbed his wrist and immediately sat upright. Turning to him, she squeezed his jaw with her other hand, opening his mouth, auditing his teeth.

"Domitian," said Marie, as she pushed his face away, "is it time?"

"Yes it is, My Love." Domitian rubbed and flexed the sting from his jaw and noticed Isaac standing like a statue at the doorway.

Marie elevated above her coffin and eased onto her bare feet. "Where is Marcel? Will he attend the council hearing?"

"He was summoned, but we cannot know for certain he will attend."

Marie glanced at Isaac and turned to Domitian with a seriousness that had always troubled him. "How many allies do we have on the council?"

"Three councilors and their respective clans," replied Domitian.

"Only three of six?" Marie laughed. "If we actually needed to win the ballot, I would be livid. Have the Romans arrived?

"They are stationed in the forest."

"How many?"

"Forty, I think."

Marie slapped Domitian across the face. "You think?"

"I am sorry, My Love," said Domitian, rubbing the sting from his cheek. He followed her to her wardrobe. "But I have not actually seen them to know exactly how many they are."

"Then how can you know they are even here?" said Marie, as she leafed through her gowns.

Domitian whispered in Marie's ear, "Is it safe to speak with *him* standing so near?"

Marie rolled her eyes and turned to Isaac. "Sentry?"

Isaac nodded. "Yes, My Countess."

"Concerning our conversation, what is the topic?"

Isaac appeared troubled. "Please forgive me, My Countess. I do not understand the language in which you and Lord Domitian speak. Is it English?"

Marie turned to Domitian. "He is the weakest vampire I have ever known, which makes him the perfect bedchamber guard. Do you not agree?"

"Not only the weakest, but the creepiest as well," said Domitian, closing his eyes and gathering his thoughts. "The

Romans assured us of no less than forty soldiers."

"Ah yes, the brash Italians. I rather like them." She selected a simple gown to wear. "Long ago, servants dressed me. They would select my apparel and jewelry, and do my hair and face. By Hades, they would even cleanse my arse." Marie's laughter echoed in the chamber.

Domitian took her hand and kissed it. "You can trust me, my beauty. I shall dress you, undress you, cleanse you, and serve you faithfully even long after I am master of this clan."

Marie's eyes scanned Domitian's face as if she were counting every pore on his pale skin.

"Need I remind you? Master of this clan is merely the first step," Marie said, slipping on the gown with her back to Domitian. When he finished fastening the gown, she turned to face him.

Domitian's smile quivered. "Why am I to rule when you are the wisest of us all?"

"Because, Domitian, men have always ruled this clan. Obtaining the vote to supplant father is challenging enough. At least you are male." Marie pinched his cheek.

"What of the laws?"

"We shall amend them."

"Child's blood?"

"Especially that one."

"The council will resist it."

"They are of no concern. Child's blood is essential to our livelihood, our accession of real power."

"Surely if all vampires were addicted to child's blood, the human species would become unsustainable," argued Domitian.

"The population of vampires will be reduced to no more than six to a clan and six clans. Human consumption will be minimized."

"Then you mean to war against our kind, to kill hundreds."

Marie grinned. "Peace is sought through war."

"Even if we were successful, how could we possibly control the chosen few that remain? How do we prevent them from growing their clans?"

"By annihilating all who defy us, and controlling the rest

with tyranny, we shall create a new order, a new League of Six. Hades, help those who do not conform."

"You are as exquisite as the night," said Domitian, ignoring the deteriorating effects of her addiction—sores, wrinkles, dingy color.

59 - COUNCIL HEARING

A crescent-shaped table of timber stood at the center of the council chamber. Trophy heads of wolves and bears adorned the walls. Seven chairs aligned the table's circumference, with the master's chair slightly elevated in the center of the arrangement.

Six council members in black hooded cloaks entered the chamber, followed by Marie and Domitian who took the floor in front of them.

The master councilor stood in front of the master's chair and raised his right hand. "Be seated." The master councilor waited for his colleagues to settle and then began. "In absence of the master of the Royal Flemish Clan, and in accordance with the bylaws of this clan and council, its members hereby form a quorum, to rule on a motion of great importance not only to this clan but to the League of Six. A majority vote in favor of the motion shall require Count Marcel Marc de Vos to abdicate his position of master of the Royal Flemish Clan. Provided there are no challengers, his proposed successor is Domitian Augustus de' Medici.

"Countess Marie de Vos, are you prepared to present evidence supporting your proposal?"

"I am," said Marie.

"Are you both prepared to face the consequences should your proposal prove unsuccessful?"

"We are," said Marie.

Domitian nodded affirmatively.

"Are there any questions before we begin?" The speaker gazed at Marie and Domitian, and then at the councilors left and right. "Very well, state your name for the record."

"Countess Marie de Vos, reborn of Count Marcel Marc de Vos."

"Duly noted," said the master councilor.

"Domitian Augustus de' Medici, reborn of Countess Marie de Vos."

"Duly noted. Countess Marie de Vos, you have the floor."

"Thank you, master councilor. Members of the council, no one appreciates Count Marcel Marc de Vos more than I do. He is my father, my master, and he was the greatest love of my life. He had been a great leader to this clan, successfully protecting its interests for over four centuries. Were it my decision, Count Marcel would never grow old and continue to rule this clan. A dear friend once told me that vampires age and die as trees do, slowly yet surely. The count is more than five centuries old now. He spends most of his time in seclusion, sleeping away the years. He knows his reign is coming to an end, for the oracle has foretold it.

"According to prophecy, an Englishman bearing peculiar birthmarks on his hands will succeed the clan master. I sent my headmistress to England to find this successor. She was successful in confirming his identity and whereabouts. I then journeyed to meet him and assess his qualities. He is impressive: young, handsome, fearless, smart, and bearing the birthmarks. I gave him the dark gift so that I may develop him, observe him, and guide him to us. I was almost convinced that he was the chosen one. However, despite my efforts, he rejected our kind, our ways, and our rules.

"He fasted, and fed only on rodents and terminally ill humans. Finally, he refused to leave England and denounced any affiliation to this clan. Yet my father would allow such a man to succeed him, thereby placing this clan and our allies at risk."

Domitian unrolled a document and handed it to Marie, who held it out for the council to see.

"This declaration bears the signature of the rouge, Pierce van Fleming, and his witness, Cedric Martens, a former castle servant. By his signature, Mister Fleming has severed any affiliation, rights, and claims to this clan," said Marie, as she handed the declaration to the councilor. "Furthermore, I have reason to believe Mister Fleming is dead, for he carelessly revealed his true nature to mortals while in a state of frenzy, a result of his incessant fasting.

"Based on the clan master's absenteeism and his belief in a false prophecy, I declare Count Marcel Marc de Vos unfit to rule this clan," said Countess Marie. "I ask the council to consider not only the evidence presented here but also what you have seen of him. Where is he? Should he not be here to defend himself? Perhaps his absence is his defense? I request the council to vote in favor of his resignation. His successor is standing before you. I present to the esteemed council Domitian Augustus de' Medici of Roma." She bowed and moved back a step.

The master councilor stood. "Thank you, Countess. Does the council have any questions?"

"Yes," said a councilor with the declaration in hand. "Where is the witness Cedric Martens?"

"I abandoned him in England," said Marie. "I suspect that he too was apprehended by the human authorities and duly punished for his part in crimes committed by Mister van Fleming."

"Any other questions?" asked the master. "No? This council shall deliberate. Let us reconvene at midnight."

In the light of a full moon, Count Marcel Marc de Vos rode through a meadow west of the castle with Sir Michael Livesey by his side. He pulled to a stop and squinted at bits of charcoal and chimney stones scattered on the ground. Marcel closed his eyes and recalled the barn that had stood there long ago and the village near it.

Marcel received the castle and its lands by rights of lineage and title in the early fourteenth century. A year after taking residence, he was made a vampire by a clan master who dwelled in a house in Brussels. Because the house was too small to accommodate his clan, he targeted Marcel. Together, they grew the clan in the catacombs, while maintaining discretion. They never hunted in the village nearby the castle; instead, they hunted in outlying villages.

A hundred years later, as Marcel spoke with the oracle in the forest, she warned of a band of rogue vampires from the east who would soon attack the village and castle. The battle would end badly for the clan master but not for Marcel. Skeptical of the oracle's prophecy, Marcel returned to the castle with no expectations. He shared the premonition with the clan master, who dismissed it.

A week later, however, six vampires from the east with blood on their breath arrived at the castle's gates. They asked for shelter and promised to move on the next evening. Curious to know if they were the ones the oracle had foretold, the clan master invited them in. His clan was twenty strong, more than a match for six foreigners.

As they conversed, the visitor's cryptic responses filled Marcel with distrust. They were boisterous, blood-drunk and condescending. When Marcel explained that it was forbidden to hunt in the nearby village, they became fractious and foul, calling him a traitor to his kind. Infuriated by his guests' rudeness, the clan master asked them to leave at once, but they refused. A vicious argument ensued. By then, twelve vampires from the catacombs arrived to remove the unwanted guests. The foreigners decided they would not leave, ever. The fight was over in a matter of minutes. All the foreigners, along with the clan master and half his clan, were killed. As a result, Marcel acceded to clan master.

Meanwhile, the surviving villagers placed the blood-drained bodies of their friends and family members in a barn and debated to burn them or bury them. Marcel met with the village elders who blamed the attacks on demons from within the castle. Marcel assured them that the demons had come from the forest where they had always fed on bear's blood, but when the bears disappeared, the demons began to starve. They left the forest in search of a new blood source. When asked if the demons would return, Marcel assured them they would not because his soldiers had killed them all.

In the end, and because the villagers feared the dead would otherwise reanimate, they burned the barn and the bodies inside it to the ground.

"This is the site of the barn," said Marcel to Sir Michael. "Inside were thirty villagers, killed by a band of vampires from the east. All that remains are fragments of stone, brick, and charcoal. You probably know nothing of what happened here because we do not speak of it."

Sir Michael scanned the meadow and imagined a village there. "Yes, I know of the village but nothing of its demise. What happened?"

Marcel chuckled. "Countess Marie de Vos happened."

"How do you mean?"

"She hunted the villagers. Before any of us had learned of it, the castle was under siege. The villagers took arms and even repaired an old siege weapon with which to attack us. To avoid undue notice, we had no other choice but to end it quickly. We eradicated all the villagers and burned the village to the ground. We stored a hundred bodies in the catacombs, and another hundred in the moat. We filled the moat, buried the evidence, and hunted down those who tried to escape. It was not the way I wanted things to be."

"Was the countess punished?"

"Not properly. My greatest weakness and greatest regret was my love for her. I should have sentenced her to death. Instead, I allowed her to live in the catacombs. Eventually, as my heart grew emptier, I sought to refill it with lust for others. I punished her with infidelity. Now, whenever I see a fire, I see the village, and I see her."

"Milord, may I remind you that she and Domitian are in council as we speak."

"Yes."

"Your absence may result in your removal from the clan."

"They cannot remove me because the chosen one has not yet stepped forward. When he does, I will gladly step down. On your advice, I requested reinforcements from the Prussian Clan. I am certain of their support, but not of the other clans'. Perhaps Marie is right; I am too withdrawn and out of touch."

"Milord, you must leave. It is not safe here."

"It has never been safe here. Yet, it is my home."

The word *home* struck a chord in Michael. "You spoke of a

house in Brussels, the home of the former clan master. Is it yours?"

Marcel smiled and nodded affirmatively. "You are quite clever for an old Englishman."

"Does the countess know of it, Milord?"

"Nay. It is my escape, my secret refuge." Marcel peered across the grassy landscape at the castle. "Whilst many believe I am in the high tower, sleeping away the years, I am really in Brussels enjoying anonymity."

"Milord, let us ride there now. I shall return to assemble your personal guard. Later, we will join the Prussians in the forest."

Marcel turned to Sir Michael. "Agreed."

Michael was surprised that Marcel had cooperated so easily. "Milord, may I ask you an unrelated question?"

"You may."

"The countess has a sickness, as you say, but is her sickness as dreadful as we are made to believe? Would you consider making child's blood an exception to the rules?"

"Never!" shouted Marcel, startling Sir Michael and riling the horses. "I have seen its toxic effects, what it does to us! It corrupts the senses and destroys the body. Rapid aging and sores on the flesh are the first visible signs of addiction. Eventually, no amount of child's blood will restore youth even to where it was before the addiction. The addicted ultimately go mad and rot from their insides out. I pray that you never experience it, old friend."

"Please forgive me, Milord," said Sir Michael, lowering his eyes.

"Imagine hundreds of vampires as sick as Marie. Now, find out which councilmen voted in my favor. Bring them to me, for they will need my protection if you are correct about the countess's intent." Following one last sweeping gaze across the countryside, Marcel turned his horse towards Brussels.

In the council chambers, voting was about to begin.

"I wish to state a comment and motion," said a councilor. "Given that neither signature can be verified, I motion to remove the signed waiver from these proceedings."

"Duly noted," said the master councilor. "All in favor of removing the signed waiver from consideration show your hand." Everyone raised their hand. "The motion stands. The signed waiver shall not be admissible. Are there any other comments or questions before we cast our votes?"

He paused for a moment and then raised his hand.

"Let it be known that in the absence of Count Marcel Marc de Vos, who had been summoned to these proceedings, and by the powers vested in this council, the clan master's right of rebuttal is hereby waived. This council shall put to motion a vote. Those against or in favor of the clan master's resignation shall state their vote when called upon—yay in favor of resignation, nay against. A majority vote in favor shall result in the clan master's immediate removal. A losing vote shall result in sedition, followed by sentencing." The master councilor sat and looked hard at Countess Marie de Vos as he facilitated the vote. "Honorable councilor of the Roman clan, what say you, yay in favor of the clan master's resignation, or nay against?"

"Yay," said the Roman councilor.

"One in favor. Honorable councilor of the Spanish Clan what say you—yay in favor or nay against?"

"Nay."

Five votes in, the ballot was three in favor and two against. The Prussian councilor voted nay to tie the vote. The master councilor smiled at Marie as he announced his vote.

"The Royal Flanders Clan votes nay." He and the councilors stood up. "Count Marcel Marc de Vos shall remain the master of this clan." The master councilor looked towards the entryway. "Council guards!"

Four guards entered the chamber behind Marie and Domitian.

"Escort the seditionists to the catacombs and imprison them. They shall remain locked up until their sentencing," stated the master councilor.

As the four guards escorted Domitian and Marie through the catacombs, Marie tapped one of the guards on the shoulder.

That was the signal. The guard quickly confiscated a guard's sword and lopped off his head. He then tossed a sword to Domitian and together they fought and killed the other two guards. The countess looked both ways and saw that they were alone.

Domitian smiled at the guard who helped them. "Well done, Fredrick. You know what to do, yes?"

"Aye, Milord. Notify the council master everything is well, and then wave the red flag atop the east tower."

Domitian glanced over at Marie who was already nodding affirmatively. "Go," said Domitian to Fredrick.

Fredrick found the master councilor still in the council chambers and assured him that the seditionists were locked up in the dungeon. After that, he ascended the east tower and waved the red flag, signaling the awaiting Roman forces in the forest to attack the castle.

60 - A LEAP OF FAITH

A rap at the door woke Cedric. He got up and opened the door to the front page of *The Gazetteer* held up to his face. It read:

MANCHESTER KILLERS IN LONDON!

"Good morning, Mister Fleming," said Cedric, taking the paper and closing the door after Pierce entered the room. Cedric stared at the page and smiled. "He really *is* quite good."

Pierce pulled his cravat over his nose. "Good? Who and at what?"

"Deputy Constable Byron's sketches of our likeness," said Cedric, tapping at the newspaper. Cedric tilted his head, opened his mouth, and sneezed three times.

"Are you all right?"

"My throat hurts and my nose is—is—" Cedric sneezed again.

"That is unfortunate," said Pierce clearly perturbed as he walked to the window and peered down at the street. "The constables arrived last night."

"Including Chief Constable Gareth Turner?"

"Yes. They are meeting with London's police..." Pierce felt a slight sadness quelled by a surge of anger at the thought of Marie de Vos and the lives she had destroyed. He lowered his cravat to test the air. "Our ship will leave in approximately five hours."

"Which ship?" asked Cedric, wiping his nose with a kerchief.

"The Cape something... The one going to Oostende."

"South Cape," said Cedric.

"Precisely."

Cedric blew mucus into his kerchief.

Pierce bounced the top of his fist on his chin and paced the small room. "The police will likely check hotel registries and post our likeness all over the city. We are not safe here." He moved to the door. "Gather your things. We are going. Oh, and dress warmly, please."

Gareth and Byron met with London's Chief Constable, Charles Blackwell, and implored him to join the manhunt. Blackwell offered only to detain the prisoners. He blamed Gareth for allowing the killers to escape in the first place. Byron was from a well-to-do family with ties to London's police. He offered Blackwell four crowns to have his men check registries and post new wanted posters. Blackwell agreed at six crowns.

Cedric walked slowly with his drippy snout buried in his kerchief. He followed Pierce's lead, lifting his collar and lowering his hat over his eyebrows. He avoided prolonged eye contact with people, glancing briefly at random faces only to see if anyone had recognized them. Cedric wondered where everyone was going in such a mad rush. The good news was they ignored the newly posted wanted posters. Unfortunately, as Pierce and Cedric turned the corner at a busy intersection, they walked directly into the path of Deputy Chief Constable Byron.

"Excuse me," said Byron to Pierce after their shoulders bumped.

Utterly stunned, they stood facing each other as people flowed past them. Pierce acted first, knocking Byron to the ground. He then took Cedric by the wrist and ran. Byron clambered back to his feet and pursued them with difficulty, for he was a heavy man with bad knees. But his whistle sounded loudly, summoning two spry deputy constables from across the street.

Cedric shook his wrist loose and tried to run faster. Pierce thought about leaving Cedric behind but allowed the ailing boy to keep up.

"Cedric, come on! Faster, please," shouted Pierce. Cedric wheezed as Pierce pushed his way through the crowds. He turned right through a narrow alley, leaving the river behind them. Whatever gains they could make were quickly eroded as the young and fit constables relentlessly pursued them. At a cross street ahead stood the hotel where Pierce had left Angelica, the girl he had rescued from the brothel.

"Cedric," said Pierce. "Do you see the hotel ahead?"

"Yes," gasped Cedric.

"You are to duck into the hotel and run upstairs to room thirty-two. Ask for Miss Angelica. Tell her Mister Pierce sent you. If she is not there, break in and wait for me there. Agreed?"

"Agreed," whispered Cedric.

As they approached the hotel, Pierce collected random wooden crates with which to stack into a blind at the hotel's entrance. Cedric slipped into the hotel behind the blind as Pierce continued on, drawing the constables across the street. After leading his pursuers for several blocks, Pierce entered a quiet alley and lunged three flights up onto a roof. Working his way across rooftops back to the hotel, he could only hope that Cedric was safe in Angelica's hotel room.

Winded and confused, Byron and the constables found themselves at a dead end. Pierce had somehow vanished. Gasping heavily, Byron leaned against a wall and struggled to regain his bearings. "Where...where is he? Where are we?"

At that moment, Pierce was approaching room thirty-two. He listened for signs of life and then knocked at the door.

"Who is it?" said a girl's voice from inside.

"Pierce."

The door opened and Angelica let him in.

"I thought I would never see you again, Mister Pierce," said Angelica brightly.

The sharp smell of Angelica's blood struck him at once. He saw that Cedric was on the bed and took in the smell of vomit and other unpleasant odors to control his hunger.

"I would not let him in until he mentioned your name," said Angelica. "Poor boy, he is very ill."

Pierce checked his pocket watch. "Master Cedric, are you well enough to leave?"

Cedric opened his bloodshot eyes and nodded slightly. Pierce saw the cloak he had sequestered from a would-be john and turned to Angelica. "May we use it?"

"Yes, of course."

Pierce helped Cedric to his feet. He lifted him onto his back and turned to the girl. "Will you please drape the cloak over us and open the window?" asked Pierce.

After Angelica secured the cloak on them, Pierce stepped out onto the roof with the boy on his back and moved swiftly along the rooftops towards the Pool of London.

The boy was barely hanging on, and it was all Pierce could do to keep moving and Cedric from falling off. Pierce ran across Thames Street and continued on to the wharf where he encountered no less than a dozen constables. At first glance, Pierce appeared as a very large person with a hunched back, which drew unwanted attention and finally recognition.

"There! Stop that man!" yelled a constable, as several others gave chase.

Pierce moved quickly back towards Thames Street with twelve constables in pursuit, blowing whistles, barking orders and warnings. They were keeping him in sight as he ran north to Fish Street Hill. Upon reaching the thoroughfare, he turned in the direction of London Bridge and ran up the incline onto the bridge from where he could look down on South Cape, now working her way into the shipping lanes.

There was no time to dither. The constables were fifty yards away and closing in fast. Pierce quickly moved to the opposite side of the bridge and tapped Cedric on the head.

"Master Cedric, hold on tightly. I need the use of my hands."

Cedric moaned miserably.

"Cedric, please!"

The boy mumbled something and managed to clasp his hands together as Pierce released the boy's legs. "Wrap your legs tightly around my waist and do not let go." Accelerating quickly, Pierce jumped.

Mid-air, Pierce felt the boy's arms and legs tighten. The ship's port side was a sizeable target. Pierce aimed for the mainmast. The boom sail was full and might have made for a softer landing, but he fell short and caught hold of a ratline instead. Their momentum swung them out over the river like circus performers. When the swinging motion returned them over the quarterdeck, Pierce released his grip.

With Cedric still clinging to his back, Pierce landed gently on the deck. He set the boy on his feet and looked back at the constables. Turning his attention to the equally stunned, but impressed, shipmaster on the quarterdeck, Pierce bowed and hoped no one had read the Gazette and not recognized them.

"Pierce van Fleming and Master Cedric Martens requesting permission to stay aboard and settle passage to Oostende as previously agreed."

"Welcome aboard, Mister van Fleming, sir!" The shipmaster waved to his first mate on deck. "Mister Jacobsen."

"Yes, sir?"

"Log and settle these passengers, then show them to their berths."

"Aye, sir."

The shipmaster turned to view London Bridge shrinking in the distance, then up at the cloudy sky from whence Pierce seemed to have fallen. He hooted and snorted and doubled over with laughter. "And fallen from the sky, he had!"

61 - INTO DARKNESS

The next day, the merchant ship South Cape arrived in Oostende as scheduled. Relieved to be a sea away from the Manchester-Killers news, Pierce went below deck to fetch the boy.

In his hammock, Cedric was asleep and still feverish.

"Master Cedric, can you stand?" said Pierce.

Cedric slowly opened his swollen eyes and nodded.

Carefully, Pierce helped the boy to his feet and up the ladder. Fresh air and sunshine lifted Cedric's spirits and his posture straightened as he made his way to the gangplank. Halfway across it, he vomited into the harbor.

Located on the North Sea, Oostende had been the subject of invasions over the centuries. Pierce observed cannon balls still lodged in sections of crumbling ramparts. If not for Cedric's illness and the seriousness of their quest, Pierce would have liked to stay and explore at leisure. Standing in front of a modest inn, Pierce considered a room, but Cedric held him back.

"Mister Fleming," said the boy. "We must go."

"You are in no condition to go anywhere. I suggest that we rest here tonight. We can leave on the morrow."

"Please, sir, we are almost there."

"Perhaps you need a doctor."

"No doctor. We must find Elida... "We must go to her."

"Who?"

"The elf-woman in the forest."

"You cannot be serious," grumbled Pierce.

"We must find her."

"Master Cedric, your elf-woman is merely a reverie. You

said so yourself."

"I was sick."

"As you are now."

"Elida was as real as you," defied Cedric, who stared at the kerchief dangling from Pierce's pocket.

"We endured an uncomfortable escape from England," said Pierce. "We need to rest and recover."

"We can rest on the way. Have we enough money for a coach?"

"We have," said Pierce unconvincingly. The truth was, Pierce had spent most of his shillings in London on food for the boy and multiple bookings to ensure their escape. He was unable to withdraw his wealth on account of Marie's thievery. Replete with odium for Countess Marie de Vos, he imagined his hands on her neck, squeezing it until her eyeballs bulged.

As Pierce and Cedric argued, the battle for Vos Castle was underway.

62 - ISAAC THE SENTRY

Roman vampire soldiers wore leather armored vests and carried a variety of weapons: wooden stakes, arrows, spears, battleaxes, swords, and daggers. Domitian ordered twelve Romans to guard the steps leading to the catacombs. With the exception of Marie and her sentry, the guards were ordered not to allow anyone in the catacombs.

Marie had little appetite for war, unless of course it was the best means for gaining power and others would fight it for her. With the battle raging directly above her, Marie approached Isaac, her favorite sentry. She controlled his mind with ease. From her bedchamber, she led him through the corridor to the counting chamber. Marie then sat down on a pile of bags and held out her arms.

"Come," said Marie to Isaac.

Isaac came to her and lowered himself beside her.

She embraced him. "Can you hear the battle above us?"

"Yes, My Countess."

"It frightens me." After a moment, she let go of him and waved him away.

He quickly retook his position at the entrance as if nothing unusual had happened. Marie sat down at her table and emptied a bag of English Broads that she had counted numerous times before. Candlelight and glimmering gold cajoled thoughts of Cedric and Pierce. She buried her fingers into the pile of riches and imagined them discovering the bodies of friends and family in her wake. She imagined their capture, public torture, and execution. Suddenly, as if an arrow had penetrated her gut, Marie doubled over in pain. Every inch of her body rippled with blisters. She had not fed on child's blood since the start of the battle. Her skin was wrinkling, her insides were churning, blisters were forming, along with an unpleasant scent of decay.

Stoically detached and blinded to her unpleasant symptoms, Isaac remained at attention.

"Sentry, come here!" she screamed.

Isaac moved to her and bowed deeply. "Those shackles," said Marie, pointing at all four walls. "Fill them. Fill them all with boys, the younger the better."

"My Countess, as a result of the battle, it is likely the servants are dead."

"Then scour the countryside for more. Where you find them is of no concern. Fill those shackles!"

"Yes, My Countess. Will that be all?"

"No. I need a young girl as well, a very special girl filled with love and hope in her bloody heart. I shall describe her, and you shall find her and bring her here." Marie paused to manage her discomfort and sat down at the table. "Have you seen Lady Abigail?"

"No, My Countess, not since before the siege."

"After you have filled the shackles and delivered the girl, find Lady Abigail and that oracle witch. Bring them to me."

Isaac took note of the young girl he was to capture, and left Marie in the counting chamber.

63 - EVOCATIVELY FAMILIAR

As the coach from Oostende shook, swayed, and creaked its way southward, Pierce scanned the countryside. Surely grain fields, pastures, crows, and scattered farming villages were as common in Flanders as in England. Cedric's vivid description of Flanders was accurate, but the details were so evocatively familiar that Pierce felt as if he had been there before. He removed the crushed onion from his kerchief and held it to his nose, inhaling slightly until his eyes watered and cheek twitched. He gazed at Cedric, who was lying awkwardly on the bench seat.

Over ruts, rocks, bumps, and holes, Cedric rested surprisingly well. After several hours of travel, the boy finally sat upright, rubbed his glassy eyes, and squinted at the scenery.

"How do you feel, Master Cedric?" asked Pierce from behind his rancid kerchief.

Cedric noticed the rag and looked for something ill-smelling. "Is it me?"

"Yes," said Pierce.

"I am ashamed, Mister Fleming."

"Never mind that. How do you feel?"

"Better, thank you."

"Good. Do you know where we are?"

Cedric noticed the dense forest and cottages in the distance. "How long has it been since Oostende?"

"Three hours."

Cedric pointed at the foggy woods. "That is the Sonian Forest. The castle is another hour from here."

"We must avoid the castle."

"But Lily…"

"My dear boy, have you no concept of planning? We cannot save your Lily while you are sick and dim-witted. Is there somewhere we can gather our strength and senses?" Pierce had hoped Cedric would not utter that Nordic elf-woman's name again, but he did.

"The old woman in the forest," said Cedric. "She might help us, or at least direct us to a place to rest, or…turn us into toads. On second thought perhaps we should avoid her."

They disembarked at the base of a ravine, three miles north of the castle. Pierce was relieved to be on his feet again and in the cover of trees. The joy of hearing and seeing creatures large and small, buzzing, fluttering, and scampering about offset the miserable stench of his onion-infested kerchief.

Following a stream for what seemed to be several hours, Elida's cottage finally came into view. As before, smoke drifted up from its chimney and Cedric froze at the sight of the vine-covered pile of rocks. Pierce watched curiously as Cedric cautiously touched the vines and then recoiled.

"They moved like—like snakes," stammered Cedric. "Ensnaring and choking me. I struggled unsuccessfully to break free of them."

Pierce ran his hand over them. Nothing happened. He then turned his attention to the cottage.

"But as you can see, this place is real, Mister Fleming. It is just as I described it," Cedric insisted, staring at the spot Elida had stood when she crept up on him. "She was right there."

Ignoring the boy, Pierce started to move towards the building.

"No, wait," Cedric whispered fearfully. "Elida may appear to be blind and defenseless, but she wields a stick like a weapon and has magical powers. There is something elfish about her. I am certain of it!"

Pierce turned to Cedric. "Wait here and stay away from those…menacing vines," said Pierce, giving Cedric his father's sword and smirking.

The building was more of a hovel than a quaint cottage, a wholly unkempt mishmash of stone, mud, and reeds. Based on the size of numerous cracks and holes in its walls, Pierce suspected pest infestation. He knocked on the door and listened intently for signs of life inside. Before he could knock again, the door unlatched and opened slightly. A hunched pale woman with hair the color of straw stared up at him.

"You are no elf," Pierce thought aloud.

"You are no human," replied the woman. They stared at each other for a few moments more and then the woman opened the door wider. "Come in. Come in!"

Pierce looked past the old woman for reasons not to enter, but saw none. He glanced back at Cedric, who was crouching and shaking his head not to go in. Pierce removed his hat and entered the cottage.

64 - TRUTH IS IN THE BROTH

Pierce saw that the floor inside the cottage was smooth, clean, and warm; the walls as well, with no visible holes, cracks, or pests. Suspended over a fire was an iron cauldron. In the cauldron was a broth of some kind that emitted peculiar aromas and purple and green coils of steam.

"Please sit with me by the fire," said the woman.

"Thank you...Elida, is it?" said Pierce, as he eased into a wooden chair.

"Why, Mister van Fleming, how on earth do you know my name?"

Pierce smirked and wagged his finger at her.

"How do you know mine?" Pierce asked, repositioning himself in his chair. "Are you the oracle?"

Elida reached for a ladle and stirred the broth. "I am no more the oracle than you are the chosen one."

"If you are not the oracle, then how can you know anything about me?"

"You seek the truth, yes?"

"As do most people, yes."

"Why do you seek the truth?"

"In my experience, truths serve better than lies."

"Then why did you not face your truths in England?"

Pierce took pause in her knowledge of his country. Then he nodded with his own explanation. "My language and accent is obviously English; thus I must be from England."

Elida chuckled as she stood up to stir the liquid in the cauldron. She put the ladle down and trained her cloudy-blue eyes on him. "You are Pierce van Fleming of Manchester,

England, son of the cotton baron Hans van Fleming. You have two sisters, a niece, and two nephews in London—"

"Correction, I have no surviving family. All were recently murdered. The cotton mills were burned to the ground. All in retribution for what I refused to do."

Elida's expression remained unchanged. "That is unfortunate."

Pierce took a deep breath.

"You have always had a keen sense of smell," said Elida.

Pierce flared his nostrils and inhaled deeply again. "Yet, I smell nothing."

"Your wretched kerchief dulls your senses. Throw it into the fire." Elida eased into a rocking chair and waited for Pierce to do as she suggested. When Pierce's kerchief landed behind the log fire, Elida looked up at the ceiling and rocked back in her chair. "You fled England for several reasons: to save yourself, to help the boy, to avenge your family and friends. But there is far more to you than you can know."

"Who are you, really? How can you know anything about me?"

"The broth will reveal the rest about you." Elida's face beamed with a genuine happiness. "I am so delighted to see you, Percy. I was concerned my plan would not work, yet here you sit."

"Your words have no meaning," said Pierce, crossing his arms.

"They will in time. You and the boy may stay the night in exchange for your help," said Elida.

"Help?"

"I alone cannot stop Countess Marie de Vos. She is trying to overthrow our clan master, Count Marcel Marc de Vos. She has chosen Domitian to succeed him. The castle is currently under siege."

Pierce felt unsettled to hear Marie's name. Who was Elida really? Was this a trick? Did she work for the countess?

Elida glanced at the door and stood up. "The boy... Is he always ill?" Elida said, opening the door. Cedric fell forward onto the floor. Startled, he backed against the wall.

"Cedric the Inquisitive," said Elida dryly, hands on her hips.

"We meet again. You must be as cold and famished as ever. Warm yourself by the fire. I will pour some broth for you."

Pierce gave him an assuring nod, pointing to a wooden footstool beside the inglenook. The warmth of the fire brought a smile to Cedric's weary face, and he gladly accepted the broth.

"Soon he will sleep and hear nothing of our words," whispered Elida. She took Cedric's cup and refilled it. "He will feel better when he awakens. This broth has many benefits."

Cedric took the broth to a table. She ladled some into another cup and handed it to Pierce.

"It smells horrid," said Pierce.

"Your sense of smell has returned," said Elida.

"How can I know this concoction will not fill my head with lies?"

"No one is forcing you to drink it," said Elida as she repositioned a log on the fire.

Pierce watched Cedric fold his arms on the table, rest his head on them, and close his eyes. Tentatively lifting his cup to his lips, Pierce sipped the broth. Elida gave him a defying simper and sipped her broth without hesitation. They stared at each other unpleasantly. Pierce gagged a bit but drank some more. Elida plugged her nose and finished hers. By the time Pierce finished his, he was feeling light headed. He noticed the fire and how it hissed, rumbled, and popped like a dragon whose lair had been forayed.

Elida eased back into her rocking chair and saw that Pierce's eyes were dilating. "You were nine years of age," she began. "Seven years my junior, you were a smart boy, sensitive, honest, and beautiful, with long wavy brown hair and a perpetual smile. You attracted everyone, like bees to honey. I— on the other hand—was neither beautiful nor charming. I lived on the fringes of your popularity." Elida leaned forward and stared at Pierce's face as if she were disappointed in him. "You see, you were Father's favorite, and I was terribly jealous of that, my immaculate brother."

Pierce shook his head, allowing skepticism to shape his expression. *Who is this woman? Why does her voice sound so familiar?*

"We were born in a village east of here," continued Elida. "Our father was a shepherd and our mother a weaver. We attended church and school as other children had. We did our chores and got into trouble as other children had. We appeared to be ordinary, but our appearance was a deception. Despite the curse we must now endure, our secret remains well-hidden."

"Secret?" asked Pierce. He saw Elida's eyes clear up for only a moment before clouding up again. "What secret?"

"We are now as we have always been—sorcerers."

Pierce laughed loudly at the absurdity of her claim.

Elida prodded on. "Not false sorcerers, mind you. Our lineage traces back to the days of the gods."

His laugh went hysterically silent as it dropped into his stomach.

"Stop it!" shouted Elida. "It is not funny."

"Siblings... sorcerers... gods... Are you not listening to yourself? It is funny!" He giggled some more then calm down and glanced at his empty cup, curious to know what was in the broth.

Elida glared at Pierce the way a mother does before scolding an impish child. "I assure you, little brother, I speak the truth. The broth—"

"Foul tasting mud."

"Do you not feel anything?"

"I feel gassy."

"Do you not feel its effect?"

"Bloating—"

"Silence!" hissed the old woman.

Pierce noticed blue and green flames in the shape of demons dancing atop the cinders. He wanted to lie but only considered the truth. "I am hallucinating, quite disagreeably."

"Go on, test it. Lie to me."

"Lie? Very well, I fan...fan...loath the smell of onions."

"You meant to say you fancy the smell of onions."

"I enjoy the smell of oni...on..." Pierce was beside himself. Dishonesty was not possible.

"You see. You cannot lie, and neither can I. Now, when we were children, do you not remember how you mocked me to tears? You had me believe that I was ugly. Because of you, mother cast a beauty spell over me—a spell that endures to this very day."

"Beauty spell?" said Pierce, glancing over at Cedric, still slumped and snoring. "The boy might call it an elf spell."

"You have not changed," said Elida disappointedly. She glared at the cauldron. "Our mother made powerful potions similar to this broth to bury your memories, change your identity, and charm our English cousins into accepting you for their own."

Pierce shook his head in disbelief. "Hexing me is believable if this broth is any indication of the power of magic, but a journey to Manchester and then finding the van Flemings and getting them to adopt me is—"

"Completely plausible for our mother," said Elida. "She was the greatest sorceress of her time. She condensed a charming potion into powder form, bottled it, and placed it in your pocket. We knew where the van Flemings lived. You were given money and instructions where to find them in Manchester and what to do when you arrived. When Hans van Fleming found you beside the pond, you blew the powder so he would breathe it in. You treated all the family members to the magic in your pocket. They took you in because of that. They were made to believe that you were an orphan sent from God—and so they adopted you."

"Farfetched! All of it! Too many things should have gone wrong."

"Mother and Father discussed the risks, but they saw no better way to save you. Do you not see? You were resurrected from the dead. The village would have killed you and the rest of us. Luckily, everything went according to plan. You lived a charmed life through your teen years and into adulthood." Abigail paused as if noticing the disbelief on Pierce's face and said, "Have you any childhood memories before the age of twelve?"

Pierce was surprised to hear the question, for he had not shared that secret with Elida.

"Struck a chord, have I? Well, brother, at eleven years of age, you were taller and stronger than any other boy your age.

Because of that *and* your charming personality, you attracted the Chief Constable's daughter, Anneké. She lived in the next village over. I envied her because everybody thought she was beautiful and witty. You fancied her, and her ugly twin brothers disliked you for it. According to Anneké, they told you to stop seeing her or they would kill you, but you and she dismissed their threats, meeting secretly at the three trees on a hill near the windmill. Do you remember?"

"The trees or the twins?"

"All of it."

"I have dreamt of being chased. I run towards the three trees on the hill, but they catch up to me—"

"Mother and I found your broken body not far from those trees. We were devastated by the tragedy, especially father. A month later, Anneké's lifeless body was found in the river, a rope coiled tightly around her neck, the other end tied to a bridge rail. Her death was ruled a suicide, attributed to a broken heart."

"Do you think it was suicide?" asked Pierce.

"In other words, do I think she was murdered? Well, I believe her brothers killed her, probably for ignoring their warnings concerning you. They were spiteful lunatics. Everybody knew it. That is why Mother decided to deal with the twins in her own way."

"*Renatus,*" whispered Pierce.

"Yes."

"I remember. Mother was always conjuring some sort of magic. She taught you to resurrect our sheepdog after the wolves killed it, but it ran off, never to return."

"Nay, the dog returned after it killed the wolves. Well, I suspected that it had killed them, for we heard no howling after. On your birthday, not long after your death, Mother and I returned to the deadwood tree. Do you remember it?"

"Deadwood...yes, an odd tree, copper in color, standing in the clearing of a dense forest."

Elida nodded. "It is called Sonian Forest. We buried you in the clearing. Father begged Mother not to disturb your grave, but she ignored him. A year after your murder, she entered the forest at midnight during the blood moon to perform the *renatus."*

Pierce felt a warming sensation in the palms of his hands and looked down to see the star-shaped birthmarks glowing.

"You were a fiery effigy, dancing round the deadwood tree as Mother negotiated your soul from Death herself. Everything seemed to be on fire, but there was no heat, no smoke—"

"Wait," interrupted Pierce, "how do you know Death is female?"

"What?"

"You said Death *herself.*"

Elida paused to think. "I am uncertain. Why do you ask?"

Pierce shook his head. "It is nothing important. I must know more. Please, go on."

"When we plucked your soul from Death's grip, it leached into the earth and flowed back up through the deadwood tree. You received your soul and everything the tree represents through your hands."

Pierce traced the markings with his fingers. "The *sabbat.*"

"Yes." Elida observed Pierce and the sleeping boy as she stirred the broth. "Though you seemed much like your former self, you were a revenant and noticeably bigger and stronger than before. You were faster and more energetic as well. Mother spoke of a power, a great power bestowed upon you. She said you will hold it in the palms of your hands."

Pierce continued to observe his hands. "What sort of power?"

"Do you remember the leather satchel?"

His eyes rolled up to see her. "Mother's leather case stowed under the bed?"

She nodded. "It contains a collection of magical memoirs, stories, potions, chants, spells, and tools linked from one generation to the next through the ages. It contains our legacy, our bloodline. This bloodline must not be broken."

"Where is it? Do you have it?"

Elida ladled more broth into the wooden cups. "It is hidden."

"I wish to see it."

She shook her head. "There are those who would kill to have it. It must remain hidden."

"I do not wish to have it. I merely wish to see it once more. It will help me to remember."

"This foul broth will help you to remember. Drink up. We have much to discuss."

As Pierce spooned the broth into his mouth, he wondered why his sister appeared so old and different. Had something gone terribly wrong with the beauty spell? Two cups of broth later, Pierce was itching to ask. "My sister's name is not Elida, and you bear her no likeness."

She stoked the fire. "Yes, of course. I can easily forget my own name when in disguise. Abigail. Abigail van Ness. Do you remember a blond woman standing across the street from Ravens Gate pub in Manchester? It was last year. She wore a beautiful, blue silk gown, and a jeweled tiara. I believe you wanted to escort her to safety."

"Yes, but she vanished before I was able to."

"She had gone to England to find you, and found you she did. She observed your duel with John O'Brian. She learned about your life in Manchester, the cotton mills, the carousing, and fighting, and those sordid tarts with whom you slept."

"Yes, yes...enough of the minute details. You have made your point. The mysterious woman was you."

"Indeed." Abigail turned to him and waved her hands over her face, removing an invisible mask. Her posture straightened. Her hair grew longer, thicker, and blonder. Her eyes became clearer and bluer.

Pierce carefully studied her changed face and poise as she explained.

"I can only appear as Elida in and round this cottage, and mother's beauty spell only works on those who wish to see my beauty. Immediate family members see me as I truly am."

Trying to make sense of her and piece together fragments of his memories, Pierce thought she appeared as youthful and pretty as when he left Flanders all those years ago. Cautiously, she moved into his brotherly embrace and pressed her face to his chest. Pierce sensed her joy, sadness, and uncertainty. He wondered if she sensed his emotions, too, and if she was to be trusted.

"Sister, you were always a compulsive liar," said Pierce. "Did the countess send you to England to spy on me?"

Abigail stepped back, struggling not to answer his question. "Yes."

"Did you encourage the countess to find me, to remake me, and to murder my family and friends?"

Abigail looked at him with affronted eyes. "Find you, yes, but the rest was none of my doing."

Pierce searched his memory for clues of his sister's deceit. "When we were young, did you not *lust* for the village priest?"

"Yes, but—"

"I told you to stay away from him. Yes?"

"Yes, but he loved me," Abigail insisted, her eyes jittering.

"You mean he loved mother's magical deception of you."

"We were in love before the spell was cast."

"Perhaps, but was it my revenge as a revenant or your love affair with the priest that revealed our secret and turned the village against us?"

Abigail slouched as if wounded. "Both. The sight of you—life resurrected—was enough, but my affair with the priest sealed our fate."

"From the revered to the reviled—oh, how wondrous are we witches now? And tell me, my licentious sister, what happened to the Elida the oracle? Where is she now?"

Abigail closed her eyes and turned away. "Sorcerers, not witches."

Ignoring his sister's words, he continued. "One who steals another's identity is surely up to no good."

"Oh, this horrid broth!" Abigail moaned, falling back into her chair. "Elida was a Nordic oracle assigned to our clan. As headmistress, I met with her on behalf of the clan master, and she revealed the prophecy of accession to me:

A Roman on strings of malice shall rule

Kingdoms of man and vampire shall fall,

Lest the strings of malice are severed by one,

All shall be lost and ever forgotten.

Those words foretold the fall of Marcel and the rise of Domitian, but Domitian was merely Marie's puppet. He and especially she were unfit to rule. I pleaded with Elida to tell me who the chosen one would be. She refused to tell me—only that he would come from an island nation."

"England," murmured Pierce. "You stole the oracle's identity to sell your version of prophesy to Marcel."

She lowered her chin and voice. "Nay. I have used her essence to appear as her. It only works here at the cottage where she is buried."

"Buried? You...you murdered her?"

"It was an accident. I only wanted the truth."

"How did it happen?"

"I added a truth serum to her tea, a derivative of this broth. It was too strong for her."

Pierce's eyes grew wide.

"Worry not, Brother. We cannot die from it."

Pierce turned to Cedric with concern.

"The boy is safe, as well."

Pierce sensed her guilt, but felt no less disgusted by it.

"I hid her in the storage cellar beneath the cottage. When I checked on her the next day she was..." Abigail shook her head. "It was an accident. I never intended for her to die." She brought her finger to her lips and scanned the room. "She haunts me."

"Good."

"Do your victims haunt you, too, Brother?"

"Do you mean the twins that mother had conjured me to kill? Or the people I have fed on because of you?"

"Me?"

"You masterminded a reprehensible charade to coax me here, knowing the countess would likely turn me and then kill my family and friends."

"I did not *know* what she would do," said Abigail.

"If not for you, Sister, I would still be in Manchester, oblivious of this place and running a lucrative business, grooming my studious niece to take charge of it someday."

Abigail turned to Pierce. "I may be a wicked creature, but there is someone far more wicked. Have you seen the hover?"

"I have. It is among the reasons I came."

"She must be stopped, Brother," Abigail said, squinting at him. "We are siblings, the last of our bloodline. As much as you hate me for what I have done, no amount of apologies will change the past. This is our reality, and a common enemy dwells in it. *The one to defeat her will come from an island nation with a power far greater than hers.* Those were Elida's words, not mine. I convinced Count Marcel that you are he, the chosen one. He believes it. *I* believe it."

Pierce's eyes found the door. "Then you believe in someone who does not believe! Enough talk. Take me to the deadwood tree."

65 - THE MONSTER

With an iron sword and wooden spear, Domitian led the Romans into battle at the castle, all the while, searching for Count Marcel Marc de Vos. "Where is he?" shouted Domitian at his soldiers. "Find Marcus and the rest of his naysayer councilmen, and bring them to me!"

After delivering six young boys and a girl to Marie's counting chamber, Isaac gathered a few men from Domitian's guard to assist his search for Abigail and the oracle. As the distance between Isaac and the castle grew, Marie's influence over him faded. His mind began to clear. His mission was still at the forefront of his mind, but its importance started to escape him. After hours of walking, the cottage finally came into view. Isaac held his arm up and everyone came to a halt. A faint glow of a fire inside the home illuminated a small window. The vampires listened, but heard nothing more than the sounds of the forest.

In her counting chamber, Marie gloated at the shackled children. Strapped to the Louis XIII table lay the girl. She fit Marie's description to the eyelash. The girl's eyes darted about the room for something to focus on, anything but Marie. In the glow of a few candles, Marie stroked the girl's messy blond hair.

"Do you know who I am?" asked Marie.

The girl said nothing.

"I am Countess Marie de Voss, daughter and former wife of the feeble clan master whose glorious reign is finally ending." She dragged her fingernail along the girl's jawline.

The child cringed and trembled.

"Stupid girl, you may look at me." Marie glanced over at the boys shackled to the walls and raised her voice. "All of you may look at me. Go on. I command you to open thine eyes and gaze upon thy master, Countess Marie de Vos."

But no one dared to look at her.

"Look at me," growled Marie.

The children whimpered and breathed nervously, pressing against the stone walls as if they might somehow push through to safety.

Marie's abscesses glistened as she stretched her gaunt skin into a grotesque grin. "Once upon a time, a boy came to this room to replace candles," said Marie in her sweetest voice. "He was beautiful, smart, and dauntless. His name was Cedric Martens." Marie swiveled to face the girl.

Lily opened her eyes and took in a waft of Marie's stinking and discolored face. The freakish nature of her appearance and bioluminescent eyes pulsating to the rhythm of her heartbeat was both terrifying and hypnotizing.

"Am I not the most beautiful woman you have ever seen?" said Marie, her tongue extending out, freakishly licking her own face like a cat. She glanced over at the cowering boys and belched a lurid laugh. Then her eyes rolled over and latched onto the girl's features. "I now see what Cedric saw in you. Did you know that he professed his love for you on numerous occasions? Alas, you shall never see him again, for he is dead."

"That cannot be," whimpered Lily, her fear melting in the growing heat of resentment of the countess, of the monster she undoubtedly was. Cedric had promised to return for her and she believed him.

"She speaks! Oh, how angelic her voice is," said Marie excitedly.

"Cedric promised to return for me," said Lily defiantly.

"Promised or lied?" said Marie, flexing her elongated

fingers. "Have you not learned that love and men is an impossible pairing? Men cannot be trusted. Sooner or later they will deceive you, as Cedric surely has." Marie lowered her slimy face to Lily's and flicked her tongue at her like a snake. "No hint of devil's piss on you. Do you know what the smelly dip is for? It is to protect you and your kind from the likes of me and my kind. You see, the royal members of this clan abhor the odor and taste of vinegar, garlic, and onion—all the ingredients in the dip known as devil's piss," said the vampire. Marie's tongue slipped out again, this time extending towards the girl's lips.

Lily closed her eyes, pressed her lips together, and tried not to scream.

Marie licked Lily's face from neckline to temple, then dropped back and laughed maniacally as she floated a few inches over bags and lockers strewn across the floor. She held out her arms and spun around, taking in the shackled boys. "The nectar of youth is divine, is it not?" she beamed. "This used to be a chamber of torment. Apart from the shackles, the original instruments of pain were removed and displayed throughout the castle. I keep a few of the exquisite artifacts in my bedchamber."

A young boy accidentally glanced at Marie's glowing eyes.

She grinned and crouched to meet him until they were nose to nose. "On special occasions, children are brought here," said Marie to the boy. "Do you know what happens to them? Do you, number three?" She waited for a response that never came. "No? Let me demonstrate."

From the table came a timid voice. "My dear countess, how many bags and lockers are there in the counting chamber?"

Marie paused to think. "Two-hundred-forty sacks and thirty-four lockboxes, why do you ask?"

"It is an impressive collection. May I help verify that count—"

"You may not!" erupted Marie, her body jolting upward above the trembling boy. "Boorish girl! This is *my* counting chamber. Only I may count here. *I* am the countess, not you!" She laughed and slinked back down to the boy, leveling her bony index finger to his face and dragging it across his quaking cheek. A teardrop squeezed from his clenched eyes. She caught the salty pendant on the tip of her finger and tasted it.

"Where was I? Oh yes, please, observe." She placed her hands on the sides of his head and penetrated his mind with hers, seeking his fears out and extinguishing them until he was more relaxed. She then tilted his head to the side and sunk her fangs into his neck. Marie felt euphoria in her stomach. She stood up and turned to show Lily how rapidly her sores healed and youthful appearance returned. As a smile formed on Marie's flawless face, she fell back into a hover, floating face up in the center of the chamber, rotating slowly a few feet above Lily.

66 - THE DEADWOOD TREE

Abigail and Pierce left Cedric to sleep in the cottage as they started down a trail through the forest. It was not long before Pierce started to recognize unusual rock formations and trees. Suddenly, Abigail sprang into a sprint and Pierce gave chase. He had never run so fast through a forest before. He nearly slammed his head into a branch and tripped over a log but managed to stay on his feet. His sister was astonishingly swift, but he kept her in sight. Then, she did something unexpected.

She stopped so suddenly that he ran past her a few paces. He turned and saw her crouching beside a buck. As Pierce circled round, it became clear that she was feeding on the deer, her mouth firmly latched to the side of its neck. The deer stood calmly, as she held on to its antler while stroking it gently with her other hand. Abigail lifted her head, wiped her mouth, and said, "Come, feed."

Pierce obliged. Deer's blood was gamier than human blood, but not bad tasting and nonetheless filling. When he was done, the deer laid down to recover.

"The animal will be up and running in two hours," said Abigail. "I have never drained a deer to death. It is not necessary. More importantly, we do not require human blood to survive. We simply desire it, some more than others." Her words rang true to Pierce. He was pleasantly surprised to see that she and he were not very different after all.

Before long, they arrived at the clearing in the center of the forest. A flood of memories brought Pierce to his knees there. It was as he remembered it. A dense stand of beech trees encircled the clearing. Tufts of ferns and wildflowers, logs with mushroom, and lichen and moss covered everything in varying shades of green. Aside from the deadwood tree, which was now a burned stump, everything looked as beautiful as it had when he was a child.

"We buried you here," said Abigail, kneeling beside a mound of stones, replacing wilted flowers with fresh ones.

Pierce thought it odd that she would place flowers on an empty grave. "In case you had not noticed, I am standing here, not lying there."

Abigail ignored him and continued to arrange the flowers, reaching over to pluck a few more. "Perhaps I do this for the crow-faced boy I once knew, and the spinster girl I once was."

Pierce looked back at the charred stump and imagined the *renatus*. "There is nothing left of the tree—or of me for that matter."

"That is not true," said Abigail. "You were a beautiful child, but as a revenant, your beauty and charms were greatly enhanced."

"A ghost conjured and solidified by dark magic is hardly beautiful or charming. I am unnatural, a threat to humanity."

"Or perhaps humanity is a threat unto itself and you are its guardian." Abigail stood and turned to Pierce. "You are as unique as the deadwood tree, and as real as any creature. Mother restored you with love and magic in equal measure. Never forget that, Brother."

Pierce returned to the stump. "Do you remember the slugs?"

"I punished you for them."

"So did Mother." Pierce had spent much of his boyhood in the forest with his mother and sister. Always anxious to climb the crusty old tree, from its gnarled branches he liked to watch his mother gather ingredients, as she called them. She scolded him for climbing the tree, explaining that its familial ties and magical powers commanded respect. Tired of policing him, she appointed Abigail guardian of the deadwood tree. Abigail would not let him near the tree and would shoo away his pet crow or toss rocks at it whenever it came near. So when Abigail least expected it, Pierce attached slugs to her back. Oblivious to the slimy land mollusks trailing across her gown, she screamed when she noticed them.

Seven years Pierce's senior, Abigail easily overpowered him. Catching him and pinning him down, she intended to feed him those slugs. Their mother intervened with an itching spell, causing Abigail to drop a slug into his mouth. She rolled off Pierce, scratching like a flea-infested squirrel. Pierce did the same as he choked on the slug. Their mother always had a few good ones to cast, including some that induced crossed eyes and numb arms.

Now, a giggle escaped Abigail. "I am still the guardian of the deadwood tree."

"What tree?"

"Do you remember the crow? You raised it from a chick. You sat in the tree with that nasty bird. It drove me mad."

"Does your loathing of the bird stem from the time it relieved itself on your head or from your prejudice of crows in general?"

"Both."

Pierce stepped back from the tree's remains and imagined how it used to be. "It was hideously beautiful, much like my invisible demon friend, Death. I was always disrespectful of Death, always taunting her. I called her pathetic and ugly. I feel ashamed."

"You ought to," snipped Abigail. "Your words destroyed my confidence if not my childhood."

Pierce huffed. "You exaggerate."

"I do not!"

"Well, I am not sorry for taunting you, Sister. You deserved every word of it."

Abigail stiffened. "What?"

Pierce chuckled. "You see? Do you not see how quickly you boil? Your temper was and still is an endless source of entertainment. When I became a revenant, I substituted you for the angel of death without knowing why. I knew nothing of her desire to recover that which mother had stolen." Pierce scoffed at his own words. "Truth is I was the pathetic one, the ugly one. I was self-centered as a child and lived a stolen life as an adult." His face turned solemn. "Yet, the regret I feel for my egregious and reprehensible deeds cannot offset my yearning for vengeance."

"Then will you help me defeat the countess?"

Pierce scanned the clearing and glanced at Abigail whose familiar expression reminded him of their inexhaustible sibling rivalries.

"What happened to our village?" he asked instead.

"Thanks to the countess—who massacred the villagers and murdered our father when she abducted me, our home is a field of barley now."

"She is like the Black Death, destroying everything in her path." Pierce looked at the marks on his hands. "And what of these?"

Abigail approached Pierce. "Mother said you would encompass untold powers dating back to the time of myth."

"Myth?"

"The origin of our kind... Pity you have not discovered at least one of your powers by now."

"I do not understand. What powers? I have experienced no magical powers."

"Mother believed that when you clasped your hands, the two halves of the *sabbat* would become whole and generate a power greater than anything known to man."

Pierce placed his hands together and waited. He felt nothing. He changed his clasp.

"See? Nothing," he finally said.

Abigail looked about the clearing and pointed to a large rock. "Pull your hands in towards your heart and imagine that rock splitting into halves."

Pierce walked over and placed his hands on the rock, concentrating with all his might, but nothing happened.

Abigail focused on the rock and held her right hand up and said, "*Ego impero agito.*" The rock trembled for a moment and then went still.

"I suppose you ought to dust off your Latin," Pierce said, as he rubbed his hands together and concentrated on the rock again. Just as he was about to give up, he closed his eyes and clearly imagined the rock splitting into two parts. His hands began to glow and suddenly, a stream of energy shot out, striking the rock.

Abigail ran to the steaming rock and saw that it was still

whole. "Impressive," she said happily. She touched the stone. "It is warm."

Pierce hunched over, placing his hands on his knees.

"Are you all right, Brother?"

"That was draining." He straightened his back and cracked his neck, noticing the warm but undamaged stone. "Not a very powerful power."

"Practice makes powerful, Brother."

"We should go before Cedric wakens," said Pierce.

67 - THE OLD GUARD

Abigail and Pierce walked in silence, contemplating and assessing everything that had transpired that night. Pierce was confounded by what his sister meant to him. Was he to trust her? Was he to join forces with her? How might they defeat Marie? And what of the boy and his quest to free Lily? What was to become of him and the orphans in the castle?

"If we possess great powers, can we not just conjure some sort of spell to make us invisible or invincible?" asked Pierce.

"Invisibility spells are seldom reliable, and no invincibility spell exists, though complete knowledge of all the magic contained in the satchel might bring us close. If you die, I can attempt the *renatus*, though you might end up a frog," snorted Abigail.

Pierce stopped walking. "Promise me you will never again resurrect the dead," said Pierce. "Promise."

Abigail nodded. "I need not promise, for I have not the skill."

"You resurrected the dog."

"An animal, yes, but not a human. I think the dog ended up... well, wrong."

"What about simple spells, like the sort Mother used on us?"

"Numb arms and an itchy bum?"

Pierce chuckled. "Yes."

"Only illusions and potions have worked on vampires. I cannot know if my magic is not powerful enough, or if vampires are not alive enough."

"You must be speaking of us. *We* are vampires."

"Yes and no. We are unlike them. Have you noticed?"

Pierce had little to compare, as his experience with

vampires was limited to Marie and now his sister, who was also a witch. "If Marie is any indication of what other vampires are like, then yes, I have noticed. Tell me about Domitian. I want to know his strengths and his weaknesses," said Pierce, as they resumed walking.

"He might appear incompetent," said Abigail, "a fool, or cowardly, but that would be a false impression. He is an exceptional negotiator and swordsman. He adores Marie and will do anything for her. Because of that, she controls him—completely. I believe his weakness is her."

"And what about Count Marcel?"

"Though physically powerful, twice as strong as you, the clan master is very old. He *has* become aloof, and seldom participates in social or business functions; however, he efficiently utilizes his advisors and the oracle, and has never been forgetful or dull in my presence."

"Why does Marie want to overthrow him?"

"Two centuries of jealousy, greed, and madness. Marie and Marcel were married. After she disobeyed him and the clan laws, his eyes wandered to fancying others. Over time, heartache and jealousy twisted her. Her incessant counting is a harmless symptom, but her addiction to child's blood is serious. How she came to taste it in the first place is uncertain. Perhaps she took a child in defiance of Marcel. Perhaps he is as much to blame."

"It was her choice," muttered Pierce.

"Yes, but he allowed it."

Pierce suddenly thought of Cedric, and what he said about a crime: *If we are able but unwilling to stop it, are we not condoning it? If we condone it, are we not accomplices?"*

"Pride and naivety," said Abigail. "Marcel is too proud to believe that Marie and Domitian would ever challenge him. He is too trusting of them, and even of me."

Before the cottage was in view, Pierce smelled something alarming. He pulled Abigail behind a thicket of ferns and crouched. "Do you smell it, too?" whispered Pierce.

Abigail breathed in. Finally, she shook her head.

"I smell trouble." Pierce quietly gathered a branch and with his folding knife whittled a point at each end. After making two spears, he handed one to Abigail.

Marie's sentry, Isaac, approached the cottage as his men hid behind trees. He knocked on the door and waited. Inside the cottage, Cedric was still fast asleep at the table. Isaac knocked again, jarring Cedric from his broth-induced slumber. He saw that he was alone and went to the door to answer it.

"Good evening, young master," said Isaac to Cedric. "My name is Isaac. I have come to see the oracle."

"She is not here," said Cedric.

"When is she expected to return?"

"Soon," said Cedric.

"May I wait for her inside? I come in the name of Countess Marie de Vos."

Cedric was alarmed to hear the countess's name, and knew the man outside was not to be trusted.

"I am sorry, sir. It is not my place to invite you into someone else's home. You are welcome to wait outside until the oracle returns."

"May I just come in for a drink of water? I am quite thirsty—" Suddenly Isaac was lifted off his feet and vanished into the darkness.

Amazed by what had just happened, Cedric stepped outside to investigate. Sounds of a scuffle alarmed him. Before he could go back inside, a hand took hold of his arm. Attached to the hand was a large man in leather armor.

Pierce was fighting Isaac when two of the sentry's men restrained him. They confiscated his stick and were about to question him when one of Isaac's men screamed. Pierce took his stick back and broke it against Isaac's armor. Isaac reeled and ran towards the cottage where his men were holding the boy. Abigail and Pierce pursued him. Two more vampires came out of the woods, wielding swords and stakes. The vampires restrained Cedric and pulled back his head by his hair.

"Stop or I shall break his neck and have his blood," said his captor.

Isaac looked down at the scratch on his leather armor where Pierce had tried to stab him. Then he looked closely at each of his three prisoners. "Who do we have here—a boy, a foreigner, and Headmistress Abigail. The countess will be so pleased to see you again, Headmistress." He gazed desirously at Abigail's beauty. "She has sent me for you and for the oracle. Where is she? Where is Elida?"

"Elida is not expected to return anytime soon," said Abigail.

"Is that so?" said Isaac, turning to Cedric. "You said she was expected to return *soon.* Which is it, soon or not soon?"

"Leave him alone," said Pierce. "He knows nothing."

Isaac turned his eyes to Pierce. "And who are you?"

"Do not tell him," said Abigail.

Isaac backhanded her viciously. "Do not think your incredulous beauty will stop me from disfiguring it!" Isaac turned back to Pierce. "Tell me your name and from where you came."

"If you let them both go, I will tell you my name."

"Kill the boy," said Isaac.

"Stop," blurted Pierce.

The sentry looked at Cedric with suspicious eyes. "I recognize this boy servant. Why is he here? Does he belong to you?" said Isaac to Pierce.

"No, he does not belong to me," said Pierce.

Isaac refocused his attention on Pierce. "Once more, who are you?"

Pierce needed more time and the right opportunity to kill them all. He also needed Abigail's help. "I am from an island—" Pierce wanted to lie but the effects of the broth lingered— "called England."

"So, Englishman, what is your name?" demanded Isaac.

"Pierce."

"And the rest of your name is...?" When Pierce paused, Isaac nodded at one of his men to press a dagger blade against the boy's neck.

"I will tell you my name. There is no need for bloodshed."

Isaac nodded and the guard removed the blade.

"My name is van Fleming, Pierce van Fleming of England."

Isaac leered up at Pierce. No longer under Marie's influence, he recalled random bits of information such as names and places. "Pierce van Fleming of England," murmured Isaac. "I have heard of you." His face grew serious as he recalled Domitian's hatred of that name. "You!" hissed Isaac.

Suddenly, Isaac and his men started wailing in pain as they collapsed, their backs impaled by arrows, their bodies rapidly decaying until only the bones of the eldest and rotting flesh of the youngest vampires was all that remained.

Abigail and Pierce stood motionless while Cedric's eyes clenched with fear. From the forest emerged a group of soldiers with discharged crossbows, followed by Sir Michael Livesey, Count Marcel Marc de Vos, and three councilors on horses with glowing eyes.

68 - THE CLAN'S MASTER

Marcel dismounted his enchanted steed. Pierce, Abigail, and Cedric stood amidst the ashes, weapons, and armor of the late sentry and his guards. To Pierce, the clan master appeared stoically ancient, his cape cascading from a fur nape attached to a finely crafted leather vest. Pierce salvaged a sword from the remains of Marie's sentry as Marcel stood his ground a few paces distant.

Marcel pointed at the remains and moved towards Pierce. "There was a time when iron mail and plates of armor donned our bodies," said Marcel. "But the iron was cumbersome. So we crafted leather armor with thin metal plates embedded inside to shield our vulnerabilities." He gazed lovingly at Abigail. "You are as beautiful as the night, my child, and I am pleased to have arrived neither later nor earlier." He looked at Cedric and then at Pierce, and came closer.

Pierce raised his sword.

"Lower it," whispered Abigail to Pierce. She curtsied and bowed her head. "Thank you for your impeccable timing and for defending us, Milord. We are honored and grateful to be in your presence. May I introduce Pierce van Fleming of England, and his servant Cedric Martens?"

Marcel stopped a few feet distant to admire Pierce, a man as large as he. "The oracle speaks highly of you, Mister van Fleming," said the count. He turned briefly to his horsemen. "Behind me are the clan's loyal councilors. The younger one is my trusted advisor, Sir Michael Livesey—English like you, though the root of *your* lineage, I believe, is Flemish. Behind them are my warriors, my trusted guard." Marcel glanced down at the remains of Isaac and his men.. "You have nothing to fear, lest you are the enemy." Marcel turned to Abigail. "Where is the oracle?"

"She left unexpectedly, Milord. The cottage is in my care."

"We shall speak inside then," said Marcel.

"Yes, of course," said Abigail, bowing her head.

Inside the tiny cottage, the councilors stood in a semicircle with Marcel at the center. Everyone stared at Pierce with great curiosity.

"Is he aware of the prophecy?" said Marcel to Abigail, cutting to the chase.

"Yes, Milord," said Abigail.

Marcel felt Pierce resisting his mind probe. "You are unusually strong for someone so young." Marcel sensed Cedric's blood but continued unabated. "We were attacked by Domitian's allies three days ago. I am at fault for underestimating his resolve. I have requested reinforcements to secure the castle."

"Reinforcements from where, and when will they arrive?" asked Pierce.

"A trusted ally and soon enough," said Marcel, evading the question. "Please, Mister van Fleming, may I see your hands?"

Pierce revealed his palms.

"The chosen one comes from an island nation and bears the mark of the eight-legged star on his hands, half the star in each hand. How is it not remarkable that you are exactly as described?"

"I have a question, if I may," interrupted a councilor with a gruff voice.

Marcel nodded. "This is Councilor Gavin of Prussia. Please, Gavin, speak your mind."

Gavin stepped forward. "Mister van Fleming, Countess Marie de Vos presented the council with a declaration bearing your signature. The declaration renounced your affiliation and all rights henceforth to this clan. You also swore never to step foot in Flanders. Yet, here you are. Please explain."

"I signed the document to release myself from the countess. She destroyed all that I cherished. She even tried to have me and master Cedric killed. I come seeking retribution."

"Or perhaps you are here because of prophesy," said Marcel.

"The countess stated that you despise our ways and intend to protect humanity at the expense of our kind," added Gavin.

That was true, and Pierce had no problem addressing it—with or without a truth serum. "Humanity is natural and I intend to conserve all that is natural in this world," reasoned Pierce.

Marcel's eyes wandered over to the boy, who was clearly struggling to make sense of their conversation.

"Or perhaps you are a friend of the countess and have come to assassinate the clan master," said the councilor.

Marcel raised his hand. "That will be enough, Gavin."

"That is quite all right," said Pierce. "The countess is no friend. She is severely depraved and rapidly degenerating into something so perverse that she must be removed for all our sakes, and if not by me, then by whom?"

"Marie has a sickness for which I am to blame," said Marcel with heaviness in his voice.

"She has committed treason," said Gavin followed by nods and grumblings from the others.

"Domitian and she will destroy everything unless they are stopped," said another.

"I will stop her," said Pierce.

"And so shall I," blurted Cedric.

All eyes turned to the boy. Cedric held his ground, returning their glances with a fierceness Pierce had never noticed before. Pierce felt as if he should speak for the boy but waited to see what he might do.

"I have my reasons to stop the countess, just reasons," said Cedric. "She is not who I thought she was."

A few men laughed at his confession of being tricked.

"It is no laughing matter," said Cedric. "She engaged me with a riddle to solve—"

"Riddle?" asked one of the councilors.

"Yes. After I solved it, she rewarded me with a gold coin. Then, she selected me to escort her to England in search of Mister Fleming. I served her well, and in return she asked me to run a stake through Mister Fleming's heart."

Laughter erupted again, but much louder this time.

Cedric shook his head. "I fail to see the humor in that. She not only abandoned me in England but must have told the constables that Mister Fleming and I had committed murder because our likeness was in the newsprints and they chased us from Manchester to London. I cannot prove the countess had committed the murders of which we were accused, but I am suspicious of her—fearful as well."

"You ought to be, boy," said a tall man.

"The countess has her ways," said a short man.

"There is something odd about her," declared Cedric. "And dare I say most people in these parts are just as odd. And... and there are monsters—"

"Monsters?" blurted Marcel. "What monsters?"

"Something or someone is killing people. Mister Fleming and I discovered victims in London. They were terribly mutilated, as if attacked by a vicious animal. I came across a similar killing in a farmhouse just east of the forest—an entire family murdered." His eyes dropped. "I have seen many horrible things. Had it not been for Mister Fleming, I would not be here."

"Courageous," said Marcel to Cedric, "smart and experienced beyond your years. I am inspired, though old and tired, and I have largely ignored the mounting problems that have brought us to our current state of crisis. It is time to take back the clan and restore order." Marcel took a step towards Pierce. "Mister Pierce van Fleming, will you not defend the Royal Flemish Clan and uphold its laws and covenants as the master-to-be?"

Pierce had no desire to be clan master and would not believe that Marcel was otherwise convinced. "With no disrespect, Milord, I am here solely to avenge the deaths of my family and friends, and to help him," Pierce turned to Cedric, "free his friend. However, I shall fight in your name until my work here is done. If I survive, I shall leave this place and never return."

Marcel rotated in the center of the group, gazing into everyone's eyes, until he stopped to face Cedric. The boy did not back down from Marcel's intimidating gaze.

"I can only hope that you will eventually believe as I do." Marcel's comment was meant for Pierce, though he continued to stare at the boy.

Pierce sensed that Marcel was trying to probe Cedric's mind. The boy was strong-willed, but not healthy enough to prevent the ancient vampire from gleaning his emotions.

Marcel finally turned to Pierce. "One cannot force another into such an arrangement and expect it to succeed," said the count. "The oracle claims that you are noble and strong, that you are the chosen one. Because I trust the oracle's vision, you must be those things. As for Marie..." Marcel's eyes squinted with emotion. "I love her and loathe her equally. She was a beautiful girl, but her elegance and sensibilities have since eroded. She and Domitian must be stopped. You will have my support."

In the counting chamber, Marie had finished draining all but one boy to death, and was hovering high above Lily in vile ecstasy.

Lily felt that the last boy would be next and then her. She tried to work her bindings loose. She tried to kill herself by holding her breath. Nothing worked. The boy was just as helpless. She tried to make eye contact with him, but he was petrified with fear. Her only hope was for someone to come and end the horror before the effects of the hover wore off.

69 - THE PIT AND PROPHESY

Early the next morning, Pierce planned to explore alternate entrances to the castle. Marcel described an airshaft. It drained excess water from the catacombs and was accessible from an outlet to the east. Marcel ordered his guard, Gandt the bowman, and his advisor, Sir Michael Livesey, to accompany Pierce.

Cedric led the way through the forest towards the northeast side of the castle. Pierce brought up the rear. The castle loomed in the distance, belching smoke of a battle in progress. Pierce took in the aromas and noticed a stench. It grew stronger as they approached a gully where Cedric believed the airshaft to vent. They found a stream and followed it into a wash, the odor growing ever sickening.

"The smell," said Cedric, cringing and cupping his hand over his nose.

"Death," said Sir Michael.

"I shall investigate it," said Pierce.

"I will go with you," said the boy.

"We shall *all* go," insisted Sir Michael.

Pierce wished he had come alone. "Very well."

The group moved out of the ravine and into the meadow towards what appeared to be a sizeable pit. It looked as if someone had dug it up and filled it many times over many seasons, probably years. Cautiously, they crawled on their bellies to the edge of the pit. What they saw turned even Pierce's stomach.

There was no telling how deep the piles of bloody sacks actually went. The sacks closest to the edge of the pit were fully or partially buried in soil that had been excavated, while others had been torn open by scavenging creatures, their ghastly contents strewn out. The gruesome scene contained entrails, ribcages, spines, skulls, and tangled hair. The horrific scene surged and swelled with the buzzing and crackling noises of insects hovering, gnashing, and gnawing. Pierce looked over at Cedric and noticed his eyes locked onto a spot directly below them. Pierce followed his stare to the bodies of women buried to their waist.

"Mum and Helga," Cedric whispered Cedric sadly, as if he had lost family members.

Pierce managed to pull Cedric away from the pit and into the cover of the forest. Cedric vomited with such force he riled the crows in the trees. Pierce took notice of the birds. They were sounding a warning. Suddenly, a stone bounced off Pierce's shoulder. Pierce looked over at Sir Michael, who was crouching and pointing at something in the forest.

"Watch the boy and keep him safe," whispered Pierce to Gandt. He unsheathed his sword and sprung forward into the forest.

When three Roman scouts sensed Pierce fast approaching, they turned and ran along a trail towards the meadow. Sir Michael kept pace behind Pierce, who increased speed and was almost upon one of the scouts when they suddenly dispersed in three directions. Pierce pointed to a scout peeling off to the right for Michael to pursue.

Pierce ran between the other two. One tripped and tumbled. Before he could recover, Pierce sliced off his head in full stride. Continuing the chase, he cut towards the second man at an angle to close the gap. A thick stand of trees made Pierce lose sight of him. Pierce had little time to react to the wooden spear, jutting out from behind a large beech tree. He jumped and tumbled to the ground, colliding headfirst into a large rock. Pierce was slow to recover, and the enemy launched himself with his spear aimed at Pierce's chest. With the spearhead nary an inch from Pierce's chest, the attacker veered violently off target with a knife in his throat. A second later, Michael cut off the scout's head.

"Are you all right?" asked Sir Michael, knife still in hand.

Groggily, Pierce rubbed his neck. "I believe so. The other?"

"Dead. Let us hope we got them all," said Michael, sheathing his knife and starting back to where they left the boy and guard.

"Thank you, Sir Michael," said Pierce.

Michael nodded. "You fight well."

Sir Michael's accent intrigued Pierce. "Are you by any chance from Kent?"

"The Isle of Sheppey, actually. Have you been there?"

"No," said Pierce, still rubbing his neck. "How did you get here?"

"To make a long story brief, I was a baronet of Kent and served in the civil wars. I fled England soon after Charles the Second took the throne. Count Marcel Marc de Vos recruited me in Amsterdam."

With a concerned expression, Pierce stopped and turned to Michael. "Were you one of the commissioners who sentenced King Charles to death?"

"Yes, but he was not king," said Michael understatedly.

"You committed high treason," whispered Pierce.

Sir Michael shook his head. "Dear, dear Mister Fleming, Charles the First was a traitor. His son sought revenge, and unjustly, considering his father had lost the civil war. What does it matter now? It happened over two hundred years ago."

"It is a matter of character, which you seem to lack."

Michael cringed. "Charles was a zealot of the Pope, who would have devolved England to the Dark Ages. Surely, you would not defend that."

Pierce drew his sword. "I would defend my king to my last breath. Have you no sense of loyalty? How can Marcel trust a regicide?"

Sir Michael drew his sword and dropped back two steps. He then crouched, gently placed his weapon on the ground, and stood up with hands out.

"If you are so righteous an Englishman, please slay me now in the name of the Roman Catholic Church."

"What is this?" said Gandt, leading Cedric to them.

Sir Michael glanced at the guard. "Gandt, Mister Fleming and I were discussing English history and politics." Sir Michael smiled at Pierce. "I am ready to move on if you are, my friend."

Pierce could not afford to lose focus. Their political differences were a separate matter.

"I am ready," said Pierce to Sir Michael.

When they reached the gully, Cedric pointed at a crust of exposed rock on the west side of the ravine. They pushed through the flora towards an iron grate, firmly attached to the rock face. Pierce examined the bars and narrow outlet, and shook his head. "This was not meant to be removed, and the opening is quite small."

The grate would not yield to any amount of pulling or prying. As Pierce was observing their efforts, he blocked out the odors of death from the nearby pit and focused on the musty smells emerging from the shaft. Hints of candles, muddy water, and rodents were expected, but Marie's scent came as a surprise. He kept the information to himself but was certain the tunnel led to her.

With the iron grate stubbornly unmoved and the sun nearing its zenith, the party headed back to the cottage.

Abigail took Marcel's arm. Under watchful eyes of his guards, the couple moved slowly through the forest near the cottage.

"Abigail, I fear for your safety," murmured the master.

"My sweet Lord, please do not—"

"Let me finish. One of my greatest fears is losing you, and as much as we try, secrecy is impossible to keep for long. Marie knows of our love and intends to end it. Beware, for she is made of jealousy, hatred, and greed. I can only pray that we stop her before it is too late."

"We shall, Milord," said Abigail, as she pulled him to a halt and gently placed her hand on his face.

"Mister Fleming will, as foretold," Marcel said, smiling. "He is an honorable man. I can feel it."

"He is."

"He asked me how I could possibly want to live for so long. Do you know what I said? I told him I slept my way through it. I want to sleep, and I do, much like a bear hibernates."

Abigail could not contain her laughter.

Yet, Marcel was not laughing. He imparted a serious gaze and said, "You went to England on Marie's orders to find him."

"Yes. I had no choice."

"I understand."

Abigail moved to look up at him directly. "My allegiance is to you, Milord. I am yours, and I shall defend you with my life. Forgive me for obeying the countess, but it was necessary to protect you."

"There is nothing to forgive, my sweet child. I trust you, and I want you to go to Spain."

Abigail's shoulders drooped. "Milord?"

"It is folly, Abigail. All of it. You are not a warrior. You are not safe here. You will return when it is safe, when I send for you."

"But I can help Pierce destroy the countess."

"My men can help him just as well."

"Nay! I know the countess's secrets and weaknesses better than anyone. Please, allow me this honor, Milord. Please."

"You have nothing to prove, my child."

"I believe I do. I need to show the countess to whom my heart and loyalty truly belongs."

Marcus shrugged his shoulders and nodded, for he knew that no amount of persuasion would change Abigail's mind. "I would prefer that you leave, but you may stay if that is your wish. I do understand your reasons for confronting her."

"Thank you, Milord. May I ask something of you, something important to me?"

Marcel gazed into her flawless face and smiled. "Anything, my child."

"No matter what happens, please give Pierce van Fleming safe passage if he decides to leave."

"Do you not believe in prophecy?"

"I believe fate and destiny are not preordained, for if they were, we would have little purpose or hope for change."

"How then can you explain countless outcomes that were prophesied?"

"It is not prophecies as such, but rather our belief in them that makes them true. If Pierce does not believe the prophecy, then it cannot be true."

"I have already said that such an arrangement cannot be forced. Besides, I have already chosen a successor."

"Sir Michael?"

"Yes. He has proven his loyalty for well over a century. Thus, Pierce van Fleming shall receive no reprisal from me by his leave."

"Thank you, Milord." Abigail reached behind his neck and placed her lips on his.

70 - PROTECT THE CHILDREN

Dusk faded to black. Marcel's reinforcements still had not arrived. Cedric put his armor on and urged van Fleming to leave at once for the castle. In Cedric's mind, each passing minute decreased Lily's chances of survival. Finally, Pierce gathered Cedric, Abigail, the stout bowman, Gandt, and Sir Michael at the table.

"We will be the first to infiltrate the castle," said Pierce. "Cedric and Abigail will enter the castle through the airshaft east of the castle." Pierce noticed Abigail, cringing discretely in disagreement.

"Correction," said Pierce, realizing her concern. The airshaft was too confining for her—a vampire and a boy—to occupy together. Her willingness to renounce human blood was never put to such a test. "Cedric will enter the airshaft alone and Abigail will pair with me."

"Mister Fleming, the iron grate," said Cedric. "We failed to remove it."

"The boy is right," said Sir Michael. "How do you propose to remove the grate? With magic?"

The men in the room laughed, but Pierce remained steady.

"Cedric will meet us inside the castle on the other end of the airshaft," said Pierce. "The rest of you will follow my lead. Abigail and I shall be the first to jump the ramparts. I will signal the next pair to do the same when all is clear. Be prepared to eliminate your enemy quickly and quietly. Your task is to assess their strength and positions and report back to Count Marcel. Do not hesitate to finish Domitian if you can. Abigail and I will hunt down Marie de Vos in the catacombs."

"The Romans are skilled fighters," said Marcel, leaning

against the wall. "Engage them in numbers whenever possible."

"Protect any child you encounter," said Pierce. "Is that clear?" Pierce waited for all to agree. "Swear that you will allow them to leave the castle unharmed. Swear it now."

Sir Michael appeared conflicted. "But if the children know of us, what we are, and are set free..."

"The law to which you refer applies to adults only," said Pierce.

"It implies all their kind," said Gandt.

"That interpretation is wrong in principle." Pierce turned to Marcel. "No one will believe them."

"For centuries, fantastical stories of us have been told," said Marcel. "We are still here."

"Exactly," said Pierce, hoping that Marcel was taking his side. "Too many children have perished because of us. It must stop. I will not be a part of this unless it does." Pierce waited for Marcel's nod of approval.

After a moment of consideration, he said, "My men will follow your lead, Mister Fleming. They will harm no child. You have my word."

"Good," said Pierce. "It is time."

Pierce led his raiders back to the gully east of the castle. He asked Abigail and the guards to stand watch while he and Cedric continued on to the airshaft.

When they arrived at the airshaft, Pierce focused his thoughts on the iron bars and brought his hands together. "Cedric," said Pierce, "turn away and close your eyes." After the boy did as he was told, Pierce imagined a wedge splitting the rock apart. From his hands, a blue beam of energy shot out at the rock face. Chards shot out round them and animals hiding in the reeds scattered. Pierce quickly took hold of the iron bars and pulled away the grate.

Cedric turned to see the results and was astounded. "But how...?"

"The warriors must have weakened it," said Pierce with a

wink. "Where does this shaft lead to?"

"It ends at a small door of stone that opens into the catacombs near the counting chamber," said Cedric.

"Counting chamber?"

"Yes. The countess spends much of her time there, counting the castle's treasure."

Pierce noticed concern on Cedric's face.

"I would prefer to go with you, Mister Fleming," said Cedric.

Cedric was a grave liability. He was no match for a vampire. "Master Cedric, you asked me to accompany you here, and I did. You asked me to help you free Lily, and I will. Now I ask you to stay the course. Will you?"

Cedric felt the issue was not a matter of staying the course as it was choosing methods suitable to achieving the goal. Cedric had no torch or candle to light his way. Shimmying through a confined tunnel in pitch darkness was a daunting task, though aside from insects, grime, and an occasional rodent, there was nothing to fear.

"My life would be inconsequential without Lily," said Cedric softly. "I will stay the course, Mister Fleming."

"Lily will be proud of you, Master Cedric. Now, where can I find the door and how does it open?"

"You will need to enter the catacombs from the stairs in the main hall. From the bottom of the stairs, follow the corridor to the right. Do not take any of the narrower passageways lest you fancy labyrinths. Eventually, you will reach Marie's counting chamber marked by a royal crest above the entrance. The airshaft is to the right about twenty paces beyond the chamber. A slight recess outlines the door, and the candle sconce above it is a lever that opens the door when in the down position."

"Very good."

"Mister Fleming?"

"Yes?"

"Please promise to let me out."

"Worry not, Master Cedric."

"Promise, please."

"I promise that you will be let out," Pierce said, cradling his hands and boosting Cedric into the shaft. "See you on the other side."

71 - THE RAID

Pierce and his small band of raiders moved quietly into the meadow towards Vos Castle. Bushes, trees, and structures provided adequate cover from the detection of guards stationed on the parapets. All was quiet and Pierce wondered if the battle had finally ended.

"They are not Flemish guards," whispered Abigail, leaning against an old cart. "They are probably Domitian's Roman soldiers."

"It seems that Domitian has taken the castle," added Sir Michael.

"This wall is guarded by only one watchman," said Pierce.

The lone watchman noticed movement near the forest. He peered at a stand of trees and saw a small gathering of deer grazing at the meadow's edge.

"It is time," said Pierce. When the guard turned away, Pierce stood up and took a running leap into the sky. Just as he had when he leaped from London Bridge to the sailing ship, he controlled trajectory and rate of descent with his mind. Before landing beside the guard, he readied his sword and then lopped off his head as he touched down. The body collapsed and began to decompose. Pierce took the guard's place near the rampart and surveyed the walls and castle. Astonishingly, there were fewer guards than he had expected to encounter. In fact, he was the only one standing on that section of wall. Pierce gave the signal for Abigail to jump.

She reached out to him when she landed. After everyone had successfully jumped and landed on the rampart, they paired up and quickly moved into the courtyard. Pierce followed Abigail into the castle through a side-door. Together they moved from column to statue and partition to balustrade. Within view of the stairs to the catacombs, they were disappointed to find a dozen castle guards stationed there. Pierce was certain he could take out three, perhaps four, on his own, but not twelve. They waited.

Finally, yelling outside the castle demanded everyone's attention. Six of twelve guards had abandoned their post to investigate the commotion outside.

Abigail whispered, "I will create a diversion. When they give chase, finish the rest. Wait for me in the catacombs near the counting chamber."

Pierce nodded and readied his sword and wooden stake.

Abigail casually walked into the main hall and stood before the guards, who ordered her to halt, but she ignored them and kept walking. All but three vampires pursued her. Pierce attacked those remaining guards, successfully killing them, leaving bones and rotting flesh behind.

Abigail ran outside with her pursuers close behind. Luckily, Gandt was there.

"Be ready," said Abigail, as she turned to face the Romans behind her. Gandt shot arrows, eliminating two guards, while Abigail fought and killed the third.

In the catacombs, which were flooded by several inches of water in some areas, Pierce made his way through the main corridor. It was too noisy to run, so he crept along the edges of the water, all the while sensing Marie's odor. Noticing the coat of arms above the archway, he stopped and waited. The smell of something other than Marie, of something sweet and delicious riled his anger—*child's blood*.

He listened intently but heard nothing. He moved twenty paces to the small door below the candle sconce. He placed his hand on the sconce and paused. If he let the boy out now, Cedric would probably insist on attacking Marie and end up dead. Pierce shook his head at that probability. If he waited too long for Abigail, a guard might show up and spoil his element of surprise. Pierce was confident he could kill Marie, and if he was the chosen one, he would require no assistance. He decided to leave Cedric in the shaft where he would be safe and to go at it alone.

Dagger in hand, Pierce crept quietly through the arched entrance into a short corridor towards the counting chamber. All was quiet. Was the countess inside? Suddenly he sensed someone behind him. He turned and pressed his dagger to Abigail's neck. Stifling his irritation, Abigail placed her index finger across his lips and led him out to the main corridor, and then far enough away from the chamber to discuss the obvious change in plan.

"Where is Cedric?" whispered Abigail.

Pierce pointed towards the shaft.

"Are you going to let him out?"

Pierce shook his head. "Too dangerous."

"You promised to let him out."

"I did not agree to when. Attack now and let him out later."

"Very well." Abigail took a sword in each hand and looked into his eyes with fearful determination. "As agreed, I will attack first and position her so that you can come in and drive a stake through her heart. Ready?"

"I am, are you?"

She forced her fear into a darker place and nodded. "Ready as ever."

72 - BATTLE IN THE CATACOMBS I

Of all the horrors Abigail had witnessed, few were as harrowing as the scene in the counting chamber. All the boys save one were dead. Tied down to the table in the center of it all was Lily. She was staring up into the shadowy heights of the ceiling. The counting chamber was the only room in the catacombs that projected up through the castle.

Marie was nowhere to be seen, but her stench hung strong in the chamber. Abigail knew she was there, probably hovering high in the darkness, oblivious to them. She quickly approached the last living boy and kneeled.

"Are you hurt?" whispered Abigail so softly that she could barely hear herself. The boy was unresponsive but physically whole. Abigail returned to Lily. Suddenly, a droplet of blood landed on the girl's forehead. Abigail followed Lily's stare into the void beyond the timber trusses. Two faint lights, pulsating, came down at her, knocking her to the ground so violently she dropped her swords.

Marie stood beside the table, her tongue jutting freakishly. She was specked with flesh and sodden with blood, a macabre spectacle of horror.

Abigail scampered like a crab over blood-splattered sacks of coins to flee. Marie was upon her in a blink of an eye, lifting Abigail to her feet by her hair. Marie spun her around and lifted Abigail's wrists behind her back. Abigail glanced at the entranceway, shaking her head at her brother. Now was not the time.

Pierce stayed out of sight, waiting for his sister's signal. He knew how child's blood affected the mind and body, producing not only euphoria but also greatly enhanced senses and physical strength. Could the countess detect him, smell him? He could not wait too long. Pierce watched intently for a moment when Marie was vulnerable.

Marie held Abigail's wrists with one hand and loosened her armor with the other. Then, she reached inside and cupped Abigail's breast. "My naughty girl," said Marie, "Marcel is nowhere to be found. Tell me, has he surrendered or fled? Or will he bring reinforcements and fight? Answer me now."

Abigail winced in pain as the woman twisted her wrists, but she said nothing.

"Answer me now or suffer a painful end," said Marie. With no response, Marie pinched off Abigail's nipple and brought it out for inspection. She put it in her mouth and rolled it cheek to cheek. "I venture to guess Marcel has never suckled thee like this." Marie cackled and stripped off Abigail's armor. "Thou must think I am so imperceptive to know nothing of thy whoring. Well, I know everything! Evidently, loyalty means nothing to thee. What shall I tear off next, an ear, a hand, an arm? Shall I flatten thy perfect face?"

Abigail remained tight-lipped.

"Very well."

Marie broke Abigail's thumbs.

Abigail whimpered and repeated, "*Armis torpent. Armis torpent!*"

"Dost Latin ease thy pain, my dear?" Marie shoved Abigail to the ground and placed her bare foot on her face. "Where is Count Marcel? Answer the question!" Just as the cartilage in Abigail's nose started to crack under Marie's weight, the countess eased up and scented the air. "What is that smell?" Before she could identify it, something slammed her into a rock wall with such force that her head cracked the masonry. Her eyes widened with surprise. She had not noticed the wooden stake protruding from her chest with Pierce standing before her.

"Percy, my sweet prince, what an unexpected surprise. I thought you were dead."

Pierce expected Marie to die, but she lifted to her feet with ease. She then removed the stake from her chest as if it were merely an annoyance and snapped it in half.

Pierce rearmed with Abigail's stake and hurled himself at Marie again, but this time he met the wall head on, splintering the stick and dazing himself. Lying flat on his face, he felt the weight of Marie's body on his back, her legs wrapping around him and her demon-like hand gripping his neck. Pierce pushed up in a great surge of power, lifting them towards the ceiling, slamming Marie against the rafters, knocking her off. When he landed, he turned to face her, but she was not there.

Pierce quickly stepped aside as Marie landed on her feet where he had stood. Pierce grabbed a sword and attacked, but Marie was incredibly fast, easily evading him. Pierce sheathed his sword and clasped his hands together, imagining her body splitting apart. A bolt of energy pushed Marie back against the wall. She locked eyes on Pierce's hunched frame and grinned at the sight of smoke curling around her.

"That was impressive," said Marie. "Perhaps thou art the chosen one after all." She charged at him. Their momentum broke a wooden pillar, causing a storage loft to crash down on them.

Abigail withdrew from the pain of her injuries and unexpectedly recalled Elida's prophecy. She heard her voice, as if Elida was inside her head, repeating the words:

A Roman on strings of malice shall rule
Kingdoms of man and vampire shall fall,
Lest the strings of malice are severed by one,
All shall be lost and ever forgotten.

At the airshaft outside the counting chamber, Abigail pulled the candle fixture down with her index finger. The small door opened and Cedric fell out into the damp corridor.

"Headmistress, what happened?" said Cedric, as he got to his feet, rubbing a bump on his head. "Mister Fleming promised to—"

Abigail quickly shushed the boy. "You are too loud," she hissed. "Listen well, Cedric. Terrible horrors await us inside the counting chamber. Ignore them. Focus on Lily. Do you understand?"

"Lily? Is she—?"

"Alive? Yes. She is a prisoner, strapped to a table."

"And Mister Fleming?"

"You must focus on Lily. Untie her bindings. I will free the boy. We will bring them here and you will escort them to freedom through the tunnel. Do you understand?"

After Cedric agreed, she led him into the counting chamber.

It was impossible for Cedric to ignore the carnage. It reminded him of all the horrors he had seen in the last year, starting with the farmhouse murders, followed by the murder of Farmer John's family, then Pierce's bankers. He imagined Pierce's family in the same state of mutilation. The monster was her, Countess Marie de Vos. He began to hyperventilate as his heart raced out of control.

Then, as he felt he might pass out, in the middle of the room, he saw Lily.

73 - BATTLE IN THE CATACOMBS II

As Abigail worked to free the boy shackled to the wall, Cedric went to Lily. Muffled sounds of struggling echoed from high. With all her strength, Abigail broke the iron shackles, releasing the boy. Cedric severed Lily's leather bindings with his sword and lifted her off the table.

"No!" screamed Marie, as she swooped down from the ceiling at Cedric. Before she could slam into him, Pierce knocked her off course, and they tumbled across the floor of scattered bags and boxes.

"Run," said Abigail, leading the boy to the entranceway. Cedric cradled Lily in his arms. She weighed almost nothing, and Cedric had always been a strong boy. They made it to the airshaft, and in the light of a torch, Cedric recognized the other boy.

"Jacob?" whispered Cedric.

Jacob was unresponsive, as if in a daze.

"Go," said Abigail.

Cedric quickly helped Lily and Jacob into the airshaft and encouraged them to follow it to the end. As this was going on, Abigail sensed danger.

"Hurry, Cedric," said Abigail, bracing herself. She ducked and moved aside to avoid her attacker's dagger. She retaliated, but the guard blocked her swing and pushed her up against the wall with his blade pressed to her throat.

Before he was able to finish Abigail, the guard reeled back in pain. He swiveled to find Cedric there, sword in hand, fear in his eyes. Cedric had brought his blade down on the guard's head, splitting it open. Not enough to stop the man, though. He lunged at Cedric. The boy tried to move aside and reposition his sword, but the sentry was too fast, and Cedric was too late. The boy braced himself.

Suddenly, the man let go his dagger. His jaw dropped, and then his head fell to the floor, followed by his body. Abigail shielded Cedric from the rapid decomposition of the remains, and ushered him back to the airshaft.

Before Cedric ducked into the shaft, he saw the remains of the guard. "What was that thing, a monster?"

"Yes. Now go save your friends. Save yourself. Leave this place forever."

Cedric thought of the farmhouse murders again. He paused to gaze into Abigail's eyes and memorize her face. She no longer appeared blindingly beautiful. She was injured with concern on her face. "I want to help you and Mister Fleming," said Cedric reasonably.

Abigail shook her head. "You must help your friends."

"You *are* my friends," Cedric said, his eyes glancing at her injured hands.

Abigail pointed to the shaft. "Quickly..."

After an uncomfortable standoff, Cedric begrudgingly entered the airshaft and Abigail lifted the candle sconce to close the door behind him.

74 - BATTLE IN THE CATACOMBS III

Abigail returned to the counting chamber to find Marie and Pierce standing face to face in a deathly embrace. Abigail rushed Marie, but the countess was ready, using Pierce as a shield. In a blur, the countess released her grip and struck Abigail in the face, knocking her unconscious. Marie leaped over Pierce, twisting and turning, landing behind him and grasping his neck with both hands.

Pierce's eyes bulged as Marie's fingertips dug in. With Abigail laying senseless on the floor, and the countess burrowing her fingers deep into his throat, the situation was hopeless. Pierce's only thought was for his old friend, Death, to come quickly.

"This is how I paralyzed thy sister," said Marie, as she fondled the vertebrae in his neck. "I made her watch as I devoured thy precious niece, Emma. She was delectable. I hovered for hours." Marie glanced at the doorway. "Where is the boy—what was his name? Ah, yes, Cedric. Cedric Martens." Marie pressed against a vertebra, causing Pierce to twitch and grimace. "If he is still alive, I will find him, and when I do, I shall tell him how I removed your head from your body, one neck bone at a time. Then I shall end his life by—"

Suddenly, hundreds of gold Broads rained down on them.

Marie immediately released Pierce and fell to her knees, frantically gathering the coins, counting aloud. "One, two, three, four—" More coins fell around her, "...eight, nine, ten, eleven, twelve, thirteen—" She quickly deposited a stack of twenty gold pieces on the table and slouched back down for more. She ignored the person standing an arm's length away from her. At eighteen coins, she finally paused to acknowledge who it was. "Well, well, look who has come to die," growled Marie.

She lunged at him.

He was ready for her, lifting the point of his sword to her stomach.

She pressed against his sword, sliding herself onto the blade, gnashing her fangs, waiving her claws towards his throat, but slowing in her advance as the tip of his sword found her spine and something about the boy's spirit weakened her.

Cedric quickly shoved her back with his boot and pulled out his blade. She was the monster. He knew it now. "You... it was you who murdered the farmers by the forest. You killed the castle servants, as well as Mister Fleming's family and friends," said Cedric, trembling with as much fear as loathing.

Marie snarled and came at him again.

Cedric stepped aside and severed her hands at the forearms.

Her face contorted with surprise and panic, and then a demented grin. "After I kill thee," she hissed, arm-stumps oozing blood the color of soot, "I shall devour your precious friends. None shall leave this place alive."

A flash of steel sliced through air and tissue as she attacked once more.

The countess stopped in her tracks, her back to Cedric, head slightly misaligned. Her arms fell limp. Then her body fell backward to the floor, the severed head rolled to Cedric's feet. Cedric's emotions were instantly entangled with horror and regret for taking a life, unfathomable disappointment for not resolving the conflict diplomatically, anger for reasons that escaped him, confusion for what his eyes saw next. The head began to change. The flesh turned rotten, then dry and gaunt. The eyes sunk into the sockets until only a leathery skull remained. Silence...unsettling like the moment his mother died. He had slain the monster in self defense and in defense of his friends, who were still lying on the floor incapacitated.

Cedric rushed to Pierce's side. His neck appeared more severely injured than when it was impaled by the O'Brian brother's arrow. Cedric placed his hand on Pierce's chest and felt no movement. He lowered his ear to his mouth and sensed no breathing. "Mister Fleming," said Cedric with a tremble. "Mister Fleming, sir, can you hear me?"

"Do not worry," said Abigail, as she slowly moved to a sitting position. "My brother lives." She creased her brow at the concerned boy.

Cedric saw Countess Marie's rotting remains and those of the murdered children in shackles. Nothing made sense, but few things ever had. His eyes paused to take in Abigail's imbalanced form. "What are you people?" asked Cedric in a less credulous tone. "Are you vampires," his eyes found the remains again, "like her?"

"We are...not like her," said Abigail, testing her balance. "We are magical beings of the forest."

His eyes narrowed with suspicion. "Magical beings...?"

"Similar in kind to Elida, the oracle." Abigail touched her nose and flinched. "Master Cedric, how did you escape the airshaft? I thought the door was locked."

"I jarred the door with my sword."

Abigail took a step. "Lily and Jacob, are they safe?"

Cedric nodded. "They are outside, but others might still be trapped in the castle. I must free them."

"You must free yourself, Master Cedric. If others are here, Pierce and I will find them." Gingerly lifting two sacks of gold coins, she handed them to Cedric.

Cedric accepted the money, and her insistence to leave. He tied the sacks together and slung them over his neck. Then he turned to Pierce. "Mister Fleming, sir, can you hear me?" Cedric saw the corner of Pierce's mouth curl. "Forgive me for parting like this, sir. You are a good man, magical or not. I hope we meet again. God be with you."

Abigail was waiting for Martens at the entranceway. On his way out, he noticed a few pendants beside a busted leather bag. As fortuitous, coincidental, or improbable as it were, all the pendants were gold crucifixes. Incredibly, one of them belonged to him. It was his gold cross, the heirloom that had been confiscated when he was brought to the castle. The bag must have been ruptured during the course of Pierce's battle with Marie. He retrieved his cross, and exited the counting chamber with Abigail.

75 - THE WAY OUT

After Abigail secured the airshaft door behind Cedric, she returned to her brother who was still lying on the counting chamber floor. She kneeled beside him and gently placed her hand over his neck wounds and chanted three times, "*vicis vigoratus totus vulnus...*" After a moment of accelerated healing, he opened his eyes. After several moments more, she helped him to his feet. As they hobbled out of the chamber and into the corridor, the sounds of violence above them echoed hollow as if the battle was miles away. Abigail's thumbs had healed well enough to hold a weapon, and Pierce's neck wounds were rapidly mending, but the siblings were in no condition to fight a battle. With torches in hand, Pierce and Abigail ventured deep into the labyrinth of the catacombs.

After an hour of wandering, they entered a large chamber in which mummified bodies in tattered dress were stacked in rows like firewood. Pierce wanted to ask her about them but decided to let his voice rest and bring it up later if they survived their ordeal. He followed her to the back of the room where a flight of steps led to an ironclad door. They opened the door and entered a cylindrical room. It appeared to be the base of a turret with no other way out. Abigail dragged her hand along the wall until she came to a stone that was set slightly askew. She pushed against it, triggering sounds of gears behind the wall and movement of a large stone. It revealed a narrow passageway on the other side.

The passageway was so narrow they could only move sideways through it. Climbing five or six levels up, they finally entered a room in which there was nothing more than a piece of lumber jutting out from the wall. Naturally, she pushed against it until it was flush with the wall, and then a section of the wall pivoted just enough to squeeze through to the other side. On the other side was a decadent parlor.

The pivoted section of wall on the parlor's side was a beautiful bookcase. Abigail took Pierce's hand and pulled him away. Then, the bookshelf realigned with the wall, concealing the room behind it. Abigail moved towards a door and turned to her brother, who had turned back to the bookcase.

"Come, Brother."

A book entitled *Metamorphoseon* caught his eye. It was identical to the one he had awarded Meghan Clark after she had won the horserace. Before he could touch it, though, he heard the sounds of a door latch and a boy's voice.

"Hello?" The boy had opened the door and was smiling up at Abigail.

Abigail shook her head at Pierce, whose attention moved to the boy. "He is not an orphan," said Abigail.

"Identify yourselves," commanded the boy.

"Come, Brother, we must leave," said Abigail.

"Not without him," said Pierce, eyes steadily affixed on the boy's starry eyes.

Abigail approached her brother. "He was born here. He and his parents live here. This is their home."

"He will be in danger if we leave him," retorted Pierce.

"He will not be harmed. Trust me. This family is a front. Without them, the clan has no home. His mother is one of us, ordered to keep her husband and son alive and oblivious."

"How?"

"No time to explain." Abigail turned to the boy. "Master Jonathan, go to your father."

As if satisfied just to be noticed, the boy obeyed, turning and running along.

"Mind bending," murmured Abigail. "Countess Gerda was turned shortly after giving birth to Jonathan. Her husband, the count, holds title to this property. Because Gerda has become so efficient at mind bending, she can wipe clean their memories on a daily basis and create a blissful life for them here. It is essential that the count remain human so that he may conduct business away from the castle, but never far from his countess, Gerda."

She took hold of Pierce's wrist and pulled him through the sunroom to the entrance door. She paused and listened for anybody that might be standing guard in the corridor outside. Relieved to find no one, they continued towards the girls' servants' chamber two floors down.

When they arrived at the girls' bedchamber, the door was wide open, and Pierce smelled no humans. He shook his head.

They moved on to the boys' bedchambers one floor down. Sensing humans inside, they cautiously entered the room and stopped to listen. Two girls and a boy were crouching behind an overturned bed.

"Children, do not be afraid," said Abigail softly.

The children trembled and huddled closer as if to appear smaller or to disappear entirely.

Abigail turned to Pierce for help.

"Children," said Pierce in a strained but disarming voice. "Do you know a boy called Cedric Martens? Do you know a girl called Lily?" He waited for a response that did not come.

"Do you know Jacob?" added Abigail.

"They are all waiting for you outside the castle," said Pierce. "We will take you to them."

One of the girls no older than nine years of age stood up. "I know Lily."

"What is your name?" asked Pierce.

She wilted back down and leaned against another girl of the same age.

"What is your name?" said Abigail

The other girl spoke up. "She is Anna. I am Katarina."

"I am Abigail and this is my brother, Pierce. We are here to protect you. Please, come with us."

Whether they believed the adults or simply gave in to authority, the children stood up and joined Abigail and Pierce.

"Everybody must stay close," said Pierce. "When we walk, you walk. When we run, you run. When we stop, you stop. Yes?"

The children nodded.

Anna waved at Pierce to come closer. He knelt to her. She

reached out to touch his neck, and pulled back. "Does it hurt?" asked the girl.

"Yes, Anna," said Pierce, "but it will heal." Pierce stood up and took her hand.

"This way," said Abigail. She led them down a stairwell in the tower. The sounds of skirmishing grew louder as they descended to the ground floor. They ran through a corridor towards the kitchen and stopped beside a column. The hallway leading to the courtyard was just fifty paces away. She nodded and they started towards the hallway just as two Roman guards came through it. The guards drew their weapons. Abigail herded the children away as Pierce prepared to fight them.

Pierce imagined the peril. Defending himself was one thing, but defending three young children and his sister was another entirely. It overwhelmed him. He lost focus. A flashback of being beaten with wooden clubs reminded him of how it all came to be. Hatred killed him. Love resurrected him. Vengeance betrayed him. Humanity delivered him.

It was over in two blinks of an eye. Pierce watched in fascination as his enemy's flesh putrefied and dried on their bones. He peeked through the side door and saw enemy soldiers waiting outside. He turned and met up with Abigail to discuss another way out.

76 - DOMITIAN

Three of Count Marcel's guards were fighting several of Domitian's Romans in the main hall when Abigail, Pierce, and the children arrived at the steps to the catacombs. As three soldiers came up the stairs, Pierce ushered the children and Abigail behind a pillar.

"The back door," whispered Abigail. Before they could move, more soldiers approached from that direction.

"We have no choice but to fight our way out," said Pierce.

"Marcel's army will enter through the courtyard," said Abigail.

"Then we will go through the front door to meet them."

Abigail nodded.

Pierce stepped out and swiftly moved forward to engage the enemy. He caught them by surprise, shoving two down the stairs and vanquishing one. Abigail ushered the children towards the massive entry doors. Before they reached them, a voice caused Abigail to freeze.

"Headmistress Abigail!" shouted Domitian from the top of a flight of stairs. Behind him were six soldiers. Domitian's eyebrow rose when he saw the children and Pierce. "Where are you going with those?"

Abigail glanced at Pierce.

Domitian took a step and paused. "Are you freeing them?"

"I am," said Abigail.

Domitian took another step, shook his head, and clicked his tongue. "Countess Marie will be displeased."

"Countess Marie is dead," replied Abigail.

Domitian paused for a moment to process the news and then shook his head. "Liar!" He shouted.

"She speaks the truth," hollered Pierce.

Domitian's eyes remained focused on Abigail. "Who is that?"

"That is my brother, Pierce van Fleming of England."

Just then, enemy soldiers flowed in from all sides.

"Run," shouted Pierce as he led Abigail and the children through the foyer and out into the courtyard with a dozen of Domitian's men behind them.

77 - SACRIFICE AND BETRAYAL

In the courtyard, Pierce dropped back to give Abigail and the children more time to flee. He lifted his swords, deflected two arrows, and prepared to fight. But the unexpected happened. Domitian ordered his men to stand down. Pierce saw that Domitian's eyes were distracted. Behind Pierce were horses and men entering through the gates into the courtyard. Suddenly, he was standing between Domitian and Count Marcel, who was riding his horse to the front of the formation.

Marcel nodded at Pierce to fall back. As Pierce cautiously moved towards the gate, he saw Abigail waving for him to join her. Outside the gates, Abigail pulled Pierce aside and grabbed his face with both hands. Pierce winced.

"Your neck will be fully healed by the morrow," said Abigail, "as the moon is full tonight." She noticed Gandt approaching.

As he rode past them, he tossed a leather bag to her and saluted Pierce.

"This is yours," said Abigail, handing Pierce the bag. "Go to Oostende and book passage to the New World."

"No. I have decided to stay and fight," said Pierce.

She glanced at the children standing nearby. "Nay, you cannot stay. Deliver the orphans to Cedric and leave straight away." Abigail's eyes glazed with sadness. She turned away. "I must go."

"Wait," said Pierce. "You are the only family I have, and I am a strong fighter. I can fire bolts of lightning from my hands, remember?"

Her smile imparted a sadness that Pierce had not seen since he had left for England to start a new life as a van Fleming.

"You must go, for you *are* the chosen one, Brother—not to rule this clan but to guard our heritage. You are the last of our kind, of our family. Someday soon, you will understand. Fare thee well."

Domitian leaned on his sword and gazed at Count Marcel sitting tall in the saddle of his charmed black steed. Over its haunches draped the count's cape, bearing the Flemish coat of arms.

"Domitian," said Marcel in a commanding growl. "It is folly to cross swords with me. Stand down. Let us discuss this deplorable misunderstanding."

Domitian's insolence manifested into a defiant grin as he watched Abigail find her place beside the count. Then he saw Sir Michael, sitting on his horse directly behind them.

"All the count's horses and all the count's men," muttered Domitian to himself as his eyes finally returned to Marcel. "The legendary Count Marcel de Vos...! Your stature, your style, your fine stallion with eyes aglow, reminds me of how I admired the legend of you. For a brief moment, I caught a glimpse of that virile warrior of my imagination, but then you opened your mouth and spoke like the feeble-minded buffoon that you are. Deplorable misunderstanding?" Domitian's expression turned sour. "Had you attended the council meeting, there would be no *misunderstanding!* Had you abdicated your chair, none of this would have had to happen," Domitian glanced over at his men. "Just look at them, exhausted, outnumbered two to one by your Prussian reinforcements." His expression turned desperate. "Our only hope, it appears, is to surrender and beg for mercy. I believe that is what Lady Abigail implied as she ushered away her *brother,* Pierce van Fleming of England!"

Domitian noticed a glint of surprise in Marcel's eyes. "Oh, dear me, had she not told you?" Domitian lifted his sword and rested it against his shoulder. "Funny coincidence, is it not, how Abigail's blood *brother* matches so perfectly the oracle's description of the chosen one?"

Arrogance filled Domitian's face. "Sooner or later, the seductress makes fools of us all. When was the last time you saw Lady Abigail and the oracle, Elida, together?"

"Enough!" said Marcel. "Unrelated observations do not lighten the crown of treachery upon your head, Domitian."

Domitian glowered. "I think you meant to say the crown of accession. Step down now, old man, and I shall spare your life. Otherwise, the extent of your ignorance and arrogance shall be revealed to all by your death."

Marcel unsheathed his sword and signaled his men to ready their weapons at which time Sir Michael lifted a javelin and hurled it with all his strength into Marcel's back, impaling his heart.

Instantly, the skin on Marcel's face began to wrinkle and darken as he twisted to look at his most trusted advisor turned traitor.

Sir Michael sat expressionless as he watched his master wither and crumble into a heap of dusty bones at Abigail's feet.

Abigail kneeled down to touch the remains of her lover and master.

"Get up," ordered Sir Michael to Abigail.

Abigail tilted her head to see Michael looking down on her from his horse.

"Why, Sir Michael?" whimpered Abigail as she rose. "Why? He loved you, as a father loves a son."

"*You* are why," muttered Michael. "You murdered the oracle to promote a fool's prophecy. Then, you made *him* the fool."

"*You* are the fool," said Abigail. "Just last night Marcel had chosen you to succeed him. See how long Domitian's trust in you will last!"

"Silence!" shouted Domitian. "Lock up that woman!" Domitian then sheathed his sword and took a step towards the Prussians. "My brave and honorable brethren, you have traveled far to bear witness to the defeat of Count Marcel Marc de Vos. I am indebted to you, and to your esteemed clan master, to whom I shall deliver payment as promised." A stagnant silence fell across the courtyard as Domitian waited patiently for their validation. Then, as Abigail was taken into the castle, all kneeled to recognize the new Clan Master,

Domitian Augustus de' Medici.

78 - THE AFTERMATH

Before the color of day, Cedric Martens roused Lily. He had stood guard over the children in the forest, including three more orphans who seemingly stumbled upon them. It was Pierce who delivered them. Cedric wanted to see Pierce once more, but knew in his heart that a new chapter was beginning and van Fleming was not to be in it.

Lily snuggled to him. "You must be tired," she whispered into his ear.

Cedric lifted a small branch and poked Jacob until he woke up. "Wake the others," said Cedric to Lily. "We must go."

In Oostende, Pierce sat on his hotel bed with the bag he had received from Abigail and started going through its contents: gloves, full change of clothes, and four plump bags of gold coins. He would waste no time in booking passage to Virginia.

In the afternoon, the children finally entered Brussels. Cedric led them to an inn and booked three rooms, one to share with Jacob, one for the three children, and one for Lily. As Marie's former personal attendant, Cedric had become comfortable and competent in a big city, knowing what to look for, where to go, and how to go get whatever he needed. That afternoon, he bought everyone hot baths, new clothes, and food to eat. By sundown, they had settled into their rooms for the night.

In what used to be Count Marie's bedchamber, Abigail was made to lie upon a wooden rack, her wrists and ankles securely tied with rope that was wound through rollers. The rack was one of several torturing devices that Marie had salvaged from the castle's former dungeon-turned-counting chamber. She had regularly lain upon it to nap.

Sir Michael inspected Abigail's bindings and then her exquisite form. Even under threat of pain and death, she exuded beauty and grace. She turned her face away when he tried to touch it. His eyes relished her mystic beauty. Yet, no amount of lust for her was going to influence him. He was going to separate her limbs from her body if needed to get what he wanted.

"Lady Abigail," said Michael softly. "Lord Domitian requires information and has asked me to extract it from you. Unless you provide it freely, I am going to torture it out of you. We can bypass this distasteful process if you simply tell me what I need to know. So please answer these questions. Where is your brother, Pierce van Fleming, and where is he going?"

Abigail closed her eyes and ignored him.

"Lord Domitian's final request is quite revealing, even to me. The late countess had told him that you are a necromancer. That the countess had intended for you to resurrect her if needed. Is that true? Do you have powers to resurrect the dead? Your silence will not save your friends, and it certainly will not save you." Michael placed his hand on the crank and turned it, tightening the tension just enough to open Abigail's eyes. "How attractive or useful might you be without arms and legs? Tell you what, wait here while I fetch Gerda. Perhaps she can mind-bend the answers out of you." Sir Michael left Abigail alone in the bedchamber.

On the outskirts of Oostende, an old woman saw Pierce through a broken window and waved him into her home.

"Doctor... The pain," whimpered the old woman.

Pierce took her hand. She was feverish and terminally ill.

"Please, doctor."

"I am not a doctor," said Pierce.

She squeezed his hand and cringed. "Bleed me of this curse."

Pierce placed his other hand on her forehead and sensed the disease. Focusing on her mind, he attempted to isolate her fondest memories, something he had not yet tried.

"What is your name?" he asked.

"Eva."

"Eva. Think of happier times." He searched her thoughts and eased her into a hypnotic state. As a result, her breathing slowed and her face relaxed. "How do you feel now?"

She smiled and breathed steadily.

"Where is your family?" asked Pierce.

"In heaven," whispered the old woman.

"Do you want to be with them?"

The woman smiled and nodded.

"Well then, close your eyes."

After she closed her eyes, Pierce lifted her arm to his mouth, bit into a vein, and bled her of her curse. When he was done, Pierce covered the woman's body with a blanket and left for port.

He boarded the merchant ship Balcluthe on a full stomach, but even the fullest stomach would not sustain him for the two-month voyage. He would have to feed again, unless he slept the entire way to Virginia. It was possible. Count Marcel had told him that it was. *When you are very old, you learn to sleep as I do, deeply and for extended intervals—weeks sometimes months.* Aside from feeding on the crew, or on rodents if he found any, there was no other option. Marcel's technique was worth a try.

Countess Gerda entered the bedchamber, followed by Sir Michael.

"Lady Abigail," said Michael as he approached the rack, "Countess Gerda is here to see you. As you know, her ability to bend the mind is unsurpassed. Your cooperation is expected."

The clanging and rasping of gears and rollers turning, and the strum of rope tensioning, jolted Abigail's eyes and mouth open.

Michael turned to Gerda and nodded.

Gerda placed her hand on Abigail's forehead and lowered her chin in concentration. "Where is Pierce van Fleming?" said the mind bender. "Please, Lady Abigail, tell me."

Michael cranked the roller three times more. The tension lifted Abigail's body off the rack.

Gerda turned to Michael. "She is trying to block me."

Michael brushed Gerda aside and brought his face to Abigail's.

"Do not think for a moment that Gerda's bedside manner or your feeble attempts to protect your mind will save you. Cooperate or I shall turn this machine until your torso is all that defines your body. Do you understand?" Michael took hold of the crank handle again.

Gerda placed her hand on Abigail's head. After a minute of silence, Michael turned the crank three clicks more. Abigail cried out as joints and ligaments began popping and snapping loose. Gerda turned to Michael with excitement.

"I know who killed Countess Marie de Vos," whispered Gerda with a shocked expression.

"Tell me."

"In the presence of Headmistress Abigail and Mister van Fleming, the boy servant, Cedric Martens of Linder, beheaded her with his sword. I do not understand... The boy fled with five other orphans to Brussels."

Michael grinned. "Well done. And what of Pierce van Fleming?"

"Nothing yet," said Gerda.

Sir Michael was let into Count Marcel's former chambers to find Domitian playing the harpsichord. The room was completely redecorated. The display of armor and weapons had been removed. The chamber appeared more like a music room, with a collection of lyre and guitars, the harpsichord, and a rectangular piano. Michael waited patiently as Domitian continued playing.

"Michael, what news do you bring?" asked Domitian, his body swaying to the music.

"I bring news of the boy, Cedric Martens, Milord."

Domitian stopped and turned to Michael. "Yes?"

"Gerda has confirmed the boy servant, Cedric Martens of Linder, is guilty of murdering Countess Marie—

"How?"

"The boy beheaded her with his sword."

"Impossible! Unless she was asleep, how can a boy slay someone as powerful as the countess?"

"I trust Gerda's findings. Do you as well?"

With a troubled expression, Domitian nodded. "What more?"

"He and five other servants fled to Brussels on foot."

Domitian's canines elongated and his face twisted with vengeance in his eyes. "I want Cedric Martens alive and unharmed. I have plans for him—big plans. Has Abigail revealed the secrets of necromancy? Do you think we can extract enough information from her so that some other stinking witch will perform it? I want to resurrect my love. I just need to know how. She spoke of Abigail's knowledge of necromancy, and I must have it."

"I expect to have answers in short order, Milord."

"Good, and where is that false prophet, Pierce van Fleming? I want him alive and unharmed, too. I wish to kill him myself. The chosen one, indeed!"

"Yes, Milord."

"After Abigail has vomited her secrets, I want her limbs torn from her body, her remains dipped in oil, tossed in a hole in the ground, and burned and buried. Is that clear?"

"Yes, Milord."

Domitian turned to the keyboard and cracked his neck to release tension. When his fangs finally receded, he said, "Count Marcel once explained that pleasures fade over time. Blood becomes less satisfying, the hunt less stimulating, the power less empowering—immortality and tedium becoming one in the same." Domitian started to play the harpsichord again then stopped to add, "I for one do not believe any of that idiocy. Thank you, Sir Michael, for silencing the old fool."

79 - MUCH TO DO ABOUT EVERYTHING

In his room the next morning, Cedric was up and dressed, considering his next move. As he stood at the window, gazing out at the city his mother had once visited worry grew into a barrage of unanswered questions. Was Brussels far enough away from the castle? Should they leave? Where would they go? To the New World, to the north, to the east?

Jacob slumped down in a chair. "What happened to us?" he asked.

"What do you mean?" said Cedric, his breath clinging to the cold window.

Jacob clenched his teeth and shook his head in despair. "I saw horrible things, impossible things..."

"Forget them."

"Why do I feel so miserable?"

Cedric turned and saw tears forming in Jacob's bloodshot eyes. Cedric was not miserable. He was motivated by will to survive and fight for a life he had yet to live. He made good on his promise to his mother—at least partially. He still had to make a life for himself and hopefully for Lily.

"There is nothing wrong with feeling miserable every now and again, Jacob," said Cedric. "But we must not let the miseries of this world defeat us." Cedric went to the door. "Come, we have much to do."

Sir Michael entered the bedchamber to find Gerda stroking Abigail's hair, and Abigail still in one piece. Gerda lifted her eyes to Michael.

"Well?" said Michael as he closed the door.

"I have your answers and more, much more," said Gerda. She quickly took Michael aside and whispered into his ear. "Pierce van Fleming is in Oostende, booking passage to the New World."

"Continue," said Michael.

"Her mother was the necromancer. Abigail was her apprentice. However, her mother was stoned to death before Abigail finished her training. Still, she resurrected a dog."

"A dog?"

"Yes and successfully."

"What else?"

"Her brother was a revenant when Countess Marie turned him, resurrected by his mother a year following his untimely death."

"Interesting... How did Mister Fleming die?"

"At twelve years of age, he was murdered by twin brothers—punishment for fancying their sister."

"How entertaining..."

"I discovered something far more entertaining than that, Sir Michael, something of a greater value."

"If it is of such value, why not keep it to yourself?"

"Sir Michael, the information would go to waste on me as I am not the strategist that you obviously are."

Michael smiled in agreement with Gerda's explanation. "What is it then?"

"Abigail is no ordinary witch. She descends from the house of Perseus, an ancient family harking back to the time of myth. I saw something else, something hidden deep within her mind: a satchel, wherein godly powers are contained."

"Godly powers?" Michael shook his head at the notion. "It is a trick. She is cunning." He glanced over at her beautiful form on the rack. "I admire her for that."

"I am not so easily tricked," exclaimed Gerda. "False images never hold their shape for long. The satchel appeared as solid as the saddle on your horse. Besides, she is starving and too weak to hide the truth from me. I know her most intimate thoughts and regrets—being responsible for the stoning of her mother; partaking in the countess's deeds and the resulting guilt that eats at her shriveled soul to this day; deceiving her brother, causing him unbearable anguish; and her hatred of you for betraying her lover—"

"Enough! If she hates me so and possesses such powers, then why has she not used them to free herself and to destroy me? Why lay there and suffer?"

"She has never studied the contents of the satchel and is not by nature a killer. More importantly, she protects her brother Pierce van Fleming. She—like him—finds our kind to be uncivilized, unworthy, and deceitful."

"Deceitful?" spat Michael. "She is one to talk after deceiving her own family." He pinched his chin and stared at Abigail. "Inside that woman is the key, the key to unlocking supernatural powers." He placed his hands on Gerda's shoulders. "I must have it, the satchel and everything in it. Tell me how."

"She has the ability to conjure the satchel," said Gerda. "Perhaps you can take it while it is in solid form. She is weak and easily manipulated."

"Yes, yes, I will convince her to give it to me." He pulled the woman close and whispered in her ear. "You have done well, Gerda. With such power, nothing can stop us. I shall elevate you, second only to me."

"I only wish to serve, Sir. I have no desire to be elevated."

Michael smiled at her. "Then, serve me. Denounce your loyalty to Domitian and pledge your loyalty to me."

Without hesitation, Gerda stepped back and kneeled. "In the name of Hades, ruler of the underworld, I swear my loyalty and life to thee, Sir Michael."

"And Domitian?"

"He is no longer my master." Gerda rose to her feet and smiled admiringly at Michael. "What is your plan, Master?"

Michael's lips curled with excitement. "Establish an empire under which humans are cultivated like crops, a world in which these rat-infested clans and insular troglodytes will have no place."

"What will you do to Domitian?"

"He and his ridiculous ideas of necromancy will be destroyed. All in this castle will be destroyed. You and I will leave this place and establish a new order in the New World. Bring the human Count and his son to me. If I cannot convince Abigail to conjure the satchel, perhaps the smell of fresh human blood will entice her. Go now."

After Gerda left the room, Michael went to Abigail. He gazed at her beauty, imagining how delicious she was when she was human. "My dear lady, you are far more precious to me than I had ever known you to be. Thank you for your cooperation. You need not worry for your brother. His whereabouts have not been shared with Domitian—as yet.

"And the children?" said Abigail.

"Too late for them. Domitian's men are hunting them as we speak. I believe he wants to feed them to Countess Marie de Vos after you raise her from the dead." Michael retrieved a chair and red silk bed linen and brought them to the rack. He covered Abigail with the linen and sat down. "I do not fancy torture," said Michael, "never have. Though it is undeniably a reliable means of persuasion, it is also barbaric and wasteful, all the terrible things we ought to despise." He crossed his legs and tilted his head. "Tell me, how powerful really is the magic contained in the satchel, and why have you not used it?"

"Such magic destroyed my family. I fear it. It is too powerful and unpredictable. It is as blinding as the sun and as dark as chaos. Not just anyone can harness such power and control it."

Michael liked what he heard and saw that Abigail was cringing with hunger.

"I know you want it," said Abigail.

"Yes," whispered Michael.

"I will agree to give the satchel to you. However, you must ensure my brother's safety."

"Agreed," said Michael.

"Agreed," whispered Abigail.

Michael stood up. "Very well, then. Conjure it."

"Sir Michael, the satchel is more than just a container of magic. It lives, it knows, it must accept its new guardian. It must accept *you*."

"Convince it to accept me! Do it for your brother's sake."

Abigail closed her eyes and began to whisper something in Latin so softly and quickly that Michael could not understand it. The image of a satchel began to form over her chest, rotating slowly, shimmering like a star. Michael's hands passed through it like smoke. Then, the image disappeared.

Michael's teeth and hands clenched. "What happened? Where is it?"

"I am too weak," whimpered Abigail.

"I grow tired of your tricks. Conjure the satchel. Do it!" When she failed to respond, Michael tightened the ropes until she screamed.

80 - DO NOT DISTURB

After boarding the ship, Pierce went three decks below to his assigned berth. It was nothing more than a canvas hammock suspended between wooden posts on the starboard hull behind the foremast. A footlocker rested beneath the hammock, and a porthole window beside the hammock allowed for daylight reading. The crew's hammocks were stacked in pairs on both sides. In the center of the deck was a large table with a scuttlebutt secured to the foremast, and an oil lantern secured tightly to a rope suspended over the table.

He took off his cloak and kerchief and placed them on his hammock. Then he placed his leather bag inside the footlocker and draped his cloak and kerchief over the bag. He closed the locker lid, eased into his hammock, and gazed out the porthole, determining how best to practice Marcel's deep sleep technique.

Marcel had described hibernation as two of three distinct planes interconnected by narrow passageways. Normal sleep occurs in the first plane, the white plane. Hibernation occurs in the second plane, the black plane. The third plane was to be avoided, for it led to the realm of chaos and no return.

To reach the black plane one must first be asleep and the mind must be clear of all thoughts but one—focused only on the narrow passage between the white and black planes. One must then go through the passageway to enter the black plane. Once inside, there are no sensations, no dreams, just a faint acknowledgement of the passageway connecting the planes.

Pierce tried to clear his mind. He struggled not to think about his life before Manchester, his life in Manchester, the love that might have been with Meghan Clark, or Domitian's rage and Marie's fingers boring into his neck. But it was difficult, and the smell of the mariners' blood was every bit distracting.

When they entered the berth, they did so indiscreetly, stomping, laughing, shouting, uncorking a bottle of wine. They spoke excitedly of a family of four who had booked a stateroom on the forward deck. According to them, the married couple's twin daughters were quite agreeable as the sailors shared their explicit fantasies of them. Pierce could not relax with braying sailors making gossip. Pierce rolled out of his hammock and went up to the main deck for a look around.

The ship's commander, Master Crowley, stood beside his chief mate. Crowley was a medium sized man, round spectacles on his nose, and a gray beard so lengthy it touched his indigo blue frockcoat. With hands clasped behind their backs, they appeared statuesque, scrutinizing the rigging with squinting eyes.

The ship was old but well maintained, with many of its appurtenances refurbished. Pierce leaned over the starboard rail and noticed a row of battened gun ports. He surmised that Balcluthe was formerly a warship, and wondered if she was still armed. It was not uncommon for merchant ships navigating hostile waters to be fortified with cannons.

Pierce approached Master Crowley.

"Mister van Fleming," said Crowley, distracted by mariners setting the sails. "I hope your accommodations are satisfactory."

"Quite," said Pierce. "However, I do have one request, Commander."

Crowley turned his eyes to Pierce.

Pierce lifted a cold coin from his waistcoat pocket and placed it in Crowley's hand. "This is consideration for your assurance."

Crowley inspected the coin. "Assurance?"

"I trust you will let no man disturb my sleep. You see, I intend to sleep throughout the entire voyage."

Crowley felt the weight of the coin and then slipped it into his frockcoat pocket. "Of course, Mister van Fleming. I will see to it that you are not disturbed. However, such a request is hardly necessary. My crew is not in the habit of disturbing passengers. It is prohibited."

"Yes, of course, however, I may appear lifeless because I shall not stir or wake for many days and weeks." Crowley's face turned serious when Pierce placed his hand on his shoulder and planted the concept into the commander's mind. "You and your men must not be alarmed. Sleeping without waking for many weeks is unusual but not impossible," said Pierce.

Entranced, Crowley responded in monotone, "Indeed, it is."

"Please inform your men of my unusual condition and order them not to disturb me or to allow others to disturb me."

"I will, sir."

"And commander, I shall pay another gold coin upon arrival provided no one disturbs me throughout this voyage." Pierce removed his hand and stepped back.

Crowley blinked a few times and smiled. "Rest assured that neither I nor my men will disturb your extended sleep. Question: in the event of an emergency, what then?"

"Wake me only in the event of fire or sinking, Commander."

"Very good, sir."

"Thank you, Commander. Pleasant voyage." Pierce moved away from the commander and noticed a middle-aged man standing a few paces aft. His features were slender and pale. Something about him looked foreign—perhaps the way he stood or his black-on-black fashion. The man smiled at Pierce and tipped his hat. Pierce responded in kind and then noticed the family of four about which the mariners had been gossiping. The parent's twin daughters dressed in wool cloaks over silk gowns with long white gloves were even more beautiful than the sailors had described them to be. They walked the main deck, arms locked, listening to their father. As he lectured on about seafaring, the girls' eyes strayed from one mariner to another.

After a once-around the deck, Pierce returned to his berth.

It was not long before the pale gentleman in black joined him. He came to Pierce and extended his hand. "How do you do, sir? My name is Elijah. Elijah Scott."

Pierce shook his hand. "How do you do, Mister Scott? Pierce

van Fleming."

"English?" asked Elijah.

"Yes."

"I was born in Kentucky but currently reside in Virginia with my wife Esther." The American removed a pewter flask from his waistcoat and extracted the cork with his teeth. "Care to drink, Mister van Fleming?" He handed the flask to Pierce.

"Corn whiskey aged in American oak?" asked Pierce, having smelled the contents.

"Why, mister van Fleming, I believe you have a nose for the finer things in life."

Pierce took a sip and handed the flask back.

Elijah leaned forward and murmured, "I've got French oak onboard this ship. I do not believe anyone has ever aged corn whiskey in French wood."

Pierce thought American oak was better suited for American whiskey but made no comment. It was not important. Sleeping throughout the voyage and preventing the crew from disturbing him was.

Elijah drank some more and offered the flask again.

"No, thank you. I am quite tired and expect to sleep the entire voyage."

Elijah chuckled and quipped, "Whiskey is my solution to the boredom of transatlantic seafaring."

Pierce placed his hand on Elijah's shoulder and stared intensely into his pale blue eyes. The man's face suddenly relaxed as he fell into a trance "Mister Scott, I have a condition which causes me to sleep for many weeks without waking. Do you understand?"

Elijah nodded, eyes unblinking, "You sleep like a bear in winter."

"Yes, Mister Scott. I hibernate, and you shall not be alarmed by it."

"I shall not be alarmed."

"You shall not disturb me."

"I shall not disturb you."

"Also, Mister Scott, you shall not allow others to disturb me. Yes?"

"Yes. You must not be disturbed."

"Thank you, Mister Scott." Pierce released him and stepped back.

Elijah blinked a few times and then stroked his beard with a puzzled look. He shrugged his shoulders and chuckled. "May the ship rock you like a cradle and conjure pleasant dreams, Mister van Fleming." Strangely convinced that Pierce possessed the incredible ability to hibernate like a bear, Elijah tipped his hat and returned to the main deck.

81 - THE GREATER GOOD

At the inn where they were lodging, Cedric, Lily, and Jacob quietly discussed their next move while the younger children chatted amongst themselves at the far end of the dinner table. Incensed with paranoia, Cedric's eyes constantly swept the room for signs of trouble.

"We cannot stay in Brussels," said Cedric. "It is not safe here."

"Are they pursuing us?" whispered Jacob.

"Not us, *me*. They are pursuing me. Because you are with me, you are in danger." He glanced over at the youngsters and then at Jacob. "I have given considerable thought to everyone's safety and—"

"No," said Lily before Cedric could finish. "I know what you are thinking. You want to leave us."

Cedric took her hand in his. "They are coming for me—"

"How can you be so certain?" asked Lily.

Cedric would not tell them of his journey to England with Countess Marie, of Pierce van Fleming and why he had slain the countess. He wanted to forget all of that, never to discuss it again.

"When you left the castle," said Lily, "I longed for you, for your return. Even when it felt as if God had abandoned me and all hope was lost, I knew in my heart that you would come. And you did."

"We go where you go," said Jacob, looking at Lily to agree.

She nodded. "Where will we go?"

"The New World?" asked Jacob.

Cedric yearned to be with Lily and to keep his friend Jacob close, but the monsters were coming, and they were cunning, fast, and merciless. They would kill them all if he stayed.

"I cannot allow it," murmured Cedric.

Lily let go of Cedric's hand and looked around the room. When she finally locked eyes with him again, she took on a serious tenor that reminded Cedric of his mother.

"We saw the monsters, too," said Lily. "We lived in constant peril and fear. The countess would have surely killed us had you and Headmistress Abigail not come. I still do not understand it—why the headmistress helped you, but I am, for one, grateful. You risked your life for me, and I will do the same for you. I am not afraid. I will die for you if that is my destiny."

"I wish to be with you, too, um, for different reasons, obviously—friendship and adventure reasons," mumbled Jacob.

It was a poignant moment, a moment of alliances and pledges among friends, but no one smiled. The paranoia and concern hung like a raincloud over them as they glanced over at the three youngsters, playing quietly, oblivious to the seriousness of their guardians' decisions.

"What of them?" whispered Jacob.

"We will think of something," said Cedric.

Three vampires walking the streets of Brussels knew what Cedric looked like. With five orphans tagging along with him, he should be easy to spot. As they went along, they checked free shelters, such as abandoned hovels, alleys, and under bridges. They were not aware of the wealth Cedric had received, and thus failed to check the inns. But as they circled round the city and inwards towards its center, they were getting closer and closer to the children.

In the morning, Cedric, Lily, and Jacob took the three youngsters to a sizable abbey nearby. Cedric asked Lily and Jacob to wait outside as he led the children through a vestibule where Cedric saw two nuns, one nearly thirty years of age and the other much older.

"Good day, Mother Abbess," said Cedric to the eldest nun.

"Good day," said the abbess.

"I am Cedric Martens."

"I am Abbess Maria Theresa, and this is Sister Claudia Dubois."

"Please to make your acquaintances." Cedric turned to the children. "These are...my nieces, and this is my nephew, all nine years of age."

The abbess tilted her head. "How may we help you, Mister Martens?"

"I would like to speak privately, if I may," said Cedric to the abbess.

The abbess observed him with her pale eyes, as faint sounds of other children drifted through the halls. Cedric desperately searched for something to say or do to gain an audience with her. He lifted his gold cross between his hands. "Please, Mother Abbess, only a word."

The abbess turned to the sister and nodded.

Cedric turned to the children and said, "Please go with Sister Claudia. I will not be long."

The sister smiled at the children and took Anna's hand. "Come, children. Let us find something delicious to eat. You must be very hungry."

The abbess led Cedric into a room with modest furnishings and said, "Are you of our faith, Mister Martens?"

"I am," said Cedric.

"Then I trust you shall speak the truth."

Cedric lowered his head and nodded. "Please forgive me, Abbess Maria, for I am no uncle to those children, though I feel for them as if they were my own blood."

"I thought so," said the abbess. "They are orphans, then?"

"Yes."

"What do you wish to discuss?"

"Abbess Maria, I wish to discuss these children. I want them to be safe, to be treated with kindness, to learn, to become pious citizens, your future parishioners. Will you please shelter them?"

She turned to Cedric. "Many orphans seek shelter here. We do our best to accommodate them all. However, certain realities cannot be ignored, such as expenses. We have more orphans than beds. We survive mostly on the generosity of our parishioners, and there is barely enough money to feed and clothe the children we already shelter. No, Mister Martens, I am afraid we cannot afford to house anymore orphans at this time."

Cedric retrieved four gold coins from his money purse. "Abbess Maria, I will buy as many beds as needed."

The abbess stared at the money. "If you are so wealthy, why not raise them yourself?"

Cedric wanted to avoid that part of the truth, but he confessed some of the sordid story. When he was finished, an hour had passed and they were both sitting in chairs in the warmth of a fire.

"The castle from whence you came...was it Vos Castle?" whispered the abbess as if the very utterance was sacrilegious.

Cedric nodded.

"I have heard of it and of such stories. Most people have. They are called fairytales: vampires, witches, the occasional elf or troll in the forest."

Cedric smiled. "Indeed, the stories are unbelievable, but one thing is as true as you and I sitting here now. The orphans in the castle are severely mistreated."

Abbess Maria noticed Sister Claudia standing in the doorway.

"Sister, Mister Martens' three children will stay with us."

"That is good news," said Sister Claudia with a surprised, but pleased expression. "They wish to see Mister Martens."

"Is there anything more you need?" asked Cedric of the abbess.

"That is all, Mister Martens. Thank you for your generous donation. Your children will be well cared for here."

"Thank you, Abbess Maria. I will speak to them now and be on my way," said Cedric.

In a room not far down from the corridor sat all three children at a table on which a tray of cheese and fruit that had been mostly picked over rested between cups of water. Cedric sat down next to Anna, who smiled at Cedric in a way that reminded him of his little sister.

"When are we leaving?" asked Anna, resting her head against Cedric's arm.

Cedric had only known the children for a few days, but had become profoundly attached to them, concerned for them, and saddened to leave them behind.

"This is your new home, Anna." He imparted glances to the others and smiled as brightly as he could as he took a piece of cheese. "Is this not a beautiful monastery? You are sure to make many friends here."

"Are you going to stay with us?" asked the boy, who was normally the silent one.

"I cannot," said Cedric, "but I will come visit you."

"Why can we not live with you?" asked Anna.

Cedric placed his hand on her slender back and rubbed it gently. "The truth is, I am leaving."

"Where to?" asked the other girl.

"To places far, far away."

"Will Jacob and Lily go with you?" asked Anna.

"Yes, Anna, and when we return, we shall bring exotic treasures for all of you."

"I want to go with you," said the boy.

"I need you to look after your sisters here at the abbey," said Cedric. "If you are not here, then there will be no one to return to. Do you understand?"

The children sat in confounded silence.

"Do you trust me?" asked Cedric, his eyes moving from one child to another.

"Yes," said Anna.

"Then please do as I ask. Wait for me here with Sister Claudia. Yes?"

"Only if you promise to come see me tomorrow," said Anna.

Cedric intended on leaving Brussels that morning. His gut told him of monsters lurking in the city. His heart told him to consider the children. He gazed into their tearing eyes and swallowed dryly.

"I promise," Cedric said, standing up from the table. The children rushed to him, embracing him and dampening his clothes with their tears. Cedric put his arms round them and struggled not to weep.

82 - PURSUIT OF POWER

Sir Michael leaned in to examine Abigail's face. She was showing telltale signs of starvation: fading beauty, quailing, and wincing. He placed his hand on her cold forehead and entered her mind. He was surprised how easy it was. He moved through a winding tunnel of her oldest recollections towards her most recent ones. At the end of the tunnel he saw a clearing in the center of a great forest. In the clearing was a gnarled little tree. Resting at the base of its trunk was a leather satchel.

As Michael approached it, the tree began glowing in brilliant shades of silver and copper, and suspended horizontally above the tree was a man, hovering face up. Michael could not identify him as he could not see his face, and as he approached the satchel, it moved away from him. Michael pursued the satchel round the tree until it suddenly lifted upwards directly over the hovering man's chest.

Michael could only watch as the satchel, the man, and the odd tree faded into darkness. Michael staggered back into the chamber and sat down in the chair, drained from the experience. Then he noticed Abigail smiling at him.

"I saw it," whispered Michael, rubbing his temples and shaking his head with frustration. "It was beside a tree in the middle of a forest. It moved away when I tried to retrieve it. It floated upwards to a man suspended over the tree."

"The satchel has a mind of its own," said Abigail. "It has chosen its new guardian, and now it is gone."

Michael jumped to his feet. "What do you mean, gone? New guardian? Who?"

"You know who."

"Never trust a witch!" Michael shouted, taking hold of the crank and turning it. Abigail shrieked as her arms and legs began to pull out of their sockets.

Suddenly, the door opened and four guards rushed in, followed by Domitian and Gerda.

"Bring him to me!" ordered Domitian.

The guards quickly apprehended Michael and brought him to Domitian while Gerda went to the rack and loosened the tension.

"Gerda told me everything," said Domitian to Michael. He cracked his neck and filled his lungs. "You are a bigger fool than I had imagined, Sir Michael, believing Gerda would betray me, or that Abigail would simply hand over the powers of the gods to the likes of you. By the way, thank you for stabbing Marcel in the back. I have come to the conclusion that no one can trust you, certainly not I." Domitian turned to his guards. "Lock him up."

Domitian joined Gerda beside the rack. He shook his head at the sight of Abigail beneath the red linen and clicked his tongue. "Sweet Abby, how terribly hungry you look. Do not fret, my sweet. We shall either feed you or kill you before the frenzy comes. All I ask is that you resurrect my beloved countess." He lifted his hand. "I know, I know. She was not your favorite. However, if you resurrect the countess in the image of your ideal vampire, with love and compassion in her heart, you might fancy the new countess and I shall pardon your brother instead of tearing his head from his body with my own bare hands. What say you, hmm, Countess Marie de Vos for Mister Pierce van Fleming?"

Abigail leered up at him. "You will never find my brother."

Domitian leaned in close to her. "In England, in America, in Asia, in Africa, where he goes, we shall go, and we shall find him. Well, what say you? Have we an agreement?"

83 - A FORTUNATE REUNION

The day after Cedric had left the small children at the monastery, Cedric, Lily, and Jacob returned by buggy.

"Jacob, Lily, choose your weapons," said Cedric, opening a large sack.

Jacob peered into the sack at a collection of wooden stakes, daggers, garlic, and onion. He fished out a dagger and wedged it into his britches. Lily lifted two daggers, a wooden stake, and a moldy onion, and started to conceal them under her cloak. Cedric hopped down from the buggy and checked his weapons beneath his overcoat.

"I will not be long," said Cedric. "As we discussed, flee at the first sign of trouble. Go north to Amsterdam. We will meet at the largest church in the town's center."

"Do not be long," said Lily.

Cedric entered the vestibule where he had met the abbesses. The monastery was quiet, very quiet. He quickened his pace through the corridors, trying to ignore the fact that he was frightened. What if the monsters are here? From the corner of his eye he saw someone sitting in a room. He stopped and reversed to the doorway to look inside. It was Sister Claudia, reading the bible.

"Good day, Sister Claudia."

"Oh, good day, Mister Martens," said the sister, putting the book down. She was about to stand when Cedric lifted his hand.

"No need to stand. I just came to say goodbye to the children. Do you know where I can find them?"

"They are attending the morning service."

"Of course." Cedric was embarrassed to have forgotten what

day it was.

"Service ends in a few minutes. Please have a seat. I will go and fetch them for you."

Cedric sat down at a table to wait.

A clock on the mantle had ticked twelve minutes before the children bounded into the room. They ran to Cedric, competing for hugs. He got up from the chair as they pushed him against the table. Anna held up a flower she had picked for Cedric.

"Thank you, Anna," said Cedric.

"Stay here with us," said Katarina.

"I wish I could, but Lily and Jacob are waiting for me."

"I like it here," said Anna. "I made new friends. We will wait for you."

"Thank you, Anna," said Cedric. "I promise to return for you and meet your new friends."

It was both emotionally and physically difficult for Cedric to leave the children as they latched on, but with the help of Sister Claudia, he was freed to bid them farewell and leave the monastery.

Outside, Cedric made way to the street where he found no buggy, no Lily, and no Jacob. It was a bad omen. Had they spotted vampires? Had they escaped? He cautiously walked round the monastery but found no signs of them. He decided to go, running northward. At the transition from cobbled street to dirt road, he saw a man standing fifty paces ahead. His back was turned to Cedric, and he appeared to be looking at something in a valley farther down the road. Cedric slowed to a walk and looked behind him to see another man.

The man in front of Cedric turned to face the boy. A whip was coiled and hanging from his shoulder. It was the guard from the detention building at Vos Castle. Those men were castle guards, and they were hunting Cedric.

Cedric took out a dagger and wooden stake, but then decided to run through a field towards a row of small houses. The vampires were upon him in a few heartbeats.

With orders not to harm the boy, the guards circled Cedric. The boy lashed out with his dagger at them. He felt the whip coil around his leg from behind. Suddenly, he was on his belly. As he quickly turned to get up, a cape was dropped over him.

Cedric slashed at the fabric with his dagger, but the vampire held his arms. They wrapped the cape and wound the whip round him and lifted him off the ground.

Cedric thought his time had finally run out. He would never see Lily or Jacob again. Just before all hope had vanished, he was dropped, landing flat on his back. As he gasped for air, the sounds of horses and fighting confused him even more. Had Lily and Jacob returned to save him? After a moment of silence, he felt hands on him again, but they were rolling him over, unwinding the whip. When the cape was finally pulled off, he saw familiar faces.

"I know you," said a man, peering down at the boy, "Cedric Martens of Linder?"

"Is it you?" asked the other.

They helped Cedric to his feet.

"Yes, it is me," said Cedric gratefully. "Thank you."

"Thank you? Is that all?" said the elder, Mr. Fortune, pointing at the decomposing remains of the attackers.

"I warned you of such monsters," said the younger.

"Youngsters these days never listen," said the elder, shaking his head.

"Thank you for slaying them," said Cedric. "They might have taken me back to Vos Castle." Cedric shuddered to think of it.

"That castle is a place to steer clear of," said the younger. "Where were you going?"

"Amsterdam," said Cedric.

"The elder laughed and nodded as if agreeing to a request the boy had yet to make. "We are, too, and of course you may join us!"

"Safety in numbers!" added the younger.

Cedric was relieved. "Many thanks," said Cedric. "I wish to travel with you. What should I call you? What are your names?"

The elder pointed to himself. "I am Fortune and—"

"I meant, what are your true names?" said Cedric.

"Ah, those names," said the younger as he mounted his horse. "You may call me Gert."

"I am Klaas," said the elder.

At that moment, the third vampire sent to capture Cedric was observing them from a great distance, too far to hear them or to catch up to them. He would instead report what he had seen to Domitian.

84 - LEGACY BESTOWED

Levitating at the center of a luxurious void, Pierce barely acknowledged the faint glow of light in the distance. It seemed so far off, just a white dot against the backdrop of oblivion. He slowly drifted towards it, or so it seemed, for there was nothing more than the spot of light to gauge distance and motion—no walls, no sound, no atmosphere. The light grew larger, until finally he passed through an enormous tunnel. From the space of darkness to the space of illumination, it was neither brilliant nor blinding, but radiant, devoid of shadows and sound.

In the vastness, Pierce saw a black dot from whence he came, a red dot to where he would not venture, and the glowing outline of a satchel rotating above him. He felt a tingling sensation in the palms of his hands from which he observed curling lines of color weeping upwards. He felt no pain, only a ticklish sensation. Suddenly, a geyser of imagery erupted from his hands in all directions filling the void with a different reality, causing his eyes to see and rousing his mind to think.

Recognizing the sounds of a ship pulling into harbor, Pierce rolled out of his hammock and made way to the top deck. The anchor weighed as he emerged into the brightness of day.

"Welcome to Virginia, Mister van Fleming," said Commander Crowley.

Pierce shaded his eyes from the light. Passengers were boarding rowboats: port side to Portsmouth, the other to Norfolk. He moved amongst the busy mariners and saw the twin sisters pointing out sights of interest, giddy that they had arrived in good health after two months at sea. Pierce smelled the sweetness of Elijah Scott's whiskey.

"Slept well, Mister Fleming?" said Elijah under a chuckle, as he moved towards the rowboats.

"Indeed I had, Mister Scott. Thank you," said Pierce. He casually surveyed the land and felt unsettled with the familiar towns' names and Georgian architecture. In Portsmouth, except for the newcomers from mainland Europe, most of the townsfolk retained a semblance of regional British accents with a distinct American vernacular that was difficult to explain, yet easily heard. He enjoyed it, for it reaffirmed his foreign status in a country far removed from England.

In a hotel lobby that evening, Pierce lounged in an armchair, dissecting aromas from the hotel's dining room: wild turkey, venison, blue crab, lobster, mussels, oysters, corn, beans, squash, butter, spices, herbs, coffee, and whiskey. His appetite for blood was unusually absent, and the possibility to enjoy a cooked meal again provoked his pallet. All was well, or at least he thought until he came across sketches of his face printed in the center of an article of the local newspaper. Alarmed by it, he turned the page to find another print of his face, and then another on every subsequent page.

Scanning the room with renewed paranoia, he noticed a young woman walking outside by the hotel. She wore a velvet green cloak with black trim, with the hood pulled over, but he saw enough of her delicate facial profile to recognize her. He quickly went to the front door and stepped out onto the wood plank walkway. He watched and listened intently to the hammering tempo of her gate and followed it.

She stopped beside a boutique window to gaze at a fashion display. Pierce stopped beside a pillar too narrow to hide behind. She glanced at Pierce, once briefly, then again, long enough to recognize him. Startled to see him, she dropped her parasol.

"Pierce?" said Meghan Clark.

Pierce was speechless. Why is she here? When did she arrive? When will she leave, or will she stay? With whom did she come? Is she wedded? Does she still loath me? Does she still love me? He retrieved her parasol and handed it to her. Then he brought his tricorne down and bowed. Before he could say a word, another familiar voice interrupted the moment.

"Brother? Is that you?"

He turned and was stunned to see his sister Abigail. She was wearing the beautiful gown and tiara from when he saw her in Manchester.

Pierce tried to speak, but a burning sensation in his throat left him voiceless.

"Percy?" said his father Hans. His mother and Emma stood beside him, with his sisters and Farmer John, his wife, and Breanne behind them. Everyone he cared for was there.

Bewildered and bewitched he turned to Meghan, but she had vanished. He swiveled round to address the others, but they too had vanished. The sounds of wheezing and the smell of rotting flesh from behind the display window caught his attention. The reflection of his throat looked as it did after Marie had nearly decapitated him: punctured, incised, and bleeding. Crouching beyond his reflection was what appeared to be a winged gargoyle with eyes of a goat and teeth of thorns.

Pierce woke from the nightmare. After a moment of self-gathering, he rolled out of the hammock and opened the side scuttle. A damp breeze entered the stale hold. It was black and brackish outside, but warm. The ship creaked like binding gate hinges as the ocean gently lifted and rocked her forward. It was dark in the berth, but he saw through it and smelled the sailors, swaying and snoring in their hammocks. Judging by the length of their beards, Pierce supposed two or three weeks had passed. The deep sleep must have worked. If only he could do it again for the duration. He would try, but first he wanted to check his belongings.

Pierce opened the footlocker. He expected to find everything as he had left them, but surprisingly there was something more...a leather satchel materializing before his eyes. He lifted it and closed the locker. Placing the satchel on the hammock, he unbuckled the flap and lifted out a very old parchment. On it was an elaborately drawn tree. Pierce retrieved a few pages of parchment and fingered through them—spells and potions in his mother's handwriting.

Through the porthole, Pierce saw the ocean and took in the salty breeze. He recalled Abigail when she was sixteen. Every Sunday, she led him across the street to church. Churchgoing was a front to appear ordinary. He recalled Abigail's adoration of the young priest. Pierce was fearful of her budding love for someone who would destroy them if he knew their secret. As a result, nothing of her appearance and character escaped Pierce's scrutiny. His goal was to make her feel unattractive so she might somehow *become* unattractive, especially to the priest. Pierce achieved the former, but not the latter, thanks to Mother's everlasting beauty spell.

Pierce reached into the leather container and retrieved two daggers his mother had called *athame*, one with a black-horn handle and the other with a white-bone handle, each with gold inlays of the symbolic eight-legged *sabbat*. The bronze blades were polished and sharpened. The *quillon*, a bronze cross-guard between the blade and hilt, extended about an inch to each side. The white athame belonged to his mother and the other to his father. He recalled his mother using hers to scratch symbols in the earth. His father seldom used his dagger that way. The first time Pierce saw his father use his athame was when they were shepherding.

Two days from home, with a large flock of sheep, dusk was nearing, and Pierce's father hungered for something other than salted venison. As their dog tended to the flock, Pierce followed his father to a nearby meadow known for its abundance of hares. Pierce readied his bow and walked slowly in hopes of flushing one out. After a while, two rodents sprung from behind a rock. Pierce took aim and shot an arrow but missed. With his *athame* in one hand and a folding knife in the other, his father threw them in tandem. Pierce saw the *athame* circumnavigate a tree and two large rocks then penetrate the hare's ribcage. Miraculously, both blades negotiated obstacles and hit their targets.

Pierce learned that his mother was far more enthusiastic about witchcraft than his father was. His father preferred shepherding and hunting—with a bit of magic—to pentagrams and complicated spells. His father raised the bloody *athame* and said with a mischievous grin, "Perseus," which is what his father oft called him, "say nothing of this to your mother."

As a boy, the satchel had been his muse. Pierce had always wanted to view its magical contents and hoped to inherit all of it one day. Now that it appeared to be his, he began to wonder if he still wanted it. He was beginning to realize how thin the line between wishes and regrets might really be.

He brought his kerchief to the scuttlebutt beside the table, soaked it with water, and wiped staleness from his face. The ship's berthing deck ought to have felt like a meat locker to him. The smell of blood coursing through suspended bodies should have driven him to feed, but Pierce took little notice. He gave no mind to the ship's relentless push towards an uncertain future because his thoughts were elsewhere.

Was Abigail still alive? Were any of his blood relatives still alive? Somewhere between thoughts of the living and of the dead a notion surfaced. He rushed to the satchel and gently removed the parchment on which the tree was so eloquently drawn. The calligraphy was otherworldly ornate, lending textures he had not previously noticed. Every detail was so legible as to cause his lips to part and his voice to utter, "Deadwood tree."

The lantern's flame, blue and languishing, finally expired into a thread of smoke as another piece of his jig-sawed life fit into place. In the darkness, the family tree softly illuminated copper and silver, emitting aromas of licorice root, sage, and leather. His hands tingled. His birthmarks glowed with a power he hoped to explore. He noticed that his favorite tree branch was rendered with the names of his grandparents, uncles, aunts, cousins, parents, and sister. Names of distant relatives formed other branches of the tree, and a single line—the bloodline—interconnected all the names. He followed the line from branch to branch and down to the base of the trunk where the first name appeared to rise from the ground—*Perseus*.

There was meaning to it. He understood some of it, but too weary to ponder all of it, he filed the parchment into the legacy satchel and locked it away. Then, he levitated onto his hammock, emptied his mind of worry, and fell into a deep, deep sleep.

Dear Reader,

It means the world to me that you bought THE HOVER, CEDRIC BOOK I and took time out of your busy life to read it. I strive to write clean prose, and edit like a traditional publisher to minimize structural and grammatical distractions. My goal is to write stories that are entertaining, intelligent, and thought provoking, to develop characters that are interesting, original, and memorable. This story is told in the third person in order to recount centuries of information and describe surreal settings in multiple, distant locations.

I would love to know what you thought of this story. Please leave a quick star rating on Goodreads and the online bookstore you purchased this from, and if you can spare the time to post an honest review, please do! Your feedback is very helpful to me as a developing author of fiction.

To learn more about my other projects and to contact me, please visit www.CALear.net or find me on Facebook, Instagram, and Twitter.

Thanks again for your support!

C. A. Lear

Made in the USA
Columbia, SC
10 June 2019